A FATED KISS

She was tempted. She wanted him to hold her, needed to know what it felt like to be loved, cherished. She needed to know she wasn't alone, that she could lean on James, but most of all, she yearned for the kiss that his eyes promised. Just this once, she told herself. This one time, she'd blame her weakness on the night, on the shimmering carpet of stars overhead and the soft cadence of insects lending their chirps to form a backdrop of soothing sound. Before the harsh light of the new day reminded her of all the reasons for guarding her heart, she had to know what it felt like to be held—and kissed—by James, the knight of her dreams, the one person who didn't frighten her.

She took that one small step, lifted her hands to his shoulders and allowed him to draw her close, his arms encircling her. One hand slid up her spine and cupped the back of her neck. She held her breath, waiting for the return of the suffocating fear of being trapped by strong male arms. To her surprise and pleasure, she felt no panic with James. Instead, strange urges flowed through her, frightening her as much as those same feelings made her lean closer to the man holding her so tenderly.

His breath, warm against her cheek, teased her. "Fate brought us together, Eirica. We were meant to be," he whispered, his lips moving closer.

White Nights

Susan Edwards

LEISURE BOOKS NEW YORK CITY

A LEISURE BOOK®

April 2000

Published by

Dorchester Publishing Co., Inc.
276 Fifth Avenue
New York, NY 10001

ISBN 0-8439-4703-9

To a special man in my life, Gary Swenson, who aside from being a great father, is one of today's heroes. He put his own life on the line each day he donned his uniform and went to work, serving and protecting the community.

And from the bottom of my heart, a special thanks goes to my editor, Chris Keeslar, who believed in me and gave me the chance to prove that dreams do come true. Thank you.

Prologue

Lower California Crossing of the Platte River
June, 1856

Icy-cold water crashed over Birk Macauley, sucking him down into the dark, murky Platte. The raging, snow-fed current shoved him downstream with gleeful abandon, seizing his clothing and boots, using the weight to hold him under. He kicked and thrashed uselessly. Terror filled him. Seconds ticked past, his lungs felt close to bursting. The waning light above his head taunted him. The surface. Air. So close. So far.

With a desperate kick he broke through the surface of his watery grave. Struggling to keep his head above water, he gulped great lungfuls of air and glanced around wildly for his wagon, but the swift-moving torrent swamped him, and pulled him ever farther downstream. He slapped his palms against the water's surface, grasping for something—anything—

11

to hold on to. His fingers slid through the frothy-white water as he tumbled in the arms of the capricious river. He suppressed the overwhelming need to breathe. A hazy gray film engulfed him. This was it. He was going to die.

Without warning, a hard object slammed into him. He gasped, drawing water into his lungs. Clutching the large log that had collided with him, Birk held on for dear life and rose to the surface, coughing, choking and spewing water. His chest and ribs ached, the rest of his body was numb with cold. He felt himself sliding off the log. Desperate, he clung to it, his cheek resting against its rough bark.

Tired, so tired. His vision blurred and his body shook uncontrollably, but inside raged a fury every bit as savage as the river carrying him farther from his wife. He cursed Eirica, shouted his fury into the growing darkness that surrounded him and left the banks shrouded in a cloak of gray mist.

Damn her. This was all her fault. Renewed disbelief swept through him. The bitch had defied him, left him while he slept off the effects of drinking too much rotgut the night before. How dare she? She and them brats belonged to him. His nails dug into the log, impervious to the pain. Curses and promises of retribution tore from his lips. It was her fault he'd been banished from the wagon train, her fault he'd been forced to cross the Platte unaided to fetch her and his children back.

In its frenzy, the river spun him dizzyingly around and around, using icy fingers to try and wrest his lifeline from him, but Birk hung on, cursing and fighting against the grip of death. The swells of dark water continued to slap at him as the last of the light faded, leaving him in the midst of a freezing watery hell. One thought echoed through his mind during the deepening night, giving him the strength to live: revenge. The bitch would pay.

Chapter One

July, 1856

Independence Rock. It rose from the sage-covered desert like some massive turtle or giant whaleback. Covered with names and inscriptions of all sizes, the oval landmark served as lookout, campsite, trail register and bulletin board to the thousands of westward-bound emigrants.

Some climbed the one-hundred-twenty-eight-foot-high granite rock to add their names to the very top, while others were content to view the next major landmark in their journey west: Devil's Gate. The high ridge of hills made of trap rock, sandstone and granite rose to a height of four hundred feet and pointed the way to the halfway mark from Westport to Oregon: South Pass.

Camped a short distance from Independence Rock and the swarm of humanity, Eirica Macauley coaxed a small flame to life by slowly adding dried grass. When the flames caught and eagerly licked at the precious sage wood laid over several fist-size rocks, she sat back on her heels, swiping damp strands of hair from her forehead. To one side of her, a canvas sack filled with dried droppings from all manner of beasts roaming the trail and surrounding land lay open, ready for use once the wood burned out. Though the droppings burned hot and ferocious, they left a great deal of ash that required removal before adding more of the dried fuel.

Taking a deep breath, she struggled to her feet—no small task when one was heavy with child. The sultry afternoon wind whipped the worn, homespun material of her faded, indigo-dyed wrapper dress around her legs and into the smoking fire. Eirica jumped back with a muffled exclamation.

Shaking out her skirts, she noted a couple of new burn holes in the fabric and grimaced. The hem was already tattered and ragged from being snagged on rocks, brush and all other matter of thorny plants, not to mention dragged through mud during the rains. After walking more than eight hundred miles during the last three months, it was no surprise that her clothing and shoes were wearing out.

Grabbing hold of a fistful of skirt to keep the breeze from billowing it up over her head, Eirica stepped well away from the fire and turned her face into the capricious wind. Her bonnet blew off and hung down her back, held by the knotted ribbons around her throat. The strong breeze played with loosened strands of long golden-red hair as she massaged her lower back. A slight tightening of her abdomen followed. Unconsciously, she smoothed her palms down over the swell of her unborn child and ignored the spasms. At twenty-two, she was eight months pregnant with her fourth child and knew these contractions were nothing more than her body's preparations for the labor that would follow in a few short weeks.

Shielding her eyes from the glare off the white canvas-topped wagons of nearby campers, Eirica turned her attention to the landmark so many emigrants held in awe. She stared at the monstrosity in the distance with pensive eyes. What lay ahead? What did the future hold for her and her children? They'd made it this far, would they survive to see their new home?

Survival. The word sent chills through her. Gooseflesh popped out on her arms. How would she manage once she reached Oregon? Fear, worry and uncertainty rolled through her like tumbleweeds racing across wide open plains. She felt lost and alone in a strange and unfriendly world. The hundreds of graves along the trail bore testimony to the harshness of the journey west.

Her throat tightened. In the last week alone, she'd recorded more than forty graves in her diary. Lives of all ages, snuffed out by cholera, measles, mountain fever and so many other hazards that struck the innocent and unwary emigrants. Each new grave site, some off-trail, others smack in the middle of it to keep coyotes and wolves from digging up the bodies, ate away at her confidence. Was she doing the right thing by continuing onward to Oregon?

How could she, a widow with three, soon-to-be four, children make it across this wild, hostile land? And if she made it to Oregon, she'd be faced with starting over, alone. She wrapped her arms protectively around her swollen abdomen. Feeling the movement of the baby nestled safely inside her brought forth another worry, but she refused to even think about giving birth out here so far from home. It was just another fear to keep her awake at night.

"Ian! Come back!"

At the sound of the high-pitched shout, Eirica whirled around to see her youngest child running away from his older sister. Giggling with delight in the chase, Ian, barely two, dodged Lara, unaware that he'd run into the path of several oxen being driven away from the crowded wagons camped along each side of the trail to find better forage.

Eirica's heart jumped into her throat. She picked up her skirts and ran awkwardly. "Ian, stop! Come back!"

Intent on dodging three-year-old Lara, Ian kept going; his little legs, brown and sturdy from nearly three months of living outdoors, flew over the uneven ground.

Hearing Eirica's panicked shouts, a short, plump woman wearing baggy men's woolen trousers and an even baggier shirt, darted in front of the oxen and scooped Ian into her arms, safely out of the path of the bellowing beasts.

Sofia De Santis carried Ian toward Eirica, holding him upside down, much to the little boy's delight. Lara skipped alongside her, her thumb in her mouth and a small square of blanket clutched in her curled fingers. Her baby-blue eyes were wide with worry.

"The *bambino* is full of energy." Sofia chuckled, tickling Ian's belly, eliciting more giggles before righting him in her plump arms and handing him over to Eirica.

Eirica hugged her squirming son, her heart still beating a wild tattoo against her breast. She smiled weakly at the newest member to join her small wagon train. "Thank you, Mrs. De Santis. I swear, Ian is such a handful. I can't seem to make him understand he can't just run off."

Ian wiggled and protested. "Down, Mama, down."

Eirica lowered him to the ground. He tried to take off again, but she held tightly to his wrist. "Ian, you cannot run off. There are far too many people and animals around. You're going to get hurt." Seeing his tiny features screwing up to protest, she pulled several carved wooden animals from a pocket in her dress. "Here, take these and go play quietly beneath the wagon while Mama tends to supper."

Rebellion forgotten for the moment, the little boy eagerly grabbed the prized wooden figures made for him and his sisters by another member traveling in their wagon party. Content for the time being, he followed Lara to the shade beneath their wagon and settled on his stomach with the toys spread out before him. Lara sat cross-legged beside him.

Eirica sighed ruefully as she watched Ian use one figure to attack another, then set both to pouncing on Lara's knee. Her daughter giggled around her thumb. At the sight of her children playing happily, a sunburst of love warmed Eirica from the inside out. *Please,* she prayed, *keep them safe and healthy.* She didn't know what she'd do if she lost one of them to the indiscriminating hand of death.

"Ah, to be so young." Sofia's long, graying black hair, piled haphazardly on top of her head, had loosened during her mad dash after Ian. She deftly removed two thin, tapered sticks and rewound her hair on top of her head, then jabbed the makeshift pins through the loose bun.

"Sure wish I had some of his energy. He's going to

be the death of me yet." Eirica bit back a yawn. Her day was a long way from being over.

Sofia beamed. "Ah, but he is strong and healthy. It's normal for him to be curious. He's a very bright child. This is good, no?"

"Ian is smart," Eirica agreed, her gaze softening on her two youngest children. "But he has no fear. He's not afraid of anything, and that scares me something fierce."

Sofia's smile faded. "My Gino was just like your little boy, always getting into mischief and running his poor mama to exhaustion when he was a wee *ragazzo*. Nothing stopped that boy; always ready to learn new things, eager to explore new places. When he left our village to travel, I used to pray for his safe return."

Her deep, husky voice broke, and a tear fell from her soft, brown eyes. The single drop of moisture spread along the lines age had brought to her face. "I worried for nothing. It wasn't his wild running about that killed him," she whispered in a broken voice.

Eirica felt sorry for this woman who'd lost so much. Two sons, a daughter-in-law, two grandchildren and her husband had succumbed to cholera within days of one another. All the poor woman had left of her once-large family was a seventeen-year-old granddaughter and two grandsons, aged twenty-two and ten. Like Eirica, she too faced starting over without the support of her family. It wasn't fair, yet Eirica knew many more women would lose members of their families before reaching Oregon. She reached out and squeezed the woman's fisted hand. "I'm so sorry, Mrs. De Santis."

Sofia squared her shoulders. "Life is not always kind, Mrs. Macauley. I thank the good Lord daily that I

19

still have Dante, Catarina and Marco. They are Gino's children and carry his blood in their veins. All I have to do is look upon them to see my son, or with Dante, my husband, Luigi." She fell silent, lost in thought.

Eirica rubbed her arms and hugged herself. The enormity of what lay ahead made her want to drop to the ground and weep with the unfairness of it all. The daily passing of mounds of dirt, hastily formed crosses and piles of stones haunted her, kept her awake at night. What if she lost Ian, Lara or Alison? She'd already lost her husband, but unlike Sofia, Eirica suffered no grief over Birk's death—a source of guilt that continued to eat at her. But no matter how hard she tried to grieve and feel sad over his death, she only felt a welcome release from a six-year marriage that had been her own personal hell.

"My Luigi, he had so many dreams," Sofia whispered.

"They all do," Eirica responded sadly, thinking about the vast number of men who'd forced their women and children to make this horrendous journey. Like so many others, Eirica hadn't wanted to leave all she'd known to journey across this wild, untamed land—but she'd had no choice. When she'd refused to go to Oregon, Birk had threatened to take their children and leave without her. Eirica pressed her lips together. Becoming a widow was the only good thing to come from this perilous trip.

Her lips twisted with bitterness. Her husband had known full well she'd never allow him to take her babies from her. Now she held their lives in her hands, she was pitted against an unpredictable land that both fascinated her with wondrous sights and frightened her with the sheer magnitude of what lay ahead. Her palms grew damp. She wiped them on her apron, her eyes filling with tears of frustration.

How she wished her mother were still alive. But Mary Newell had died two years ago, helped into her grave by a cold, indifferent husband who wouldn't even allow an old sick woman to spend the day abed, gathering her strength after falling ill during the harsh winter. Memories of the woman who'd spent her life waiting hand and foot on her husband and eight sons brought tears to Eirica's eyes.

Old resentments welled up inside Eirica. Birk had refused to allow her to go care for her mother during the day, even though they were neighbors. She'd defied him once, sneaked out to take her ma some fresh bread and honey. He'd found out, though, and that act of disobedience had earned her a broken arm and bruised ribs. It was the last day she'd seen her mother alive. A month later, Mary had just given up, laid down and died, a broken woman.

Eirica fought back tears of regret. If only she'd stood up to Birk, done something to help her mother, maybe her ma would be alive today.

The need to talk to someone who understood what she was going through overwhelmed Eirica. She glanced at Sofia. Though the woman was more than twice her age, Eirica felt a closeness to her that was missing from the other women traveling with her. Jessie and Coralie were younger, childless and newlyweds. Anne was older, but she was happily married.

"What are you going to do, Mrs. De Santis? Are you going to continue or head back? Barnaby Thurston and his sons are turning back. Can't bear to go on after losing his wife. Heard several other families are considering joining them."

Sofia straightened and met Eirica's worried gaze, her own fraught with determination. "I shall go to Oregon. It's what Luigi wanted. I'll claim the land he dreamed of and make a new life for my grandchildren." She considered Eirica through narrowed eyes. "You aren't thinking of turning back?"

"I wish I could." Though Eirica spoke the words aloud for the first time, she knew it was fruitless. Thanks to Birk's laziness and drinking, she had no home to return to. He'd lost their farm and their small, crude cabin, leaving them no choice but to move into her father's home before they'd taken to the trail.

"You have no other family? No *madre* or *padre*?"

Eirica brushed her tears away, furious with herself for wishing for things that could never be again. "No one who cares," she said, leaving it at that. She'd spent her whole life trying to please her father and brothers, but it was never enough, never appreciated. All her long hours of work and devotion to ensure their comfort had been met with more demands, contempt and indifference toward her own wants and desires.

As she'd quickly discovered after she and Birk had been forced to move in with her family, nothing had changed in the five years she'd been gone. Though her three older brothers had married and lived in homes a short distance away, five of her younger brothers still shared space in the cramped three-room farmhouse along with her pa. And with her ma gone, they and her pa had expected her to step in and wait on them. She wasn't a daughter or sister to them. She was a slave, someone they ordered around. They'd even started making demands of Alison who'd only been four, having her fetch and carry for them as they were too lazy to get up and do it themselves.

Sofia nodded as if she understood what Eirica left unsaid. "Then you and I must be strong and help each other." A shout from one of her grandsons made Sofia smile. "I have much to live for." With that, she excused herself to go finish her supper preparations.

Eirica did likewise. Moving to the back of her wagon, she pulled off the tailgate and struggled to move her wooden box of cooking utensils.

"Ere, lass, let me lift that down for ya."

Eirica turned to Rook, the cook for the men hired to drive west the wagon master's cattle. "Thanks, Rook," she said, stepping back, hiding her smile when he continued to frown at Sofia's retreating back. Why those two didn't get along puzzled her. They both seemed so friendly and at ease with everyone else.

Rook muttered something beneath his breath then lifted her box down. "Point out what else ya needs."

She pointed to a large sack and another box. He lifted those from the back of the wagon as well. Wiping his hands down the front of his buckskin breeches, he studied her, his bright blue eyes intent as he pulled at his bushy white beard. "You's frettin' again, lass. Ain't good for you or that babe you's carryin'."

Rook's fatherly concern touched her. As with Sofia, she felt as though she could talk to Rook and he'd understand. With sudden insight, she realized these two special people had taken the place of her parents. Rook was much more a father than her own had ever been. The feeling warmed her, allowed her to open up to him.

"I try not to think of tomorrow or of what it will bring, but I just can't help it." Despite the heat of the afternoon, she shivered.

Rook pulled her into his burly arms and hugged her awkwardly. His deep rumbling voice drifted over the top of her head. "Now, lass, ya has ta trust yerself. Ya come from good, hearty Scottish stock, like me, and we Scots is survivors." He put her from him and gave her a stern look. " 'Sides, we's yer family now and not a one of us is gonna allow anythin' to happen to ya or them young'uns of yers. So no more frettin'."

Touched by his concern and the emotion he tried to hide beneath a gruff exterior, Eirica hugged him back. "You're a wonderful man, Rook. I wish you'd been my father," she said impulsively.

Rook turned beet-red. With shaking hands, he pulled three small wooden objects from his shirt pocket and awkwardly handed them to Eirica. " 'Ere. For them young'uns."

In her palm lay three carved puppies, each in a different position. Sleeping, sitting and standing, all had incredibly realistic features. She would add these to the other wooden carvings he'd made for the children. "Rook, these are lovely. The children will love them." Her second hug embarrassed him even more. "You're spoiling them, you know."

Rook stepped back, blinking rapidly. He stuck his pipe between his lips, then shoved it back into his shirt pocket, his movements jerky. Finally, he stilled and met her teary gaze with determination and love. "Hell, lass. The lot of ya deserves ta be spoilt and I might as well be the one ta do it."

Without another word, Rook walked away, his short, stocky legs carrying him to his wagons and the long trench fires that sent waves of heat rolling along the ground. A moment later, his loud voice boomed over the area when he shouted for two of the hired hands to "git out of the stores."

Amused to see grown men scurrying away rather than face Rook's displeasure, Eirica shook her head. No one dared to argue with or disobey Rook. The crusty old trapper ruled all within his domain with an iron fist. Yet beneath his rough demeanor lay a heart of gold and a sharp mind filled with the wisdom of his years. And as he'd so gently reminded her, she truly wasn't alone. A second good had come of this trip. For the first time since marrying at the age of fifteen, she had friends—lots of them—something Birk had never allowed.

But then, Birk Macauley had never loved her. She'd been nothing more than a slave to see to his every whim and a convenient vessel to slake his needs. For six long years, she'd worked his farm, borne him children he neither loved nor wanted, and endured his jealous nature, childish tantrums and violent rages.

She shuddered, fighting nightmarish memories of protecting her young children by drawing her husband's fury from them to herself. Placing one hand on her chest, in the hollow between her full breasts, she spread her fingers upward, feeling smooth, raised scars hidden from sight beneath her bodice.

Her other hand absently rubbed her healing ribs, some of which had been broken, others badly bruised during Birk's last beating. She'd shielded her son's small body from her husband's rage with her own body. That had been a month ago—the day before Birk died.

She dropped her hands to her side. Scars. Pain. She wanted to shout with the joy of knowing he'd never take his fists to any of them again. If starting over was the price she had to pay for that freedom, she'd gladly do it. A gentle roll from within her womb brought a sigh to her lips. Her baby was safe, as were her other children. "No one will raise a hand to you in anger," she vowed, easing the tight flesh with her fingers.

She thought again of Mr. Thurston and the others who were turning back, disheartened by the loss of loved ones, lame oxen or dangerously low supplies. If she joined them, she could just as easily start over back east, maybe find a job as a seamstress or school-marm. Eirica paced, walking in a tight circle, careful to keep her skirts out of the fire. Three young boys ran past, shouting with youthful abandon, but she paid them little heed.

Closing her eyes, she searched her soul for the right answer, feeling the pressure of knowing that only she could make this decision. It occurred to Eirica that most who turned back had one thing in common: They'd lost hope, lost their dreams. She straightened her spine. A few short months ago, there had been no hope for her. Now she had a future. There were choices, maybe even dreams.

For the first time in her life, she was in control of her destiny. She'd be a fool not to grasp her chance for a better life with both hands. With nothing waiting for them behind her, somehow, she must find the courage and strength to make it to Oregon. Nothing mattered now except giving her babies a brighter future.

As if sensing her mother's troubled thoughts, three-year-old Lara crawled out from beneath the wagon and ran to her on matchstick legs, wearing only a simple, worn chemise and no shoes. Eirica picked her up and spun in a slow circle, hugging her daughter tightly. She smoothed the child's wispy strawberry-blond curls from her face. "Mama loves you, Lara girl."

With solemn eyes the same shade of blue as her mother's, Lara wrapped her arms around her mother's neck and whispered, "I wuv you, too, Mama."

From the corner of her eye, Eirica noted the coals in the fire glowed white-hot. She lowered Lara to the ground, picked up a Dutch oven containing the bread dough she'd mixed that morning, and set it among the burning embers glowing in the fire pit. With two forks, she covered the lid with coals—for even baking—then stood back, pleased her "light" bread, made with saleratus instead of yeast, had risen nicely during the warm day. It would be wonderfully tasty served with warm milk from the milch cow they'd purchased in Westport, the place they'd spent the winter preparing for this trip.

Lara followed her mother to the back of the wagon, her hand fisted tightly around Eirica's skirts, her blanket held in the other. "Where's Ali?" She stuck her thumb into her mouth and stared at her mother, worry clouding her baby-blue eyes.

Eirica pointed toward Independence Rock. "Your sister went to see the names on the rock with Mr. Jones and his sister, sweetheart. She'll be back soon. Now go watch over your brother while Mama finishes supper." For the moment, Ian seemed content to dig in the sandy soil with a spoon, but his attention never stayed on any task long.

Lara walked back slowly, sat on the ground beside Ian and stared at the rock where her sister had gone. Eirica's heart twisted. This child was a worrier by nature and Eirica couldn't blame her for fretting whenever her big sister was out of sight. Alison's harrowing experience of being kidnapped three weeks earlier wasn't something Eirica would soon forget.

Eirica still had nightmares borne of those long days and even longer nights when she hadn't known if she would ever see or hug her firstborn again. She closed her eyes, grateful for the happy ending to that episode. With a sigh, she tossed a slab of bacon into a frying pan and set it over the coals. With any luck, the second half of the trail would be downright dull. Between the kidnapping, Birk's drowning, storms, difficult crossings and stampedes, she'd had enough excitement to last a lifetime.

A tug to her skirts drew her gaze downward. Ian yawned and lifted his little arms up to her. "Is my boy ready for bed?" She smiled and picked him up, loving the feel of his soft, cuddly body next to hers. With a sleepy sigh, he slumped against her. Eirica ran her hand up and down his back. Contentment washed over her as Ian imitated his sister and stuck his thumb in his mouth. With a heart measurably lighter, Eirica hummed softly and swayed side to side in front of the fire.

Lifting her gaze to a sapphire-blue sky marbled with wisps of white clouds just turning gold and pink from the sun's descent, Eirica forced herself to relax and put the past behind her, to enjoy the beauty of the approaching sunset and the feel of her son snuggled close. For the first time in her life, she had a future of her own making. She'd been given a second chance for a better life and she planned to reach out and take it.

"All I want is to reach Oregon, find a piece of land to call my own and settle down to raise my children in peace." Over and over, she repeated those words, trying to draw courage from them.

Chapter Two

High atop Independence Rock, James Jones surveyed the land spread out before him with his sister, Jessie, on one side of him and five-year-old Alison Macauley on the other, her small hand tucked securely into his own. From the crowd around them, whispered words of awe mingled with shouts of jubilation.

James sucked in a deep breath and whistled, unable to contain himself in the face of the incredible view and the history surrounding him. "Whoo-ee, great sand and sagebrush! Look at all the wagons down there, Ali girl." He pointed at the white-topped wagons dotting the area as far as the eye could see. Oxen, mules and horses foraged for food while men, women and children moved with purpose, reminding him of ants scurrying back to their ant hills.

Alison stepped forward, closer to the edge and leaned over. "Where's Ma's wagon, James?"

James tightened his hold and pulled the little girl

back to his side. As an extra precaution, he rested his free hand on her shoulder. "Not so close to the edge, Ali. It's a long way down and if anything happens to you, your ma will skin me alive."

Giggling, Alison glanced up at him, adoration shining in her eyes. "I won't fall, James. You're holding my hand tight."

Still nervous, James backed up a step for good measure and squatted, encircling her with his arms as he pointed. "Your ma's wagon is way out there."

"Everything looks so tiny." Alison leaned into him, her wide eyes taking in the expansive scene. James savored the bond between him and this child. If he had his way, he'd soon be a part of her life—he just had to convince the girl's mother to give him a chance. After several silent minutes, the youngster pulled away from him and dropped to her knees. She crawled over the rock behind him, using her fingers to trace the names etched into the rock upon which they stood. Relieved that Alison was safely away from the edge, James turned sideways so he could divide his attention between the child and the view.

Jessie's exclamations echoed his own awe. "Look how the Sweetwater River twists and turns before tumbling through Devil's Gate."

From his lofty perch, James studied the Oregon Trail as it followed the winding river. The trail detoured around the deep chasm because wagons wouldn't fit between the two high ridges. To the west rocks and boulders, some of incredible size, littered the land as far as the eye could see. The prospect of negotiating those zigs and zags and rocks left him breathless with anticipation. No sooner did they meet one challenge the land threw at them, than there was another. And if the terrain snaking westward was any indication of things to come, he had the feeling the trip was about to get rougher.

Some said Ash Hollow, that hidden paradise of green grass, pink roses and abundant water that they'd passed through a month ago, was the entrance to hell, and Devil's Gate the exit, but staring at the rough trail ahead, it looked as though they were about to enter something far worse.

"How can there be so many different and wonderful sights?" Jessie breathed. "I never imagined a world so different from our home. Look at those towering rocks. I didn't think anything could beat Chimney Rock for being spectacular, but I was wrong."

James stared down into eyes that not only mirrored his own sense of wonderment, but were also the same deep shade of green as his. Right now, they sparkled with enthusiasm, echoed the underlying excitement running through his own blood. He rolled his eyes. Trust Jessie not to have the good sense to fear what lay ahead.

Never mind that he, too, felt his blood race in anticipation. He loved the constant change, the need to be on his toes. After living a quiet life on a small farm, he knew he'd never forget this trip. Just thinking about the swollen river crossings, steep hills requiring them to lower wagons by rope, and all manner of weather made his blood pump. He ruffled his sister's medium-length black hair.

"You scamp. You've said the same thing of all the landmarks we've seen since leaving Westport."

Jessie giggled and spun around, her face animated, her arms outstretched as if embracing all she saw. "Oh, James, this has been so exciting, such an adventure. I'll never forget it."

He pulled her to him for a quick hug. Dressed in a

blue flannel shirt with the sleeves rolled up past her elbow, woolen trousers that concealed her womanly curves and scuffed boots, she seemed the same old Jess. "Neither will I. And you, my lucky sister, get to travel all this once more when you and Wolf return to his home in the Nebraska Territory come spring." He sobered. "Life won't be the same without you, Jess."

She dropped her arms and stared at him with tears in her eyes. "Oh, James," she whispered before turning around so he couldn't see her face.

James shoved his hands in his pockets and stared at the sky above them. He'd seen the tears in her eyes, felt the pain in her heart. How could he not? His own eyes burned and his heart protested the inevitable separation. This time next year, she'd be gone and he might never see her again.

He took a deep breath, fighting the emotion curling through him. The Jones siblings were close, always there for one another. Nothing and no one had ever come between them, not even the wagon master and his no-single-women-allowed rule. Jessie being Jessie, had simply refused to be separated from her brothers. He fought back a chuckle. None were as resourceful as his little sister, though she wasn't so little anymore.

Watching her and Alison studying the inscriptions, pride filled him. At seventeen, Jessica Naomi Jones was a grown woman newly married—a fact he still had a hard time believing. Who would have guessed his little tomboy sister would fall in love and marry before they reached Oregon? Just the mention of some would-be suitor coming to call had sent her running several months before.

But she'd fallen in love with the wagon master,

Wolf White. James's lips twitched when he thought of the shotgun wedding he'd insisted on when he'd found out the pair were lovers. Jessie had been furious, but James had no regrets. It was a brother's responsibility to make sure no man took advantage of his sister and if James had to do it all over again, he would.

He paced, not seeing the view or even the other emigrants moving around him as he struggled with the pain of change. He listened to Jessie reading Alison the names and dates of emigrants who'd gone before them and sighed with a mixture of regret and longing. His siblings no longer needed him, and that realization made him feel much older than twenty-four.

For so long, his whole life had revolved around them. At sixteen, he'd buried his parents and stepped into their shoes, becoming both mother and father to two brothers and his sister. Now that his responsibility was complete, his future loomed, bleak and endless, like the horizon stretched out beyond forever.

Akin to the excess furniture and food littering the trail, he felt cast off, no longer needed or wanted. It wasn't the truth. In his heart, he knew his brothers and sister loved him as much now as they had when they'd depended upon him to provide for them, but they were ready to branch out and start their own families.

Yep, life went on and with each of his siblings seeking their own futures, it was well past time for him to do the same. Both Jordan and Jessie had married in the last three months, and if he had his way, he'd join them in wedded bliss.

Alison jumped up, breaking him out of his musings. "James," she squealed, her voice high with excitement. "Look! Right here, there's no marks on the rock. I want my name here."

Grateful for the distraction, James hunched down beside the red-haired girl who promised to one day become as beautiful a woman as her mother. Just thinking about Eirica filled him with warmth and purpose. After years of avoiding simpering, giggling girls who'd set their sights on him, he'd finally found the woman he wanted to marry.

Alison tugged on his arm, her wide eyes filled with doubt, some of the sparkle dimming when he just knelt there, silent. "Maybe this isn't such a good spot." Her voice wobbled with uncertainty.

He hastened to reassure the little girl. "This is the best spot on this whole da-darn rock, Sweet Pea."

It bothered him that she always expected disapproval, but considering what a bastard that Birk Macauley had been, James wasn't surprised. The child tried so hard to please and wanted—no, needed—so much reassurance, his heart ached. He ran a finger down her freckle-covered nose then set to work, carving her name as deep and as big as he could in the small area she'd chosen. While he worked, he vowed to see that both mother and daughter would only have cause to smile and laugh from now on.

Finished, he stood, noting the waning of the afternoon sun. "Time to head back, you two. I need to return to the herd and relieve Wolf." With Jessie on one side of the little girl and James on the other, they descended the rock and wound their way through the throng of wagons and tents taking up most of the available ground close to the landmark. The farther out, the more space they found—and dried grass among clumps of sagebrush.

Shading his eyes against the lowering sun, he searched out the dark blur of cattle moving lazily in the distance and noted their position. Lack of grass along the trail drove the herd out several miles in search of more bountiful supply. At least they no longer had to worry about the poisonous alkali ponds. Water was once again fresh and abundant. Satisfied that things were fine, he relaxed. He'd check on Eirica before heading back out.

When they arrived at the circled wagons, Jessie stifled a yawn. "Should've taken a nap instead of sightseeing. Guess I'd best give Rook a hand with supper or you boys won't be eating tonight."

James grabbed her by the arm before she took off. "Please, don't let Coralie bake the bread."

Jessie laughed, her eyes lit with mischievous delight. "Now, James, our dear sister-in-law has to learn to cook sometime. Just think of the abuse poor Jordan's stomach endures when she cooks for him."

Shuddering, James scowled. "Coralie is *his* wife. Let her experiment on him, not me. Remember the last time Rook let her bake the bread? It was gooey in the center and burnt black on the outside and we were stuck with just beans and pork for supper."

"And you boys were so nice, telling her how good it was."

James scowled. "The dog wouldn't even eat it."

"No promises." Jessie punched him in the arm, then sprinted off toward the supply wagons, the ribbon holding her shoulder-length hair away from her face slipping. The sight of that one touch of femininity still caught James by surprise. He'd never known Jessie to have any use for hair ribbons, preferring a length of leather when her hair had been long.

Change. So many things had changed since leaving their farm.

"Evening, James," a soft husky voice greeted him.

Shaking off the melancholy mood, he nodded at

Catarina, Sofia De Santis's granddaughter. He quickly continued on his way before the girl waylaid him. Each time he came into the camp, she found an excuse to speak to him. Though she was nice enough, she didn't interest him in the least. He had eyes only for Eirica.

He sniffed the air, his stomach rumbling in response to the scent of fresh bread and other savory smells. Passing close to Rook's fires, he grimaced. Bacon and beans. His appetite fled. He was heartily sick of the trail staple. A man needed variety, and Rook's meals tended to be monotonous and plain. Fresh meat would be a welcome change, but game was in short supply.

Glancing down at Alison who skipped contentedly beside him, he winked. "Let's go see what your ma's cooking. Maybe it'll be better than Rook's beans."

"Prob'ly not. All we get is beans and bacon, too." She made a face equal to his own and the two snickered. James ruffled her red curls and held out his hand.

With Alison's fingers wrapped around his, James threaded her way around camps, wagons and people going about their evening chores with a preoccupation that bespoke of drudgery. Whistling tunelessly, he spotted Eirica and quickened his pace.

She stood, her profile to him as she rocked Ian in her arms. But as he neared her, he slowed his steps, telling himself he didn't want to startle her with his sudden appearance. She was still skittish around him and he didn't want to risk having her drop the boy. And, in truth, James wanted a moment to watch her, to feast his tired eyes upon her beauty without making her uncomfortable.

It also gave him a chance to catch his breath, slow his heart and plan what he wanted to say. Maybe then, when he spoke to her, he wouldn't sound like some great big lubber who'd never been around women.

He drew courage from the fact that back in Westport, the ladies had found him attractive—as did several single women on the trail. When the emigrants gathered for an impromptu potluck and night of music and dancing, he never lacked partners. But this was different. He'd never actively courted a woman before. He had never wanted more than the entertainment of the moment. Working his struggling farm and raising his siblings had taken all his time and energy.

But now, the closer he got to Eirica, the tighter the neck of his faded blue shirt seemed. He removed the bandana he kept tied there so he didn't have to breathe the dust from the cattle and unbuttoned the top two buttons. After running his finger around the inside of the collar, he checked to make sure his hands were reasonably clean. There wasn't much he could do about the dust coating his clothing. When he realized what he was doing, he stuffed the square of material in the back pocket of his well-worn denims. Damn, facing a herd of stampeding cattle seemed easier than exposing his heart and soul to the woman who'd captured both.

His gaze slid over her profile. Her haunting beauty stole his breath. The glow of the sunset brought her hair to life and heaven's goodness shone in her ethereal features. She was an angel, sweet and gentle— vulnerable—made more so by the swell of her rounded belly where her unborn babe nestled. The miracle of that new life made him sigh.

He longed to put his hands on her and feel the movements that could sometimes be seen from beneath the apron she wore over the long skirt of her dress. An unexpected memory of his parents sitting on the wide porch swing in the evenings slid through his mind. Their zest for life had filled their home with love and laughter. James remembered hearing shouts of laughter one night from the porch and having gone to investigate. He'd found his pa sitting with his big hand spread over his wife's swollen belly, exclaiming with delight every time the baby—his sister, Jessie—had moved.

And when his ma had invited him to also feel, he'd done so, not expecting anything. But the bumps and movement of his baby sister had given him that first rush of wonder that came with the discovery of life. He'd never forgotten it, and had looked forward to the day when he could have his own family, feel his own babes' movements before holding them.

Eirica shifted her position. James felt his heart thud against his rib cage. His blood raced anew as their gazes met across the short span separating them. Conscious of her wariness, he stopped a respectable distance from her, content with the sheer pleasure of gazing into eyes as blue as bittersweet nightshade. Tendrils of golden-red hair framed her small oval face and he fought the urge to reach out and sweep the silky strands away from her face.

"Afternoon, ma'am." He jerked the felt-brimmed hat that had seen better days off his head and clutched it tightly between his fingers.

"Mr. Jones." She dipped her head then hesitated, as if about to say something more. But she remained silent, staring down at her son, her front teeth nervously pulling at her lower lip.

James allowed his eyes to dip to her moist mouth. Full and soft, her lips drove him crazy with desire. A man could spend a lifetime tasting her lips, discovering the hidden charms of her inner mouth, and never learn all her secrets. One part of him strummed with life, causing him to shift uncomfortably.

He swallowed a sigh of intense desire and reminded himself to go slow, have patience. More than anything, he longed to see love and trust replace the wounded and wary look in her eyes—and after eight years of raising his sister, he figured he had the patience of a saint.

Alison tugged at his hand. "Mama, we're back!"

Eirica smiled gently at her elder daughter. "So I see. Did you have a good time?"

The little girl let go of James and jumped up and down between the adults. "Oh yes, Mama. We climbed that big rock and everything looked so very tiny. I tried to see you but I couldn't. And guess what, Mama? James cut my name into the rock. Right on the very top for everyone to see!"

Eirica's head jerked up and around to face him. She pinned James with wide eyes gone smoky-gray. "You took Alison to the top of that rock?" A frown tilted the corners of her vulnerable lips downward.

James fiddled with his hat and tried to smile reassuringly. "Yes, ma'am, but don't fret none. Jess and I kept Alison close. She was never in any danger."

"We had fun, Mama." Alison pouted, glancing from one adult to the other. "James and Jessie made me hold their hands." She folded her arms across her narrow chest. "But I could've done it all by myself. I'm a big girl now!"

Eirica shifted Ian in her arms and visibly relaxed. She drew a deep breath. "Yes, sweetheart. You are a big girl. Your ma is just fussy as a hen with one chick."

Alison giggled. Eirica shifted Ian in her arms and

smiled down at her daughter. "I think Lara missed you. Why don't you go tell her about your adventure."

"Yes, Mama." Alison skipped over to her sister and chattered nonstop.

James stared at Eirica, noting her pale, pinched features. He gentled his voice, spoke slowly and carefully as one might to a frightened doe. "I'd never let anything happen to her, Eirica."

Eirica shifted Ian in her arms again, her gaze skittering away from his. "I know. I'm sorry, Mr. Jones, I truly trust you and Jessie. It's just that I worry so. She's so young and I feel so guilty for what happened to her."

James frowned. "Why should you feel guilty for something you had no control over?"

Eirica lifted tear-filled eyes to his. "If I had gone with Alison and Jessie to Fort Laramie, or not allowed Alison to go with your sister, that horrible woman and her brother might not have kidnapped them. Without my little girl as bait, Jessie might have been able to get away from them." She broke off and closed her eyes.

"If I'd lost Ali—"

"But you didn't," James interrupted, moving closer, drawn by the pain and guilt in her eyes. "Jessie and Alison weren't hurt. Everything turned out all right."

He glanced over at Alison, who was telling her sister about her climb up the rock. Though he sought to reassure Eirica, the memory of her daughter and his sister in the hands of the vengeful criminals still haunted his own nights.

Eirica glanced up at him, opening her mouth as if to protest. James stopped her by placing one finger gently over her lips. "Don't torture yourself, Eirica. What's done is done. Leave it where it belongs—in the past." He removed his touch, grateful she hadn't flinched from him. His heart lightened. She *was* coming to trust him.

"You can't convince me you don't still think about what happened," Eirica whispered.

James replaced his hat and pushed the brim up. "Yeah, I do. I go through hell just thinking about the what if's, but none of us knows the future, and we can't wrap those we love in cotton wool."

He grinned ruefully. "Though Lord knows, I tried with Jess when she was younger. I guarded her fiercer than a she-bear her cubs, so scared she'd hurt herself and them town folk would come take her away. But most of the time, my good intentions to protect her weren't appreciated."

A genuine and amused smile curved Eirica's lips. "I imagine Jessie was a handful."

James snorted. "Hah, Jess is willful, stubborn, rash—"

Eirica interrupted with a soft chuckle. "And you wouldn't have her any other way."

He grinned back, loving the sound of her laughter, grateful the sad, melancholy mood that normally shrouded her had lifted. "True enough. Your Alison reminds me of Jessie. Always out for an adventure."

James rocked back on his heels. Now that Alison was no longer under her father's oppressive thumb, she'd blossomed. Her confidence grew daily and she showed every sign of becoming as adventurous as Jessie. But the kidnapping had been too much for a young child. Worry for her sobered him. "Have her nightmares stopped?"

Eirica nodded. "I think so. She hasn't had one in more than a week now." A companionable silence fell between them. Finally, Eirica glanced at the fire. "I'd best see to supper."

The aroma of fresh bread set his stomach to growling. He longed to wrangle an invitation to stay and eat with her and her children, but he didn't want to rush her. Noting her tent hadn't yet been erected, he nodded. "I'll see to your tent before I go."

Eirica glanced up and shook her head. "No need, Mr. Jones. You're a busy man. I'll see to it after supper." She carried Ian to a blanket spread out on the ground. Before she bent to lay the sleeping toddler down, James, who'd followed her, reached out.

"Here, let me." He took the boy in gentle arms and lowered him to a pile of quilts. The day was warm so he didn't bother to cover him. Standing, he turned, not realizing Eirica stood so close to him. His arm brushed against her swollen belly.

Startled by the suddenness and the unexpectedness of his touch, she jumped back and lost her balance. James reached out to steady her. He released her arm when he saw the flash of fear in her eyes. He flinched against the stabbing pain in his gut. Damn, her instinctive reaction to his touch stung, and though he knew she couldn't help it, her reaction felt like someone had slammed a fist into him, knocking the air from his lungs. Not all men were mean drunks like her first husband.

But knowing she'd married young, and therefore had no other experience with men, gave him hope that one day she'd realize that all he wanted to do was love and cherish her. He took a deep, steadying breath, and left his hands hanging loosely at his sides where she could see them. "Eirica, you have nothing to fear from me. I'd never hurt you." He kept his voice low and soft, his body still.

Color crept up her neck and stained her cheeks. She

lifted miserable teary eyes to him. "I—I'm sorry, Mr. Jones. Sometimes I just react."

James tried a smile to lighten the tension between them. "I know." Again, the silence stretched between them, this time fraught with tension. He rubbed the back of his neck then adjusted his hat, trying to work up his courage. "I thought we'd agreed to drop the formality between us. I'd be honored if you'd just call me James. Please?"

Eirica twined her fingers together, her gaze locked with his. "All right—James." She picked at the fraying edges of her apron, but she didn't move away from him.

A wave of happiness stole through him. He held out his hand. "Friends?"

Hesitantly, she placed her hand in his. "Friends."

Quelling the urge to draw her close, James relished the feel of her small hand in his big calloused one. It thrilled him that she'd taken this step. He released her immediately, though he could have stood there all night holding her hand and gazing into the blue of her eyes. Her gaze was so full of emotion, he felt her thoughts, her pain and her uncertainty.

"Thank you, Eirica." Going to the back of her wagon, he reached in and grabbed the rolled-up canvas, brushing aside her second protest that she could see to her own tent. Time would heal her wounds. For now, he'd take it nice and slow and show her he could be trusted, that he would take care of her and cherish her. One way he could prove his good intentions was to ease her hardship on the trail. Whistling, he pushed up his shirt sleeves and unrolled the canvas tent.

Chapter Three

Eirica glared at James, who went about setting up her tent with a tuneless whistle. His cheerfulness made her long to march over and demand he stop, but she swallowed her pride. What else could she do? Aside from truly being tired from the long day, she'd learned during the past month it did little good to argue or protest when James decided on a course of action.

James Jones was too used to taking charge. She just wished he'd listen to her, consider her wishes, but like most males, he didn't think her serious, thought he knew best. And maybe he was right, but it hurt that he ignored her.

Turning away from him, she removed the Dutch oven from the fire and checked the bread. It was done, so she pulled it from the pan and set it out to cool. Then she put a pot of water over the hot coals for some tea. Minutes later, she sat on the wagon tongue, stretching her swollen feet out before her and cradling a tin cup of sweetened tea in her hands. Though she had a few precious minutes to sit and enjoy the peace, her growing debt to the Jones family, in particular to James, left her too edgy and restless to relax. Being a burden to others weighed heavily on her conscience.

Eirica understood the hardships of the trail, had witnessed the fate of women forced to continue alone after the loss of their fathers, husbands or children. So many women struggled with no help from their wagon train. If they fell behind, they were left to fend for themselves.

Eirica knew she could so easily have been in the same position if not for the generosity of James and his willingness to share his wagon and supplies. He'd made it possible for her to leave her husband and strike out on her own. Birk had made it very clear during their marriage that everything they owned belonged to him, that if she ever left him, it'd be with the clothes on her back and nothing more. Of course, he'd never thought she'd actually leave. Her lips thinned. She'd proved him wrong.

At least she had her wagon and supplies back, though Birk had nearly lost them when he'd tried crossing the river alone. Unwilling to think about him or what he'd put her through, Eirica gnawed on a hard-as-rock biscuit while slanting James a look from the corner of her eye.

She had to admit it felt heavenly knowing someone cared enough to step in and do what needed to be done—but that was the problem. Her growing dependence on James and the others scared her. Once they reached Oregon, they'd all go their separate ways and she'd be left to survive as best she could.

For her own peace of mind, she had to know she could be self-sufficient, physically and emotionally. It was time to stand up for herself, and stop relying on others, including James. But how to tell him without offending him or hurting his feelings? How could she make him understand how important her independence was to her?

Alison and Lara ran past, begging James to let them help. Watching him with her girls, she admired his patience at the small hands that hindered more than helped. The sight of the genuine affection between him and her daughters tugged her heart-strings, forcing Eirica to fight harder her growing attraction to him—another source of worry plaguing her mind and heart. His kindness and gentleness touched her, tempted her to reach out and take what he offered.

How could any woman not be drawn to this fine man? She shifted so she could watch him without craning her neck. He'd stopped working to roll up his sleeves, revealing tanned arms dusted with thick, dark, curly hair. Her gaze continued downward to skim long legs encased in faded and worn denim pants that fit snugly over narrow hips. Noting the holes in the knees, she made a mental note to mend them on the next wash day as a way to repay her debt.

Her attention slid back up his long, lean frame to his hair, black and silky-looking, falling in soft waves past his collar. The breeze ruffled the gently curling ends like a woman's fingers. When he reached up to steady a pole, his flannel shirt pulled taut. Muscles rippled from one side of his back to the other. A tiny quiver of appreciation darted through her. James was a man in his prime. He wasn't pretty-boy handsome like Coralie's brother Elliot but more rugged, earthy.

Staring at him, it was apparent he'd spent his days outdoors in the sun, wind and rain, even before heading west. A fine form such as his didn't happen overnight.

James chose that moment to glance over his shoulder. He caught her staring at him and had the audacity to grin, revealing strong white teeth in stark contrast to his darkly tanned face. The lines at the corners of his eyes crinkled with hidden amusement and the two grooves etched on either side of his mouth deepened. Her breath quickened. Unlike most other men on the trail, he kept his face shaved, revealing a square jaw that warned of a stubborn nature.

But oh Lord, that face of his. How had she managed so far not to be affected by the sheer beauty of it? He held her gaze with his own. Heat seared her cheeks. Flushed, Eirica glanced away, her breathing quickening. He could have any woman he wanted. So why her? She wasn't worthy of someone like James. She was too damaged, too worn in mind and body. But how to convince him that she wasn't interested? How to convince *herself* she wasn't interested!

Part of her rebelled, hating the thought of him with someone else, but knew it was best for him to turn his attentions elsewhere; Eirica could not allow herself to ever fall in love again. Though he was gentle and patient, he, too, would eventually consider only his own needs. The fact that he refused to listen to her sat like a lead ball in her stomach. He was just a man—a man like all others—and men weren't to be trusted, not even nice, handsome ones like James.

Though James wasn't mean like Birk, he would expect to dominate his wife and children. He was too used to being in charge, and she could never put herself under the dominance of another male, especially one with the same tendency to override her wishes, as he was doing now with the tent. It didn't matter that he believed he was doing her a favor.

In fact, that made him even more dangerous in her eyes, for Birk had been just as sweet and kind when they were courting. He'd won her over with fistfuls of wildflowers, store-bought gifts, sweet words and sweeter compliments followed by declarations of undying love. Eirica had believed she'd found her knight in shining armor, her hero, someone who'd love and cherish her forever.

How wrong and so very, very foolish she'd been. Heroes didn't exist outside the pages of some stupid books. As soon as Birk had what he'd wanted from her—someone to cook, clean and take care of all his needs—he'd revealed his true nature, one he'd carefully hidden from her during their courtship. It had only taken that first night alone with him to have her dreams of love, romance and happily-ever-after crushed.

Hunching over as if in pain, Eirica's eyes burned with remembered humiliation and terror of those first weeks of marriage. But she was wiser now. She knew better than to believe a man's promises of love and devotion. She'd learned her lesson, but the suppressed need to be swept off her feet lingered, reminding her of the innocent and naive girl she'd once been. Troubled, her fingers smoothed the material of her bodice over the worst of her scars.

Taking deep, slow breaths, Eirica calmed herself, forced her hands back into her lap. She wouldn't think about the past. With effort, she shoved the painful memories back into the dark recesses of her mind. Needing activity to keep the haunting nightmares at bay, she struggled to her feet and walked slowly to the back of her wagon, rubbing the tightening skin of her abdomen. She couldn't help stealing one last look at James.

How she longed to be proven wrong, longed to find true love, but the stakes were just too high. It was time to face reality. She was a widowed woman with three children, and soon she'd give birth to number four. With so much to be done to prepare for an infant, she didn't have the energy or time to waste on wishing for what could not be.

She peered inside the wagon, found the small, beat-up trunk that contained baby clothes and quilts. But it rested against the side, just out of reach, with heavy sacks of flour and rice piled around it. She frowned. Now what? She couldn't climb into the wagon anymore. With a sigh, she glanced over her shoulder and saw that James was finished setting up her tent. He was deep in conversation with his brother Jordan. She hesitated to interrupt, hating to ask anything else of him, yet she had no choice.

But before she could go to him, the two men walked away with Jordan leading his horse.

Eirica planted her hands on her hips. "Bother!"

"What's up, Eirica?"

Shifting her stance to face the woman who'd come up behind her, Eirica smiled. "Hi, Coralie," she greeted the pretty blond girl, then motioned in the direction of the two men. "Your husband just left with James."

"Yeah, he has first watch tonight, which means I'm stuck helping Jessie and Rook cook."

Jordan and Coralie had married days before setting out for Oregon. Eirica remembered Coralie's first few weeks on the trail. The newest Jones family member hadn't been at all enamored of outdoor life and hadn't hesitated to let everyone know. She'd been spoiled,

petulant and nearly impossible to be around. But
slowly she'd changed, matured into a caring woman.

Eirica shaded her eyes and glanced around. "Is
Jessie already helping Rook?"

Coralie grimaced. "Probably. As I should be. Do
you need her?"

"No," she sighed. "It can wait. I planned to go
through the baby clothes I brought with me tonight.
Figured they might need airing and some mending, but
I can't climb into the wagon to get them." She patted
her belly.

Scoffing, her friend stuck her nose in the air. "You
don't need Jessie for that. I can get them just as well.
Where are they?" She clambered into the back of the
wagon after adjusting the skirts of her beige wash-day-
length calico dress.

Eirica hid her smile at Coralie's obvious need to
compete with Jessie. She pointed out the small trunk.
Sisters by marriage, Jessie and Coralie were as different as night and day. Jessie was a tomboy skilled in the
outdoors and Coralie a city-bred lady spoiled by her
father. The two had started the trip as mutual nemeses,
but their longstanding feud had finally come to an end,
leaving Eirica free to enjoy both her new friends, their
easy banter, and now-friendly rivalry.

"Here we go. See?" Coralie gave one final pull and
fell back on her bottom, puffing and panting. "We don't
need Jessica for this." Wearing a pleased grin, she
hopped down from the back of the wagon, then swayed.

"Coralie!" Concerned, Eirica reached out and
grabbed the girl's arm. "Are you all right?"

Coralie leaned against the wagon and closed her
eyes briefly while fanning her cheeks with her hands.
"I'm fine. Just a bit dizzy."

"Dizzy?" Eirica frowned, then did some fast calculations. "Have you been dizzy before, I mean, recently?"

Coralie lowered her voice to a mere whisper. "I haven't said anything to Jordie because I don't want him to worry, but I've been feeling sick and am so tired. I'm so afraid I'm going to take ill and die." She closed her eyes. Tiny tears clung to her lashes.

Her own problems forgotten, Eirica put her arm around the younger woman's narrow shoulders. "Coralie, when was your last flow?"

Coralie's gaze flew open, clouded with confusion. "My last—" Understanding dawned in her baby-blue eyes. Her gaze went wide first with shock, followed by disbelief, then absolute joy.

"I haven't paid it much attention out here, traveling each day. It's been a couple of months, I think." She paused, grabbing Eirica's fingers tightly. "Oh, Eirica," she breathed, "you don't suppose—could I be with child?" Her hushed voice tingled with suppressed excitement.

Laughing, Eirica hugged her. "Don't think there's any supposing about it. Looks like you're going to be a mama."

As sudden as it had come, Coralie's joy fled and a look of horror washed over her features. "I can't be with child. I don't know how to be a mother. I've never even tended a baby. How will I know what to do? I can't do this." Her voice rose and ended in a panicked squeak.

Eirica rolled her eyes. This was the Coralie Eirica knew well. Overemotional and melodramatic. "Calm down, Coralie. You'll do just fine."

Seeing that her words didn't reassure her, Eirica put her hand on the other woman's shoulders. "Look, my baby is due in a month. You'll have plenty of time to learn how to diaper, bathe, hold and care for an infant. I'll show you everything and you can help me and practice." She lifted the lid of the trunk. "By the time yours is born, you'll be a pro, and I even have lots of baby clothes for you to use—"

Eirica's voice trailed off abruptly. An odor of rot filled the air and made her gag. "Oh no," she moaned, staring at the mildew-covered baby things in disbelief. She lifted out what had once been a tiny white gown. It was now black with a hole through it where the material had rotted.

"The dampness from all those storms got into the trunk." Eirica pulled out layer after layer of moldering cotton. "They're all ruined." Even the tiny blankets and quilts on the bottom were covered with holes and black dots of mold.

Coralie covered her mouth, obviously fighting the urge to gag. She moved away. "Oh, Eirica, how terrible. What are you going to do? Will you have time to sew more before the baby comes?"

Feeling the weight of responsibility return to sag on her shoulders, Eirica blinked back tears of helplessness. "I don't have any material. Birk wouldn't let me buy any to bring. I was counting on these lasting until I reached Oregon." She bit her lip and just stared at the ruined layette.

Coralie patted Eirica on the arm. "We'll figure out something. I have some material from Pa's store that he insisted I bring, even though he knows I can't sew. We can see if there's anything there you can use."

Hearing a shout across the way, Coralie glanced over her shoulder and grimaced when Jessie motioned her over. "Guess it's time to start cooking. Those hired hands of Wolf's are worse than a swarm of locusts. I swear, they'd eat their tin plates if they could."

Standing, she awkwardly patted Eirica on the shoulder then hurried over to where Jessie and Rook were busy preparing supper.

Eirica closed her eyes, unable to face the prospect of sorting through the ruined clothing. She thought of Coralie's offer of material and just as quickly rejected it. Even if she paid for it—not that she could afford to do so—she wouldn't take it. Coralie would need her supply for her own dresses and baby things in Oregon. Eirica would just have to cut up one of her woolen blankets for nappies and infant-size blankets. As for clothing, she'd have to do the same with one of her old dresses or use Birk's old shirts, which she'd saved to reuse the material.

With frustration coursing through her, she slammed the trunk lid closed and stood. She'd deal with this later. She just couldn't think about it now.

Alone once again, she faced the enormity of her situation. Anxiety churned in her stomach and a chill ran through her. Her palms were slick with sweat. She wiped her hands on her apron, then wiped the moisture from her eyes, feeling scared and overwhelmed by the knowledge that the survival of her children rested squarely on her slim shoulders.

How could she do this? She had some money stashed away in a hidden compartment beneath the floor of the wagon—not nearly enough, though. Birk had dug into it, spending a good amount of it on the trail to purchase liquor from anyone willing to sell it to him.

Now she was glad she'd risked Birk's fury by taking some of that money herself every time he got into it, tucking it into her sewing basket. She'd also kept a portion of the payments she received for doing laundry for some of the single men in her wagon party. She would really be in desperate straits if she hadn't. Luckily for her, Birk had believed he'd spent more on his drink than he truly had, which kept him from depleting their resources further.

But even by adding the two stashes of cash together, the funds wouldn't last long setting up a farm in Oregon. Things would be tight until the first harvest. By her calculations, there wouldn't be anything to spare.

So what was she going to do? A hard knot of dread formed in her throat. She swallowed, fighting panic. No. She would not give in to her fears. Closing her eyes, she slowed her breathing by taking a deep breath, feeling the air flow clear down to her toes. Then she released it, imagining all her fears and worries leaving her as she exhaled slowly and completely. She continued to breathe consciously until she felt her heartbeat calm and the tightness in her throat ease.

"Life goes on," she whispered under her breath. She thought of Sofia and the woman's determination to carry out her husband's dreams. Then she thought of Jessie. Nothing stopped her young friend from going after what she wanted.

Eirica struggled to her feet, determined to prove to herself and everyone else that she was strong and in control. She'd survived this far: she'd taken the steps to free herself and her children from Birk's violent nature before he'd drowned. Love for her children had given her the courage then, and that same love and determination to give them a better life would give her the courage to make it to Oregon and find a way to survive once there. Her babies would have what she hadn't had as a child: happiness and laughter and all the love they could ever want.

A gentle rolling movement came from inside her

womb, as if her unborn child was trying to reassure her that everything would be all right. It made Eirica smile. She patted her stomach. This infant, helpless at birth, would be dependent on her for warmth, nourishment and love. This child would grow, learn and someday be ready to face life on its own.

And like her unborn child, Eirica was a babe in the woods when it came to survival. She'd been thrust into a harsh situation, an unfriendly world, but she'd learn. She'd grow. She'd survive. And like those baby clothes she had yet to go through, she'd salvage what she could from her life and start anew.

Doling out cold bacon and slabs of hot, buttered bread, she sat down with Alison and Lara. As they ate, she asked her daughters about what they'd seen that day. Each night for the last two weeks, she'd gone through the same ritual and slowly, her girls had started to talk openly and voice their thoughts.

But tonight brought forth a wondrous milestone and tears to Eirica's eyes when her girls' shy, hesitant giggles turned to uncontrollable laughter.

White Wolf rode into the wagon circle, tired, dusty and hungry. But it wasn't food that led him to where Rook, his long-time friend, prepared supper. No, he hungered for the sight of his wife.

His wife.

Would he ever get used to those two words? He hoped not. The thrill that filled him each time he saw Jessie, thought of her and realized they were husband and wife, partners in life, made him feel alive as never before. No other man could be so lucky or happy as he was. He dismounted and tied his black stallion to the back of a supply wagon.

Jessie, with both hands immersed in a sack of flour,

smiled when he approached. "You're early. Supper won't be ready for a while yet."

Her eyes sparkled with joy and humor—and as her gaze slid over him, lingering on the golden expanse of chest showing through the open buckskin vest he wore with no shirt beneath it, they darkened. And when her gaze slid lower to the front of his buckskin breeches, her tongue snaked out to wet her lips. Recognizing her hunger, her need for him, sent his blood racing through his veins.

He scooped her up into his arms. "Supper can wait. Your husband cannot."

Jessie giggled and tried to shake the flour from her hands. Fingerprint-size spots of flour dotted her cheeks and nose. She shoved her hair out of her eyes, leaving a wide streak of flour across her forehead. She finally gave up trying to rid herself of the flour and circled her arms around his neck, leaving him coated with the powdery stuff. "Wolf, put me down."

"You have flour all over your face," he teased. Her attempts to brush it off made it worse, hiding the tiny brown freckles sprinkled across the bridge of her nose. He laughed, low and private. "Leave it. I'll wash it off later. I'm getting used to seeing my wife covered with either mud or flour."

Her eyes darkened to forest green, reminding him of their first meeting, when she'd been wet with mud from her head down to the toes of her boots. Jessie mistook the reason for his humor. "Watch it or you'll be wearing some as well. Now put me down. I've got work to do."

"Nope. It's our first-month anniversary and I'm taking you away. Rook will have to do without you tonight." He glanced around and spotted Jessie's sister-in-law. Wolf's smile turned wicked. "He has Coralie to assist him tonight and in the morning."

Jessie's brows rose with full understanding. "You rat. You purposely assigned Jordan first watch knowing if she didn't have to cook for Jordan, she'd help me and Rook."

Wolf affected a look of innocence. She knew him well but that didn't mean he'd admit as much to her. "You wound me, Jessica. It was his turn."

Her eyes narrowed and she reached up to tug none-too-gently on a strand of long, flowing, golden-brown hair. "You, my husband, are devious. Simply devious." She grinned, her fingers tangling in his hair as she pulled his lips to hers in a long, ravenous kiss.

Behind them, Rook snorted in disgust. "Git yerselves outta here. I has a meal ta fix and the pair of you are in my way."

Wolf didn't hesitate. He strode away, eager to have some private time alone with his wife. The one aspect of trail life he disliked was the lack of privacy. No matter where he turned, there were people. Lots of them. But not tonight. While out hunting for fresh meat, he'd found the perfect spot an hour's ride from Independence Rock.

"Wait, Wolf, put me down."

"Why?"

Exasperated, she twisted out of his arms and landed on her feet. "Knowing you, you've probably found some nice, romantic, out-of-the-way place to spend the night. I need to grab some clothes." Her gaze turned dreamy and, without giving him time to argue, she sprinted away, hopping into the back of a wagon.

Wolf returned to his horse and pulled down the antelope he'd killed for the evening meal. At his feet,

Wahoska—his companion for the last seven years—
eyed the carcass with gleaming eyes. "You'll have to
wait old man," he told the wolf. The animal growled
low in its throat but shuffled off.

Wolf grabbed the hind legs of the antelope and
hefted the dead animal over his shoulder and took it to
Rook. "Figured the men might be getting sick of your
beans and bacon."

Rook whistled and rubbed his hands together. He
wagged his bushy white brows. "Nice of you to think
of us while you go off to celebrate." He ambled toward
one of the wagons and returned with a canvas sack.
"Here's some grub. Figured ya would take the lass
away t'night, seein' as it's been a month since ye was
hitched."

The old man didn't miss anything. Rook knew him
too well. But before he could thank his friend, the
crusty cook stalked away, muttering beneath his
breath about the foolishness of youth.

Wolf loaded up the supplies and paced. What was
taking Jessie so long? Impatient to be off, he spun
around, ready to go haul his wife out of her wagon. He
came to an abrupt halt. His jaw dropped. For the second time since he'd known her, Jessica Jones had discarded her normal male garb—for a dress in pale blue
calico. She'd also piled her dark curls on top of her
head—revealing her long slender neck kissed to a
golden brown by the sun—instead of leaving it to
frame her face or blow wildly in the wind. Standing
with the setting sun behind her, she took his breath
away.

Growling, he swept her into his arms, set her sideways in his saddle and leaped up behind her. He pulled
her across his lap and wrapped his arms around her.

"Vixen. I give you no guarantees that we'll make it to the spot I found for us."

Jessie's eyes glowed with mischief. She reached up and threaded her fingers through his long, golden-brown hair. "You're the one who showed me there are definite advantages to wearing a dress," she whispered, licking her lips teasingly while wiggling in his lap.

Wolf groaned and spurred his horse into a full gallop.

59

Chapter Four

Rook chewed on the end of his pipe and watched the newlyweds ride off. Grumbling, he scowled at Coralie who stared after her sister-in-law with a contented smile. "Quit ya grinnin'! They's leavin' all the work to us."

Coralie giggled and wrapped her arms around him. "Poor Rook, you have me. I won't abandon you."

Heat crept up his whisker-covered cheeks. He waved his hands helplessly at his side. Just as quick as the impulsive hug began, it ended. Coralie twirled away from him, leaving him torn between relief and regret. His own daughter, had she lived, would have been about the same age.

He shook his pipe at her, thrusting away old pain and bitterness. "If'n yer young man rode in here right now, you'd leave this old man without a second thought and don't tell me different, lass. I'm surrounded by a bunch of swarmy-headed, lovestruck young folk." His momentary regret at how Lady Fate had cheated him of a family faded for the moment when the young woman before him crossed her hands across her chest, her baby-blue eyes narrowed.

"That isn't true." She lifted a hand, ready to denounce his accusation then, realizing Rook had baited her, Coralie grinned impishly. "I'd at least think *twice* before abandoning you."

Rook eyed the carcass at his feet, hiding his smile. "Sassy and impertinent, too," he muttered, peeping up at her.

Coralie slanted him an arched-brow look. "Oh, quit your griping. You don't fool me, Rook. All bluster and a heart bigger than that rock everyone went to see." She walked around the antelope, holding her skirts well away from it. "We shall have a fine meal tonight. Should I go tell the others? There's more than enough for everyone to have some."

"Good idea, lass. I'll dry what don't git eaten." He pulled a long hunting knife from a sheath around his waist and knelt beside the carcass, laughing beneath his breath when Coralie shuddered and practically ran from his cook area.

Rook set to work. He stuck his pipe back between his lips, chewed the stem and shook his head in bemusement. He'd broken one of his steadfast rules on this trip. He'd allowed himself to care for the folk he was traveling with, particularly Coralie and Jessie. He'd come to regard the two young ladies as his adopted daughters. Each made him think of the family he'd lost so long ago.

Hot coals of emotion burned in his gut and brought painful memories to his mind. Once more, he found himself standing on the edge of a familiar dark, bottomless pit. He teetered, fighting waves of despair.

Standing abruptly, he shoved the past back into the hollow shell of his heart.

But it was too late to stop the flow of need, of longing. Being around Jessie and Coralie made him realize just what had been taken from him. Hell, he might have been a grandfather by now if Lady Fate had looked kinder upon him and his. Though it was pointless, he couldn't help but wonder what kind of woman his own daughter would have become had she lived. And his other child. Would it have been a son or another daughter?

No one had known Annabelle had been with child, not even Wolf. And he had been with him that fateful day when they'd returned to Rook's cabin and found his wife and daughter dead, murdered. It was cold consolation that he and Wolf had tracked the bandits responsible and taken care of them. Nothing could bring back his family.

Ah, he'd missed out on so much. Regret for what he had no control over bowed his shoulders. He stabbed a hunk of meat and added it to the growing mound on the cut board. For years, he'd closed himself off from as much contact with humanity as he could get away with, never allowing himself to care or be cared for—with the exception of Wolf. And he'd succeeded—until now.

Hell, he'd done it this time all right. He glanced around the camp, his gaze lingering on each and every person. There wasn't a single person in this wagon party he hadn't come to care for. They were family, this group of emigrants. Across the way, Alison and Lara Macauley chased one another, their childish giggles wresting a smile from his gruff features and intensifying his anguish. He shook his head. "Must be gittin' old and senile." He attacked the antelope carcass with a vengeance born of desperation.

A soft nose pressed into his side. He glanced down to see a black-and-tan dog staring up at him, her soulful brown eyes soft, intent on him, as if sensing the sadness in his heart. "Ah, Sadie, lass, what's come over me? Past is past."

The dog belonged to Jessie and her brothers. She whined, then stuck her nose in the air, sniffing. Rook grinned, the gloom in his heart lifting. "Hungry, are ya?" He eyed her swollen belly. "I expect so seein' how that rascal wolf got you pregnant." On cue, a large white wolf joined them. Wahoska licked Sadie's muzzle, then growled low in his throat, as if demanding food for his hungry mate.

Grumbling about randy young men, newlyweds and old wolves who had nothing better to do than make more work for him, Rook grabbed two fresh, meaty bones he'd set aside. "Here, this ought to hold the pair of you until after supper's fixed." The dog and wolf grabbed their treats and ran beneath the wagon to gnaw in delight.

Behind him he heard steps, then Coralie's voice. "I'm back. Lars will be by shortly and so will Eirica. Mrs. De Santis—"

Without looking at her, afraid she'd see the inner turmoil he battled, Rook growled low in his throat at the mention of that woman's name. He sliced off a large slab. "Take this ta her. Don't want her coming 'ro—" His voice faltered when he saw two pair of legs encased in baggy trousers come to a halt before him. He straightened, embarrassed to see the woman in question standing beside Coralie along with her elder grandson, Dante. She smiled smugly.

"This should do for ya, Mrs. De Santis."

"*Si.*" She took it and passed it to Dante who carried it back to their wagon.

Coralie cleared her throat and glanced nervously from Sofia to Rook. "Sofia, uh, has offered to help us tonight."

Rook sat back on his heels, pulled on his white beard and glared at Sofia from beneath lowered white brows. He took stock of her glittering black eyes, the haughty tilt of her nose and a bulging sack of God knew what foreign spices and food she clutched in her right hand. His hackles rose.

"Help? Hah." He graced her with his best don't-mess-with-me frown. It sent grown men running but had no effect on this woman. He set the knife down and jabbed a finger toward her, but he addressed his comments to Coralie. "Ya tell that woman we don't need her help nor her fancy spices. We's got it covered between us."

He glowered when Coralie shifted on her feet. "An extra pair of hands might be nice."

"Bah!" This was his domain and as far as he was concerned, there could only be one cook—and it wasn't going to be her. The woman could find another way to repay Wolf.

The wagon master had insisted she and her grandchildren join his group when he'd learned that she'd been left behind to nurse her sick family. He'd come across her, a-month after she'd lost most of her family, fighting a group of rough-looking men who were trying to rob her and rape her granddaughter. The thieves had gotten away with her money, leaving her unable to offer any payment for Wolf's assistance, not that his friend would have taken the woman's money. Still, Rook couldn't blame the woman for wanting to offer recompense, but he didn't need or want her help, and he especially didn't want her around him.

Undaunted by Rook's blatant dismissal, Sofia lifted

a thick black brow then glanced around, noting that the slab of pork needed to be sliced, the pieces already frying were quickly turning brown and two pots of water were boiling away. She indicated the hunks of fresh meat he'd set on a wooden board next to the pots. A sack of dried beans sat on the ground.

"You would ruin perfectly good meat by cooking it with beans and pork? No. I will make *agnoletti*. It will be delicious." She kissed her fingers with a loud smack.

Rook had no idea what kind of meal she was thinking to fix and didn't care to find out. "*My* boys don't need some fancy foreign dish they can't even say. My grub sticks ta their ribs. Tha's what they need: Food that'll stay with them." He pursed his lips and added, "Ain't nothin' wrong with beans."

"Nothing unless that's all you eat," Coralie muttered beneath her breath, eyeing Sofia's bag of spices with interest.

"What was that, lass?" He shoved his hands down onto his hips and stood.

Coralie jumped. "Ah, nothing, Rook. Nothing at all." She glanced around, then smiled. "While Sofia cooks whatever she's planning and you cut up the meat, I'll start the bread."

Both Rook and Sofia protested at the same time, for once in agreement. Repressing a shudder, Rook jammed his pipe into the pocket of his buckskin shirt. "No, lass. I'll do it." The men would skin him alive if he let Coralie make the bread. "Add the beans and rice to the water and finish cookin' the pork." He turned to glare at Sofia. "I'm still in charge around here and I says we's having a nice stew of beans, pork and antelope meat."

Coralie folded her arms across her chest and tapped

65

an impatient foot. "You don't trust me to make the bread." Her big blue eyes filled with tears. "How am I supposed to learn if no one lets me practice?" She sniffed and glanced first at him, then Sofia from beneath golden lashes darkened by tears.

Rook knew Coralie too well, had seen her produce tears at will without even blinking an eye. The lass had perfected that pout long ago; it had got her whatever she wanted before she could walk! But Sofia fell for it.

"Now look what you've done. You've made the child cry." She glared at him and shook her finger. "She's right. I'll teach her to make bread so light, it floats."

"No," Rook bellowed, taking a step forward. "I'm in charge of cookin' and I say who fixes what." He glared at Coralie who had the audacity to blink her innocent blues at him. Despite her penchant for complaining, the lass really tried. The spoiled little-girl demeanor she adopted hid a tender, sensitive soul.

As if sensing his weakness, Coralie sniffed and turned away, shoulders hunched for good measure. Rook ignored Sofia who stood with her arms crossed, her eyes challenging him. Unwilling to allow this dark-eyed woman to worm her way further into his territory, he hacked another chunk of meat from the carcass, using more force than needed. He sent Coralie a fierce frown from over his shoulder.

Had he seen real dejection in her eyes before she'd turned away? Working with her so closely since he'd volunteered to teach her to cook, he knew it was a sore spot with her that she hadn't managed to master bread-baking and had to endure a goodly amount of teasing with each failure.

"Well, what're ya waitin' fer? That bread ain't gonna bake itself." Coralie was his protégée and he'd be damned if he'd allow that *woman* to teach the lass how to bake bread—not when his trail bread was the best.

With a cry of happiness, Coralie spun around and hugged him again. "Thanks, Rook. I won't burn it this time, I promise."

After Coralie released him, Rook stuck his pipe between his lips and moved back to his work area, keeping Coralie close so he could keep an eye on the bread making. Chopping up bits of meat to add to the boiling pot of beans, he refrained from watching Sofia. He was cooking his stew, no matter what.

But as he hovered over Coralie, repressing his shudders as she spilled flour and made a gummy mess of the dough, loneliness assailed him. The love surrounding him brought home just how empty his life had become. At his age, wandering from place to place no longer appealed. He longed to put the past behind him and settle in one spot to live out the remainder of his years. He slid his gaze to the black-haired widowed woman working not more than five feet from him.

Sofia glanced up from a frying pan of sizzling meat and lifted her eyebrow as if she read his mind and knew the unrest in his heart.

The tantalizing scent of spices reached him and made his mouth water. He sent her a disgruntled glare, gave his attention to Coralie and started telling her one of his tales to keep his mind from wandering down forbidden paths. There was no other woman for him. He was destined to roam alone until he met his maker.

For the women traversing the trail, their day commenced before night released its grip on the world to the light of the sun. No matter how tired or how far they traveled the day before, the women left their tents to prepare for the new day long before the sun peeped over the eastern horizon.

Eirica, snuggled between her quilts, woke to the sounds of muffled chatter outside her tent. She wanted to open her eyes but they refused to cooperate. Surely it couldn't be time to rise already. She felt as though she'd only just gone to bed. Between the hard, rocky ground and her heavy, cumbersome womb, sleep usually came in fitful bouts, leaving her feeling tired and achy in the mornings. What she wouldn't give for a soft feather bed.

She huddled deeper into the warmth surrounding her, dozing lightly. Outside, noise continued to disperse the fog shrouding her senses. Somewhere on the other side of the canvas walls, the sounds of clanking pans and the harsh whirl of a coffee grinder made her wince. Groaning, she ran her hand through her disheveled hair and rubbed her gritty eyes. Precious time was wasting. There was much to be done before the signal sounded to hit the trail.

Slowly, she worked the stiffness from her back, shoulders and neck and thought of the decision she'd made during the long night while sleep eluded her. It troubled her greatly that she had to rely on others so much. Each person traveling west had their own load to carry, it didn't seem fair that she added to it.

So this day, her eighty-first of traveling, marked her first step toward independence. Anne and Lars, Jessie and Coralie, Wolf and Rook, and all the others had been there for her and her children while her ribs healed and she came to terms with what Birk's death meant to her life. They'd all been so wonderful, but good conscience deemed it time—past time, in fact— for her to stand on her own two feet. After all, when she reached Oregon, they'd all be spread apart and she'd truly be on her own.

Alone. On her own. Those words sent frissons of fear darting through her. Knowing if she dwelled on it, she'd take the easy way and continue as she had for the last month, she put it from her mind. Quickly, she unbraided her hair, combed her fingers through the long golden-red ripples that fell to her waist then twisted the strands into a tight bun at the nape of her neck. As much as she'd like to dally, to put off starting the new day, certain bodily functions couldn't be ignored a moment longer. She left the tent.

In the predawn grayness, she eyed the shadowy figures of women moving about. Some headed for the river with dinged and dented pots swaying in their hands as they walked, while others grouped together in small, silent clusters. A young woman, also pregnant, motioned for Eirica to join them.

She joined the five women who stood in a tight circle facing outward. Each held their skirts fanned out to the sides and in the center, they shielded a woman relieving herself. When the woman stood, she smiled at Eirica and motioned that they should trade places.

Eirica took care of her bodily needs in the same fashion and when done, she traded places with another woman, fanning her skirts out to the sides. She stayed until another woman came and took her place. This method of women providing one another some measure of privacy worked when they camped together. When her group was off alone, the men erected a canvas latrine. With only her and Coralie wearing dresses, they couldn't shield each other very well.

Back at her tent, she started a fire in the cold pit from the night before, then put a pot of water on to boil. This was her favorite time of day—before children and the trail made demands on her. Cradling a cup of hot tea between her palms, she used the last of her cherished moments before the sky turned gray-blue to gather her thoughts and plan her day.

By the time she roused her children, the aromatic scent of roasting coffee beans and frying bacon mingled with wood smoke. Men left their warm cocoons of quilts and grabbed cups of coffee before driving out oxen and mules from wagon enclosures or rounding up stock left to wander and graze at will. After the animals were yoked, wagon wheels and axles had to be checked, tents taken down and wagons packed.

Watching the bustle of activity increase around her, Eirica hurriedly washed down two dry biscuits with the remainder of her cold tea. Her children ate their meal of cold bacon and biscuits topped with butter and a thin layer of precious jam while kneeling around a wooden box that served as a table. Brushing crumbs from her apron, she sighed, longing for the day when she could fix a real breakfast again: Thick slices of ham, fresh eggs and hot slices of buttery bread. And coffee. Hot, strong, sweet, with just a tad of cream.

But making a pot of coffee just for her consumption didn't seem worth the effort, and cooking in the morning following a sleepless night required more energy than she usually possessed. Soon, she promised herself.

A glance over her shoulder confirmed her children were done with their meal as well. Three faces with jam smeared on their cheeks and white mustaches on their upper lips greeted her. Smiling, she washed the sticky fingers and faces. "Now, go play while Mama finishes cleaning up. Alison girl, keep an eye on your brother."

"Yes, Mama." Alison grabbed hold of Ian's hand and they ran off. Lara followed more slowly, clutching her tattered blanket.

After wiping off the tin plates and rinsing the cups, Eirica packed the leftover bread from the evening meal and the cold meat from the antelope Wolf had provided the night before into an unbleached muslin pouch for the noon stop. After placing it and the Dutch oven with rising bread dough into the wagon where she could easily access them, she rubbed her lower back to ease the lingering stiffness.

A sharp jab inside her prompted her to caress her swollen belly. Soon, she'd hold her babe in her arms. Impatience to have her pregnancy come to an end warred with the fear of giving birth on the trail. She sighed. It could be worse. Some women traveling had no one to assist them. Both she and Anne had each assisted in several births on the trail, fetched by frantic husbands. Thankfully, she'd have Anne and Sofia when her time came.

Laughter from a family camped nearby drew Eirica's attention. Like most of the emigrants making the long arduous journey, the fertile green land of Oregon had lured Lars and Anne Svensson from their struggling farm as well.

Eirica watched Lars tease his two young daughters, Kerstin and Hanna. Both girls shrieked with delight. Witnessing the bountiful display of love caused a ball of envy to wind tight inside her. How she longed for the carefree happiness so many families took for granted. Not so much for herself, but for her children who'd never known the tender loving attention of a doting father or relaxed, fun-filled mealtimes.

Neither had she, she realized, turning away when Lars unashamedly kissed his wife on the lips in front of their children. Mealtimes in her father's house had always been silent affairs, broken only by the noisy, rude, eating habits of her brothers and their demands for more food. And sitting down to eat at the same table with Birk always tied her stomach in knots. Would he be displeased with the food, or would one of the children spill their milk or start fussing? It had never taken much to set him off. And if his day had gone badly, then nothing any of them did pleased him.

Suddenly, she was thrown back in time, caught in the bruising grip of a daymare as images from her haunting past played before her eyes. She shook with remembered pain, recalling the time Birk had come in from the field and found supper not on the table. She'd just given birth to Alison days before, and caring for her newborn had caused her to fall behind in supper preparations.

Birk had been furious and in his rage, he'd thrown the pot of boiling water at her, burning her stomach and half of her chest. A low sound from her throat brought her back to the present. It took several minutes to calm herself. Birk was dead and could no longer cause them pain.

With her breathing steadied, she repeated her vow to see that love and laughter filled her children's hearts. She glanced around, checking their whereabouts. Lara stood at the edge of the Svenssons' camp. Kerstin ran over and led her to Hanna.

Eirica smiled. Her quiet little Lara adored Anne's two daughters and surprisingly, none of the boys scared her. The Svenssons had four strapping sons. Bjorn, fifteen, bent down and tweaked Hanna's long blond braids, then reached for Kerstin's, but she slapped him away. To Lara's delight, the boy also reached over and tapped her on the nose before sauntering away, leaving three giggling girls behind him.

The sight of her love-starved daughter saddened Eirica. Could she ever make up for what her children had lacked in their short lives? Fighting off the ever-present guilt that she hadn't taken steps to stop Birk a long time ago, she turned in a slow circle, searching for Alison and Ian.

Ian moved faster than a jackrabbit these days and required at least three sets of eyes to keep him out of mischief. She breathed a sigh of relief when she spotted him running from Alison a short distance away. She stole a few moments to watch them as well.

Alison trapped Ian next to a wagon wheel that was taller than he was. Unwilling to lose to his elder sister, Ian dropped to his hands and knees and crawled between Alison's spread legs, then straightened his own sturdy limbs and took off, shouting in triumph.

Eirica chuckled as their gleeful laughter filled the morning air. She shook her head. Those two were so full of energy, just watching them left her feeling exhausted. But witnessing their carefree abandon gave her hope that over time, the memory and affects of their father's abuse would fade into oblivion.

Reassured her children were fine for the moment, she put out the fire, then turned her attention to the tent. She ran her hands down over her swollen middle and grimaced. Dealing with the tent was the one chore she dreaded each day. Getting down on all fours was hard enough but getting up again was another matter. With a resigned sigh, Eirica gathered the blankets and quilts and arranged them on the floor of the wagon, near the front to form a padded sitting area for her three children.

Minutes later, the tent lay in a heap on the ground. Huffing and puffing, Eirica rolled it up. Using the wagon wheel to hold on to, she struggled to her feet.

But before she could bend back down to pick up the heavy rolled canvas, two voices stopped her. She turned to see Alberik, Anne and Lars's eldest son, and Dante, Sofia's grandson standing there. They eyed each other their stances competitive.

"Excuse me, Mrs. Macauley, but I'd be happy to load your tent for you." Red crept up Alberik's neck. "You really shouldn't be doing this in your, um, condition."

Eirica smiled gently at the eldest Svensson boy, marveling at how nicely his parents had raised him. A woman's "condition" had never stopped her father, brothers or husband from making their demands on the women in her family. It was life as normal, before the birth and after. She liked this concern on her behalf, believed it good for the young man to help others, though she warned herself not to get used to it. "Thank you, Alberik. I'd appreciate your help."

She watched the nineteen-year-old heft the tent effortlessly into his arms and load it into the back of the wagon. Without asking, Dante, three years older than Alberik, took charge of her supply boxes and sacks. Both boys reached for the tailgate at the same time, neither willing to give in to the other. Eirica swallowed her laughter as they both placed her tailgate back into the slots. Alberik managed to grab the strings and draw the canvas cover closed to secure the load so nothing could bounce out of the back while traversing the rutted and rocky trail.

Eirica plucked at her apron. "Thank you, again, Alberik, Dante."

Alberik blushed again. "I'd be happy to come every morning and give you a hand with anything heavy."

For the first time on the trip, Eirica realized that Anne's eldest was only a few years younger than herself. She felt so much older. The last thing she wanted to do was encourage him. "I don't want to impose or take you from your own chores."

He glanced up at her, giving her a shy smile. "It's no trouble."

Not to be outdone, Dante shuffled his feet. "Same here."

Anne joined them, her eyes alight with amusement. "I can't believe I haven't thought of you needing help loading up in the mornings, Eirica. I feel terrible."

Eirica smiled. "I've managed just fine, Anne, though I must admit, it's getting harder to deal with that tent." Wanting to be fair to the two young men— each vying to be the one to help her, she had an idea. "With two of you offering to help, I wouldn't feel as though I were taking so much of your time." And now she wouldn't be quite so beholden to James, either. The thought made her feel both good and guilty.

Anne nodded, met Eirica's eyes. "What a good idea. Alberik can help you in the mornings. I have his father and brothers to load our wagons and can do without him."

Dante grinned. "And I'll take the evenings."

Nodding to each other, the two men left, each with shoulders thrown back and swaggering steps. Eirica had misgivings. She didn't want to cause any trouble between them. "I hope I'm not encouraging either one of them, Anne." Realizing belatedly how it must sound to her friend, she groaned. "I didn't mean it like—"

Anne put her arm across Eirica's shoulder. "Don't say it. I know what you meant, Eirica. Both of them are young, but—" she smiled wickedly—"A little healthy competition won't hurt either one of them, and neither will learning some manners around a lady."

Eirica joined Anne in soft laughter. She admired

Anne who had raised four sons who would someday make wonderful, considerate and loving husbands. Of course, they had the perfect role model in their father.

Conscious of the time, Anne hurried back to her wagons while Eirica set off to catch and yoke her own oxen. By the time Wolf rode up to the circle on his great black horse to visually check each wagon and team of oxen, each member of his party stood ready.

Eirica quickly herded her children to the front of their wagon. "Climb in, girls. Quickly, now." Alison and Lara scampered onto the wagon tongue and clamored over the wooden slats into the padded area Eirica had prepared. But when she tried to lift Ian, he protested and slid out of her arms.

"Me do it." His little face scrunched with determination.

"All right." She stood behind him, ready with a helping hand. Finally, he, too, was safely inside. Alison poked her head out and glanced around. "Where's Jessie? I want to ride with her."

Lara joined her sister. She took her thumb out of her mouth long enough to say, "I wanna ride with Rook. His beard tickles when he holds me." She giggled.

Eirica smiled gently at her daughters. A month ago, they wouldn't have dared voice their desire to spend time with others. Birk had hated and resented any outside interference with his family.

Her socializing and allowing her children to be around others on the trail had infuriated Birk, who'd seen it as a deliberate attempt to thwart his control. In six years of marriage, he'd never allowed her to form friendships or attend Sunday church services, and over the years, contact with her family had also grown scarce. But even he'd realized he couldn't knock them around with so many people about; he'd ignored all of them during the day. In the evenings, when they were more or less on their own, he'd once again rule with a heavy hand.

But that was behind her now. She and her children were free to make and have friends. Now Eirica worried that the girls, so enamored of their new freedom, would make too many demands on the generous natures of the other adults. Adjusting Lara's bonnet, she leaned in and kissed both girls. "It's not polite to ask. You must wait for Rook or Jessie to offer. Go sit with Ian and play quietly. I'll let you out to walk later."

"Yes, Ma," the girls replied in unison.

Eirica donned her own wide-brimmed sunbonnet with its long tail to protect her neck, then picked up the short whip. With the sun, weak but already beating down on her, a trickle of sweat gathered beneath her bodice. The day promised to be another scorcher.

Taking her place beside the oxen, she grasped the reins and waited. Her hands trembled. This was it. She could do this, she reminded herself. She'd managed the oxen and wagon for a week when her husband had fallen prey to a nest of angry hornets and been too sick to walk. The venom from their stings had caused him to swell and run a fever.

But she'd only been six months pregnant then, and the trail hadn't been quite so crowded or rough. Doubts as to the wisdom of taking charge of her wagon slid through her mind, eating away at the confidence she'd felt in the dark hours when she made this decision.

Each morning in the month since Birk's death, someone had come to take charge of her wagon during the day. She squared her shoulders, determined to manage on her own. It was important for her to know that she could handle whatever tasks needed to be done. After all, in Oregon, she'd only have herself to rely on.

When Gunner, the youngest of Wolf's men, arrived on horseback to drive her oxen, she took a deep breath and waved him away before he dismounted. "I appreciate all your help, Gunner, but I can manage on my own now."

The short, wiry man looked uncertain as he glanced from the three yoke of oxen to her. "Pardon me, ma'am, but I has my orders."

Eirica smiled, showing more confidence than she felt. "You may tell Wolf I'm perfectly able to handle things on my own now."

Frowning, Gunner scratched his head. "It's Mr. James Jones who'll have my head, ma'am. I has my orders from him."

Eirica frowned and tightened her grip on the leather reins. James again! His continued high-handedness over the last month strengthened her resolve. Though she appreciated all he'd done for her, he wasn't her keeper. It was long past time for him to know she could take care of herself and her own. Tipping her chin, she replied, "You may tell Mr. Jones I no longer require help during the day."

Gunner still looked uncertain but he rode back the way he'd come. Eirica breathed a sigh of relief. But when the signal to roll—a loud, piercing whistle—sounded, nervous anticipation seized Eirica. As her wagon had led the march yesterday, today she'd take her place at the rear. The rotation was supposed to give each family a rest from walking in the dust of the preceding wagons, but when the trail narrowed, it made no difference. The dust lingered in the air like a low floating cloud.

Each wagon pulled out of the circle and lumbered

past, falling in line. Today, Elliot Baker, Coralie's older brother, took the lead. Blond and blue-eyed like his sister, he planned to open a mercantile in Oregon. Lars and Alberik Svensson followed. The Svensson family had two wagons, the only ones in their group to boast spring seats. Most of the time, they still chose to walk rather than ride. Anne followed the wagons, walking between eleven-year-old Kerstin and ten-year-old Hanna, an open book held out in front of them as each young girl took turns reading aloud. In front of the girls, four milch cows swished their tails.

One belonged to Eirica, one to Anne, and the other two provided dairy products for the men driving Wolf's herd of cattle west. Because the cows gave better milk if they were allowed to walk freely during the day rather than be tied to the back of the wagon and pulled along, each morning, the girls gathered the cows and took charge of them during the day. Eirica knew they loved working for Wolf like their older brothers. They, too, were earning money, which would help their family start their new life in Oregon.

Rook, along with Nikolaus and Bjorn, two of the Svensson's sons, came next with the supply wagons followed by Rickard, the youngest Svensson's boy. At fourteen, Rickard was in charge of the wagon belonging to the Jones siblings, which left Jessie free during the day to gather fuel or hunt for fresh meat. Sofia and Catarina waved to her as they passed by. Sofia led a cantankerous mule. Dante cracked his whip over the backs of the oxen. He nodded to her and Marco ran ahead to join his new friend Rickard. At last, it was Eirica's turn. Taking a deep breath, she tightened her hold on the reins and snapped the leather. "Gee haw," she ordered firmly.

Nothing happened.

Chapter Five

Frowning, Eirica repeated the command to the team of oxen, lifting her voice and snapping the reins. The lead ox turned belligerent eyes toward her before swishing his tail and lowering his head in search of grazing.

"Drat," she muttered, swatting the beast lightly on his rump with her whip. Birk had always been overly cruel to the animals when he wielded his whip, but when her gentle tap produced no results, she swatted harder. "Gee haw!" she shouted. The animals ignored her.

Eirica glanced around frantically, noting that the other wagons were pulling further ahead, leaving her behind. The fear of falling behind, having no one notice, and not being able to find them later sent blind panic running through her. She snapped the reins hard, jerked on them and swatted the ox. She begged and pleaded to the great beasts, but to no avail. Wiping a bead of moisture from her brow, she relaxed her hold on the reins and gasped when without warning, the ox took off with an angry bellow. The rest of the team, spread out ten feet from each yoke, followed, picking up the pace.

"Good oxen," she praised. Grabbing the trailing reins, she breathed a big sigh of relief. Elation rolled through her. She'd done it. Pride made her steps light as she walked at a fast clip. Realizing belatedly that the oxen were going too fast, that she'd never be able to keep up this pace, she tugged on the reins. "Whoa! Slow down."

Eirica's smile died as once again her efforts to control the team were ignored. They pulled her along as though she were nothing more than a rag doll. Grabbing the reins with a firm grip, she pulled back with all her strength. Scanning ahead of her, she noticed they were fast catching up to the others. "Please slow down," she moaned, her arms aching from the constant pull of the reins, yet she didn't dare let go. Her satisfaction gave way to worry.

Maybe she'd been hasty in thinking she could do this, but last time she'd had no trouble. In fact, trudging alongside the beasts all day had been downright boring. Loud, playful shrieks sounded from inside the wagon. Eirica ignored them, all her concentration focused on slowing the six huge animals with minds of their own. But when the noise inside the wagon increased, she turned her head and shouted, "Alison! Lara! You children settle."

"Yes, Mama." Lara giggled.

Eirica rubbed her belly when she felt the strong kicks of her unborn child.

"You settle, too," she muttered, frustrated, already exhausted. The day had barely begun.

* * *

The morning sun inched higher into the blue sea spread out from horizon to horizon. James finished saddling his chestnut gelding, snugged his gloves and hung a canteen filled with cool water from the Sweetwater River over the mantel. It wouldn't take long before the water grew warm, but when a man had a thirst, had a throat clogged with trail dust, even warm water tasted like nectar. With fluid grace, he mounted and gathered the reins in one hand.

The horse perked his ears and shook his head, letting James know he was eager to begin the day's work. But James hesitated, staring westward where he knew Eirica's wagon would already be underway. Just thinking about her, knowing she was there, so close, yet, during the day, so far, drove him crazy. What if she fell? Went into labor? He longed to be with her, watching out for her, protecting her, easing the hardships of the day.

Whenever he felt he could be spared for the day, he gave in to his need to be with her, but now that the trail was turning rough again, his duty and responsibility lay with the herd and the ten men he was in charge of. Wolf had hired him and his brothers and eight other men to see the cattle to Oregon. James was in charge—second to Wolf.

With a sigh, he contented himself with the knowledge that he'd see Eirica at day's end.

"Let's ride, Mister," he commanded his horse. With a slight nudge, the animal moved into a slow trot, then into a canter, as James rode alongside the meandering herd. Whistling as he rode, James ran an experienced eye over the livestock, searching for signs of disease and exhaustion. Considering they'd come more than eight hundred miles, they didn't look too bad. They'd started out with five hundred head and he figured Wolf had lost a few dozen to disease and other trail hazards such as treacherous river crossings and stampedes.

Spaced along the long length, the men were in position, sitting in their saddles, waiting patiently. His brother Jeremy, and another hired hand, Leroy, were positioned in the flank position while Sunny and Claude, further down the line, rode swing. James rounded the tail end of the herd where Bart sat hunched in his saddle, his hat pulled low over his head. Bart and Gunner rode drag. Their job, to keep the stragglers from falling behind, was the least desirable. This morning, Gunner was absent, as James had assigned him to Eirica's wagon.

Duarte and Shorty waited several yards away, keeping the herd of horses from wandering. The horses, also called the *remuda* or remounts were crucial to the cattle drive. Each hired hand needed to change his mount at least once during the day, if not more often, depending on trail and weather conditions. Behind the herd, another wagon sat, this one held supplies for the livestock.

Unlike the cattle and the emigrants' oxen who were hardy and could survive on what grass and forage the trail offered—it was sometimes plentiful but more oftentimes scarce—the horses could not. The wagon carried grain and shoeing equipment. Saul indicated the wagon was ready to roll. Satisfied that everything was in order, James headed back to the front of the herd where Jordan and Wolf, who'd returned, waited.

As he rode up, he noted with envy the relaxed and satisfied grins of both his brother and brother-in-law. Everyone knew Wolf had taken Jessie away last night, and James knew Jordan had returned to Coralie after his watch. A surge of longing took hold. Again, he wished he'd gone to help Eirica instead of sending

Gunner. Forcing his mind to the job at hand, he nodded at Wolf. "All set, boss."

The black stallion Wolf rode pranced and fought the bit. He reared, pawing the air, making it clear he still didn't like the close proximity of the cattle. Wolf brought him back under control with practiced ease. "Let's head out."

Jordan and James singled out the lead steer and a couple of others, waved their hats and shouted. Their loud voices sent the animals surging forward with bawls of annoyance. The bell attached to the lead animal jangled, signaling the rest of the herd. Without a hitch, the cattle followed. Gradually, the herd swelled to six across and formed a column nearly half a mile long.

Wolf eased his stallion alongside James. They discussed the trail ahead. Out of consideration to their fellow travelers, Wolf tried to keep the cattle off the main trail, but oftentimes it was impossible. Also, night stops had to be chosen carefully. Grazing and water availability were deciding factors.

With the day planned, they fell silent, each lost in his own thoughts. James glanced at the wagon tops billowing in the distance. Keeping his distance from Eirica was becoming harder and harder, but it was too early for him to state his intentions, so he had to content himself with seeing and talking to her under the guise of friend and protector. She'd only been a widow five long weeks—he could wait longer, however long she needed. After all, society back home wouldn't even allow her to consider a new husband for many months yet.

His comfort lay in the fact that this wasn't some town filled with bored matrons who had nothing better to do than rule other people's lives. They were heading into unsettled land. Who knew what awaited them in Oregon? But one thing was as clear to him as the sky above: a woman with four children could not make it on her own. She was vulnerable, a target.

Normally James was a patient man. He longed to give her as much time as she needed to come to know and trust him, but feared her wariness and mistrust of men in general would take more time than he had. He wanted to marry her, start his new life in Oregon with her at his side. They'd be a family she a cherished wife, and he the happiest man alive. He envisioned a houseful of children. Her four plus more. His and hers. Black-haired and redheaded. Blue eyes and green. Children who would be loved and treasured.

"Didn't you assign Gunner to drive the Macauley wagon?"

Wolf's question drew James from his heartwarming reverie. "Yeah. He and Bart have been rotating."

Wolf pointed. "Looks like there might be trouble."

James frowned when he saw Gunner loping toward them. He and Wolf surged forward, riding to meet the young man.

When all three came to a stop, James demanded, "What's wrong?"

A pained look came over the young man's face. He grimaced, revealing yellowed teeth. "She sent me back. Says she don't need help no more."

James exchanged puzzled glances with Wolf. "Who's driving her wagon?"

"Um," Gunner hesitated. "Said she could do it herself."

"What!" The bellow tore from James's throat before

he could stop it. Unable to believe he'd heard right, he narrowed his eyes. "She can't handle those oxen in her condition."

Gunner swallowed nervously, his gaze shifting from James to Wolf who'd remained silent. "I tried to tell her, boss, but she refused to listen."

Wolf wheeled his horse around with a shake of his head that bespoke his inability to understand women any better than James. "Go," he ordered. "I'll stay with the herd."

Grateful, James rode off, his heart in his throat.

Eirica wiped the sweat from her brow and glanced around, seeking help. In the distance, she noticed a horse galloping determinedly toward her. She groaned and swallowed past the lump of failure lodged in her throat. Though the rider was too far to see who it was, in her heart, she knew. James was coming after her. Truthfully, she expected him to either send Gunner back or come himself. And she'd planned to show him that she was able to take care of herself just fine.

Why, oh why couldn't things have gone as planned. Of all people to see her predicament! She swallowed a moan of dismay and blinked back tears of frustration. Frantically, she once again yanked at the reins, trying to regain control over the unruly team before he caught up with her.

"Come on, please, don't do this to me, not now." Her answer came in the form of one ox's snort, a baleful glare and no letting up of the pace. Now what? She didn't want James to witness her dismal failure. Only now did she realize how important it was to her to have him view her as a capable woman, a woman in control, a woman who could manage anything life threw her way—like his sister.

She didn't want him believing her incapable of taking care of herself or her children. To fail at something so simple as driving the oxen, a task Jessie would have handled without blinking an eye, left a bitter taste in her mouth and ignited frustrated anger inside her. It shouldn't matter what he thought, but it did. As quickly as that realization hit, she dismissed it, buried it and refused to even examine why his opinion mattered.

A glance over her shoulder confirmed James was nearly upon her, riding as though he were a knight on a white horse out to save a maiden in distress. Once again, she was that helpless maiden, but this time, she didn't want someone stepping in to make things right, especially James. But what she wanted and what would happen were two different things. She faced forward, determined to keep her pride intact. At that moment, she was very much afraid it was all she had to protect her heart against this big man who seemed determined to play the hero-knight to her damsel-in-distress.

Without a word, James rode up alongside her and jumped off the moving horse, landing on his feet in front of her. He reached out and took the reins without a word. Digging the heels of his boots into the hard, rocky ground, he gave one loud snap and sharply voiced command and snapped the bullwhip in his hand over the heads of the oxen. To Eirica's consternation, the stupid beasts obeyed. They slowed to a normal, easy walking pace.

Eirica ignored the pain in her side and her breathlessness from running beside the team. She snatched the reins back from James, ignoring the thunderclouds gathering in his stormy green eyes. While some part of her felt grateful for his timely arrival and how easily he'd regained control of the oxen, she resented the fact that he hadn't asked her if she needed help. Though her reaction smacked of ingratitude, she couldn't help it. Wolf or Jessie would have asked, even if the answer was obvious. They'd have shown her some consideration, not made her feel incompetent.

She held her head high, her shoulders thrust back. "Thank you, Mr. Jones," she said, her voice stiff with pride and anger. "I can handle it from here." To her relief, the oxen kept to a normal walking pace.

James clenched his jaw, led his horse to the rear of the wagon and tied the animal to the back. Eirica knew by his brooding silence he was angry. Fine. That made two of them. Seconds stretched into minutes.

Finally, he rejoined her, frowning fiercely. When he realized he was walking too fast, he slowed his long-legged stride to match her shorter one. He held out his hands for the reins, but Eirica tightened her hold on them as if holding on to a lifeline. Her stubborn defiance surprised him.

He dropped his hand to his side. "Want to tell me why the hell you sent Gunner back and what you're trying to prove? You're in no condition to handle a team of oxen and you know it."

Eirica shrank from him, some of her bravado dying. She bit her lip and eyed him warily. Used to gauging the degree of Birk's rages instantly, she usually only had a few seconds to brace herself or step in front of her children to protect them by taking the blows aimed at them. But to her surprise and relief, she saw no sign of uncontrollable fury or outright rage. And with that realization came another.

With a lifelong fear of angering the opposite sex, she'd always taken the easy route and did whatever her father, brothers or husband demanded. But she felt safe with James, safe enough to rebel. He'd never lash out at her or hurt her. With James, she felt free to express herself, including allowing her own anger to surface instead of forcing it to remain below the surface.

This time, she studied him—really looked. She searched out each line stretched across his forehead, noted the lines bracketing his mouth. His features conveyed concern, a good amount of determination and stubbornness in the hard set of his jaw. But what left her feeling ashamed and guilty was the disappointment lurking in his dark green eyes.

With effort, she tore her gaze from his and stared straight ahead, a thread of worry weaving through her. There'd been something else, some other emotion lurking in the depths of his eyes. She'd seen it before, knew it existed, and so far, had refused to acknowledge it, for the unspoken feelings James harbored toward her were in direct opposition to her own need to be free and independent.

"Well, Eirica?" James prompted, his voice gentling, reminding her she hadn't answered him. His emphasis on her given name reminded her that she'd agreed to drop the formality between them last night.

Eirica took a deep breath. "Thank you for your assistance, *James,* but I can manage on my own now," she said, eager to have him gone. His close presence unsettled her. Though they weren't touching, she felt him as though they were. Walking side by side, she felt his warmth shoulder to thigh. With each step she took, the skirts of her dress fluttered, grazing his denim-clad leg as if luring him closer.

James lifted a brow, gently mocking her. "I saw how well you were managing. If you'd gotten yourself tangled in those reins or fallen, you'd have been dragged beneath their feet." He closed his eyes as if in pain.

His obvious concern touched her and made her feel ungrateful. After all, it wasn't his fault she was inadequate for the task at hand. But she could learn. *Had* to learn. She forced a smile. "Don't think me ungrateful. I'm very indebted to you for all you've done."

He tore off his hat, bit back a curse then raked his fingers through his hair. "We'll deal with *gratitude* in a minute. Right now, I want to know why you sent Gunner back? You've got young'uns who need watching, and in your condition—"

Uncomfortable with his once again bringing attention to her expectant status, she moved a few inches away, pretending to give the oxen her attention, and spoke primly. "Mr. Jones! It is not proper for a gentleman to discuss a woman's delicate condition. I appreciate all you and your family have done for me and my children, but I can't accept any more charity. It's time I took care of me and mine."

James stopped in shocked disbelief, then caught up with her in one long stride. "Charity? What nonsense is this?" Disbelief mingled with anger and a hint of hurt. "I thought we were friends, Eirica. Friends help each other."

Eirica's fingers fisted over the reins. "Friends respect each other's wishes and don't barge in without asking."

"What are you talking about?" James shoved his hands into his pockets and scuffed the tip of his boots in the hard, packed dirt.

"You didn't ask if I wanted help." She spoke the words bravely, her voice dipping to a whisper. She chanced a look at him.

"I didn't need to ask. It was obvious that you—"

"And yesterday, I said I'd take care of my tent." Afraid she'd lose her courage, she took a deep breath and plunged forward. "You ignored me yesterday and did as you pleased."

Wearing a look of incredulous shock, James jammed his hat back onto his head. "Are you telling me you don't want my help any longer?"

The fight left her. Weariness laced her words. "It's nice to be asked, to have my wishes considered and not be run roughshod over."

A long silence fell between them. James poked his hands into his pockets. "Am I really that bad? So bad I've driven you to taking risks?"

"Oh, James." Frustration lent a sharpness to her voice. "You mean well. I admit that, but please try to understand. I need to stand on my own two feet. When we reach Oregon, I won't have you and the others to rely on. It's been a month since Birk drowned, and well past time for me to stop relying on everyone else to do what I should be doing myself."

James looked stunned. "But you'll have . . . I mean, you don't need—" He broke off, as if realizing he was saying more than he meant to.

There it was again, that unspoken, unnamed something between them. Eirica met his embarrassed gaze. "James, this has nothing to do with you or anyone else or even what the future holds. For my own peace of mind, I have to prove I can make it on my own because I will never—"

"How will endangering your health help you or your children?" He cut in, stopping her from saying she would never remarry. If she didn't say those words, he still would have a chance. All he needed was time to win her trust. "If something happens to you, what will become of them?"

Before Eirica could think of a reply, Ian poked his head out the front of the wagon.

"Mama. Out!" He leaned out over the wagon tongue.

Eirica turned and gasped. "Ian, get back inside." She pulled on the reins to stop the oxen, but as before they ignored her.

Ian started crying, leaning out farther, his arms begging for her to come get him.

To Eirica's horror, one of the wagon wheels hit a large stone in the path and the wagon jerked.

Ian toppled over the front edge of the wooden slats.

Chapter Six

Eirica dropped the reins, her eyes wide with horror. Around her, everything spun out of control as she helplessly watched Ian fall. Seconds passed with excruciating slowness like some horrible nightmare in which she couldn't move or even scream. A loud buzzing in her ears garbled James's shout.

Beside her, James dove toward her son, reached out and snagged the falling toddler by one hand, then hit the side of the wagon hard with the force of his forward momentum. Unbelievably, when he straightened, he held Ian clutched to him.

He tucked the screaming boy securely under one arm and staggered toward her, his features twisted with pain and pale with the fright her son had given them both. He passed her without a word, grabbed the trailing reins and in a harsh voice, halted the oxen.

Eirica shook with lingering fear and heart-thumping

relief. The sight of Ian's body falling into the path of the wagon wheel, creaking and groaning beneath close to two-thousand-plus pounds, would forever haunt her. If her son had hit the ground, the wheel would have rolled over him, crushing his head. Bile rose and burned the back of her throat. "James—"

Her voice faltered when James came toward her, his chest heaving, hot emotion shimmering in eyes gone dark as a forest on a stormy day.

"Want—to tell me again—you don't—need—help?" The words came out clipped, stark and harsh, as if he'd just run a mile at full tilt.

Around them, wagons, animals and people filed past, eyes averted, none stopping to see if they needed help. A vein near his temple beat in time to the clenching of his jaw. His quiet anger engulfed her. She tried to speak but her heart thudded painfully in her chest, leaving her short of breath. Long familiarity with angry men made her take an involuntary step away from this man who'd saved her son's life. Moments ago she'd felt safe with James, but the raw emotion swirling between them was too much for her.

Long seconds passed as they stared at each other. Harsh gasps of air mingled with Ian's continued cries. Her gaze slid to James's hands, measuring his state of mind. No fists. No clenching and unclenching, no bulging of muscles in his arm and his face hadn't turned red and ugly, all signs that with Birk warned of some sort of physical attack, either with hands or feet—or both, depending on the extent of his rage.

Eirica remained still, afraid to move or speak. But beneath her frozen fear, warmth and a sense of renewed amazement curled from her toes to her heart.

Though James was angry, he was in complete control of himself. His hands, still holding her son gently yet firmly, didn't seem quite so frightening anymore. As earlier, his anger didn't terrify her or make her duck for cover. There was no urge to brace herself for a blow or turn and run.

For the first time in her life, Eirica felt no fear and could even acknowledge that James had every right to be upset, angry even. Her own foolish pride had nearly cost her son his life. She owed much to this man whose quick actions had saved her baby.

James had saved her son's life.

Ian was alive. Safe.

A deep shudder tore through her and she forced from her mind the memory of Ian's near death. She desperately needed to feel her son's soft body cradled close to hers. "Thank you, James," she whispered, holding out her arms for Ian.

James ignored her and set the crying two-year-old down on the ground, keeping him from running to Eirica. Kneeling on one knee, he forced Ian to look at him. "Ian." The deep, no-nonsense tone silenced the boy. With wide eyes, Ian stared at James, his lower lip trembling.

Eirica stepped forward, ready to protect her child. "James, he's just a—"

"Don't hit him." From the back of the wagon, Alison's shrill voice drew the attention of both adults. "He's just little." Alison and Lara watched the adults with trepidation.

The combination of fear and agitation in her daughter's voice brought tears to Eirica's eyes. Her Ali had tried so hard to protect her younger siblings from their father's wrath, sometimes by hiding them when he was in one of his drunken moods. Once she'd even suffered a beating in their stead until Eirica arrived to stop Birk.

Alison's frightened plea seemed to affect James as well. He glanced from the girls to Ian, then to Eirica. Four pairs of blue eyes framed by various shades of red hair watched him warily. His gaze lingered on Eirica. "No one will ever hit any of you again." His voice deepened with emotion and there was no doubting him.

While not much else might be clear to her, she trusted James and took a step toward him. When James shook his head, she hesitated. It was easy to acknowledge trust, much harder to prove it.

With gentle fingers, James forced her son to look at him again. "You scared your ma and me something fierce, Ian. Leaning out of a moving wagon is very foolish and dangerous. You must never, ever do that again."

Rather than leave his rebuke at that, James pointed to the wagon wheels and went on to explain to Ian—and the two little girls watching and listening—what had nearly happened. When he finished, after making sure all three of her children understood the dangers, he stood, lifting Ian into the cradle of his strong arms.

Ian's bright blue eyes were wide, but not with fear as Eirica expected. In fact, her son stared at James with what looked to be awe on his face. Straddling the wagon tongue, James deposited Ian back inside with his sisters, then removed his hat and dropped it onto the little boy's head. Ian giggled and pushed up the wide brim as the hat completely covered his eyes, nose and most of his mouth. Still grinning, Ian played peekaboo with Lara. Alison stood to one side, watching James intently.

James wiped his forehead with his arm then reached out to draw her to him. The child threw her arms around his neck. Watching the two, Eirica felt her eyes tear up. Her daughter and this gentle giant of a man shared a deep bond, forged when Alison had been kidnapped and James had helped rescue her and his sister.

He put Alison down and stroked her curls. "Ali, you're the eldest. Your ma needs you to help her by watching Lara and Ian when she's busy. Will you do this for me?"

The little girl's mouth dropped open, then she nodded solemnly. "I'll help Ma, James, and I promise to be good. Maybe Lara and I can play with the beads Jessie got us at Fort Ke'rny."

James ran a hand down her pale cheek. "That's a great idea, Alison." He stepped away from the wagon.

With her children settled, seemingly none the worse for the scare, Eirica was torn between gratitude for James's quick reflexes and the lingering thread of resentment at his interference. But it was hard to be angry at a man whose very interference had saved her son's life. On top of that, his handling of her children had been right. She'd have coddled Ian, too relieved to have him safe after his near brush with death to scold him. But not James. With no sugarcoating or anger, he'd made his point without lifting a hand against her children or causing them to obey out of fear. Her resentment died.

She peered into the wagon, needing to reassure herself they were indeed all right. They were sitting quietly, watchful but not afraid. She walked around to the back of the wagon where James had unhitched his horse. Though he seemed calm, the tightness etched around his mouth and the lines around his narrowed eyes conveyed the anger residing within. Her knees shook. He had every right to lash out at her. Her hand fluttered to her throat. "I'm very grateful—"

Her heart stopped when he lifted his hands. She couldn't stop the automatic flinch from a blow that she knew wouldn't come. A long pause fell between them, then James reached out slowly to grasp her shoulders. There was no force or pain in his grip. Only the gentle massaging of her tense muscles. The look in his eyes let her know he'd seen her instinctive reaction, but he didn't acknowledge it verbally. Instead, he pulled her to him, held her tightly, his voice, taut with emotion, fanned her ear.

"That was too damn close," he whispered.

Eirica felt some of her shakiness fade beneath the soothing warmth of his embrace. For a moment she allowed herself the luxury of accepting the comfort he offered.

She needed his touch, his secure embrace and the brief moment to lean on someone. What would she have done had her son been injured or worse, killed? A stab of pain went through her heart. She couldn't bear to think of what might have happened. James tightened his hold and for a long moment, they stood there, wrapped in each other's arms. Then he put her from him, keeping hold of her shoulders, his fingers firm but not hurtful.

"Look at me, Eirica."

Slowly, she lifted her gaze to his, saw the sadness he couldn't hide.

"I don't want your gratitude. I want your friendship, your trust." He threw his head back as if in pain. "Hell, I want more than that and you know it, even if you won't admit it." His fingers slid up the sides of her neck until they tenderly cradled her jaw. His hands were large, his fingers spread from her chin to her temple. He tipped his head down and searched her face with eyes that mirrored his soul, revealing all that he felt.

Seeing the naked love exposed in his darkened eyes, Eirica opened her mouth to deny what he felt toward her, then shut it. What could she say? For to respond verbally to the anguish etched in lines on each side of his mouth, in the tautness of his jaw and staring at her from his sad, haunted gaze, meant opening the door to feelings he'd only hinted at but not put into words—words she didn't want spoken aloud. The very thought of him loving her frightened her. She shook her head slightly, denying what she knew to be true.

"Yes," James whispered, using his thumbs to caress the lines of her jaw. "But I won't say the words, not yet, not until you're ready to hear them."

Eirica's heart raced with excitement and fear. He couldn't—she wouldn't—"James—"

With a groan, he closed the space between them and lowered his head to brush a tender kiss over her lips, the contact no more than a feather-soft caress, yet time seemed to come to a halt. Her lips parted, his lingered. Their breath mingled. Then he stepped back, released her and jammed his hands into his pockets.

Wide-eyed, she stared at him, forgetting all the reasons why she had to deny herself a second chance at love. Was it so wrong to want what she'd dreamed of as a young girl? To have a love as strong and lasting as the Svenssons'? To have a home filled with love and laughter? And family?

James drew in a deep breath, his nostrils flaring as he fought for his own control. Agitated, he ran his fingers through his hair. "Don't ask me to apologize for that. If Ian had fallen beneath those wheels, you'd have buried your son today."

Reminded of what her own foolish actions had nearly caused brought Eirica back to reality—and her senses. A sob rose and stuck in the back of her throat. "You don't need to remind me how close I came to losing him, James." She turned her back to him.

James gently spun her to face him. "There's no room out here for misplaced pride, sweetheart. Your family's survival depends on you knowing and accepting your limitations. When you need help, damnit, ask for it. Don't sacrifice your health, or the safety of your children for pride's sake." He fell silent, his gaze holding hers.

Eirica tried to speak but was so overcome that she could only stare at him, her face hot with humiliation, shame—and the emotions kindled by his kiss. Deep inside, a curl of hope swirled in a buried recess of her heart. She locked it away to take out and examine later, when she was alone. Right now, the enormity of what had nearly happened left her paralyzed.

What would she have done had James not been there? In her condition, she'd never have reached Ian in time to prevent a tragedy. Staring at the distant eastern horizon, she thought of the many graves of children she'd duly recorded in her daily journal entries. So many lives lost so young. It made her ill just to think how easily Ian could have become another woman's journal entry.

James mistook her silence as refusal and, as if afraid of saying or doing more than he should, he released her and mounted. Eirica felt lost and alone. Wiping the tears from her cheeks with her apron, she tried to pull herself together. There would be plenty of time to think about the tragedy her actions had nearly caused.

She placed a hand on her belly, ready to admit she just wasn't able to handle the oxen in her condition. James was right.

But where did that leave her? If she couldn't manage out here, how would she manage alone in Oregon? Worry wound through her mind, leaving her feeling panicky. Taking a deep breath, she shoved it aside. Right now, her first priority was catching up to the others and to do that, she needed James. Lifting her head, she stilled her nervous jitters and placed a hand on his knee, then jerked away at the warm hard feel of him. Embarrassed, she put her hands behind her back. "Don't go."

His smile warmed her. Shyly, she lowered her eyes. She didn't deserve such thoughtfulness and consideration. He dismounted, moved close and lifted her chin once more. Her heart lurched. Was he going to kiss her again? Lord help her, she wanted him to, but he didn't.

"Thank you, Eirica." He stared into her eyes for a long moment then released her, handing her the horse's reins as he strode to the front of the wagon. First he lifted out Lara and Alison, settling them both on the back of the horse. Next, he swung Ian onto his broad shoulders. Eirica listened to the sweet giggles of her girls and her son's delighted laughter and felt lighter of heart than she had in a long time.

James really was a nice man—too nice—she thought, resisting the urge to touch her fingers to her mouth to feel where his lips had brushed hers. Eirica fell into step beside him, leading the horse. She snuck a glance at the silent man walking next to her. He chose that moment to look her way. Their gazes meshed, hers shy, uncertain, his filled with longing and desire.

Eirica felt herself drowning in eyes that reminded her of a spring field of dewy green grass. It was so easy to imagine running, twirling and spinning freely across that field, her laughter ringing out as he gave chase. Together, they'd fall onto the carpet of softness and he'd lower his head once more, touch her lips with his.

As if he knew where her thoughts had taken her, James smiled, revealing an unexpected, but sweetly appealing dimple in his left cheek. Her pulse raced. Oh Lord, no man should have such a powerful smile.

His hand lifted, his thumb brushing a wisp of hair from her face. "A man of honor should state his intentions up front. You have no male relatives for me to speak to, so let there be no doubt between us, Eirica. I aim to court you. I want to start a new life in Oregon with you at my side, as my wife. I've raised my brothers and sister and I'm not getting any younger. A man needs a family of his own."

Eirica felt adrift in a sea of conflicting emotions. James seemed to be everything she'd ever dreamed of, longed for, but she knew first-hand how fast a man could change once he had what he wanted.

But James isn't anything like Birk. He's different. He's kind.

He's the hero I've dreamed of all my life.

Tears gathered in the corners of her eyes. The pain of knowing she'd once thought the same of Birk made her wary. How could she trust herself to recognize the truth? "James, I don't know what to say—"

He reached out to place one finger tenderly against her lips. "Don't say anything. I won't rush you, but it's best you know now how I feel. Just think about it, about us. Give me a chance. That's all I ask." His finger slid down past her lips, lingered just beneath her chin before he turned his attention back to the trail, whistling softly.

Eirica touched her cheek, then her lips. Things would never be the same between them. Before, their attraction had been unspoken, something neither had acknowledged. But now, with his boldly spoken words, it hung between them.

James wanted to court her. He wanted her for his wife.

She longed to put her trust in him, to allow herself to dream of love and happiness. She wanted what he offered, what his heated gaze promised.

Eirica forced her mind away from such foolish notions. Her weakness made her angry. If she married James, she'd lose the independence she'd gained with Birk's death and her dream of owning land would also die.

And it was that dream, the need for security, that gave her the courage to face each day and continue on. Like Sofia, she would lay claim to her share of land, as was her right as a widow, and in Oregon, she'd have what she'd never had before: security—land—in her name, not a husband's. Not even for love could she give that up.

Coralie walked behind her wagon, the merciless sun beating down on her. She stifled the complaints gathering in her mind. She was hot, tired and so sick of the dust. But what good would it do to protest day after day that she was tired of walking? It wouldn't change the fact they still had weeks of travel left.

Weariness glazed her eyes and thirst left her tongue sticking to the roof of her mouth. She eyed the water barrel on the back of the wagon several feet in front of her, but the effort to quicken her steps for a taste of tepid water seemed too much. No, this trip had not been anything like she'd thought it would be.

She shuddered, grateful her friends back in Westport weren't there to see how awful she looked. If Sarah or Becky ever saw her wearing plain calico and thick, clunky boots instead of fine slippers made of the softest kid leather, they'd just about faint.

Coralie sighed with longing. Someday, she'd don the fine silks and satins she'd worn all her life. She had one last delicious creation hidden in her trunk. Thank goodness she'd been smart enough to save it for her arrival in Oregon City.

She dabbed the beads of sweat forming along her forehead and grimaced at miles of white-capped wagons stretching out beyond forever. If she never saw another covered wagon, slept in a tent on the hard ground or cooked bent over a fire with the wind whipping her hair and skirts, it'd be fine with her.

And while most emigrants had to continue that existence through the first winter, she'd already decided to find herself and Jordan a room in a hotel or boardinghouse. Surely, Oregon City would have something decent? Everyone else could share a one- or two-room shack until they could build permanent homes come spring. Not her. She planned on sleeping on a nice soft bed in a warm room and having what she missed the most—privacy.

Coralie wanted Jordan to herself for a while.

Images of her husband's handsome face and hard, lean body made her sigh with longing. She rarely saw him during the day, forced to be content with his presence on those evenings when he wasn't on first watch. And even when he did spend the evening with her, between the long grueling hours it took to prepare a meal and the rest of the evening chores, there was little time for talk. Most of the time, when they retired, they both fell into an exhausted slumber.

She frowned. Last night, cuddled close, she'd tried to tell Jordan about their baby, eager for his reaction when he learned he was going to be a father, but he'd fallen asleep! Tonight would be different. Just imagining his reaction made her smile and chased away the tiredness. She gave in to her need for a drink to ease her parched throat and swallowed two ladles of warm water, then joined her brother who flicked his whip to keep the sluggish oxen moving.

"What's the grin for? What have you done now?" Elliot asked, his blue eyes narrowed with suspicion.

Coralie affected a look of outrage. "I haven't done anything." Well, she'd done something, as had Jordan, but she planned to keep that news to herself for a while. Instead, she threaded her arm through Elliot's, her step light. "I'm happy, brother dearest." And that was no lie, despite the dust and heat and long boring days and longer, lonely nights.

"She's in love, Elliot." Jessie spoke from behind them then dismounted Shilo, her black horse and led her.

Elliot made a disgusted sound and quickened his steps. Coralie shot a warning glance at her sister-in-law. Poor Elliot. He suffered from a broken heart. She narrowed her gaze as sisterly indignation rose. How dare that mousy pastor's daughter lead him on, letting Elliot believe they would marry once they reached Oregon.

The chit had no backbone, allowing her father to end their courtship just because Elliot didn't belong to their church. Well, that was her loss. She had no doubt Elliot would find someone else, someone special. He'd already caught the eyes of several young women.

As if to prove her right, two giggling girls ran past, eyeing Elliot. Coralie scowled when they looked as if they were going to stop and chat. One narrow-eyed glare from her convinced them to keep going. A jab to her side let her know Jessie had seen her.

"What?" Coralie widened her eyes but determination filled her. Those two were simpering, giggling chits with heads filled with cotton and air. Neither deserved someone as wonderful as her brother.

Coralie couldn't help glancing behind her to where Sofia and her three grandchildren walked beside their wagon. She focused on the older girl, Catarina, who was the same age as herself and Jessie.

"Mind your own affairs, Cory," Jessie muttered beneath her breath, but she, too, eyed the DeSantis girl with speculation.

Sniffing, Coralie whispered, "Don't tell me you haven't thought the same thing."

Elliot glared at them from over his shoulder. "What are the two of you plotting now?"

"Nothing," they answered in unison.

"Don't get any ideas, either one of you."

Coralie quickened her pace and caught up to her brother. She hooked her arm through his. "Oh Elliot, love is wonderful. You'll find someone else, someone worthy of you, maybe before we reach Oregon."

Elliot pulled free. "Not a chance, Cory. I'm not interested in acting like a besotted fool again and you'd best remember that. You, too, Jessie." He sped up the oxen, deliberately distancing himself.

Respecting Elliot's desire to be alone, the two women dropped back. Glancing behind them, Coralie spotted Eirica walking beside James with Ian in her arms. Coralie laid her palm on her still-flat belly, glad she'd be in Oregon before she swelled with child. Life on the trail was difficult enough without the added burden of being so near birthing time.

Thinking of Eirica reminded Coralie of the woman's mildewed baby clothes and blankets. If only she could sew—But she'd never seen the purpose in learning when her father owned a store and could either buy what she needed or hire the work out to a seamstress. She glanced at her sister-in-law. "How skilled are you with thread and a needle, Jessie?"

Surprised, Jessie lifted a brow. "Don't tell me you want me to mend all those ruined gowns of yours? Not a chance. I hate mending."

Coralie waved her to silence. "Not mending, sewing from scratch."

Jessie grinned. "Well, James made me sew a shirt for him once. He thought it was important for me to know how. He gave me a good shirt to use as a pattern so I took it apart and made him a new one." She giggled. "He wore it once. An hour. One sleeve was too short and tight, the other long and baggy. And the seams in the side had already started pulling apart."

Laughing, Jessie slid Coralie a look of pure devilment. "The shirt was hopeless, as was the good one I'd taken apart. After that, whenever he or the others needed shirts, he paid someone else to sew them. Figured it was cheaper than wasting good material on my feeble skills. Why?"

Coralie wrinkled her nose. "I want to make Eirica some baby clothes. I suppose I could ask Anne to teach me."

Jessie elbowed her. "I thought you were knitting a blanket for her baby."

"Please, let's not talk about that. By the time I finish it, her babe will be grown! Sewing has to be easier."

Jessie rolled her eyes and shook her head. "Eirica probably already has everything she needs, Corie."

"But she doesn't, Jessie." Eirica's dismay at finding the baby clothes in ruins still worried Coralie. Her friend had looked so beaten and with all she'd gone through, Coralie wanted to do something to make it right. Quickly, she told Jessie what had happened. Then she grabbed Jessie by the hand and pulled her in the direction of the Svenssons. "Come on. Let's go talk to Anne. She can teach both of us to sew."

Groaning, Jessie pulled back. "Not me, Cory. I don't sew."

Coralie ignored Jessie's protests. "If I have to learn to cook and sew and knit and heaven knows what else, you can learn to wield a needle right alongside me."

Night had fallen when James shifted in his saddle then stood in the stirrups. The guitar slung over his back chimed with the motion. His mount, a mare this time, tossed its head and side-stepped, as if telling him to settle down. But he couldn't. Thoughts of Eirica filled his mind and the need to see her made him restless. Knowing he had to give her time to adjust and accept his intention to court her, he'd volunteered for first watch, hoping it'd keep him too busy to think about her. But nothing could erase the feel of her lips against his. It didn't matter that it had been brief, the barest brush of her silky mouth against his. The memory lingered, leaving him thirsting for more.

He ran a hand across the back of his neck. No matter how sweet the memory, kissing her had been a big mistake. For the first time since he'd met her, he'd had the opportunity to spend a whole day in her company and what did he do? Opened his big mouth and ruined it, sent her fleeing from him as soon as she'd been able to get away.

Depressed, he slumped in his saddle. "Way to go, you damn *palooka*." Duarte, one of the horse wranglers, favored the term for a dumb lout and right now, James felt as though it fit him like a second skin. At the noon stop, Eirica had shared her cold meal with him and allowed him to watch the children while she rested, but when they resumed travel she'd avoided him, choosing to walk with Anne or Coralie. The same happened when they stopped for the night. She stayed away from his wagon.

Heck, he didn't even get the chance to talk to her, to ask if he could set her tent up. Dante had taken care of it and unloaded what she needed for the evening. "Young whelp." But there wasn't any heat in his words. Sofia's grandson might have eyes for Eirica, but he was too young for her—in life's experience if not in age.

No. The person he lashed out at was himself. "Scared her off. So much for courtin' and goin' slow." He slapped his thigh with the palm of his hand. Both his mount and the nearby cows started, but James didn't notice. Over and over, he replayed the events of the morning, starting with Eirica's stubborn attempt to handle the wagon. When he saw her struggling to control the team, witnessed the lines of defeat on her face and the tears in her eyes, he'd wanted to scoop her into his arms and reassure her that she didn't have to do a man's work, she had him to take care of her.

Yet, she didn't want his help. Didn't want his charity. Charity! The word still stung. As did her comment that friends didn't barge in where they weren't wanted. He shook his head, trying hard to understand her, but she didn't make sense to him. Why would she try to handle the oxen in her present condition? Especially when she didn't have to. It was just plain foolish in his opinion, as proven when Ian had toppled out of the wagon.

His heart still pounded when he thought of what might have happened. Seeing Ian fall had taken ten years off his life, and worse, had made him forget that Eirica was fragile, that she needed to be treated gently. He'd yelled at her, accused her of being so cussed stubborn that she'd endanger her children before swallowing her pride. Then he'd had the gall to kiss her and state his intentions.

No doubt. He'd really made a mess of things now.

Swinging his guitar from around his back to his front, he absently strummed the strings, seeking an uplifting song to chase away his depressing thoughts. What drifted over the herd of cattle were the soft chords of a mournful love ballad.

Nearby, a lone cow lifted her head in response and lowed at the sliver of moon hanging among bright glittering stars in a sky of translucent black. James closed his eyes and sent his baritone voice sliding through the night, soft and silky as the fur of a newborn calf. When the last note left his lips, James dropped his hand with one last strum across the strings. His gaze lingered on the shimmering sheet of light above him.

"You got it bad, brother," an amused voice intruded.

James twisted in his saddle, frowning. "Shut up, Jordan." He didn't bother to deny it. He turned his back on his sibling and hoped he'd leave it be. Of course, it was too much to ask.

"Never thought I'd see the day when my big brother carried his heart on his sleeve. Ain't love wonderful? Cooeee!"

James rolled his eyes. Wonderful wasn't the word he'd choose. Frustrating, painful and depressing were more like it. "You lookin' for a fist in your yapping jaw?"

Undaunted by his brother's bristling, Jordan pulled his mouth organ from his pocket and sat back in his saddle, his eyes shadowed by the night. "Your watch is over, big brother. Go on, get out of here." With a self-satisfied grin, Jordan lifted his hands to his mouth and launched into a jaunty tune.

James wheeled his mount around and rode off, fighting envy that his brother and sister had both found love. But he was happy for them. He thought of Jeremy—the youngest—who seemed to be content to be alone. With all the single women on the trail, Jeremy could certainly take his pick—including Sofia's granddaughter. She seemed nice, the sort of woman who'd make a man a good wife. But so far, Jeremy had stayed clear of her, never once even trying to flirt with her or get to know her. Well, his brother would find love when the time was right.

When James reached the spot where the rest of the hired hands had bedded down, he turned his mare out with the other horses and retrieved his bedroll from a pile on the ground near the supply wagon. But instead of laying it out, he hefted it over his shoulder and started walking, his guitar slung over his back.

He picked his way around wagons, tents and wandering animals, using the light from above, mixed with the glow of campfires to find his way to the wagons. From inside canvas tents, hushed murmurs and soft chuckles reached his ears. Husbands and wives talked or judging from some of the sounds, made love before sleep claimed them. The noises intensified his own single status, which made him feel so alone. He stopped and tipped his head back. Hundreds of thousands of stars winked down at him.

Foolish mortal. They seemed to mock him. And they were right. Only a fool fell in love and willingly opened himself to the heartache and pain that accompanied it. James slapped his hat against his thigh, understanding fully the pain Jordan and Jessie had gone through before finding love. And like them, he vowed to carve out his little bit of happiness with the woman who held his heart, even if it took a long time to win her love and trust.

As quietly as possible, he entered the wagon circle, found the wagon that belonged to him and his siblings and unrolled his blankets beneath it. Sitting on the ground to remove his boots, he paused, his gaze sliding toward Eirica's tent pitched outside the circle two wagons down. He could see only a portion of it. No light burned inside. She'd be asleep by now but at first light, James planned to go to her and apologize for his earlier behavior. He'd also be on hand to assist her with her wagon and oxen.

James started to pull one boot off, then froze when a dark shadow crept up the side of Eirica's tent. It was too tall and thin to be from one of the wandering oxen in the middle of the corralled wagons. So, who was sneaking around her tent this late at night? And for what purpose? Crime on the trail ran rampant, and rumors of a thief stealing food and clothing had recently traveled from wagon to wagon.

Around him, soft snores gave testimony to the fact that everyone else was fast asleep. Whoever was moving silently beyond his line of vision couldn't be up to any good, especially hanging around so close to a single woman's tent.

Crouching down, staying close to the wagons, James crept forward to find out.

Chapter Seven

Rounding Eirica's wagon, James strained to see into the darkness encroaching on the tent. His heart hammered against his chest and sweat trickled down his back. Who was there? He *had* seen someone or something move, but whomever it had been, it appeared they were gone.

Chastising himself for his needless worry, he told himself it was probably just someone out taking care of nature's business and that they'd returned to their own camp. He relaxed, stood, then yawned. His jaw snapped shut when one dark shadow detached from the surrounding darkness, moving across the gray of the canvas, tall, distorted and sinister. He moved to the other side of the tent, ready to tackle the intruder.

Ready to take a flying leap, he tensed to stop himself when the orange glow of the fire outlined Eirica. She paced, arms wrapped tightly against her body, her hair loose, hanging down her back. James sagged mentally as relief poured over him. His poor heart had already leaped to his throat and had to be forced into calming. He knew he was overreacting. After all, what were the chances that someone would dare target this camp to rob? They were too large and, aside from that, most emigrants traveling along the same part of the trail as Wolf's group knew they had a dog and pet wolf—not to mention the fact that Wolf was a "breed," his family Sioux Indians. There was nothing like boredom of trail life to spread gossip quickly.

James still heard snatches of conversation about the stir Wolf's family had caused when they showed up at Fort Laramie to help rescue Jessie and Alison from criminals on the run. The prairie telegraph had come in handy. Since then, no one had dared to harass any of Wolf's wagon party or try to steal their livestock.

He focused his attention back upon the woman he loved. She stood, head back, staring blankly at the glittering array of stars overhead. He knew he should go, give her time to come to terms with the changes in her life. Once more, he castigated himself for declaring his intentions before she'd been ready to hear them.

So go, leave her be.

He turned away, but she looked lost, alone, like she needed a friend. He stepped out of the shadows with his hat between his hands and cleared his throat.

Eirica jumped back from the embers, the woolen shawl around her shoulders slipping, drifting to the ground. "Who's there?"

She kept her voice low, but he heard the quaver, the hint of fear. There, now he'd truly done it. He'd frightened her. He should just tattoo the word *palooka* across his forehead. Hastening to reassure her, he stepped out of the shadows. "It's just me. James," he called out softly, so as not to wake those sleeping around them.

Her hand fluttered to her throat. "James! Land sakes, you gave me such a scare."

"Sorry. I just finished my watch, saw you were still awake and figured I'd check to see if you and the children were all right." It was a small lie, but he didn't want to frighten her by reminding her of the thief lurking in the night somewhere. He stopped before the fire. They stared at each other, his gaze searching, hers evasive. A sudden flare from an ember catching fire to a piece of unburnt fuel bathed their fronts in an orange glow while darkness shrouded their backs.

Eirica glanced over her shoulder toward the tent. "The children are fine, sleeping." Her voice broke and tears filled her eyes.

James stepped around the fire, merging his shadow with hers. "What about you? Why aren't you asleep?" He longed to pull her into his arms, soothe her worries and fears, reassure her that he'd be there for her. Instead, he watched her chew on her lower lip and blink back tears. "Eirica?"

Translucent tears fell from her eyes. Angrily, she brushed them away and gave a short bark of laughter. Hugging herself tightly, she turned so her profile was to him. "You want to know? I'll tell you why I can't sleep. Whenever I close my eyes, I see my son falling beneath the wheels of the wagon. I see his broken body and I feel sick. Sick. It could have been his grave some woman would notice come the new day."

She pressed her fisted hands into her stomach, pulling tight the skirt over her abdomen. Twin trails of moisture slid down her cheeks and her jaw trembled with the effort to control her pain, but the words poured from her. "When I close my eyes, I can't hide from the fact that I nearly killed my son today. If it hadn't been for you . . ." With a cry of despair, she whirled around, as if too ashamed to face James.

The agony in her voice tore at him, echoed in his own heart as he knew the truth of her words and ached for her. He tossed his hat on top of her shawl and went to her, lifting his hands to her upper arms. Gently, he ran them up to her shoulders and tried to ease the tightness he felt. "What's done is done. The boy is safe," he said gently.

Her shoulders shook. "Only because you were there." Her voice broke on a sob. "I can't do this, James. I'll never make it to Oregon, and what will happen while I'm there? If I can't even keep my children safe here, how will I manage there?"

His own eyes stung and he blinked furiously. Bowing his head, he breathed in her scent, one of sunshine, lavender and wood smoke. His fingers slid toward the slim column of her neck, his thumbs pressing in at the base of her skull. "You will make it to Oregon." He spoke the words with confidence. She'd make it or he'd die trying. It was too important to him, *she* was too important.

"But today—"

Unable to stand the self-recriminations in her voice, James swung her gently around to face him. With one finger, he tipped her chin and stared down into her gleaming eyes. "Today took courage."

She shook her head but didn't pull away. "Today was a disaster. I wasn't being brave. I was selfish, self-centered, thinking of only myself, not of my children or what was best for them. My stubborn pride nearly cost me my son!" She closed her eyes and swayed toward him, sending more tears cascading down her face to glisten in the starlight.

James pulled her close, let her cry for a few minutes, then stepped back so he could dry her face with his thumbs. He loved touching her, loved the feel of her skin, soft and smooth beneath his calloused fingertips. "Look at me, Eirica." He waited until she complied then smiled tenderly. "No one said it would be easy, sweetheart. We all make mistakes, but you're strong and willing to learn. Survival out here and in Oregon will depend on that strength, and on being willing to do what it takes. But it also requires knowing your limits, knowing when to ask for help. None of us can survive alone. We all need help on occasion."

Eirica backed out of his hold and angled her head, hiding her gaze from his. "I'll be alone in Oregon, just me and the children.

Her declaration pierced his heart, left him bleeding with despair. His voice roughened with pain. "You'll never be alone, not unless you choose to be. I'll be there for you, Eirica. If you let me, I'll be there for you, forever, I promise this on my parents' grave." His unspoken desire to marry her hung between them, thickening the air with tension.

Eirica rubbed her arms. "James—"

Agony went through him. Again, he couldn't bear to hear her denial. "No. Don't say anything, not yet." They had a future, one that would be wonderful, if only she'd give them a chance. He just needed time to convince her that he loved her, would never hurt her or the children. James stooped to pick up his hat and her shawl. Jamming the hat on his head, he draped her woolen shawl around her shoulders. Though the days were unbearably hot, the nights tended to be colder the higher they climbed.

Eirica drew her shawl around her. It had to be close to midnight and for both of them, their day would start before the sun rose, yet he sensed she wasn't quite ready to retreat. Taking a deep breath, he held out one hand.

"A short stroll might help you sleep. Would you care to join me? It's a beautiful night."

Eirica stared at James, her emotions in turmoil. Throughout the long afternoon and evening, her mood had shifted from disappointment to relief that he hadn't shown up. And here he was. It was the perfect opportunity for her to tell him not to waste his time on her and yet, she found she couldn't do it.

"Eirica?"

The promise of the stars shone in his gaze and she couldn't help but remember his kiss—a brushing of lips that couldn't really be considered a kiss, but unlike any she'd ever experienced, it left her yearning for the forbidden. Her heart urged her to take his hand.

What harm could one short stroll beneath the stars do? Her pulse raced a little faster as her imagination took hold. No, she couldn't. Didn't dare. She fell on the only excuse she could think of. "I'm sorry, James, the children—"

His mocking smile held no malice. "Are asleep. We won't go far. Please say yes."

His warm words of reassurance and the hint of romance blanketing them made it impossible for Eirica to refuse. She placed her hand in his and allowed him to draw her close and lead her away from the fire into the dark shadows. For a long while, neither spoke. Then Eirica could stand it no longer. She had to be honest, couldn't lead him on. She didn't want to hurt him. "James, I do think you're a nice man."

He tipped the brim of his hat back and smiled down at her. "I sense a but in there."

She sighed and glanced down to where her hand rested on his arm, her fingers curled slightly along the rough fabric of his wool shirt. Her gaze shifted to his hands, his fingers, the nails cut short and square instead of ragged and sharp. He kept himself clean— as clean as any of them were able to manage on the trail. He even took time to shave, unlike most men who just grew beards while traveling.

And she meant what she'd said. He was incredibly sweet, always showing her kindness and consideration—even if she didn't want it—or deserve it. Eirica knew the problem lay with her, not James. Suddenly, that was crystal clear. James wasn't like Birk or her family. The differences between them and James were as different as night and day, good and bad. In all her life, not one of the men in her family had ever shown her an ounce of consideration or appreciation for her or anything she did. It was something she tried to forget, but had never forgiven. That kernel of bitterness lay in her heart, rotting.

Then along came James, eager to help ease her load and what was her reaction? Ungratefulness and resentment! She felt so confused. Too many changes in her life had destroyed her very foundation. What did she want? What did she need? She felt herself changing, but whether for the good or not remained to be seen. The only certainty in her life was the uncertainty she faced each day. Somehow, she needed to rebuild that foundation, gain a firm footing on her life.

Eirica's gaze skittered away from his. How could she commit herself to another man when she herself felt so torn as to what she wanted. "I'm sorry, James. Please don't think it's you. It's not. It's me. I can't tie myself to another man right now, maybe not ever."

He stopped and took both of her hands in his. "Can't or won't?"

She shuddered at the softly spoken question. "Does it matter?"

He lifted his hand to gently force her to look at him. His breath fanned her cheeks and his thumb slid along her jaw. "Don't you know I'd never hurt you? I'd cherish you. I'd protect you." His voice lowered. "I'd love you as no man ever has."

A thrill ran through her at his words. She heard the sincerity, knew he spoke the truth, but she also knew how much she had to lose by accepting that love, that protection. Once it would have been enough. Maybe even a month ago she'd have jumped at the chance to have that security, but not know. Too much had happened. Things had changed. "I know you would, James. But I need more than that. I need my independence and all that goes with it." Her heart went out to him when he bowed his head.

"Please understand, James. The law gives everything to the husband. He has absolute control. But as a widow, I'm in control. When we reach Oregon, I'll be allowed to own my own piece of land. Land and security that no one can ever take from me."

She closed her eyes, feeling again the helplessness of being at Birk's mercy, of having no choice but to stay with him because she hadn't anywhere else to go, a fact he'd taunted her with by threatening to kick her out of his house without her children if she didn't please him.

"Eirica—"

At the sound of his pain-filled voice, she covered her ears and spun away, determined to stand firm even as her heart sided with James. "No! I won't ever again allow any man to have a say over me or my children."

James pulled her back to face him, his feet planted

121

apart in the stubborn stance she found endearing. "I won't give up, Eirica. I meant what I said earlier. I'm going to court you and win your heart—and your trust."

The words both thrilled and scared her. Her gaze searched his features, seeing the determination, and the love he felt for her. "Why me, James? There are so many others you could choose from. I have three children, soon I'll have four. You deserve better. You've been tied to your brothers and sisters and now you're free. There are lots of women out there eager to marry and raise a family. Why saddle yourself with me? I'm scarred, inside and out. I'm not even much to look at, especially now." She held out her arms and indicated her bulky form.

James didn't hesitate. He grabbed her hands and held them out, allowing his gaze to roam her figure. Glancing up, he saw her genuine confusion. He pulled her toward him and kissed the backs of her fingers. "You are the most beautiful woman I've ever laid eyes on, even more so with child." His voice softened and slid over her like silk.

"Fancy words," she whispered, tugging at her hands, reminding herself of all Birk's sweet-talking while he courted her. He'd made her feel good, desirable, worthy. Then came her wedding night and the days that followed where Eirica learned that her husband's words had meant worse than nothing—they'd been lies. All lies.

James released one hand and brushed a strand of hair from her face, tucking it behind her ear. "It's the truth, Eirica. I don't lie and I don't say things I don't mean. Not ever."

Eirica felt long-lost hope flare to life. Hope and happiness. Both had shriveled long ago to be buried deep in the cold recesses of her heart. Now they stirred in response to the warmth in his voice, the gentle touch of his hands, and the promise in his eyes.

Wonder suffused her and for just a moment, she savored it. James found her attractive. Birk had always thought her ugly when she was with child, and he'd made sure she knew it. She'd long suspected he resented the intrusion of his children in her body. In hindsight, it explained why his beatings had always grown worse the further her pregnancy advanced.

But there was no mistaking the awe and desire in James's voice or in his tender gaze. Though even if she said yes to all he offered, it couldn't bring back the dreams she'd lost. Nothing could erase the past. The naive young girl with romance in her eyes was no more. She'd grown up, forced to shed her naive shell under the harsh glare of reality. She was a woman now, a woman with children who depended on her.

What she'd told James just minutes before took on new meaning and importance. She had to do this for herself, her own growth as an emerging woman. She knew full well that life didn't hand out guarantees. What if she allowed James to do as he wanted and take care of her? What if something happened to him in Oregon? She'd be in the same situation—alone, scared and unprepared.

James, for all his outward kindness and sincerity, would take over her life, the way he had taken over the oxen, or handled Ian on his own without consulting her, and step in to tell her children what to do. It didn't matter that his actions had been prompted by concern or that he'd even been right in how he'd handled both her and her kids. She'd never learn to stand on her own two feet with James at her side. He'd raised his siblings, was used to being in charge. It wasn't a habit he would break.

"Eirica?"

"Yes?" Warily, she waited.

James slid his hat off and worried the brim of his hat between nervous fingers. "I said earlier I wouldn't apologize for kissing you. I was wrong. I overstepped my bounds. You weren't ready, the time wasn't right and I don't blame you for being scared of me. For that I apologize."

His admission took her by complete surprise. Seeing his unease made Eirica reach out and touch his arm. Heat crept up her cheeks as he watched and waited for her to gather the courage to speak. She tipped her head to one side. "Your—kiss—didn't scare me. It just took me by surprise." She leaned forward, searching his gaze. The hurt she saw that she'd placed there with her honesty saddened her. Bringing him pain was the last thing she wanted. She truly valued his friendship. "Why—why did you kiss me? You were angry."

He lifted one hand to the side of her face and cupped her cheek. "No," he said faintly. "Scared."

That was the last answer she'd expected from James. Nothing seemed to scare him. "You kissed me because you were scared?"

"Yeah. No. Hell, I kissed you because I wanted to. I've wanted to kiss you since the night I saw you standing in the moonlight at Fort Kearney, when everyone had left the camp and you and I were there alone."

Eirica's jaw dropped. This was not what she'd expected. Fort Kearney seemed a lifetime ago. She wanted to ask him how, why? But she didn't know what to say or even think. Finally, she blurted, "But I was married."

Derisive laughter came from James. "Hell of a spot to be in, right? I finally found the woman I wanted to call wife, raise a family with, and she's already married." He scrubbed a hand over his jaw. "I fell in love with you, I wanted you—but you were off limits. I could have accepted that, except when I saw how your husband treated you. Then, my feelings became a living nightmare because you deserved better."

Eirica's eyes widened with shock, then narrowed with growing anger. If he was telling the truth about his feelings, why hadn't he done anything to help her, to protect her from her husband? His actions when Birk had been alive weren't those of a man in love.

She pulled her hand from his arm and stepped back. He was feeding her a bunch of lines after all, and she'd fallen for it. "I don't believe you. If you'd cared, you'd have done something to help me or my children. No one did anything, except your sister." Bitterness edged her voice.

James stared at his hat then slapped it against his thigh. "That's not true. I did what I could." He fought the memories of Birk's maltreatment of Eirica and her children and his own helplessness to prevent it. Guilt still ate at him. He'd wanted to do something, but Birk had had the law on his side.

"I went to Wolf, along with Jordan and Lars. Wolf agreed to tell Birk to lay off you and the children." James paused. "I'd have confronted him myself, but I was afraid if Birk knew how I felt about you, he'd take it out on you or maybe even leave the wagon train. At least with you there, I could watch over you as much as possible."

He shoved his fingers through his hair. "I had to wait until Birk violated Wolf's orders, hoping that if he were thrown out of the wagon train, you'd decide to leave him and stay—which you did. I was ready to step in and offer my protection and help."

Eirica closed her eyes, hearing Birk's boasts that no one could tell him what he could or couldn't do with what belonged to him. "You thought it would be that easy? That he'd listen?" Her gaze trapped his. "It made no difference who gave the order. Birk did as he pleased. Wolf's interference made him more determined to exert his dominance. He just made sure he left bruises—his marks of ownership, he always told me—where no one could see them." Shame made her turn her head. More than a month later, she still had marks on her body that hadn't fully healed.

James ran a hand through his hair. "Damn it, Eirica, I'm sorry I didn't do more. No one blames me more than I blame myself. I even tried drugging—"

His voice faltered. Eirica shot him a startled glance. "You what?"

He stared at his boots, then met her gaze boldly. "At Fort Kearney I drugged Birk's drink. I knew he'd get drunk and beat on you, so I added a few drops of laudanum to a flask of whiskey and had it delivered to him." He winced, looked guilty.

"You did that for me?" She remembered how Birk had slept most of the day following that night and how relieved she'd been.

"Yeah, and I guess I should tell you, Jessie drugged him that night as well. Wolf found out and laid into both of us."

Her eyes widened. "Both of you drugged him?"

"Neither of us knew the other had done so. But we each had the same idea—to protect you." James twisted his hat in his hands, but he stood tall and proud, not the least bit repentant.

Searching his gaze, Eirica could no longer ignore

the emotion she'd seen before and saw now. There was no doubting his feelings for her. A small bubble of happiness formed inside her and pushed past her misgivings.

James had cared enough to drug Birk, speak to Wolf on her behalf and watch over her. Knowing he'd at least tried to help left a warm, wonderful glow in her heart, like holding her newborn babes for the first time. She also admitted he was correct in believing that Birk would have taken his family and left the wagon train had he felt threatened by James or believed any man had designs on her. Shyly, she stepped close to him. "Thank you for caring, James. I'm sorry I doubted you."

He opened his arms. He could so easily have pulled her into his embrace, but he didn't. He waited, his gaze soft, inviting her to take that one small step that would bring them together.

She was tempted. She wanted him to hold her, needed to know what it felt like to be loved, cherished. She needed to know she wasn't alone, that she could lean on James, but most of all, she yearned for the kiss that his eyes promised. Just this once, she told herself. This one time, she'd blame her weakness on the night, on the shimmering carpet of stars overhead and the soft cadence of insects lending their chirps to form a backdrop of soothing sound. Before the harsh light of the new day reminded her of all her reasons for guarding her heart, she had to know what it felt like to be held—and kissed—by James, the knight of her dreams, the one person who didn't frighten her.

She took that one small step, lifted her hands to his shoulder and allowed him to draw her close, his arms encircling her. One hand slid up her spine and cupped the back of her neck. She held her breath, waiting for the return of the suffocating fear of being trapped by strong male arms. To her surprise and pleasure, she felt no panic with James. Instead, strange urges flowed through her, frightening her as much as those same feelings made her lean closer to the man holding her so tenderly.

His breath, warm against her cheek, teased her. "Fate brought us together, Eirica. We were meant to be," he whispered, his lips moving closer.

His words wove ribbons of hope around her. She stared at his mouth, wanting so badly to feel his lips against hers again even as that scared part of her heart warned this was wrong. For her. For him. She couldn't give him what he wanted.

But he can give you what you want, what you need, what you've never had.

James lowered his head, his eyes holding hers, sucking her into their desire-laden depths. His mouth enticed hers; his lips soft, full, tender. Hers parted in response.

"You can say no, Eirica. I would never force you."

Eirica's heart pounded, blood raced through her and a strange heaviness settled between her legs, the blood collecting there, pulsing with each beat of her heart. She fought her panic—terror born of her fear of a man's passion and superior strength. Underlying that same fear came another. Would James find her lacking?

Birk had never been one for much kissing, which she hadn't minded. The few times he'd kissed her had been totally repulsive, a smashing of his mouth against hers, leaving her lips swollen, bruised and bleeding. She shuddered inwardly, fighting the memories of Birk's sweating, grunting body on top of her as he entered her forcefully, uncaring of the pain he caused, eager only to find his own quick satisfaction.

She wasn't sure she could ever let a man touch her again, yet the tenderness with which James had kissed her earlier, held her now, left her yearning to experience more. Realizing it was up to her, that all she had to do was say no gave her the courage to lift her head shyly to James. "I'm not sure I can do this."

James's lips twitched, his mouth lowering until he was but a mere breath from hers. "Sure you can, sweetheart." He wrapped his arms more firmly around her, still loosely enough so she wouldn't feel trapped or held against her will. "Close your eyes. Don't think, just feel."

Taking that leap of faith, Eirica put her trust in James and waited with bated breath. It seemed like a long time before James touched his mouth to hers. Slowly. Softly. Tenderly. His lips claimed hers without pressure. Without pain. His lips moved over hers. Nibbling, tasting, showing her a side to lovemaking she'd never experienced, but had dreamed about. Warmth and incredible sensations rushed through her, leaving her weak-kneed and breathless.

The kiss went on, a sweet mating of mouths. She twisted her body around so she could lean into him, get closer than what her stomach would allow. He shifted as well, supporting her as they stood close. Eirica marveled how broad-chested he was, how hard against the softness of her swollen stomach. Her nipples tingled when he moved ever so slightly. Her fingers dug into his shoulders as his mouth continued to move over hers with gentle persuasion. At any time, she could have pulled back, but the sheer sweetness of his kiss enthralled her.

Her own lips parted and without even realizing it, she kissed him back, moved with him, tasted him as he did her. His fingers feathered across the sides of her face, stroking and touching. Her arms slid around his neck, holding him closer. She moaned—or was it him? She didn't know, didn't care.

Then, with one last stroke of his tongue, James lifted his head.

Eirica's eyes fluttered open when his fingertips drifted over her lips, across her cheeks and slid into her hair. She stared at him, trembling with need, lost in a sea of unfamiliar emotions. She'd never imagined a kiss could be this tender or that it could leave her feeling shaky, weak and in such need of another kiss that she felt as though she'd die without it. Here, wrapped securely in James's arms, she felt alive and desirable.

James drew an unsteady breath. Though he smiled, Eirica could tell the kiss had shaken him as well. Her fingers continued to thread through the silky, wavy hair at his nape. She forgot about all the reasons why she shouldn't be there as she rested her cheek against his chest, felt his every shuddering breath, heard the thudding of his heart. Sheltered in the secure circle of his arms, she didn't even think about his size, how strong his arms were, how small and fragile she felt against him.

Nothing mattered except the urge building inside her to pull his head down so she could sample another of his incredibly tender kisses. He tilted her chin so he could gaze down into her eyes, and he stroked her hair. "That wasn't so bad, was it?"

His words broke through the unfamiliar fog of desire. She backed away, stared at him, seeing a wonderful, tender, gentle man unafraid to bare his soul to her.

What had she done? She covered her mouth to stifle her cry of pain.

He was wrong, so very wrong. That kiss they'd

shared had been a cruel joke, for she'd glimpsed heaven in his eyes, tasted ambrosia on his lips and felt the first burst of sweet desire pulse through her blood. Combined, they left her aching for more. But worse, her awakened heart yearned for the romance and love he offered even as her mind slammed the door shut to protect her heart from further heartbreak.

But it was too late. She feared she'd already lost a part of her heart to the man who'd renewed her dreams of love and happiness. Backing away, she picked up her skirts and ran as fast as she dared in the inky darkness toward the safety of her tent and the bleakness of her future.

Chapter Eight

James followed Eirica, saw that she made it safely to her tent, then returned to the bedroll beneath his wagon, his mind seeking the wisdom of his actions like a dog chasing its tail. Round and round he went. Had he moved too fast? Had he scared Eirica off for good now? Had he ruined his chance with her?

But he always came back to how right it'd felt. Earlier, he'd feared his timing was off, but not tonight. She'd come to him, willingly, and Lord almighty, she'd responded to his kisses and touch with a passion and need that pushed this own to the breaking point. It had taken everything he possessed not to do more than kiss her and touch her gently.

And it made it so hard to back off and let her return to her tent. They'd be so damn good together, but those same passions, feelings, frightened Eirica. Which began the round of endless worry anew. Was he back where he'd started? Would Eirica rebuild her barriers? Could he find a way to convince her that they were meant to be? He rubbed his face with both hands then combed his fingers through his hair, tired and disheartened at the thought.

Without undressing, he crawled between the worn quilts his mother had made before her untimely death and cradled his head in his hands. Though the quilts had seen better days, should be relegated to the scrap bin, he always felt comforted surrounded by her love. She'd have loved Eirica, he thought. She'd have approved of his choice for a wife.

Staring up at the bottom of the wagon, his gaze absently picked out the shadowy farming implements he'd loaded and tied there for a new start in Oregon, James tried to regain his focus. From his pocket, he pulled out a well-worn rock and rubbed it between his thumb and forefinger, drawing comfort from the soothing action and the stone's polished surface between his fingers. His mind wandered.

He'd left behind all the material things he'd held dear: the farm, furniture crafted by his father, a house lovingly decorated by his mother, and memories. So many memories were scattered throughout that small house, so much love, joy and laughter.

The prospect of starting over, building his own home, creating new memories, scared him and took on new meaning now that he knew what his parents had felt when they'd come to Westport at a time when it was still considered the wilds of the west.

Like them, he was laying the foundation not only for himself and his family, but hopefully, generations of Joneses would draw their first breath in that new home, in a new land. He'd pulled up his roots, taken what he could of his parents' belongings, hoarded his memories, and would soon start a new chapter to add to what his parents had written. New traditions, new joys and new struggles to overcome.

He thought of Eirica, his dream of standing on rich fertile soil, staking out their new home, deciding together where the kitchen would go, where they would sleep, where to put the children's rooms. He wanted a big house, with lots of space. With Eirica at his side, he'd have a houseful of little girls with red hair like their mother. They'd have sons, too, strong like his own brothers and just as adventurous and curious about life as little Ian.

Closing his eyes, he held the image to his heart. Someday, he comforted himself, refusing to believe otherwise. If Eirica couldn't bring herself to love and trust him, his future stretched out bleak, empty and lonely. He rolled onto his side, clutching the warm stone in his palm. His thumb rubbed a worn groove down the center of one side.

While he understood Eirica's need to be independent, her fear of men and of being controlled, he also knew just how tough life would be without a husband to take care of her and her children. She needed him, she just didn't know how badly. Again, he damned Birk for treating her as he had. There wasn't a person in this wagon party who hadn't known what went on in that marriage. Hell, they'd all heard Birk forcing himself on her night after at night, staking his claim, proving she belonged to him.

James tensed, fighting the guilt and fury that came from knowing there hadn't been a single damn thing he could do about it. He'd finally stopped coming into camp at night. But that hadn't stopped him from laying awake, his imagination running wild. Nights had become his own personal hell, sleeping beneath the same stars at the same time that the woman he loved was being brutalized by her own husband. What Birk had done with Eirica wasn't making love. Her bruises and the haunting shadows in her eyes had been proof of Birk's violence and her own helplessness, which matched James's own, ate at him.

It didn't surprise James that Eirica vowed never to be involved with another man. But there had to be some way he could prove to her that he wasn't like Birk. There had to be some way to win her trust. Restless, he flipped over onto his back again. He'd come close to gaining her trust tonight. There'd been longing in her eyes when he'd offered her a stroll in the starlight. She'd responded to his touch with shyness, but with a need that matched his.

He'd already decided to court her, woo her with gifts to prove his love was sincere and his intentions honorable, but he sensed those alone wouldn't win her heart or her trust. Somehow, he had to show her what real love was like between a man and wife. Like kissing. It'd been obvious to him that kissing was something new to her. He'd sensed wonder and awe in her reaction, and he'd seen the stars in her eyes.

She'd enjoyed his kiss and his touch had filled her with a wonder she hadn't been able to hide. It made sense. From what he knew of Birk, it was a good guess she'd never been shown the gentle, tender wonders of love and romance, nor the gentleness and tenderness.

He snuggled down between his covers, holding close to his heart Eirica's sugar sweet response. She had no idea how it could be between them, didn't understand that her body knew and yearned for what he could give her. But none of this dealt with her belief that she had to be independent, had to go it alone to maintain the control and security she sought.

Suddenly he realized that overcoming her fears of

him, of his touch, wasn't the problem. He had to prove that if she married him, she wasn't giving up control or her independence. How could he convince her of that? She was right. The law would give him control, and right now, she didn't trust him not to take advantage of it as Birk had done. He thought of her accusation—one she'd made twice today—of how he barged into her affairs. But what was he supposed to do: let her struggle, fail?

He thought of Jessie, how when she'd been younger, he'd had to force himself to allow her to learn on her own, to make mistakes and to deal with the consequences. But that was different. It was in a controlled environment. Out here, a mistake—like today's—could cost lives. Asking him to let her put herself or her children at risk was out of the question, which brought him back at the beginning. What to do?

Faced with a bigger problem than he'd suspected, he scooted over to one of the wagon wheels and leaned against it, his body scrunched down so he wouldn't hit his head on the wagon bottom. Pulling his knees up, his boots resting on the spokes of the wheel across from him, he slid the stone he'd been caressing back into the pocket of his denim pants.

"Trust yourself. Believe in yourself."

The words came from nowhere, a voice from his distant past that gave him courage and hope. Unable to sleep, knowing it would be a while before he could hope to find slumber, he grabbed the guitar resting against the side of the wagon and cradled it across his lap. He strummed a chord, then another, and another, tuning as he went until a low soothing melody drifted from beneath his wagon.

Unknown to him, several yards away, Eirica lay in her tent, listening. By the time the last note faded, she'd fallen asleep with a smile on her face, her fingers touching her lips.

Burning embers from another fire several miles away sent long, grotesque shadows dancing into the night, across the earth and over a bulky shadow creeping stealthily across the dark land. At any sound—the cough of a man, the soft whisper of a woman soothing a child—the figure dropped to the ground, silent and still.

Only when total silence prevailed once again did he rise from his prone position. Each forward step was made cautiously, his movements slow as he passed one camp after another. Passing a large white tent, Birk Macauley froze at the sound of a childish giggle. His lips curled with hatred and he glared at the unseen family who inadvertently reminded him that he'd lost his. Thanks to that damn meddling Wolf White.

"God damned nosy breed," he muttered. "It's none of his business how I deal with what belongs to me. Gave her airs, made her think she could leave me. Nobody takes what's mine." Birk stopped to control his breathing, knowing that to give in to the hatred raging through his body could be dangerous. His wandering alone in the dark of the night would rouse suspicion; questions would be asked.

But controlling his hatred of Wolf White wasn't easy. The bastard had interfered one too many times in Birk's affairs, starting with the day they'd left Westport. Eirica had allowed Wolf to nose around in their wagon, and the wagon master had discovered Birk's stash of whiskey—more than the allotted amount. The bastard had ordered the excess taken back to town and traded for food. If that hadn't been bad enough, Wolf had later had the nerve to order him to lay off hitting his woman and children.

Birk's lips twisted with remembered fury and resentment. "A man has a right to treat his family as he sees fit." His fists clenched and unclenched as he dealt with the fact that he no longer had his family. Just wait until he had the bitch back. She'd never leave him again. His loins tightened with need. Just imagining her fear, her submission to whatever punishment he decided to deal her hardened him to the point of pain.

Sweat popped out on his face and his hand went to his groin as his vision glazed over. But instead of easing his erection, allowing his body to spill its seed, he fought the pulsing need. Later. When he was somewhere by himself where he could vent his rage without fear of being heard. Then he'd allow himself to enjoy the images filling his mind, luring his lust. Right now, he needed to concentrate on matters at hand: surviving, finding food and, if he were lucky, drink. What he wouldn't give for a flask of whiskey. Hell, he'd even take snake-head whiskey. Cheap rotgut drink was better than none.

Finally, Birk reached his objective for the night—a lone wagon and single tent set apart from the others, far enough from the trail that it was no longer crowded with tents pitched practically on top of one another. He had no idea who these people were and didn't care. They were alone, not traveling with a larger group and therefore, an easy mark. He glanced around cautiously. Their fire had burned down, and from the tent came the reassuring sound of soft snores.

Hungry as he hadn't eaten all day, Birk approached the back of the wagon and pulled from his waistband a small empty canvas sack he'd lifted from another unsuspecting traveler. Luck ran with him. Remnants of the evening meal lay where any beast, two-footed or four could help themselves. He slid slabs of cold bacon and bannocks into his sack. His gaze shifted side to side as he added the knife that had been used to slice the soft chewy bread, even though he had two other knives hidden in his boots. One more wouldn't hurt.

Moving silently, he reached into the shadowy interior of the wagon and grabbed another sack sitting within arms-reach. Inside, he found pilot bread and added the hard tack to his cache of stolen food. That was all he could find without the aid of a light to see better. Scowling, he turned, ready to move on. What he had now would see him through for a few days. The sudden loud cocking of a gun turned his blood cold.

"Stop, ya damn thief. I'll teach ya to steal from me."

Birk turned cautiously and faced an elderly man wearing a white nightshirt that fell to just below his knees. In his hands, he held a shotgun leveled at Birk's chest.

"Drop the sack," the man ordered, moving closer.

Birk licked his lips, his gaze shifting, searching for escape. He bent down slowly and set the sack in front of him.

"Back away, you thieving scum."

Birk took a step back, his foot scraping against a cast-iron frying pan. When the old man bent down to pick up the sack, Birk snatched up the pan and jumped forward, swinging his weapon hard. He knocked the rifle from the man's hands then backhanded the pan across the side of the man's head.

The emigrant toppled to the ground. A shrill scream rent the air as the man's wife emerged from the tent.

Her cries slashed the quiet of the night. Birk grabbed his sack of pilfered food and the man's shotgun, then ran away from the trail toward a gully he'd found earlier. If he could just make it, he'd be safe.

Over the next nine days, Eirica and the other emigrants traveled steadily, their wagons creaking over nearly ninety miles of sagebrush-covered plains. They passed Devil's Gate, and Split Rock. The second resembled Devil's Gate, except its split was at the top of a ridge. With those wondrous sights behind them, another treat awaited: Ice Slough, a boggy marsh where ice abounded. All the emigrants had to do was reach into the muck to pull out a chunk of ice—in July!

Hot and tired, the travelers enjoyed cold drinks for as long as they could make the ice last. Finally, the Sweetwater River brought them to their objective, the most important landmark of their trip: South Pass. Not only did it bring them to the frontier of Oregon country, the pass was the key to the success of the westward journey.

Most emigrants had imagined a high ridge of mountain with some narrow defile and dramatic crest as they'd experienced with other passes. Few had expected the nearly imperceptible climb through a broad, grassy valley astride the continental divide. Most might not have even known they'd reached the summit but for the noticeable cooling of the atmosphere and the myriad white-capped lofty peaks of the Wind River Range, looming large some twenty miles away.

Eirica, along with Jessie, Coralie and Anne stopped to survey the nondescript pass. "Never thought it would look like this," Eirica said, staring around her where the earth seemed to meet a sky gone dark and menacing. She ran her hands over the swell of her child then massaged her lower back. Though eager to rest and look around, the last place she wanted to be was standing on top of the pass if a storm broke. The last couple of days had been hot and muggy with torrents of rain and thundershowers in the afternoons and early evenings.

Jessie stood with hands on hips, her green eyes alight with excitement as she eyed the darkening sky. "There is going to be a spectacular show up here when that storm breaks. Too bad we won't be here to see it."

Eirica, Coralie and Anne all rolled their eyes. "Thank the good Lord for that," Anne breathed.

Coralie smacked Jessie on the shoulder. "It figures you'd think putting yourself in mortal danger is exciting, Jess. You are truly sick in the head."

Not put off, Jessie laughed. "Hey, I didn't say I wanted to be up here when it breaks. I'm not stupid. I just said it'd be spectacular."

"Well, I for one am thankful that this is all there is to South Pass." Coralie surveyed the area, speculatively. "I don't know what all the fuss is about. It sure doesn't look all that important to me."

Eirica and Anne hid their smiles and waited. The byplay between the two young women never failed to amuse Eirica, and with Coralie feeling the exhaustion that came with the early stages of pregnancy, she provided lots of ammunition for her sister-in-law. Jessie had no tolerance for complainers.

Sure enough, Jessie responded to Coralie's negative comments. "Cory, are you blind? Open your eyes. Look beyond the spot of earth we're standing on. There, down there, lies Oregon. We've made it to the *Oregon Territory*. From here on, water flows toward the Pacific. It's a grand adventure." To emphasize her feelings on the matter, Jessie spun around, arms out. Her hat, old, dusty and full of teeth marks, flew off. She grabbed for it but the wind swept it away.

Sadie, her very pregnant dog barked sharply and waddled after it. Jessie laughed softly when the dog couldn't move fast enough to snatch it from the fingers of the playful breeze. Wahoska chased it down and brought it to Sadie who took it from her mate and carried it back to her mistress, albeit with a few more teeth marks than had been there before. Jessie took it and jammed it down on her head, then she gave both animals an affectionate hug. Though the wolf tended to be standoffish with most of the emigrants, he'd accepted both Jessie as his master's mate and Rook who snuck him prime bits of meat and thick bones.

Coralie shied away from both animals as they left Jessie's side to chase the wind. "Jessica Jones, you're disgusting. Everything's an adventure to you!"

"White, dear sister. Jessie White, now," she reminded, pride ringing in her voice.

Anne smiled and retied her bonnet ribbons. "I have to admit this has been an adventure, one I shall never forget, though I'm eager to find myself with a roof over my head once again. But now, I actually believe we'll make it." Her smile faded. "If we don't lose all our oxen. We've lost two already and the rest are looking beyond weary."

Silence fell between the women as they resumed walking across the wide summit, each contemplating the hardship of the trail. Heat, lack of good grass and exhaustion were taking their toll on the livestock. Eirica glanced behind her. Alison and Ian were in the wagon under James's watchful eye while Lara rode with Rook. From the looks of it, her three-year-old was fast asleep.

Eirica smiled. Today was the first since that kiss beneath the stars that James had arrived to take charge of her wagon. Bad weather had kept him tied to the herd. Glancing at the sky, she was surprised to find him here today. Once more, she peered over her shoulder at him. This time he spotted her and lightly tipped his hat in acknowledgment.

Her cheeks burned and she turned away. He might not have been around much during the last week, but one night he'd ridden in to give her a fistful of wildflowers with a couple of long feathers added to it and tied together with a strip of leather to form a posy. She still had it, tucked safely in the wagon where it wouldn't be crushed. He'd been so endearing when he'd presented it to her, all flushed and awkward and very appealing to her susceptible heart.

The wind gusted, reminding her of the impeding storm. Loose dirt swirled at their feet. Eirica coughed, then covered her mouth with her handkerchief. The other three women did the same, except Jessie, who wore her handkerchief tied around her neck like the men did. Jessie pulled her red triangle of calico up and over her mouth.

Coralie sniggered. "I swear, you look like a bandit, Jessie." The three women laughed in agreement, each looking at the bullwhip coiled at her waist and the long wicked knife hanging from its leather sheath. Jessie shrugged off her sister-in-law's good-natured teasing and suggestions that now that she was a married woman, she should dress accordingly.

Eirica for one disagreed. She envied her young friend. Here was a woman who knew how to take care of herself. Twice she'd witnessed Jessie's skill with that whip. Just thinking about the first time Jessie had come to her rescue made gooseflesh rise on her arms.

Nights with Birk on the trail had been far worse than those in Illinois. In such close quarters with other people, Birk had grown even more jealous, sure that every man who came near them was looking at her. He'd accuse her of encouraging their attention, punish her for sins she hadn't committed, then prove his dominance over her by claiming her body with his.

The worst times had been when Birk had had too much to drink and couldn't perform. He'd blame her and make his punishment far worse than if he'd been able to expend his sexual energy on her. At home, she would have gotten up and gone outside her cabin to walk or light a lantern and sit on the porch with her sewing or mending—anything to keep her hands busy. Out here on the trail, there were too many people around to witness her despair. She'd waited until Birk fell asleep, then left the camp to walk off her demons and release her tears of hopelessness where no one could hear.

What Birk did to her with his hands or objects left her feeling dirty, ashamed and oftentimes, in incredible pain. She'd despaired of even surviving her marriage. Only the knowledge that she stood between him and her children had kept her tied to him. She'd been tempted, oh so tempted to run away, to leave him and hide where he could never find her.

On those long solitary walks she'd dreamt of freedom—just her and the quiet of the night—until the one night she'd come across an unsavory drunk who'd decided she was fair game since she was alone. That was the first time Jessie had saved her. With her whip alone, she'd sent the horrible man running.

The second time Jessie had used her whip to help Eirica had been that last night, when Birk had gone into an uncontrollable rage and refused to leave her and Ian alone. Eirica remembered how helpless she'd felt, lying on the ground, covering Ian's small body with her own to shield him from Birk's boots and fists. As before, Jessie had fearlessly stepped in to stop Birk—with the full support of the rest of their wagon party. Birk had finally overstepped what the others could tolerate. And when he turned the whip on Jessie, Wolf had furiously stepped in. After a fight with the wagon master, Birk had been banished.

An arm around her shoulders brought her head up. She met Jessie's worried, dark-green gaze. No words were needed between them. Eirica smiled reassuringly to let Jessie know she was all right. Though Jessie didn't know it, Eirica suspected her young friend of playing the role of her protector on more than just those two occasions.

There had been that hornet attack that had left Birk bedridden for a couple of weeks. And, of course, she now knew that both Jessie and James had slipped sleeping potions in her husband's drink at Fort Kearney.

Knowing others cared about her eased past pain. An impish grin curved her lips. "I've never thanked you for all you've done for me and my children, Jessie."

Jessie lifted a brow. "I didn't do that much."

"Keeping my children out of Birk's way during the days, watching over me night after night, saving me from that drunk, drugging Birk, that's not much? And if I'm right in my suspicions now that I know you better, I'm willing to bet you were behind the hornet attack." At Jessie's start of surprise, Eirica nodded. "You didn't have to do any of that."

For a long moment Jessie remained silent, her gaze focused on the sky above.

She kicked a rock, wincing when it nearly hit the person in front of her. Then she sighed and glanced at Eirica. "Yeah, I did. It wasn't my place, I didn't even think my actions through, or the possible consequences, but I couldn't sit and do nothing. Wolf got real angry when he found out. How'd you know I was behind the hornet attack or that I'd drugged his drink?"

Eirica smiled. "I guessed about the hornets—it seemed too coincidental. And James confessed he drugged Birk and said you'd done the same." She still marveled over the discovery that James had cared enough to try and prevent Birk's nightly terrorizing of her and the children.

Jessie stopped dead in her tracks. "Are we talking about James, as in my brother, my do-no-wrong brother?"

Threading her arm through Jessie's, Eirica pulled her forward. "Yep. The very same. Surprised me as well." Thank goodness she no longer had to worry about Birk or fear what he'd do if he'd ever learned to what extent her young friend—or James—had gone to in order to protect her from his abuse. The last thing she'd wanted was to have someone put themselves at risk for her. She didn't think she could live with the guilt.

"Well, maybe there's hope for my big brother yet," Jessie responded.

Coralie asked something of Jessie but Eirica let their conversation pass over her. She rubbed her arms against the bite of cold in the air. She shifted her gaze to the north, to the high, rugged, snowcapped blue mountain peaks towering in the distance, a dramatic change in terrain. Did they have to go over those? She didn't even want to know. Ignorance, in this case, seemed bliss. One day at a time, she reminded herself.

"Look, Eirica, there's Pacific Springs." They'd left the pass behind them, were easing down the western slope. Jessie pointed toward a green oasis a couple of miles ahead of them.

"What a paradise," Eirica whispered, comparing all that greenery to the sage and scrub terrain they'd traversed for hundreds of miles. It reminds me of Ash Hollow. She glanced at the marsh. "I wonder if we'll be stopping for a day of rest. The washing needs to be done and there's so much mending piling up."

Just that afternoon, Alison had torn her dress. Of course, with the dress being so old, it was literally falling apart. She needed to make her children new clothes but had no material to do so. She'd have to sell her mother's china when she reached Oregon—if there were buyers. She just needed one bolt of cloth, but with very little money, it seemed out of reach.

Coralie fell back and sniffed. "Washing and mending is not what I'd call rest, Eirica. That's a full day's work. I think I'd rather walk all day." She glanced at her hands, grimacing, but didn't say anything.

Jessie put her arms around her. "Don't fret, Cory. Your hands are fine."

The other girl sighed. "No they aren't. They look like a farmer's wife's hands."

Eirica, Anna and Jessie exchanged amused glances once again, then looked down at their own rough and reddened hands. None took offense but Jessie laughingly reminded, "You *are* a farmer's wife, dear sister."

Jessie and Coralie continued to banter and bicker

good-naturedly. Eirica ignored them, concentrating on putting one foot in front of the other. *Just a bit farther, then we can stop,* she reminded herself.

A single wagon passed them. An elderly woman sat on the bench seat, holding the reins with both hands, bracing her feet against the front for balance. In the back, leaning against a thick pile of quilts, blankets and pillows, her husband rode, a white bandage wrapped around his head.

Eirica eyed them, worried. Word had flown from one camp to another, warning of a desperate thief, but up until nearly killing this old man, no one had gotten hurt. The thief had been reported to just take small items: clothing, shoes, food and knives. But now he had a gun. With so many strangers moving among them, it was impossible to know who the culprit was. "I still can't believe someone attacked them," Eirica said, looking at the others. "It's just horrid. What if the thief tries to get into one of our wagons?" She couldn't help but worry over the brutal attack.

Jessie frowned, her hand going to the whip at her side. "We're pretty safe, Eirica. That couple is traveling alone, which makes them an easy mark. Besides, we have Sadie and Wahoska to warn us of intruders."

Once again, a companionable silence fell. Just being together lent silent support and now that the end of the day was at hand, energy flowed as they each contemplated their evening. The faster they reached the spot Wolf had chosen, the sooner they could steal a few moments to rest before starting the night's meal.

By the time they reached a small creek a short distance away from the main springs, Eirica was too exhausted to protest when James unyoked the oxen and saw to her family's needs. It almost made her smile when Dante, spotting James, ran over to grab her tent and pitch it. The young man had made it clear to James that this was his duty.

James walked past her, his lips twitching with amusement. "Damn puppy," he whispered for her ears only.

Eirica rolled her eyes. James obviously didn't perceive Dante as a threat. He rejoined her, unloading a box of supplies from the wagon. She avoided his gaze, afraid she'd burst out laughing.

To make cooking and cleaning easier, she'd put together several days' worth of flour, bacon and other foodstuffs so she wouldn't have to unpack her wagon to get into the various sacks and barrels each day.

"I've got to go." He glanced at the sky. "The cattle are going to be edgy tonight. We're taking them as far from the wagons and people as we can in case they stampede again. Wolf thinks we'll be in for lightning storms tonight. Will you be all right?"

Eirica couldn't help the glow of warmth that came from his concern or the flutter in her chest when his gaze dropped to her mouth. Nor could she stop her tongue from wetting her lips, or halt the yearning that rushed through her. Instead, she put her hands behind her and stepped back. "I'll be fine, James. Go. You have your duties to see to."

He smiled, his eyes darkening with desire. "You know I want to kiss you again."

At the low, seductive hum his voice, Eirica's pulse jumped. She swayed toward him. God forbid, but she wanted to kiss him as well, wanted him to stay. She liked his company. But she also knew she couldn't have it both ways, not and be fair to him. Yet, that hint of promise in his eyes, her own body's anticipation of another kiss made her want to take what he offered. She stepped toward him. "James—"

James reached out and stroked the side of her face with the back of one hand. "Yes. But not now, not here. Just know that I will kiss you, and soon." He fingered her braid. "You're the fire my soul needs to survive."

There was no doubting the sincerity in his voice. It touched a chord deep within her that left her feeling more confused than ever. Oh Lord, she wanted the comfort and security of his arms around her, more than she wanted security and independence. She craved the taste of his lips on hers and wanted badly to know what it felt like to be loved and cherished. Staring into his smoky green eyes, she longed to throw aside all her fears of the future and beg James to kiss her, right here, right now. She wanted the heaven his eyes promised.

James cupped one of her hands in both of his. He pressed an object, something small, hard and warm into her palm, then folded her fingers over it and kissed the curl of her fingers.

"I've carried this stone in my pocket since the day I buried my parents. The man who gave it to me knew the enormous responsibility I was taking on by keeping my family together. He said I'd have many days of worrying ahead of me, but if I carried this stone and remembered that day, my determination, the vow I made to my parents as I buried them, I'd get through it. Trust yourself, he told me, and when you don't know what to do, or where to turn, focus your problems on this rock. Let your instincts guide you."

James paused, his thumb caressing the back of her hand, his smile wry, his eyes filled with sadness. Eirica held her breath, spellbound, waiting for him to continue. She had no trouble envisioning James at sixteen, standing proud, daring anyone to stop him from raising his siblings. Jessie had told her some of the problems he'd encountered when folks in the town thought him too young to take on that responsibility.

"Well, he was right. I had many doubt-filled days and long, lonely nights when I fretted myself sick till dawn because there wasn't anyone to ask if I was doing right by Jordan, Jeremy and Jess. And when the worry and doubt got too much, I'd remember this friend of my father's and his simple gift and even wiser words.

"I want you to have it, use it. Trust yourself, listen to your heart. I got through some difficult times, Eirica, and so will you. But unlike me, you don't have to go it alone. I want you to know that." He brought her closed hand back to his mouth to brush his lips softly over her inner wrist.

"Think of me tonight." He released her hand, tipped his hat, and mounted his horse. With one last look, he rode off.

Eirica watched until he faded from sight, her heart going out to that scared boy of sixteen who'd taken on so much and had so much yet to give. And the fact that he wanted to give that love to her both confused and frightened her. Eirica desperately wanted to be that woman.

An overwhelming need arose. It shoved aside all her other needs and vows. She was fighting a losing battle, had known it since the night they'd shared that incredibly tender kiss. She'd faced the inevitable in the following days when all she'd been able to do was think about his declaration to court her, and her dreams of their next kiss.

How could she resist this man? James wasn't anything like Birk. Not even when Birk courted her had she felt this way. Over the last week, she'd had plenty of time to examine and ponder her growing feelings and her past. Honesty forced her to admit that she'd been eager to leave home, get out from under her father's domineering rule. She'd have fallen for anyone who'd courted her with flowers, gifts and declarations of love.

But she was older now, wiser, right? Two needs raged inside her, fighting for supremacy—but only one could rule. If she gave in to James, she'd be loved and cared for, that she no longer doubted. But would it be enough? Would he, with his good intentions of taking care of her, taking charge, smother that part of her trying to emerge after years of suppression?

She didn't know. She only knew what James made her feel inside was too special to ignore or deny herself. In fact, she hungered for more of those throbbing urges that had settled low in her abdomen when he'd kissed her. For the first time in her life, she knew what desire felt like.

But could she go further, past the kissing stage? She didn't know. She didn't fear James but she didn't want him to see her body, to be touched by the ugliness that was part of her. Another reason for her to not marry James was her worry that James would find her lacking, inadequate if he made love to her. But at least he'd be gentle, wouldn't he? Or were all men rough and mindless when it came to bedding their mates?

Realizing where her thoughts were leading, she reined herself in. Things were moving too fast, including her own desires. Somehow, someway, there had to be a middle ground, a way to have James beside her without sacrificing the woman finally free to emerge and spread her wings.

Remembering his gift, she opened her palm and

stared at the polished, brownish-red rock. Both sides bore a worn groove in the center, testimony to the hours of worry James had gone through. Fisting her hand to keep the warmth—James's warmth—in, she pressed it to her heart. And as she turned to go check on her children and start supper, she couldn't help but think about his promise, that he that he would kiss her again soon.

Her stomach fluttered and she hoped it wouldn't be too long before he kept that vow.

Chapter Nine

Charcoal-gray clouds roiled across the sky, dipping low enough to make the travelers feel like ducking. Without warning, jagged spears of lightning slashed the heavens in two followed by blasts of thunder. Hard on the heels of the initial breaking of the storm, torrents of water fell from the sky, lit up by one lightning bolt after another.

The suddenness and violence with which storms hit no longer surprised the emigrants, or even caught them unaware. Most were already safely ensconced in their tents, prepared to wait it out. Knowing it could be a short storm or one that lasted into the night the wagon circles had been chained to keep the livestock inside, wagon tops lashed securely and food for a cold meal stashed in the tents. As it was still light out, most of the travelers used their enforced inactivity to nap or write in their journals. Overhead, streaks of lightning continued to zig across the sky before plunging to the ground to shake the earth.

Alone in her tent, using the precious oil in her lantern to work by, Coralie concentrated on taking small, neat stitches to form a delicate design on the satiny pink bodice in her hands. Sitting in a pile beside her, several plain, serviceable white linen baby gowns sat. Now she was glad her father had insisted she bring material with her. When he'd told her he'd packed several bolts of cloth, including some fine white linen, all carefully packaged to withstand the elements, she'd scoffed. After all, she'd thought then, if she needed clothes she would pay someone to make them for her. She held the small item up, pleased with her painstaking work.

Coralie shook her head and laughed at the irony of her situation—exactly the opposite of what she'd always imagined. She wished her father could see her now. He'd be surprised. Heck, he'd be shocked to see all the changes she'd gone through over the last few months. Lowering her needlework to her lap, a wave of homesickness took hold. She fingered the fine gold chain around her neck and the heart-shaped locket hanging from it, both going-away gifts from her father.

She missed him. Her father, ever the optimist, always had a kind word for others. His outgoing personality made his store back in Westport a warm and friendly place, something she'd never realized or appreciated. Most of all, she missed his hugs, those all-engulfing embraces that had always embarrassed her. She even missed his stern lectures when he declared that her "airs" were becoming a bit too much. Right now, she'd give anything to see him and tell him how much she truly loved him.

She'd oftentimes disappointed him, she knew. But he'd loved her no matter what and had done his best by her. She didn't remember much of her ma who'd died when she was young, leaving Coralie and her brother to the care of their grieving father and stern grandmother who'd been firmly entrenched in Boston society—but she did remember the fight between her grandmother and father when he'd announced he was taking his children west to start over.

She'd cried, sulked and pouted when they reached Westport, but her father had been strong. He'd opened his store and settled to raise his children in what he deemed "real America."

Coralie snickered. How unpredictable life was. Her father had come from farmer parents and here she was, married to a farmer as well. Full circle, she supposed. Ah, but what a farmer Jordie was. She giggled softly, recalling last night's tender lovemaking after she'd told Jordan he was going to be a father.

He'd been ecstatic and then so very tender. Overhead, a furious explosion of thunder made her dive for her quilts. When the shaking of the ground stopped, she lifted her head. How she hated storms. "Oh, Jordie." She wished he were there with her and not off with a bunch of stupid cows. It would be completely dark soon and she didn't relish sleeping alone with a storm unleashing its power around her. Storms scared her, had always sent her running to her bedroom closet.

She couldn't even call on Jessie to keep her company as her sister-in-law and Rook had ridden out to take food and coffee to the men who were guarding the cattle round the clock. Not even for food would Wolf's men leave the herd. Over the last week, Jessie and Rook had even camped out there, closer to the men. Wolf was taking no chances that the herd might stampede again, especially now that the trail was much more crowded.

To keep her mind off the thunder crashing above her head, she concentrated on the small piece of pink fabric in her hands. A loud voice sounded outside, and Coralie hurriedly slid her project into a large canvas bag and shoved it beneath her pillow just as the tent flap opened and Jessie and Anne dashed in out of the rain.

"Hey, thought we'd join you if you don't mind." Jessie removed her gutta-percha poncho and sat, pulling out her own sewing. Anne did the same.

"We finally got away, left Rook out there in the rain to boss everyone around. The cattle won't stampede. Let Wolf and them others stay up all night watching." Jessie bent her head to her work, threading her needle and picking up where she'd left off mid-seam.

Coralie narrowed her eyes, taking in Jessie's flushed appearance and flashing eyes and dry clothing which meant she'd been back long enough to change out of her wet things. "You big liar," she snorted. "Wolf and James sent you back because they *do* think the cattle will stampede." She'd never forget the frightening experience of having the herd stampede shortly after they'd left Westport. If not for Jessie's quick thinking, they might have lost all their wagons; the cattle had been heading right for them.

The silence and set of Jessie's jaw confirmed her suspicion. "Hey, it's not so bad just being one of us girls, you know. At least we're dry." Coralie waited, surprised by her need to cheer Jessie up. She knew how hard it was for her sister-in-law to be excluded in activities that before her marriage, no one would have thought twice about.

After a minute's sulk, Jessie grinned wryly. "All right. Wolf ordered me back. Said watching me almost die once was enough to last him a lifetime." Her mouth firmed. "But, damn it, I'm as good as any of them, and he—and James—know it."

"Doesn't mean they want to see you put yourself in danger. Face it, sister dearest, you are a woman, whether you want to admit it or not. And men aren't going to let a woman do anything dangerous, especially one who seems to land herself in trouble more times than not." The last was said softly, gently even.

"You scared all of us when you were kidnapped." Coralie's voice hitched as she suppressed the remembered fear she'd felt for Jessie. Another change. She now looked up to her new sister-in-law and at the same time, felt protective of her.

Jessie still frowned down at her attempt at making Eirica's baby a gown. "That wasn't my fault. It just happened, that's all. I was even on my way to find Wolf to tell him about that wanted poster I saw at Fort Laramie. Not like I tried to take on that trio by myself."

"Yes, but in true Jess style, you ended up in the thick of things anyway."

"Yeah, I did, didn't I?" Jessie sighed. "All right, I'll make the best of it. Who knows, maybe I'll ride back out in a bit to check things out." Her impish grin made Anne and Coralie groan.

Anne pulled out tiny colored squares of calico that she was sewing into bigger blocks for a quilt. Coralie reached out and took one square and studied the patterns in greens and blues. "Ohhh, Anne, this is so nice. I wish I could make a quilt." She traced the tiny squares with her finger.

The older woman smiled. "It's easy, Coralie. I'll help you. You certainly have enough material."

"But I want to make baby clothes, too. She indicated a stack of four gowns all in white linen. Eirica's going to need some bigger things, too." She brightened. "Maybe I can do both. It'd certainly give me something to do when Jordie's on watch." She fingered the squares again with longing. "But a whole quilt would simply take forever."

"Perhaps you and Jessie can do one together, with each of you doing portions to form a small baby quilt. Eirica will need more than one." Anne deftly threaded her needle and looked at Jessie who was in process of ripping out a seam.

"Damn. Count me out. I can't sew worth sh—" Sheepishly, she glanced up. "Sorry. But this is so frustrating." She held it up. The seam was bunched and puckered down the back.

"Don't pull so tight on the thread, Jessie," Anne advised, taking the fabric and easing the seam with her fingers until it lay flat.

"And you want me to do a quilt? I don't think so."

"Yes you will, Jessica," Coralie said, her tone brooking no argument. "We are going to do one together." All of a sudden, she wanted to do all those things women did that she'd previously scoffed at and belittled, boasting that her father could afford to buy her ready-made clothing or hire out to a seamstress to make what she needed, like new curtains for her room. She didn't want to pay some stranger to make her baby's clothing. She wanted her child to use items made by her own loving hand.

Jessie glared at Coralie. "Anyone tell you that you're bossy?" At Coralie's pout, she rolled her eyes.

"Don't bother. I guess I need to learn to do this. There won't be anyone to do it for me when Wolf and I return to his home."

"Thanks, Jessie. What colors should we use?"

"I don't think it matters, Cory. I've got some old shirts we can cut up. Most are blue or brown." Jessie stuck out her tongue as she concentrated on rethreading her needle.

Coralie shuddered. "No, not those colors, not for a little girl. I think we should use pink." Coralie thought of the pink linen shift that matched the dress she'd saved for Oregon. It would be perfect, especially with the white linen. Eirica deserved something pretty for this baby.

"Blue and brown are just fine for a *boy*," Jessie argued.

Another voice joined them. "Ah, figured you ladies would like a nice hot cup of tea, seein' as how this weather ain't gonna let up any time soon." Rook stuck his head in, interrupting Coralie and Jessie from their sparring.

Coralie grinned at Rook. "Did they kick you out, too? Or did you come back because you missed us?"

Rook lowered his thick brows at her. "Someone's got ta be in charge here. I brought back the wagon. Wolf don't want the supplies anywhere near them cattle tonight." Anne reached out and took the sweetened tea from Rook so he wouldn't get things wet by coming inside.

Jessie glanced up. "That bad? Maybe I should ride back out."

Rook winced. "Can't, lass. Yer husband took back yer horse ta keep ya put. *And* he gave me orders ta see that you stayed here."

Coralie couldn't help the snicker that escaped her

Thrill to the most sensual, adventure-filled Historical Romances on the market today...

FROM  LEISURE BOOKS

As a home subscriber to the Leisure Historical Romance Book Club, you'll enjoy the best in today's BRAND-NEW Historical Romance fiction. For over twenty-five years, Leisure Books has brought you the award-winning, high-quality authors you know and love to read. Each Leisure Historical Romance will sweep you away to a world of high adventure...and intimate romance. Discover for yourself all the passion and excitement millions of readers thrill to each and every month.

SAVE AT LEAST *$5.00* EACH TIME YOU BUY!

Each month, the Leisure Historical Romance Book Club brings you four brand-new titles from Leisure Books, America's foremost publisher of Historical Romances. EACH PACKAGE WILL SAVE YOU AT LEAST $5.00 FROM THE BOOKSTORE PRICE! And you'll never miss a new title with our convenient home delivery service.

Here's how we do it. Each package will carry a 10-DAY EXAMINATION privilege. At the end of that time, if you decide to keep your books, simply pay the low invoice price of $16.96 ($17.75 US in Canada), no shipping or handling charges added*. HOME DELIVERY IS ALWAYS FREE*. With today's top Historical Romance novels selling for $5.99 and higher, our price SAVES YOU AT LEAST $5.00 with each shipment.

AND YOUR FIRST FOUR-BOOK SHIPMENT IS TOTALLY FREE!*

IT'S A BARGAIN YOU CAN'T BEAT! A Super $21.96 Value!

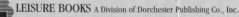 **LEISURE BOOKS** A Division of Dorchester Publishing Co., Inc.

GET YOUR 4 FREE* BOOKS NOW—
A $21.96 VALUE!

Mail the Free* Book
Certificate
Today!

4 FREE* BOOKS ❧ A $21.96 VALUE

Free Books Certificate*

YES! I want to subscribe to the Leisure Historical Romance Book Club. Please send me my 4 FREE* BOOKS. Then each month I'll receive the four newest Leisure Historical Romance selections to Preview for 10 days. If I decide to keep them, I will pay the Special Member's Only discounted price of just $4.24 each, a total of $16.96 ($17.75 US in Canada). This is a SAVINGS OF AT LEAST $5.00 off the bookstore price. There are no shipping, handling, or other charges*. There is no minimum number of books I must buy and I may cancel the program at any time. In any case, the 4 FREE* BOOKS are mine to keep—A BIG $21.96 Value!

*In Canada, add $5.00 shipping and handling per order for first shipment. For all subsequent shipments to Canada, the cost of membership is $17.75 US, which includes $7.75 shipping and handling per month. [All payments must be made in US dollars]

Name _____

Address _____

City _____

State _____ *Country* _____ *Zip* _____

Telephone _____

Signature _____

If under 18, Parent or Guardian must sign. Terms, prices and conditions subject to change. Subscription subject to acceptance. Leisure Books reserves the right to reject any order or cancel any subscription.

Get Four Books Totally
F R E E* —
A $21.96 Value!

(Tear Here and Mail Your FREE* Book Card Today!)

PLEASE RUSH
MY FOUR FREE*
BOOKS TO ME
RIGHT AWAY!

Leisure Historical Romance Book Club
P.O. Box 6613
Edison, NJ 08818-6613

AFFIX
STAMP
HERE

lips at Jessie's look of outrage. Fur would fly tomorrow. Luckily for them all, Jessie held her tongue, but her eyes flashed the promise of words to come.

Rook stared at the gowns Coralie and Jessie were sewing. "You lasses are doin' a right nice thing."

"Yeah, it's a surprise, so don't go telling her," Jessie warned, her voice stiff with anger.

Eager to regain the light and friendly atmosphere, Coralie asked, "Rook, what do you think Eirica will have, a boy or girl? I say it's going to be a girl."

Rook fingered his white beard, sending drops of water flying. "Girl," he said at length.

Jessie shook her head. "Nope. Boy."

All looked to Anne. "What do you think, Anne?"

Anne shook her head and laughed. "My wish is for a healthy child, boy or girl."

Rook chuckled. "Yer a wise woman, Mrs. Svensson, not ta get b'tween these two." He backed out and saying good night, he left Jessie and Coralie to their friendly bickering.

Rook made a mad dash for his wagon which was parked a short distance away. He was soaked to the skin and cold. He never bothered with a tent, preferring to sleep out in the open, unless it rained. Tonight, he'd sleep inside one of the supply wagons. Before he reached it, his feet slid out beneath him and he fell with a startled yelp.

He landed on his forearm. Pain shot through him. A dizzying array of stars floated before his eyes. Struggling to sit, he fell back. "Damnation," he whispered, blinking against the steady fall of rain upon his face.

"What have you done to yourself, you old coot?"

Rook turned his head toward the sound of that hateful voice. Trust his luck to have *her* find him stretched out flat on his back. "Nothin'." He struggled up, forcing himself to sit. He bit back the cry of pain when he tried to move his arm.

Sofia De Santis ran her hands down his injured arm, her fingers surprisingly gently as they probed his flesh. "It's broken, you damn fool."

"Well, thanks for the news, woman. Now, git away from me so's I can git up."

"And go where?" Sofia ignored his grumbling and called over her shoulder, "Dante, help me get him into my tent. We'll have to set his arm. Fetch that sheet I've been using to make bandages."

Rook blinked against the rain and the throbbing in his arm. "I ain't goin' ta go into yer tent. Wouldn't be proper."

Snorting, Sofia took her position in front of him while Dante went behind. Together, they lifted him. With Dante's support, Rook managed to walk the few steps to her tent. "I'll make a deal with you, Rook. If my reputation is tarnished, then I'll let you marry me," Sofia said.

They stopped just inside the tent. This time Rook snorted. "Not damned likely, ya old witch." He bit back a moan as his arm throbbed painfully from wrist to elbow.

Sofia only lifted a brow. "I'll fetch what I need. Dante, you get this stubborn old goat out of those wet things. Put him in my bed. I'll take Catarina's bedroll to your tent. The three of you will have to bed in there. Rook isn't going anywhere tonight."

Rook sputtered and protested but it didn't do him any good. Sofia marched back out with an armful of bedding, leaving him with Dante who only shrugged.

"We'd best do what my *nonna* says. It makes life simpler to humor her."

"That woman is a witch. She's bossy and always interferin', stickin' her nose where it don't belong." He blinked against the pain. "Did I say bossy?" It was difficult to concentrate and when Dante started to help him undress, he didn't have the strength to argue. In truth, he was starting to shake like a leaf, his teeth clacking together.

"Yep, you said bossy. Twice. But *nonna* knows how to set a broken arm. She's had lots of practice, first on my dad, then me. So far, Marco hasn't broken anything."

Settled between the covers, Rook closed his eyes, immediately aware that this was Sofia's bed. Her scent surrounded him, and though he found her personality objectionable—after all, she was bossy, always nosing in his territory, he relaxed. When she returned and started working on his arm, he didn't protest or make any snide remarks. Not even when she finished and made him sit so she could slide a large nightshirt over his head.

He even accepted a shot of whiskey laced with laudanum. Drifting off to sleep, he didn't see her release her long dark hair and take a seat beside him. She pulled her brush through the long strands, her gaze never wavering from his sleeping form.

Alone with her sleeping children, Eirica glanced out of the doorway of her tent. The storm had finally passed, leaving behind a cold nip in the air. She rubbed her arms and stared out into the crystal-clear darkness. Though tired, she felt too restless to sleep so she wandered around the camp, picking her way carefully across the wet and muddy ground. Passing Coralie's tent, she stopped when she heard whispered giggles coming from within.

She recognized Jessie's laugh. Over the last couple of weeks, she'd noticed how much time the two women spent together when their husbands were on duty. Though happy for her new friends, she couldn't help the twinge of envy. No matter what happened, they had a large, supportive family.

Maybe she could join them? She bit her lip. No. That would be intruding. She didn't belong. Feeling a bit depressed and sorry for herself, she returned to her tent, blaming her pregnant state for her sudden weepiness. "You're tired. That's all. You just need a good night's sleep," she comforted herself.

Climbing between the covers in the midst of her sleeping children, she rolled onto her side and closed her eyes. Somewhere close by, she heard a low howl, followed by a voice ordering Wahoska to shut up. A few seconds later, the sounds of the wolf's padding footsteps passed her tent, making her feel safe and secure.

Just as she drifted off to sleep, a noise had her bolting upright. She strained to hear. Was it inside, one of her children, or had it come from outside? Had the thief come to their camp?

A whimper broke the stillness and Eirica realized Alison was having a bad dream. She moved Ian to one side and gathered her elder daughter close, whispering until the little girl calmed.

The full extent of what lay ahead kept Eirica from sleeping. So many decisions. So many choices. And the well-being of her babies depended upon her making the right choices. She felt so alone. Then she recalled James's words that she didn't have to be alone. He was there for her.

Take him. He wants you, he loves you. He'd be a good father, a good husband. Eirica reached into her pocket and pulled out the stone. In the dark, she remembered his advice to trust herself.

Trust yourself.

Two simple words but they were oh so complicated and so hard to do.

Thinking about James, about her feelings, she tried to analyze them. What did she feel for him? *Gratitude?* Yes. *Friendship?* Most definitely. *Resentment?* Yes, when he barged in and took over. But there was more. Did she *trust* him? Absolutely. But what about love? Did she love him?

And that was the crux of the matter. She'd thought herself in love with Birk but now knew she'd been in love with the idea of love. But what she felt for James was different, deeper. Harder to put a name to. She only knew she felt *something* for the man set to win her heart. He'd changed her. She no longer felt frozen, and there was an eagerness within her to live, to experience the joys of life that had once been denied her. Was it due to James or her freed state? Though she suspected both were responsible, she had to be sure. This time, she had to be sure of her feelings. Holding the warm rock in her hand, Eirica closed her eyes. Her mind conjured up James's image and her imagination ran wild as she dreamt of their next kiss. As sleep claimed her, she thought maybe this time, she'd really, truly fallen in love.

Chapter Ten

Birk Macauley kicked a discarded tin cup that had been smashed flat by a wagon wheel and ground into the trail by countless feet. The sharp toe of his boot loosened it, sending it skittering ahead of him. When he reached it, he gave it another kick, uncaring that it narrowly missed a group of women walking ahead of him. The third time, it struck a gray-haired woman in the back.

The trio turned to glare at him, but when he glared back at them, baring his teeth in a leering smirk at the two younger women, they hooked elbows and moved off the trail, their steps hurried, as if afraid of him. Their fear made him feel good, started an ache deep inside of him, one he was having trouble subduing. There was only one woman he wanted, only one who could slake his lust.

Trudging alone, he scanned the men and women plodding along ahead, heads bent, steps slowing as the long day took its toll. Before him, he noticed a wagon painted completely blue, including the canvas top. He recognized that wagon. Damn. He'd seen it many times and knew it was the same as on both sides of the painted cover. Large black letters proclaimed their family name and city they were from. With hope rising, he carefully studied the faces of his fellow travelers. Yep, by damn, there was another group he recognized—three large families traveling together. He figured there had to be nigh on thirty children between them, ranging from screaming infants to lanky youths.

He quickly passed the noisy group, hating the sound of whining and crying brats. But for the first time in weeks, he was seeing familiar faces and wagons, which meant he was gaining on Wolf's party. Without a heavy wagon and slow oxen to contend with over crossings and the rough, rocky parts of the trail, he'd put in more miles on foot per day than most of the emigrants were able to average.

Excitement rose within. Soon, he'd catch up with his runaway wife. He curled his fingers into tight fists and sent a cloud of sandy dust into the air with the toes of boots two sizes too large. He ignored the angry shout that came from behind. As he walked, he scanned the distant scenery, searching for large herds of cattle.

"That bitch will be sorry she left me." The fury in his voice caused several nearby giggling girls to move away. Birk ignored them, heading toward a group of men pushing handcarts. With so many men traveling in small groups during the day, it was fairly easy to blend in, to look as though he belonged.

He spat on the ground, then wiped his cracked and dry lips with the back of his sleeve. As the day wore on, his heart jumped each time he spotted a red-haired woman or small child. Each time it turned out to be a stranger, his fury grew. If Eirica thought she could just up and leave him, hide behind the skirts of her new friends, she had another think coming. He'd teach her who was boss, and this time, he'd make sure they were alone so no one could stop him. When he got through with her, she'd never dare leave him again.

By the time dark swallowed up the last of the light, he knew he had to stop for the night. Aside from the possibility of missing his family in the dark, it was too risky to travel alone at night. He smirked and ran a hand along the barrel of the shotgun he'd taken from that old man. Easing his makeshift pack of supplies from his back, he glanced around for a place to bed down.

"Hey, you, move on," a threatening voice ordered.

Birk scowled at the man, noted the gun pointed at him and hefted his pack onto his back. Threading his way around wagons, cattle and tents, loud, raucous laughter from a group of men drew his attention. His ears perked. Damn, he knew that barking laugh. He moved closer, heard another voice, rough and gravelly make some ribald comment. More jeers and laughter followed.

Birk rubbed his hands together. Ah, things were looking up. He'd caught up to his old drinking buddies from before. He smacked his lips, easing into the circle of flickering light from the small fire to eye the three men hunched close to its warmth and light.

"Hey, Zeb. Long time no see." He'd spent many a night before his near-drowning drinking with this ragtag group of men headed for California's gold mines.

"Who's that?" Zeb squinted in the growing dark.

When recognition dawned, his eyes widened. "Well, boys, if it ain't ol' Birk. Ya ain't been around for a spell. Figured ya'd gotten way ahead of us when we had to stop on account of Matt gettin' hisself sick."

Birk glanced at Pete and Rat. "Where is Matt?"

Zeb shook his head. "Tha' son of a bitch didn't make it."

"That's too bad." He didn't care if Matt died or not, it just meant there was more booze for him. Birk eyed the flask in Zeb's hands and the pan of beans sitting off to one side of the fire. "Can a man join ya? I ain't eaten yet."

"What, wife ain't fed ya?"

Birk scowled. "We gots separated."

Zeb lifted a bushy brow, but he didn't ask any questions. Instead, he motioned for Birk to sit and help himself.

Birk dropped down before the fire, keeping his meager possessions close. He licked his lips and scooped up the cold, crusted-over beans with his fingers. When he'd scraped the last one from the burnt bottom of the pan, he noisily sucked his fingers clean. With the edge of his hunger eased, he turned his attention to the flask of amber liquid sitting between Pete and Zeb. Without a word, Zeb tossed it to him.

He took a long swallow, felt the warmth slide down his throat and warm his belly, then passed it back. Secure among friends, he settled more comfortably on the hard ground, stretching his feet out before him, his boots close to the outer edge of embers. This was more like it. He eyed the three men, his brain working overtime to find a way to turn this bout of good luck to his advantage.

Stroking his chin, he played with the idea of joining them. Not only would he have food, he wouldn't be as conspicuous as he was traveling alone. "Might like ta consider joining ya."

Zeb leaned back on one elbow. "What about yer wife and kids?"

Over the fire and between chugs of whiskey, Birk told Zeb how he'd nearly drowned. He blamed it on Eirica, telling the three men that she'd left him, forcing him to come after her to reclaim his children. "The bitch watched me from the other side, her and them friends. Wouldn't help me git across. Jest watched me fall. It's their fault I nearly drowned, but I gots news fer them. I's alive and I's gonna take back what belongs ta me." With each long swallow of cheap whiskey, his words slurred even more.

"She left you?" Zeb shook his head. "Had myself a pretty filly once." His voice trailed off.

Pete spat in the fire. "Yeah, found herself some young, rich, han'some man," he slurred.

Birk stopped in mid-swallow and lowered the bottle. Eirica wouldn't do that, would she? The thought of her with another man sent blood pounding in his ears. Not once had he ever really considered that. She was too meek, too afraid of him. He'd trained her right, as his ma had trained him. Memories of his ma flooded his drink-hazed mind. As a child, she'd demanded that he "kiss the rod" before she beat him with it. And he had. He'd always accepted her beatings, her punishments, meekly. And during those times when her anger overrode all else, he'd envision doing the same—not to her, she'd been too strong, too domineering—but to someone else, like Eirica, his nearest neighbor.

The pleasure that came from pretending to do what his ma did to him had made his beatings bearable.

Even as a grown man, he'd been able to stop her, could have struck her and ended her dominance over him, but he hadn't. By then, he'd come to see those beatings as a release. After his ma staggered away, drunk, he'd go off by himself and release the raging fury inside by thinking of his beautiful neighbor and how she might someday meekly accept whatever he doled out to her.

From the time he'd met her, he'd been drawn to her quiet nature. Finally, after his ma died, he'd married her and had taught her to fear him—just as he'd feared his ma. He'd be damned if he'd allow anyone to take her from him. Realizing that he was hardening just thinking of Eirica and the punishments she deserved, he drew up his knees.

But now, he had another worry. Had she found herself another man? In his mind, he thought of the single men in the wagon train. He had no problem dismissing them all—except two. The eldest Jones and that too-pretty Baker boy. His breathing grew fast and shallow. If she dared to look at another man—

Zeb broke into his red-crazed vision by moving closer to take the bottle lying beside him. "That what she done?" His expression held pity and tore Birk from his dark thoughts.

Birk opened his mouth to deny it. She wouldn't be stupid enough to let another man touch her, would she? Only now did he wonder if she hadn't left him for another. That Jones family had been against him from the beginning. Though he refused to believe it was the truth, Zeb had handed him an easy way to garner sympathy.

"Don't matter, I'm gonna get her back. Law says she belongs to me." Let the other men believe Eirica

171

had left him for another. Though it galled him to let Zeb think he couldn't hold on to his own wife, he fell silent, watching the man stroke the ugly raised scar covering one cheek from the corner of his mouth to just below his eye. "So, how 'bout it? Will ya let me join ya until I gits what's mine back?"

"I dunno. Seems there ain't nothin' in it for us. Why should we give you food?"

Birk narrowed his eyes. "When I catch up to my wife, I can pay ya then. She gots it all: the food, money, everything in the wagon." He didn't know if what he said was true or not. When he'd fallen into the Platte, he'd lost everything. He had no idea if the wagon had survived being stuck in the middle of the river. Was it gone?

"Seems pretty risky to me. What if she don't come back to ya or let you have any money to pay me? Then me and them boys is out of food."

"She can't stop me from claiming my property. Neither can anyone else."

He watched Zeb absently finger his scar. "Sure is an ugly scar. Someone ought to teach that Jones girl to mind her own business." Birk knew it had come from Jessie Jones and her damn whip. It hadn't taken Zeb long to discover that the 'boy' who'd stopped Zeb from having fun with some woman out wandering alone—obviously some whore, seeing as no decent woman went wandering in the dark—and sliced his cheek open with a whip had really been Jessie Jones. Whenever Zeb got drunk, he talked on and on about getting his revenge.

Birk's own resentment against the Jones girl reared its ugly head. Jessie had butted into his own affairs as well, and for that, he owed her.

Zeb shook his head. "Ain't gonna be me. I ain't gonna mess with that half-breed husband of hers. Me and the boys keep far away from him and his party. Don't wanna mess with him."

Birk paused in taking another drink. "Husband? She ain't married."

"Boy, you's been gone too long. Should've been at Fort Laramie when all hell broke loose. That damn woman got herself and some kid kidnapped. Me and the boys was there, you know, enjoyin' the fort and some of the willin' women when all these injuns showed up—family of that breed. No sirree, I ain't messin' with him.

Birk digested this news. Besides getting his wife back, he had a score to settle with both Jessie and Wolf. Maybe, just maybe, he and Zeb could team up. "Folk should still mind their own business. After all, a man's entitled to a bit of fun," he said, the words calculated to rile the other man into anger.

Zeb took a long drink, then spat on the ground, narrowly missing Rat, who'd bedded down a short distance away. "Yep. A man's entitled. I'd have had me a beaut that night. Was out all alone, jest sittin' on the bank, all lonely-like. Now, you and me, we knows no decent woman goes wanderin' by herself. Nope. She was lookin' fer action and I'd have shown her a good time. Then that damn boy—Jones woman—ruined it all." Zeb fell quiet, then closed his eyes. His voice turned wistful.

"Ah, what a woman that li'l angel was. All this long red hair that felt like silk." He grinned and squinted at Birk. "Had a nice set too, what with that bun warmin' in her oven. But man, I ain't never seen a face like hers. Like an angel. An angel, I tells ya, came down

173

from heaven that night jest waitin' fer me. If that woman belonged to me, I wouldn't let her out'a my sight for a moment."

Birk froze with the flask halfway to his lips. Zeb had never described the woman he'd tried to rape that night. Just called her his angel. But now, listening to him talk, it suddenly sounded like his pal was describing Eirica, his own wife.

Suddenly, it all made sense. Eirica and that damn Jones woman were friends. Hadn't Jessie Jones come to Eirica's aid with her whip the night Birk had decided to teach his wife a lesson, the night he'd been banished? He also knew that Wolf had warned Zeb away. Birk had just assumed that Wolf was once again butting in where he didn't belong. But if Eirica and Jessie had been there together, it made perfect sense.

He also recalled the few times he'd woken to find Eirica gone from the tent. When she'd come in, she'd claimed to have gone out to relieve herself. Her being with child, he'd never doubted her. He'd just taken her again to help him get back to sleep. But now, he wondered.

What had she been doing out wandering around so late? Had she gone to meet someone, another man? Had she and that Jones woman been plotting to get rid of him? Red edged his vision and his heart sped up. It was just too much of a coincidence that Jessie had been there for it to be anyone but Eirica.

And what about Wolf? Had he been in on it, too? He'd warned Birk to lay off his wife. The gall of the man to dare tell him what to do still raised his anger. But all this pointed to the fact that it had to have been Eirica Zeb found near the river that night.

Then it hit him that the man sitting across him had

lusted after his wife—had tried to *rape* Eirica. No one looked at his woman, let alone touched her. And now, listening to the lecher go on and on about what he wanted to do to his "angel" made Birk want to smash the bottle he held over Zeb's ugly head.

He lowered the bottle, fighting to keep his rage under tight control. Right now, he needed a clear mind to think. He passed the bottle back to Zeb, then pulled his knife from his boot. Cleaning his nails with the sharp tip, he thought maybe he could use the man's desire for Eirica to his advantage. His grip on the handle tightened.

"I'll make ya a deal. I have a score to settle with both Jessie and Wolf. Best way to get Wolf is by using his wife. Ya let me travel with ya, share yer supplies, and I'll find a way to get her for ya."

Zeb stared at Birk with drink-dulled eyes. "I dunno. I'd really like to find that woman, that angel. Sometimes, I think I must've dreamed her." He ran his finger down his face. "Till I feel this."

Birk stuck the knife into the dirt in front of him. "Ya know, ya never said much 'bout that woman. What if I know who she is?"

"Ya know?"

"Well, my wife has red hair and is with child. She's also friends with that damn Jones woman."

Zeb straightened, his gaze on the knife within Birk's reach. "Hey, I didn't know that angel was yer wife. Maybe it wasn't. The woman was sitting all alone, crying. All I tried to do was comfort her and she panicked. I didn't do nothin'."

" 'Cause you were stopped." Birk hid his fury. If he played his cards right, he'd get what he wanted. Then he'd take care of Zeb. The man was as good as dead for touching Eirica. He shrugged. "Don't worry. I won't hold it against ya even if that woman was Eirica. The bitch probably went out to meet someone. Seems ta me she was askin' fer trouble. Now what about our deal? I'll get ya the Jones woman and some money when I get my wagon and family back."

From the other side of the fire, Rat poked his head up and smirked at Zeb. "Hey, Zeb, seems that ugly scar on yer face is his wife's fault, too. She's the one who done led ya on, playin' the helpless female. She owes ya."

Birk stilled, the implication burning through the fog of his mind. But he wasn't drunk enough to give in to the fury building inside him. If he did, he'd be back on his own. He glared at Rat then turned neutral eyes back on Zeb whose eyes had widened. "If it were her, she'll git what's coming to her."

This time, Pete added his comments. "Seems ol' Zeb should get ta do the punishing."

Though it went against everything in Birk, he had no choice but to agree. The growing lust in Zeb's eyes gave him the perfect weapon to use. "Ya boys has a point."

Zeb leaned forward. "What're ya sayin'?"

"If yer Angel was my wife, I'll let you punish her for what she and that Jones girl done to you."

Distrustful, Zeb pulled back. "I wants one night with my angel. Tha's what I want. Seems ta be fair. If I can even the score with that Jones woman, fine. But as I said, I ain't messin' with her husband or his injun family."

Birk picked up the knife and fiddled with it. To get Eirica back, to have what he needed in order to bide his time, could he agree to Zeb's demands? No one said he had to allow the other man to go through with it. As far as Birk was concerned, Zeb was a dead man already.

Then he thought of Eirica's punishment. What if he let Zeb have at her? That'd teach her not to go out lookin' for trouble. Just imagining her fear as he watched sent the blood surging between his legs. Then, before the man actually raped her, he'd kill him. He'd kill him for even thinking about her, let alone touching her.

"Might teach the bitch a lesson she won't never fer-get." He allowed a long silence to stretch, then poked the fire with the tip of his knife, stirring the embers. "But ya has to wait 'til she births the kid. Don't want no son of mine damaged."

He watched the flash of lust in Zeb's eyes grow, eyed the man's trembling hands that he rubbed together, and knew he had him. "Might have to wait 'til we reach Oregon. With all them friends of hers, might be hard to git her back, and even if we does, they'll find us too easy on the trail. Too many people to try and stop us."

Zeb's eyes narrowed with mistrust. "How do I know you'll really share yer wife? Ya don't seem the type." He eyed the knife in Birk's hands and licked his fleshy lips.

Birk shrugged, resisting the urge to shove the blade deep into the other man's gut. But he needed Zeb—at least for a while. More than once, he'd been run off by men and women, suspicious of a lone man traveling with just a pack of supplies. And it was getting near impossible to steal food. Since word of his thefts had spread, folk were locking up their stuff and standing guard. No. He needed to belong to a group, have food and supplies and not be out wandering alone. Zeb had several pack mules instead of a wagon. He'd fit in just fine with this group of ragged-looking men.

"The bitch took my wagon, children and money. I want 'em back. Don't much care 'bout her, she's jest a woman and a man's got ta have hisself a woman to cook, clean and warm his bed at night. Let's jest say this is part of my revenge for what she done to me. If she wants to spread her legs fer another man, might as well be ya."

"What if she don't wanna?"

Birk stared at the knife, mesmerized by the firelight bouncing off the metal edges. "What she wants or not has never been important. She spreads herself when I says, or she pays." He glanced up, cold and calm. "The bitch will do as she's told or she won't see them brats again."

Zeb nodded and licked his lips. "We has lots of supplies with Matt gone. Ya can have his share."

Birk put his knife away and lowered his voice. "Deal is, we takes our own supplies and follow. Let them other two go on. Don't want too many people knowin' I'm following or what I'm plannin'."

"Well, I dunno. Rat and Pete and me, we's a team." Zeb frowned, eyeing the other two men snoring on the far side of the fire.

Birk shrugged. "Fine. Long as you don't mind sharing yer night. Seems theys gonna feel they're owed fer sharin' and all, and I'm only giving ya one night with that bitch. Ya might have ta share with yer buddies."

Zeb took another swallow, his movements turning jerky. He stood, swaying. "Nope. That angel is mine. I gits one night with her, alone."

Birk reminded. "And maybe some fun with that Jones woman."

Zeb's head wagged side to side. "Deal. One night with yer woman, and if we gits the other, she's mine, long as I wants."

178

After Zeb settled down to sleep, Birk continued to stare into the fire, making his plans for revenge. He glanced over at Zeb and fingered his knife.

No one touched his woman but him. Not ever.

The next day of rest came one day before the trail turned southwest toward Fort Bridger. Men took advantage of their free day to do maintenance on their wagons. During the night, they'd soaked the wagon wheels in water. With the wood swollen, the rims were replaced. This kept the wheel from drying out and the rims from falling off during the hot, dry days. While some men oversaw chores, others grabbed their rifles and shotguns and headed out to try their hand at hunting. Still others gathered together with greasy, well-thumbed packs of cards to settle in the shade of wagons or tents and played Pinochle, Euchre, or Old Sledge.

After the morning meal, the women put pots of water on to boil and started in on the long, tedious process of doing laundry. Knowing the routine, the single men in Wolf's party arrived early, bringing their dirty garments to Anne and Eirica to wash, each man eager to pay rather than do his own. No male wanted to be seen scrubbing his own clothing.

Jessie and Coralie split Wolf's, Jordan's, James's and Jeremy's soiled clothing between them. Sofia joined them with Catarina at her side. She had Rook's in addition to her own family's wash.

Eirica smiled at the dark-haired girl who held herself aloof. Her smile wasn't returned and Eirica knew why; Catarina regarded Eirica as a rival for James. How could Eirica blame her? James was more than easy on the eyes and his deep baritone was enough to send shivers up her spine, especially when he sang.

She swallowed a sigh of pure pleasure. Watching James had become her favorite pastime, especially when he played his guitar or mouth organ—and last night, she'd had ample opportunity to watch and listen to him.

For the first time, she'd been free to attend one of the impromptu dances held on the trail. In the past, Birk had refused to allow her to go. While everyone else went to have fun and meet fellow travelers, she'd had to stay in camp with the children. But last night, she'd taken the children and gone with Coralie and Sofia.

The dancing and music had lasted far into the night. What fun it had been to dance and feel carefree. She'd danced until her condition had forced her to sit and rest. A small grin hovered on her lips. Both Dante and Alberik had made sure they'd each gotten their share of dances, until James had claimed her, then ordered her to sit and rest. For once she hadn't minded his bossiness. She'd been exhausted but hadn't wanted to turn down any of the hopeful men looking for a dance partner and a break from the dreary days of travel. She'd sat the rest of the evening out, content to listen to the music and gossip with other women.

To her surprise, James and his siblings had provided the music with mouth organs. Several men had joined in on fiddles, including Lars. Then, to the surprise and delight of all, Sofia's grandsons had shyly produced their instruments and performed a folksy tune to which Catarina had danced. Eager to learn new dances, a horde of women and young girls had talked the shy girl into teaching them the intricate steps.

Once more, Eirica eyed the sullen girl and tried to befriend her. "I really enjoyed your dancing and your brothers' music last night, Catarina. It was a lot of fun." Eirica meant the words. She really liked the girl and her mother. Even Dante was nice, and Marco was a funny child who had a gift for making others laugh.

Coralie glanced up at the black-haired girl. "I think Elliot had a good time, too. I haven't seen him laugh or smile in a long time." She leaned forward and whispered, "Not since that preacher's girl gave him the mitten."

Catarina blushed, then looked at Coralie with interest. Jessie jabbed her elbow into Coralie's side. "What?" Coralie demanded.

Eirica exchanged amused looks with Anne as Coralie, ignoring Jessie, lowered her voice and told Catarina about her brother's broken heart. They, too, had seen Elliot dancing with Catarina, and when Dante put her on the spot by asking her sing to one of his tunes, Elliot had looked as though someone had pole-axed him.

Leaving Coralie and Jessie to their sparring while a much more animated Catarina held her own against them, Eirica turned to Sofia. "How's Rook?"

The older woman smiled. "Grouchy. He snaps and snarls and complains."

Anne chuckled. "Most men don't like being laid up."

"He will just have to get used to it. Foolish man. He should know better than to run around in a storm." Sofia rolled up her sleeves.

Sighing, Eirica started the long, dreary process, too. Talk turned to general topics, then died altogether as the sun beat down on them and the heat of the water left everyone too hot to talk. By the time Eirica— accompanied by both Alberik and Dante who'd insisted, to the amusement of all the other women, on

181

helping Eirica by lugging the heavy, sodden laundry—finished hanging the clothing out to dry on the line strung between the wagons, her back ached, her feet hurt, and her hands felt chapped and raw. And beside all that, she was starving; she hadn't stopped for a noon meal, wanting to get the work done.

Both Alberik and Dante insisted Eirica sit and let them finish. She was too tired to argue. Moments later, Jessie and Coralie joined her with their last arm-loads. Sofia and her granddaughter had left to start cooking the evening meal for the hired hands. Rook's bellows could be heard as he argued with the DeSantis woman.

"I'm not, I'm telling you, I'm not going to help those two tonight. Listening to them bicker drives me crazy," Coralie stated, shuddering.

"I don't know, I think they're kinda sweet together," Jessie said, plopping down on the ground. She stroked Sadie who reclined beside her, panting. Under her mistress's lavish attention, the dog rolled onto its side, resting its head in Jessie's lap.

Coralie rolled her eyes. "Now I know the sun has finally gotten to you, Jessica. Will you listen to them carry on? I do declare, one would think they were children the way they argue."

Jessie grinned. "Yeah. So do you think Rook's sweet on her?"

Coralie giggled. "I don't know but I've never seen him get so worked up with anyone else." Both looked to Eirica for her opinion.

Eirica loved being included. After so many years of being on the outside, never being allowed to have friends—let alone asked to give her opinion—felt as though she belonged, as if she mattered to these people. "I think Rook doesn't stand a chance. I think Sofia is smitten."

"But she's only been a widow a month."

Eirica smile faded. "So have I," she whispered, keeping her voice low so Alberik and Dante wouldn't overhear. What would others think if she allowed James to court her after so short a time?

Jessie threw Coralie a glare, her hands stopping in mid-rub, to the dog's annoyance. "I don't think it matters, especially out here. First, there's no one to know when and how each of you lost your husbands, and it's not like we're going to a settled town like Westport or St. Louis. Oregon is primitive and needs are different. Besides, I think Rook and Sofia will be good for each other. I'd really like to see Rook find someone to love again. He deserves a bit of happiness."

While Eirica privately agreed, she also decided she had to think a bit about her widowhood status and how others might view her and her children. Sofia was older, her grandchildren nearly grown. She patted a cold cloth against her cheeks and the back of her neck, scanning the area for her kids. Alison and Lara were sitting in the shade of a wagon with Hanna and Kerstin, playing with their dolls. The two Svensson girls, faced with the choice of tending the youngsters or helping their mother with laundry, had quickly chosen to mind Eirica's children. Anne's youngest son, Rickard, along with Marco, chased after Ian.

Eirica turned to Anne who'd just joined them. She pointed to Rickard who'd caught Ian and tossed him high into the air once more. "Your son is good with little ones. Not many boys his age would be caught dead baby-sitting."

"Rickard has always been good with youngsters."

Anne watched her son with pride in her eyes. "Of all my sons, he seems to have a natural way with young uns."

A group of men on horseback rode into camp. Eirica spotted James riding between Wolf and Jordan.

"Ah, our saviors," Coralie murmured, straightening her clothing and smoothing her tangled blond curls from her eyes.

Jordan was the first to dismount. He stopped in front of his wife and held out his hand. With a sigh of relief, she went with him. The pair left with arms twined around each other.

Wolf hunched behind Jessie and rubbed her shoulders. The sight made Eirica sigh with longing. Both Coralie and Jessie had husbands who were concerned with their welfare and not afraid to show their love. What she wouldn't give for someone to lean against, to soothe away her aches. She eyed James's hands. Once, not too long ago, the sight of hands that large would have instilled fear in her, but not now, not with him. She imagined how good it'd feel to have someone massage away the tired achiness.

As if he read her mind, he smiled down at her. She glanced away. To her relief, the conversation between Wolf and James turned to the trail.

Jessie leaned into Wolf and glanced up at him. "We're not taking the sublet cutoff are we?" Half-listening, Eirica watched Sadie head to one of the wagons and the scant shade it offered.

"No. It might be shorter, but water between the Big Sandy River and the Green River is scarce. We might have to go fifty miles without water. I don't want to stress the cattle more than necessary. We're doing fine time-wise so we'll head for Fort Bridger. We might even be able to sell some of the weaker stock there."

Again, feeling like an outsider, Eirica glanced away from the couple's tender looks. It was long past time for her to relieve Anne's girls. "Well, I had best collect my children."

James cleared his throat. "I'd be willing to bet you haven't eaten yet."

She sighed. "Not really. Just some biscuits and tea. Rook managed to feed my children and Anne's while we washed. But none of us women stopped to eat."

Dante and Alberik walked around James, blocking him from Eirica's view.

"All done, Mrs. Macauley," Alberik began, "is there anything else I can do?"

"I can start the fire for you." Dante, looming taller than Alberik, squared his shoulders.

But before she had a chance to assure both young men that they'd done enough, James placed a hand on each man's shoulders and stepped forward. He then draped his arms across their backs and smiled with all the confidence borne of a man who had no need to be jealous but had decided to make his intentions crystal clear. "I'm mighty glad Eirica had help today, but now that I'm here, I'll take over."

Alberik looked like he wanted to protest but Dante rolled his eyes and grabbed the younger man by the arm. "Come on, mate. We're being warned not to overstep our bounds."

Dante grinned and inclined his head toward Eirica. "Let either one of us know if you need any further assistance tonight, Eirica."

"Impudent pup," James muttered, shoving past them to hold out his hand to help Eirica to her feet. With a guilty grin that reminded Eirica of a little boy who'd absconded with a plate of forbidden cookies, he pointed to a pouch handing from his saddle.

"I nabbed some food. Come on, we'll go somewhere quiet where you can eat and rest." He led her to his waiting horse.

Eirica held back. "James, I can't leave the kids. Lara and Ian need to lie down. They've been running wild since they woke this morning." She missed the look that passed between James and Jessie.

"Wolf and I will watch them for you, Eirica. You deserve to get away for a bit."

Before Eirica could reply, Alison, who'd run over, squealed with delight. "Can we go riding, Jessie? Oh, please?"

"Well, maybe for a bit, if your ma says it's okay. Then you have to promise to lie down and rest."

"I don't need no naps no more." At Jessie's frown, she hastily added, "But I could lie down and keep Lara company while *she* sleeps."

James grinned. "See? They'll be fine. Come on."

Wolf stood and pulled Jessie up. "Get Shilo, Jessie. We'll take these youngsters for a ride."

Alison demanded his attention. "Can I ride with you, Wolf? I like your horse. He goes ever so fast."

Eirica's eyes went round, but James pulled her away. "Quit worrying, Mama. That horse of Wolf's might have been unbroken when we started out, but he's the best dam—dang horse I've ever seen."

Before Eirica could protest further, he maneuvered her into the saddle, cradled sideways in his arms as he guided his horse along the river, heading downstream. Resentment rose. Once more, he'd ignored her wishes and desires. Worse, he'd run roughshod over her in front of the others, never giving her a chance to agree or refuse. The more she dwelled on it, the madder she got. She fought back tears of frustration. Finally, she could stand it no longer. "Let me down, James."

"We're almost there. I found the perfect spot—if no one's claimed it for the night yet. I even have a nice quilt for you to sit on.' " Oblivious to her feelings, he kept going.

"Stop!"

Startled, he glanced down at her, saw the tears trickling from her eyes. "Eirica? What's wrong? Are you in pain?" He carefully dismounted and lifted her down. "What's wrong, sweetheart?"

Eirica shoved him away. He stumbled back, nearly landing in the water before he regained his balance. Too furious to even consider what she was doing, she advanced and poked a finger in his chest. He backed up until water lapped at the heels of his boots.

"How—how dare you? Who do you think you are? I'm—I'm sick of people ordering me around. You— you're no better than my father or brothers, always telling me what to do. Just leave me alone." Feeling herself falling apart, Eirica tried to turn and run, but the realization of what she'd done held her rooted to the spot. She felt the heat of anger blanch from her face and her suddenly wary gaze wouldn't leave the silent man standing before her. Instinct warned she'd better run or at least brace herself, but she didn't. Instead, she squared her shoulders, tipped her chin and waited.

The seconds passed painfully slowly. What would he do? Would he yell back, or would he shove her as she'd nearly shoved him into the water? Or would he walk away from her forever?

Her heart pounded, her stomach twisted and churned, and her knees shook so hard that she had to lock them to keep them from buckling. Why didn't he say something, do something? But he didn't do or say anything, just stared at her, his expression unreadable. Unable to stand the uncertainty any longer, Eirica clutched her hands in the folds of her skirt to dry her sweating palms.

"James?" Her voice faded to a hoarse whisper. "Say something."

Chapter Eleven

James shook himself from the trance that had held him immobile. The sight of Eirica, her eyes darkened to the slate-blue of a winter sky, caught him by surprise. Watching those eyes snap, words failed him. Indeed, he hadn't been able to move, held immobile by the sight of this woman laying into him in all her righteous fury.

Everything about her had come alive: Her face had flooded with a pink that complemented her eyes, enhancing the blue, a shade he found mesmerizing and hoped to see again and again. And the rest of her, advancing on him, so small, so delicate, yet she hadn't hesitated to poke and shove him, forcing him to back up. The soft soil beneath his boot warned him that he wasn't far from toppling backward into the river.

Now she stared up at him, her features pale, her eyes wide with horror—and she wanted him to speak?

Hell, he was breathless—and pleased beyond measure. She'd stood up to him. He chuckled, then realized his mistake when she narrowed her eyes. He stepped forward—away from the water's edge—and reached out to take her trembling fingers in his hands, trying but unsuccessful in his attempt to wipe the grin from his face. "I think you are the most beautiful woman I've ever seen."

His comment took her aback. Her jaw dropped, then firmed. She yanked free. "This isn't funny, James Jones. I—I'm serious. You're trying to control me, dominate me. Even if you are nice about it, even if you'd never strike me, I can't live like this anymore."

Recognizing that this was a big step for her, that probably for the first time in her life, she'd stood up for herself, James sobered. She was right. Once again, he'd barged in with what he thought was best without considering her wishes.

He moved closer but didn't try to touch her. "I'm sorry, sweetheart. I wasn't laughing at you or making light of your feelings." At her look of disbelief, he yanked off his hat and raked his fingers through his hair. So much depended on her believing him.

"Hell, Eirica, I don't want to control you or dominate you. I want you at my side. Working alongside me, walking on my arm. I want you to be a part of me, not beneath me. He frowned down at his hat. "I should have asked and waited for your answer."

As he spoke the words, he also accepted this was something he'd have to work on. He was just too used to giving orders and having everyone obey—well, except his sister. He glanced up, willing Eirica to believe him, to give him another chance.

She sniffed, wiping away the tears that had tricked down her cheeks. Her fingers twisted in the material of her apron. "All I want is for people to consider my feelings, to ask. I'm so tired of being ordered around and not given choices."

James tossed his hat to the ground and held out his hands, feeling low as a snake for not considering how his good intentions might come across. "I know I tend to barge in and take over, Eirica. I don't mean to, I just don't think. I was truly thinking about you and what you needed. I only wanted to take you away, give you a few hours free, and let you take a rest without being interrupted."

Eirica stared at his outstretched hands. She sighed. "I know, James. No one has ever shown me the kindness and consideration you've shown." She stepped forward and placed her hands in his. "Once it would have been enough to have someone like you see to all my needs, to make all the decisions." She hesitated when he gripped her hands firmly, yet lightly, letting her know she could pull away if she needed.

"But now?" he asked.

"Oh, James, I'm so confused. I'm not sure what I need or what I even want. I finally have something I've never had—freedom. Freedom to make my own decisions, to think the way I want, to do what I want. You have no idea what this means to me and I don't want to lose it. Yet there's a part of me that yearns for what you're offering. I lay awake at night, worrying about what I'll do in Oregon. How can I manage on my own with four little ones? What kind of work can I get, how can I farm land on my own? I can't afford help. And here you are, ready to step in and help me. You want to marry me and part of me is thrilled. You are everything I ever wanted. But it may be too late for me, for us. I don't know. I need time, James. Time to figure out what I need."

James started to turn away but with a gentle touch, she stopped him, her eyes beseeching him to understand. "Please, James, don't think I'm treating you or your intentions lightly, but there's more for me to consider. What will happen to me, to the children, if something happens to you?" Her fingers stilled his protest. "I could lose you by accident or illness. What then? Don't you see? I have to be able to stand on my own two feet. I need to know how to survive, especially in a place like Oregon. If I were back east, I could find work in a big city. I could survive as a widow with four children. But out here? I'm so afraid." Her voice trailed off.

James drew a deep breath and pulled her close, brought her hands to the hard wall of his chest. "Then I will teach you all you need to know. We will work together, be a team." He paused, his gaze searching hers. "I'm going to ask you something, but don't answer now. Think about it for a while. Give me a chance to prove myself. I want to marry you, be a father to your children, have more children with you—a houseful of red-haired and black-haired Joneses. I love you and your children and I want to adopt them."

"Oh, James." Her gaze turned tearful.

James brought one of her hands to his cheek. "I want to take care of you, provide for you, but I don't want a doormat for a wife. What you just did, the way you stood up to me, made me want to swing you up in my arms and shout. When you're angry, you're absolutely beautiful and you had every right to be mad. I deserve it. In fact, I thought for sure you were going to push me into the water."

He smiled tenderly down into her confused eyes. "That's not to say that every time you get angry I'll react so. Sometimes I'll disagree. Hell, I might even shout back. But I don't ever want you to fear me, nor do I ever want you to hide your anger or any other feelings you might have because you're afraid of me. So, let me be upfront. You know how I feel. I'm asking you to marry me. Don't answer. Wait. And in the meantime, I'll be patient. I won't push you."

At her lifted brow, his lips twitched. "Well, I'll try to be patient and if I forget my manners, you let me know." He twined their fingers together and brought them down between them. "You can poke me in the chest anytime. Now, would you like to go for that walk, find a nice secluded spot to sit, talk and rest, or should I take you back?"

He smiled wolfishly. "I'll even cook your meal so you can spend time with your children—if you let me stay and eat with you."

Eirica took a deep breath, feeling amazingly light of heart. Standing up for herself had felt good though James's reaction still amazed her. *He liked it?* He'd told her to do it again if he forgot himself. Suddenly, she wondered what it would be like to shout at him, to argue with him and have him shout and argue back— without ever having the fear of being struck? Whenever the men in her life yelled, she'd had to back down or risk a cuffing from her father or brothers—or worse from Birk.

Glancing around, she saw they were still alone. There were wagons, lines of them, further upstream and down and spread across the endless prairie as far as the eye could see, but here, in this one spot, it was only her and James, peace and quiet, no intruding voices, no crying children. She fought back a yawn, tired from the back-breaking chore of laundry. The thought of returning to start the meal, mind the children, listen to their shouts and cries as they tired made her long for just a few stolen moments alone—not to mention his offer to cook dinner. Could he cook? Well, heck, she'd soon find out. "I'd like to stay with you for a while." She indicated the spot where they stood. "How about here?"

James smiled, revealing strong white teeth in a face deeply tanned and rugged from his days outdoors. His sheer handsomeness stole her breath. Eirica felt a thrill go through her at the knowledge that this man wanted her. She watched him remove two blankets from his horse. One he spread on the ground, several feet from the river, the other he set aside. Holding out a hand, he waited for her.

Eirica joined him. Together, they sat on the grass-cushioned quilt beneath them. She sighed. It felt so good to sit, to be off her feet. James moved in front of her and took one of her feet in his hands. To her surprise, he removed her shoe.

"James, what are you do—? Ah, never mind." Sheer ecstasy flowed through her as he took her swollen foot between his big, warm hands and rubbed. Eirica closed her eyes. Never, not once, had anyone done this to her, and it felt heavenly, absolutely sinful. She leaned back on her hands and let his fingers work their magic. When done with her left foot, he repeated the process on her right. She slid down to her elbows and sighed when he set her stockinged foot down on the blanket.

"Here, sit up, sweetheart." His deep, soothing voice came from behind her.

Eirica sat with a protest. "That felt so good. I never imagined . . ."

"Anytime you want your feet rubbed, you just tell me." He settled himself behind her, drew her back into the cradle of his hips, supporting her with his

chest, his arms wrapped around her, resting his fore-
arms on the shelf of her stomach, just below her
breasts. Her head lolled back, finding a perfect hollow
near his shoulder.

He spoke, his mouth so close to her ear that she felt
the warmth of his breath. "I remember the evenings
when my pa used to set my ma down in her rocker in
front of the fire and take her shoes off. He'd rub her
feet and tell her about his day. Sometimes, he told her
stories—most were blarney and she'd laugh, but that
time in the evening belonged to them. None of us, not
even Jessie, dared to intrude."

Eirica tipped her head back to glance at him. "You
miss them still, don't you?"

He smiled down at her. "Yeah, I do. It's been a
long time but I still remember all the love and laughter in our home. Once a week, we'd gather and sing,
dance, play our fiddles or mouth organs, or just sit and
take turns telling stories. Ma was one for family
togetherness. She also insisted we learn to appreciate
music."

He hesitated, then took a deep breath. "My guitar
belonged to her. She used to play on the porch and
sing and I'd leave my window open so I could hear
her."

"That's sweet, James. You play well." She blushed,
remembering the night he'd played, as if playing for
her. Maybe he had been. The thought, so lovely and
romantic, made her smile with pleasure and forget her
hesitancy in speaking of her own family. "I wish I had
the same good memories that you do. There wasn't
much love or laughter in our house." She fell silent,
not wanting the taint of her past to spoil the mood of
the moment.

"Tell me about your family."

Eirica shook her head. "Someday—maybe. Let's just say my children will know the love and laughter you had. I made that promise after Birk drowned. But I don't want to talk about the past. Not now."

James tightened his arms around her. "All right. Close your eyes now and rest."

He reached with one hand for the other blanket and covered her. Then to her surprise, he rested his cheek against her hair and sang a soft, sweet love ballad. Eirica gave herself over to her exhaustion. One thought ran through her mind before sleep claimed her. If she married James, she'd have love and laughter and someone who'd set her down in a rocker each evening, rub her aching feet and sing to her.

James watched Eirica sleep, content to just hold her and dream of their future. And as he did, for the first time in a long time, he thought of his parents, of their marriage. Suddenly all their shared looks, flushed cheeks and laughter took on new meaning. Only now did he realize just how happy his parents had been.

He'd grieved for them when they died, but now he knew that it had been best and they'd been happier dying together. They'd been that close, that in love, that he couldn't imagine either one of them without the other. Somewhere along the way, he'd closed himself off to feeling that himself.

Raising his siblings had made him afraid to be open, afraid he'd forget his responsibilities if he relaxed. Consequently, he'd been hard on his brothers and overprotective of Jessie—all because he feared failing. In his attempt to be both mother and father, to keep the same rules and standards, he'd forgotten the laughter and joy of tossing some of those rules out of the window.

Another memory struck. Late one night, when he'd been sixteen, just months before the accident that had taken his parents' lives, his ma had come to the room he shared with his brothers. She'd woken him and quietly urged him outside. Jessie had been there, too, in her bare feet. Together, Ma led them to the barn where their favorite dog, Meara, was having puppies.

They'd spent the long night with the dog, coaching her, stroking her and finally, just before dawn, she'd had her litter—four squirming, hungry pups. Jessie had immediately claimed the first-born, a brown and black female who looked like Meara. They'd taken the dog and puppies into the kitchen where his ma already had a nice fluffy bed waiting near the stove.

They were all still up, had been up most of the night when his pa and brothers awoke. James had been tired, had known he had a long day ahead of him, but his pa had surprised him by insisting that the three of them go to bed for a few hours. Jessie, unwilling to leave the puppies—her puppy, Jo-Jo—had brought her bedding to the kitchen floor to sleep.

Both Meara and Jo-Jo were now gone: Meara to old age, Jo-Jo to a fatal attack by a coyote, but by then, there'd been another litter of pups. Jessie had kept Sadie, also the first-born.

An hour passed, then two, with James alternating between half forgotten memories and visions of the future. When he noticed the sun was lowering, he nudged Eirica awake. "Time to wake up, sweetheart. I think there's going to be three hungry young'uns waiting for us."

Eirica woke with a start. She'd have bolted upright,

but James held her tight. "Shh, easy, we're not in that much of a hurry. Look." He pointed to the horizon where all that remained of the sun was a last burst of brilliant red color streaking toward them, shading the world in hues of bright orange to the deepest red. Behind them, to the east, the color faded to a golden-yellow with a faint hint of blue-gray.

"Oh, James, what a glorious sunset."

His lips moved against her hair. "Not as beautiful as you." He shifted her slightly so he could stare down into her face. Mesmerized, she stared back, her lips parted.

"I want to kiss you," he whispered.

She caught her lower lip with her teeth. "I think I'd like that." She lifted her hands to his neck and pulled his mouth to hers.

His kiss started off slowly, a tender melding of flesh. One of his hands cupped the back of her neck, the other caressed the sides of her face and her neck. He stroked down her back as he turned her sideways so that she was cradled in his arms, pulled over his lap. His lips darted from her mouth, slid to her jaw, nibbled their way down her throat to the pulsing hollow there, then back up the smooth, soft skin beneath her chin, full circle back to her parted lips. Her soft sighs and moans fueled his need for more.

This time, he claimed her firmly, a man hungry for the taste of his woman. He angled his head, his mouth slanted over hers as he explored. Even with her kissing him back, moving with him, tasting him as he drank of her, it wasn't enough. He needed more, much more. Slowly, giving her time to object, he used his tongue, feeling her start of surprise when he traced her lips, then probed a bit deeper, stroking inside, reveling in the moist silky softness of her upper lip. "Open your mouth, Eirica. Let me taste you, all of you."

Eirica heard the plea in his voice. Hesitantly, she complied. The few times Birk had kissed her this way, he'd brutalized her mouth, left her bruised and bleeding, but James's kiss left her feeling drugged, lightheaded ecstatic. And his brief foray into her mouth made her long for more. She wanted to know, to experience with James this intimate form of kissing. James would show her exactly how it should be done.

She pulled him to her, giving him free access. At first, the invasion of his tongue seemed strange, but it also felt right. He moved slowly, giving her notice of his intent as he stroked her along her teeth, the inside of cheeks, the roof of her mouth. Eirica settled back in his embrace and shifted against a deep ache in her belly. Warmth flowed in her veins and pooled between her legs. Suddenly, it wasn't enough to let him do all the work. Hesitantly, she moved her own tongue, touched his, then retreated. His followed and to her delight, they danced around each other.

His lips moved over her face, her neck, below her ear, leaving her needing more. She wanted him as he'd had her. Tugging his head up by threading her fingers deep in his thick hair, Eirica pulled his mouth to hers and demanded entrance to his mouth. Once there, she tasted, drank and set about chasing and stroking his tongue, and sucking on his lower lip. He groaned, or was it her? She didn't know, didn't care.

Their breathing grew heavy, loud. Soft moans, deep groans filled the air. Pulling her mouth from his, she traced the line of his firm jaw with her fingers, kissed the soft spot below his jaw until he tipped her chin and claimed her mouth once more.

As the kissing went on, they grew frantic, their desires deepening. Eirica felt the urge to move her legs, squeeze them together in response to some nameless ache that overwhelmed her. Beneath the blanket, James's hand trailed down from her throat to the swell of her full breasts. She held her breath, but didn't stop him. Slowly, his palm cupped her, his warmth sinking through the fabric of her bodice. She gasped for air when his lips moved down her throat, her head resting against him as he shifted her so he could fill both palms with her aching breasts.

Part of her knew she should stop him, stop this madness. They were out in the open, where anyone could wander past, but his tenderness, his gentleness held her enthralled as did the raging needs of her own body. The foreign feelings demanded more. "James, I—I've never felt like this." Again, she shifted her lower body.

He lifted his head, his eyes glazed with emotion and need. But there was nothing there to frighten her. Only pained understanding. "That's desire, sweetheart. Your body knows what it wants and knows I can give it to you." He shifted slightly, letting her feel the hard length of his own need. He stroked the side of her face with his hand.

"I ache and throb, just as you do, but there's no reason to fear me or what you feel. I won't hurt you. I'll prove that to you, but not now. When we make love, we'll be alone, just you and me." He took a deep breath, rested his forehead against hers. "We'd best stop before I forget my good intentions."

The thought of him doing more, of somehow easing the throbbing between her legs made her moan. She knew full well how'd he'd slake his own needs but wasn't sure how he could ease hers. With Birk, she'd never felt this powerful urge for more, had never felt anything but shame and humiliation and pain. Would it be the same with James? Would he forget himself in his own blind need and simply use her body as a vessel?

Staring into his face—his eyes—and seeing only love shining there, she knew he wouldn't. Somehow her body knew he'd show her what real love was between a man and wife.

James leaned down and took her lips in another slow, thorough kiss then stood, pulling her up. He encircled her with his arms, holding her loosely. "Ready?"

"Yes. And James?"

"Yes, sweetheart?"

"You don't have to worry over Alberik or Dante. They are just trying to be helpful." Eirica knew that wasn't entirely true, but she didn't want to hurt either one of them or cause problems between them and James.

To her surprise, he threw back his head and laughed. "Me, worry about those two pups?" He took her hands in his and brought her fingers to his lips, his eyes twinkling with impish delight that reminded Eirica of his sister. "However, it doesn't hurt to make sure they understand the way of things," he added.

Eirica giggled, caught herself, and stifled her laughter, recalling Dante's wry acceptance and Alberik's endearing readiness to take James on.

James was right. Though she wasn't sure her future lay with James, she did know that as nice as Dante

and Alberik were, she could never feel more than
friendship with either younger man. As she and
James returned to camp, Eirica rested her hands on
her swollen abdomen and let James rest his arm
across her shoulders, drawing her close. In that
moment, she knew she was ready. Ready to trust
again.

A short distance away, concealed beyond the wagons
parked for the night, two men threaded through the
throng of people, watching the couple walk along the
water. They moved among the wagons, careful to keep
their presence concealed from the man and woman as
they followed from a safe distance. Zeb fingered his
scarred cheek and nervously watched the man beside
him. "That yer wife?"

"That bastard. He's dead," Birk growled.

Zeb wasn't sure if it was the same woman who'd
haunted his dreams. They'd been too far for him to
know for sure, but Birk had claimed it was his wife the
moment they'd seen her standing in the other man's
arms, kissing him. Zeb eyed the woman's pregnant
belly. She looked ready to pop.

He glanced at Birk, wondering if he'd made the right
decision to leave his buddies in order to seek revenge.
Birk Macauley was mean as billy hell and Zeb felt like
a dog caught in the dough. He doubted this man would
actually share his wife, especially after seeing his reaction to the sight of her kissing another man.

But it didn't really matter. Zeb was in it now and he'd
make sure he looked after his own interest. After he and
Birk got his wife and that breed's woman, Zeb would
take care of Birk. The man was a lazy drunk, boastful
and filled with self-righteous complaints and indigna-

tion. Zeb was tired of listening to him. Birk cared only for Birk and that was okay with Zeb. To each his own. Again he fingered his scar. But them women owed him and he planned to collect—from at least one of them.

Aware of Birk's growing fury, Zeb pulled him away, noting that the couple had disappeared from view. "Ya can't do nothin' now. At least we's caught up with them. Now we jest has ta follow and wait."

Birk shook him off. "Did ya see that? She kissed him. She's my wife. Nobody else touches her."

Zeb lifted a brow. "Not even me?"

The violent rage lessened from Birk's eyes. "Only ya. Only who I says and only one night, just to teach that bitch a lesson she'll never forget."

Zeb didn't believe him, but that was okay. He'd get his and Birk would get what he deserved as well. Deciding he needed to get the man away from his wife and her lover, he stated, "We's takin' the sublet cutoff. With that herd of cattle, your wife's party will head southeast, by way of Fort Bridger. We can git ahead of 'em. And travelin' faster, we'll have time to plan afore the two trails meet back up."

"I ain't gonna let that bitch outta my sight."

"You goin' to risk havin' them or someone else spot ya and warn 'em? If we split off and git ahead, we can watch fer 'em, check out the trail for places to nab her and that breed's woman. Don't let yer anger ruin everything."

Birk considered Zeb's suggestion. "Yer right. She ain't goin' anywhere. We'll go ahead and wait fer' em." He stormed off, heading back to where they'd left the pack mules, muttering, "He's gonna die. He's a dead man."

Zeb followed slowly to give the other man a chance

to calm down. He rubbed his hands together and formulated his own plans. First, he'd get Birk drunk enough to pass out, then he'd go in search of the woman and see if she *was* his angel. He fingered the knife on his belt, knowing he had to watch his back.

Chapter Twelve

"Beans, woman, beans. Good food, tha's what them boys need, not yer fancy noodles," Rook bellowed at Sofia. She ignored him and continued slicing her dough into long strips and hanging them over strung line to dry.

Using a thick wooden dowel, she rolled out another chunk of dough. Adding the last of the noodles to the rest of the drying strands, she turned. "The men like my noodles. Don't you ever get tired of beans, rice and pork, day after day, meal after meal? Have pity on those poor men. Now, why don't you go sit and rest? Catarina, Coralie and I can handle the rest of the meal."

"Rest? Rest! That's all I've been doin' woman. This is my domain and yer interferin'." Even as Rook shouted, he eyed the sauce bubbling in the huge pots with interest. He couldn't stop himself from sniffing. To cover his interest, he scowled and poked a wooden spoon into the pot and drew it out for a taste. His stomach rumbled in response to the spicy meat broth. "Fancy. Damn fancy cookin'."

"But it tastes wonderful." Coralie peered over his shoulder.

He lowered his brows. "Ain't ya got somethin' ta do, lass?'"

"Yes, I do. Bread." She sauntered off, oblivious to the three pairs of identical grimaces.

Rook turned to Sofia. "Ya goin' a let her ruin—ah—bake the bread, again?"

Sofia winced. "How can I tell her no?"

"Please, *nonna*," Catarina begged, you've got to do something."

Rook smirked. "Yer grandma here insists she can learn with practice."

"And the poor *ragazza* will learn, with more practice." But even her voice lost its confidence. "Lots more practice," she muttered, shaking her head.

"Well, it'll be burned, doughy, flat, or heavy as a rock unless one of us does something." With that pronouncement, Catarina went to where Coralie was dumping flour into a bowl.

Rook chuckled when he heard the girl ordering Coralie to measure carefully. He turned to Sofia. "Yer granddaughter is a right fine young woman."

Sofia lifted one brow. "A compliment? From you?" A smile wreathed her face, taking the sting of sarcasm from her words.

Staring at this woman who matched him in height, and nearly in girth, Rook's lips twitched. Since she'd joined Wolf's party, his life had turned very lively. With a start he realized he enjoyed sparring with Sofia. The woman gave as good as she got and kept him on his toes, even if she had the unfortunate and irritating habit of sticking her nose in where it wasn't wanted. And she did have a nose on her. Studying her, he couldn't help but compare her to Annabelle, who'd been small, and dainty with a face as delicate as Sofia's was strong. Still everything about Sofia fit her. Her height, her ampleness, the strength of her features. She was a force to be reckoned with.

Of course that didn't mean he'd stand by and let the woman boss him around and take over. Nope. This was still his territory and even one-armed, with his wrist broken, he could still do his job. He glared at his bandaged arm resting uselessly in the sling Sofia insisted he wear.

Ignoring Sofia, he set out a couple of pans over the fire and tossed slabs of pork on to cook. It rankled that the men did indeed seem to prefer her fancy noodles and stews but he was paid to do a job and cook he would: good, hearty, stick-to-your-ribs fare.

Jessie and her brother Jeremy arrived. Without bothering to find out what they wanted, Rook set them to work before Sofia could nab them. The threesome chatted until Jeremy whistled a low catcall.

"Cooeee, will ya look at that?"

Rook and Jessie both turned their heads to see James, his arm around Eirica's shoulders as he escorted her back to her wagon where Wolf had the three children sitting in front of him as he told them a story, using lots of hand motions. Ian had fallen asleep in his lap, Lara leaned on one side of him, her thumb in her mouth, and Alison sat in front of him, her eyes wide.

"Think our brother's gonna get himself hitched?"

"I hope so," Jessie sighed softly.

Rook grunted, though he agreed the couple looked mighty fine together. Butting in as usual, Sofia joined them. "Ah, they are in love. That boy will make a fine husband and father."

All watched James take Ian and put him to bed, then to the amazement of all, he started a fire and unpacked the Macauleys' box of foodstuffs while Eirica took her daughters down to the water to bathe.

"She's letting him cook supper? Wow." Jessie watched openmouthed.

Rook, distracted by the other pair, smelled burning. Spinning around, he frantically turned the meat. "Now look what the lot of ya made me do? Blathering on and such." But he couldn't help sneaking another glance at James. His bushy beard hid his pleased grin. Them two would make it. The lad was just what the lass and them young'uns of hers needed.

He jerked around when he heard Sofia order Jeremy and Jessie to do some chore. Glaring at her, he pointed the knife he used to turn the meat over to brown. "I already gave them work ta do."

Sofia narrowed her brown eyes and folded her arms across her ample bosom. "You can have the boy. I'll take Jessie."

"No!" he bellowed. "The lass is mine." He jabbed his finger at Jeremy. "You help her, and by damn, don't you go sneaking any of my biscuits or stewed peaches."

Rook smiled smugly at the look of ecstasy on the boy's face. He'd traded some woman a hunk of sugar and some dried antelope meat Wolf had killed for some jars of peaches and some other dried fruit he'd hidden so *she* wouldn't find it. God knew what she'd do with it.

Leaving Jessie to finish cooking meat that would probably not be eaten until noon the next day, Rook ambled over to the milch cow. Some thickened milk, sweetened with sugar, might go nicely with the evening meal.

Four days later, Eirica and Sofia trudged along the trail with Eirica keeping a watch on her children to make sure they didn't become a nuisance to the others. Up ahead, Dante carried Ian on his shoulders while Lara rode with Rook. Marco led a mule with Alison perched on its back.

Eirica was grateful for the attention the others bestowed on her children. Walking all day was impossible for them, especially Ian, yet in her condition, carrying him for long bouts of time was out of the question. That left the wagon, which none of them liked; Eirica still worried about Ian falling out of it again.

Sofia shook her head, her gaze on Rook. "That old nag of Rook's should've been sold to the glue factory long ago." Her voice carried just loud enough for the old cook to hear.

He turned, proving there was nothing wrong with his hearing. "That mule of yers ain't no better. Least I can ride Bag 'O Bones." The mule flattened its ears and let out a long bray as protest. Alison giggled and rubbed the offended animal between its ears.

Eirica coughed to hide her own amusement. When she noticed the look of soft satisfaction on Sofia's face, she studied the two anew. How could Sofia, who'd just just lost a husband she'd loved, be involved with another man so soon?

Sofia caught her speculative stare and took a deep breath as she repinned her hair on top of her head. Bonnets weren't for her, she'd claimed when Anne had offered her the use of one, and with her golden-brown skin, she didn't burn like Eirica. "You're won-

dering what an old woman like me sees in an old
grouch like him, aren't you."

The other woman's directness caught Eirica by
surprise. She shook her head. "No. Rook is pretty
special." She hesitated to pry, but there was something she had to ask, had to know. "You can tell me
it's none of my business, but weren't you happily
married?"

"Ah. Did I love my Luigi? And if so, how can I be
thinking of someone else so soon?" A faraway look
came into her eyes. "Our marriage was arranged—but
it was a good one. We grew to love each other. I'll
miss my Luigi, we had many good times and so many
dreams. He wanted so much to go to Oregon, to plant
his feet in new soil and live out the rest of his life. His
health wasn't the best, but for him, I said 'yes' and we
all packed up.

"But now, all I have left of my family are three of
my grandchildren. I must think of them." Seeing
Eirica's frown, she put her hand on Eirica's. "Do not
get me wrong. I'm not taking advantage of Rook. He's
a wonderful man, even if he's afraid to show it.
Sometimes, love grows from friendship. And sometimes, it just happens between two strangers who don't
really know each other. With Rook, I feel it here." She
fisted her hand and hit her chest above her heart then
laughed softly. "Even if the old coot is too blind to see
it. This is right."

Eirica thought about her own situation. She hadn't
loved Birk, didn't know what it was like to share a
friendship with her husband as Sofia obviously had.
But she, too, had been given a second chance, and
more than anything, she longed to reach out and take
it. Yet part of her still held back. She had young chil-

dren to consider. What if people talked? Would her children suffer if she married again so soon?

"Aren't you afraid of what people will say?"

Sofia hooted with laughter. "I'm an old woman. I can do as I please." She sobered suddenly and turned to Eirica, her nearly black eyes piercing. "You're worried what others will think of you if you finally give in to that love-struck young man who's courting you." It wasn't a question.

Put like that, it made Eirica feel weak and foolish. "Not for me, but my children. I don't want them to be outcast or to bear any shame because of me."

Sofia pursued her lips. "Do you love him?"

Faced with the moment of truth, Eirica could no longer deny what her heart had felt for a long time. "Yes. Oh yes."

"Then you must reach out and take that love and hold it to your heart." Her hands mimicked her words. "Do not worry about what others will say. Who will know? No one. All these people traveling alongside us have either lost a loved one themselves or are too worried about their own survival to pay attention to such trivial matters."

Relieved and lighter of heart, Eirica relaxed. "You must think me foolish."

"No. You've survived what most would not have. The easy path would have been to use James or any other willing man. Instead, you have been determined to stand strong."

At that moment, Eirica felt closer to this woman than she'd been to her own mother. Glancing ahead at Rook, she acknowledged how fortunate she was indeed.

An hour passed, then two. Dust and the hot sun

made talking difficult. Catarina joined them and soon, Jessie and Coralie fell into step as well. Sofia wandered off, to rejoin her grandsons—and Rook, Eirica suspected.

With the oxen tiring, the women had nearly caught up to Elliot. He sat on the wagon tongue, letting the oxen pick their own path. There was no danger of them running out of control. They, too, felt the heat and had to be reminded to keep going.

To their right, a group of three young women headed their way, their steps surprisingly spry and energetic. Even from this distance, Eirica could hear their giggling.

Coralie spotted them and scowled. "Lord save us from more simpering giggling girls," she moaned. "I do declare, if they come over here to ask about Elliot again, I shall scream."

Jessie looked pleased. "Your brother is certainly sought after. Maybe you'll have a new sister-in-law before we reach Oregon."

"Please, Jessica, let's be serious. None of them will do. Not at all. He needs someone who has a brain in their head, right, Eirica?"

Before Eirica could say anything, the young women rushed over. "Yoo-hoo, Coralie, can we join you? We'd like to have a word with you."

"Gee, doesn't this sound familiar," Jessie muttered beneath her breath. Coralie jabbed her hard with her elbow.

One of the girls got right to the point. "Tell us about your brother."

"Would you be so good as to introduce us? Now?" The questions came rapid-fire.

Beside Eirica, Catarina narrowed her eyes and turned her head. "*Elliot* is busy. I believe he'll be occupied for the rest of the day." Her height and her dark, self-assured good looks silenced the chattering visitors as they watched her walk toward Elliot with a sway to her hips. When he saw her approach, he hopped down and waited for her with a smile.

Jessie grabbed Eirica by the arm. "Come on. Let's go check on Rook, see if he's doing okay with his arm and such."

Behind them, Coralie sputtered, "Jessie, don't you dare leave." She didn't want to be stuck with these simpering, empty-headed, foolish girls.

Eirica joined Jessie's gleeful laughter as they hurried away. It felt so good to belong.

The stopping point for that night was along the Green River, downstream a mile or so from the point where they had forded. Instead of forming circles or squares, each emigrant pulled away and found a spot along the river for some much-needed privacy. Eirica helped James unyoke her oxen and check their backs for sores. After watering them, he took them out to graze. Tonight, the emigrants would take turns guarding their oxen.

Conscious of the safety of the children, Eirica sat on a stump near the water's edge. She and James had chosen a spot where the bank was flat, with a small shallow inlet. Even so, Eirica worried about the fast-moving current. Alison splashed water high into the air with her feet. "Don't go any farther, Alison girl," Eirica cautioned. Lara watched from the bank, thumb in mouth, her small remnant of blanket clutched tightly in her hand.

James rejoined Eirica. "Would you like me to see to the meal so you can rest?"

Eirica stood. Though James was a very good

cook—he'd learned while raising his siblings—she still found it hard to have a man offer to cook for her. She longed to accept and let him coddle her, but she didn't want to take advantage of his good nature.

"I'll cook, if you'll watch the children. I'm worried Ian will fall into the river." No sooner had she spoken than Ian ran past to play in the water with a pan and spoon he'd taken from the box of supplies.

James scooped him up into his arms and tickled him. "Deal." He set Ian down. Content, Eirica set about fixing a meal. But her attention kept wandering to the river where James played with her kids.

The normally serious man was gone. He seemed younger, more carefree. She loved to watch him laugh and chase her children. The sight warmed her bruised and battered soul and filled her heart with joy. She'd prayed for this, prayed for the Lord to give her children the happiness they so deserved.

She remembered her conversation with Sofia and she knew she couldn't deny any of them this chance for a new beginning. Her hand crept up her chest, felt the burn scar tissue she'd bear for the rest of her life. Her hand clenched into a tight fist. Using all her strength, she shoved the memory away, steadied her breathing, and reminded herself that it was over, past.

But part of her wondered if she'd ever be free of the past, of the pain. What if she couldn't put the nightmares of her marriage to Birk behind her? She'd never be able to forget those six years of hell she'd endured, and she would always bear the physical marks. How could she go on, move forward with so many reminders of the brutality she'd borne?

Love.

That was her answer.

Love and a gentle, sensitive man named James Jones.

An intense desire to move forward took hold. Somehow, she'd fight her demons. To have no hope, dreams or love, to never laugh or know joy in her life made existence pointless. She wanted it all, and the only way to get it was to go after it, not run from it. Eirica smoothed her hair, then shook off the crumbs from her apron, as if shaking off her fears and doubts.

Hours later, the children were finally asleep. Eirica emerged from the tent, groaning at the thought of having to tackle the dirty pile of dishes. To her surprise, the plates were washed, dried and put away along with the foodstuff. Her gaze flew to James. "You didn't have to do that."

He shrugged. "You cooked. Seemed only fair."

She shook her head. "Why in heaven's name hasn't some woman snapped you up?"

He winked at her, a twinkle in her eye. "I was saving myself for you."

Her heart fluttered and a warm, cozy feeling swirled through her. Just being near him took her breath away, but to hear him say things like that made her go weak in the knees. "You, James Jones, are either full of blarney or you are one of the most romantic men the world has ever seen."

He shuffled his feet, put his hands behind his back and muttered, "Shucks, ma'am, you're going to embarrass me." He then ruined his pose by glancing up, his lips twitching.

"Oh, you!"

He held out his hand. "Found a right nice spot by the river. Care to join me for a spell?"

Eirica placed her hand in his, her heart thudding against her chest. "I'd love to, James." She glanced at the tent.

"We won't be far. We'll hear." He led her past the stump to where an old, stunted tree flanked by waist-high bushes formed a secluded nook. On the ground lay a thick layer of quilts.

Eirica stared at it and remembered the last time they'd sat together by a river. Just thinking about kissing James started her blood pumping. She bit her lower lip, anticipation running through her.

James drew her into his arms and tipped her chin up with his fingers. "I'd like to kiss you."

Eirica chuckled at the familiar request and wrapped her arms around his neck, threading her fingers in the soft waves of hair falling below his collar. "Some things don't need to be asked."

James didn't need any further urging, but before he could lower his head and claim her waiting lips, he felt a jab to his lower abdomen. Startled, he glanced down between them, saw movement in the swell that kept him from pulling Eirica tightly against him. He realized he'd felt her baby kick. "Was that—?"

Eirica's mouth curved. "Yes."

With Eirica still holding on to him, James slid his hands down her sides and across her extended belly. The baby within her moved again, a gentle rolling motion. He pressed a little harder and received a jab back. "Wow." He glanced up at Eirica. "Did you feel that?"

She rolled her eyes and he felt silly. Of course she'd felt it. But she didn't laugh at him. She stroked the side of his face, her eyes intent, even if her lips trembled with the effort not to laugh.

"James, that was probably an elbow and if you don't get back up here and kiss me, I'm going to jab you with my own."

He tipped his head back and roared with laughter. "Ah, a woman who knows what she wants. Let's sit. I want to hold you close, but *somebody* is in the way here."

James pulled her down across his lap, her baby forgotten as he stared at her mouth. Without another thought, he lowered his head. As before, their kiss started off slowly. Each took their time relearning the touch, taste and contours of the other. Then it wasn't enough. He needed more. Lifting his head, one hand cupped the side of her face, his thumb brushing against the corner of her mouth, his fingers stroking the sensitive skin behind her ear.

"I love you, Eirica." Though he'd said he wouldn't push her, had tried to hold himself back, the words slipped out, needing to be said as much as his body needed air to breathe.

Eirica used both her hands to frame his face, her fingers feathering lightly over his features, lingering against his lips as if to stop the words, then sliding up into his hair. Her lips trembled, and her eyes held a sheen of moisture.

"I love you, too, James."

Those words were the sweetest James had ever heard. The knowledge that she loved him rocked him. They stared at each other, barely able to see as clouds blocked out the light of the moon and stars. But he didn't need to see her. He felt her, felt the love she'd spoken of. It was in her touch, in her breathless whisper and in her body's response as she pulled his head back to hers.

Her hands fell to his shoulders, trailed down his arms and back up the front of his woolen shirt, freeing each button in turn. A breath of cold air made him

217

gasp but the warmth of her palms sliding against his bare chest heated him to the point where he longed to shrug out of the shirt.

His hands followed her lead, finding the buttons down the front of her bodice. But when he began to unbutton them, she tore her mouth from his.

"No." She gasped for breath, her features stricken.

"Eirica?" Disappointment laced his words. He wanted her so much, wanted to show her how good it could be between them but he didn't want to scare her. He took one of her hands in his and brought it to his lips. "I want to see you, touch you—but I understand if you aren't ready."

Eirica uncurled her fingers and traced his lower lip. "You don't understand. It's not you. I—I don't want you to see—I'm ugly." She lowered her head in shame.

"No, you're the most beauti—" She stopped him with her fingers against his lips.

"Not there." The stark, pained words hung between them.

Sensing there was much more going on than shyness about her body, James forced her to face him, seeing only the glitter of tears in her eyes. "Why not there? Tell me, Eirica."

She drew in a sharp breath. "I can't. I don't want to ruin this. I don't want *him* to ruin this."

"Birk?"

She nodded, tears falling down her cheeks, splashing onto his hands. "You couldn't understand. I'm not pretty there. I'm ruined. He ruined me." She covered her face with her hands.

James felt a cold calm go through him. What had the bastard done to her? Knowing they had to deal with this, he pulled her close. "Tell me. He can't hurt

you or us unless we let him, sweetheart. He'll always
be there, always a part of you, a part of your children,
but he doesn't have to come between us. Not if we talk
about it and learn to deal with it. If you don't, in a
small way, he'd still own you."

Eirica used her skirt to wipe her eyes. She settled
into his arms her face resting against his bare chest,
her breath warming the spot just above his heart.

"You're right. I don't want him to ever come
between us." Her words came out fiercely.

Slowly, haltingly, she told him how Birk had
thrown boiling water at her and the damage he'd done
to her. But that wasn't the only scar she bore. "So
many scars," she whispered. "They're mostly from
bites, and sometimes he used his nails to cause pain."

She shuddered. "Birk liked to see his marks on me
the next day."

As she talked, her voice grew fainter, nearly
drowned out by the rushing river. James formed a pic-
ture of a sick man intent upon not only beating his
wife, but mutilating her as a way to keep other men
from ever wanting her. His fury rose, his heart
pounded and he wished with all his might that Birk
was alive for one last fight. He would kill the man for
what he'd done to this sweet, helpless woman.

Imagining her fear, her pain and humiliation
brought tears to his eyes. Eirica lifted her head and
saw them. "James, I don't want you to pity me. It's
done and there's no way to repair it. You don't have to
look at me there or touch me. I understand."

James shifted her around so he could look fully at
her. "I'm not pitying you, Eirica. I'm grieving for you.
No one should have to go through what you did. If
your father or brothers were here, they'd get a piece of
my mind—and maybe feel my fist. They failed you,

Eirica. Your family betrayed you and the shame is theirs for dishonoring their responsibilities." He glanced up, and around them. It was dark, and no one was near.

He spoke quietly. "No matter what's been done to you, you are still beautiful, because it's what's inside that counts. I love you, all of you." Lowering his hands once more to her bodice, he asked, "Will you trust me, allow me to prove it to you?"

Chapter Thirteen

Eirica nodded. She held her breath as James undid the buttons one by one, then pulled the bodice away and slid it down her shoulders. Next he untied her shift, the only undergarment she owned. She closed her eyes.

"Eirica, look at me. Trust me. Don't hide from me."

The bitter bite of bile rose to the back of Eirica's throat. She trusted James, loved him, but she longed to be perfect for him. He deserved that. But, she thought to herself, he also deserved someone who loved him, and she did. How she loved this sensitive man. And for the first time, she realized she deserved the love he offered so freely. The tenderness in his voice made her meet his shadowed gaze.

He gave her a reassuring smile. "That's it. Now breathe."

Holding her gaze, he slid the shift from her shoulders, baring them, then the generous swell of her heavy breasts. His fingers swept over her collarbone and upper chest. She knew when he felt each scar, for his fingers trembled slightly. He edged beneath the shift, pushing it down inch by inch. And when he felt the raised, rough mark of her burn, he paused and did the unexpected. He leaned down and kissed her blemished skin, starting with the small round scar just below her throat. He lowered her to the ground and kissed each and every scar he encountered.

And as he revealed her breasts, James gave them the same care, the same soft, tender kisses as a mother might use to kiss away the pain of a hurt child. Finally, he returned to her mouth. "Don't ever be ashamed of your body."

Before she could accept or protest, his head slid back down to her breast. This time, his mouth closed over the swollen nipple. His tongue circled and laved, his lips suckled, not to ease past pain but to give new pleasure—and the promise of more to come.

One hand held the flesh to his mouth while his other hand kneaded her other straining breast. Eirica bit her lip to keep from crying out with the sheer joy of his touch, but when his thumb and forefinger rolled her nipple, a moan slipped from her lips.

James covered her mouth with his, swallowing her soft cries of pleasure. The air brushing against her wet breast intensified the feelings surging through her. She shifted her legs, trying to ease the growing ache.

"I want you, sweetheart. I want all of you," he breathed into her mouth.

Eirica slid her palms over his chest, greedy for the feel of him. He slid down beside her, half leaning over her. Soft, springy curls cushioned her palms and hid his male nipples. She found them. Each forefinger rubbed a hard bead so small, but oh so enticing. His low moan made her smile. "I want you, too, James."

He gasped for air when her fingers slid down his taut belly. "I don't want to rush you."

"Maybe I want to be rushed." She tried to capture his lips but he held back, his look a mixture of amusement and pain and intense desire.

"Not a chance," he murmured, "I've waited a long time for this." He ran his palm over the rise of her pregnancy. "I'll stop anytime you tell me to."

When his hand shifted to her thigh and down to her knee, her insides fluttered with the need to have James make love to her. She lifted one knee. "Don't stop, James."

Her plea ended on a gasp when his lips reclaimed hers and his palm slid up her leg then back down: thigh to knee, around the back, finding a sensitive spot that made her sigh. Then down to the curve of her buttock. Over and over he caressed her, gave her time to adjust to his touch. So lost was she, she never gave thought to her state of undress or the fact that they were making love out in the open.

Then his hand changed course, shifting to her inner thigh. Desire shot from his hand to her center with such a jolt she'd have cried out had his mouth not been on hers, leaving her too breathless to do much more than gasp. Of their own accord, her raised knees fell to the side. From one inner thigh to the other, he traced her softness, brushing against her center with just enough of a touch as to make her jerk with need. Her hips moved, circled, seeking his touch, but he stayed just out of her reach.

"James—"

"Shh, slow. I'm going to give you pleasure tonight."

"If you don't kill me first," she groaned.

"Rest assured, I'll be right behind you, sweetheart," he assured, bending back down to swallow her breathy

Susan Edwards

cries. Finally, he slid his hand beneath her skirts and covered the part of her that ached most for his touch. Instantly, her hips lifted, pressing her mound hard against his palm. Thank God she didn't have drawers to worry about. She didn't think she could have waited a moment longer for his intimate touch.

James held his hand still, allowing her to respond to the soft pressure of his touch. Her hips rose, they circled, they jerked until it wasn't enough. Her hands fluttered to her side, her mouth tore free from his and her head moved restlessly side to side.

"James," she whimpered, feeling herself climbing toward an unfamiliar peak.

"Soon. Soon, just feel." He lifted his hand, but before she could voice her protest, his fingers returned to caress the swollen heat of her. He stroked, rubbed and played his fingers over her, stroking from her a response as sure as he coaxed a melody from the strings of his guitar. He matched the frenzy of her rotating hips, then he deepened the pressure, sped up those hip-lifting circles until she felt as though she'd scream. Each breath became a low gasp as she panted and climbed, higher than she'd ever imagined. Pleasure turned to pain, but not the kind that hurt or frightened. This was different. She sensed it led somewhere and she desperately wanted to go there, had to go there. She wanted whatever was just beyond her reach. She wanted it all.

Then, without warning, her hips lifted high, her legs stiffened, then her body flew apart in a burst of color and incredible sensation. She soared high, sure that time had come to a standstill in a place where there was only beauty and wondrous music. How long she hovered in that marvelous state, she couldn't have said. Then it faded, and she floated back to reality slowly, becoming aware of her surroundings, of James, his lips pressed to hers as he'd muffled her cries. "That was—incredible."

She felt his smile against her cheek. "There's more. But we won't go all the way. I don't want to hurt your babe."

She reached up to stroke his cheek, then turned onto her side to face him. Her knee slid between his legs, resting against the hard bulge of his erection. She felt the same pressure there, his squeezing, his need. She didn't want to bring Birk into this, it was just too wonderful, too beautiful; she had to relieve James of his worry.

"You won't hurt the babe." She hesitated. "B—he never paid my condition any mind." She sensed his fear, his struggle with his own desire. "Trust me, James. You won't hurt me or the babe." She moved her knee against him. He jerked in response. The idea that she could cause him the same pleasure, the same all-consuming need, thrilled her. Reaching downward, she stroked the hard ridge beneath his woolen trousers.

He shuddered and lowered his forehead to hers. "Are you sure?" His voice was hoarse with need.

"I'm sure." To her delight, his hands moved to stroke her anew, this time, sliding inside her and out and around her sensitive, swollen bud. As he touched and roused her, she did the same, touching him through the fabric of his trousers. Her tentative touch grew firm when she felt him respond. It pleased her beyond measure to hear his own breathless gasps and moans when she stroked the hard ridge from root to the soft tip. Soon, they were both gasping. Freeing himself, James turned her gently onto her other side and curved his body up against hers.

Eirica couldn't help holding her breath against the

expected pain. No matter how much it hurt, she'd give this to James. But to her surprise and delight, when he entered her moist sheath from behind, there was no pain, only a smooth entry that left her trembling with need.

"God, you feel so good around me."

Eirica tipped her head back, rubbing her cheek against his. "You feel so good inside me." She should be embarrassed to be talking during this most intimate act between a man and woman, but she wasn't. His whispered words excited her, drove her closer again to the brink.

With each careful thrust, he stoked her desire to the breaking point. Hovering on the edge, she whimpered. James's ragged breath fanned her ear. "Now, sweetheart, now. With me."

He gave one final thrust that touched off her own release. "James," she sobbed. And with that, she let go to soar with him to that special place he'd shown her.

A short while later, James sat and adjusted his clothes, leaving his shirt open. Then he helped Eirica rise and buttoned her bodice. Gathering her close, he drew a blanket around his shoulders to ward off the night chill and pulled it tighter around him to engulf the woman he loved. He crossed his arms below her breasts, holding the woolen blanket in place.

She leaned back, her knees drawn up. Neither spoke, each content to watch the silvery sheet of river as it flowed past. The clouds above alternated between thick and thin, releasing narrow beams of light to tease the land before enclosing it once more in darkness.

He shut his eyes, feeling incredibly happy, so full of joy he didn't know if he wanted to shout it to the sleeping world or just weep with wonder. The thought of a man weeping tears made him grimace. Unlike his brothers who vented with outrage and fine shows of tempers, he'd always held his emotions deep within himself. He had a sensitive soul, his mother had often said, before he'd learned to hide that weakness from the outside world. But right now, he didn't care who saw or who knew. Eirica trusted him.

She loved him.

I love you. Could any three words be finer? Not to him. Could he be happier? Nope. He sighed with contentment.

"James?"

Eirica's hands rested on top of his. Feeling the coolness, he covered them with his own. "Yes, sweetheart."

The endearment made her sigh. "I do love it when you call me that."

He smiled, his lips against her hair. "Then I'll have to do so often."

"I'd like that."

She hesitated. He felt it in her body, in the subtle dipping of her head. "What is it, sweetheart? You don't have any regrets, do you?"

Her head snapped up, nearly catching his chin. "Oh no." She shifted around to look at him. Then, feeling brave, she turned and encircled his neck with her arms. "No regrets. It was beautiful. I wish—"

"What do you wish?"

Her breasts rose with the deep breath she took. "I wish I'd met you a long time ago. Except you'd have been too busy raising your brothers and sister."

"And you wouldn't have the three wonderful children you have right now."

"True. I love my children. They were the one good thing in my life, my reason for living. Now I have you, too."

"Me and junior here, who should be asleep." James

227

ran his hand over the bulge of her pregnancy, marveling at the feel of her unborn babe. When Eirica struggled to sit straight, he helped her. To his surprise, she didn't stand or move away but straddled his legs so she could face him.

"James, you said—" another deep breath. "You said to let you know later but I want to tell you now— I'll marry you." The words rushed out.

His lungs collapsed. They must have since he couldn't breathe. Once again, the clouds parted and all James could do was stare at Eirica. Had he ever seen a woman more beautiful? The shape of her eyes, so wide and trusting, framed by golden lashes and finely arched brows. His gaze drifted down to her nose; small, straight, with a sprinkling of freckles across the narrow bridge and scattered over her cheeks. He ran a finger along her jaw, lingered at her firm and stubborn chin, then reached up to caress skin that felt soft as the wool of a newborn lamb. He could sit there and gaze at her beauty forever.

And he had forever. The thought that she was his, that she'd given herself to him, loved him and now agreed to marry him seemed too much to take in. He feared he'd wake up, find out it had all been a dream.

"James? Do you still want to marry me?"

James laughed with sheer joy. She'd said yes! He wrapped his arms around her, needing to be sure. "Absolutely, sweetheart, but are you sure you don't need more time?" He squeezed his eyes shut in case she agreed.

Eirica pulled back to look at him. Her fingers feathered over his closed lids, then down his jaw. "No. I know what I feel. You told me to trust myself. Well, I do. But more importantly, I trust you."

He opened his eyes, feeling moisture gather. Her trust was a precious gift, one he'd treasure for life. "I love you, Eirica. I love you so much."

She sighed. "Don't make any mistake, I still have worries and concerns. Part of me is fighting this, the part that fears being helpless again. I wanted my own land so I'd always have a place to call home. When Birk drowned, I vowed to never fall under a man's dominance again.

"But with you, I know I can find a middle ground. I want to share my life and my children with you. I want what Anne and Lars have, what Sofia had with her husband. Coralie and Jordan worked out their differences, and Jessie and Wolf's love for each other is so strong, anyone can feel it. I want what they have and with you, I'm willing to take a risk to get it."

James played with a long strand of her hair that had fallen over her shoulder. Using his fingers, he combed her hair, staring at the silky softness he'd pulled over each shoulder. Bringing a handful of her hair to his face, he kissed the satiny strands, then leaned forward to kiss her. "I won't let you down. Be my partner, be my friend, be my wife."

"Yes. Oh, yes." Eirica bent down to kiss him soundly on the lips.

She ended the kiss way too soon in his opinion. He was hard, throbbing with renewed need, but feared making love to her a second time would be too much for her. He tried to steady his breathing.

"James?" Eirica wore an impish grin.

"Yeah?"

"Just remember if you get too bossy, I'm going to poke you and shout at you."

He chuckled, then winced when he thought about

poking. Damn, he ached. He thought he'd hid his growing desire, but then she reached down and stroked him through his trousers.

"Oh, sweetheart, you'd better not do that."

"I want to. I want you to love me again."

His eyes widened with surprise and then hooded beneath the need coursing through him. "Are you sure? It won't be too much?"

"Never. I don't think I can ever have too much of loving you."

James freed himself, then lifted her skirts and urged her over him. "Then you take charge this time. Take me as deep as what's comfortable so I don't hurt you."

Delight shone on her face as she lowered herself over him and rode, taking him to heights he'd never imagined.

When Gunner arrived the next morning to take charge of her wagon, Eirica couldn't help feeling disappointed that James hadn't come. But she knew he had to oversee the cattle. He'd stayed with her until nearly dawn, talking, kissing and just holding her while she dozed in his arms. She fought back a yawn.

Today was going to be a long day, but last night was worth some weariness. She smiled to herself. James had been incredible. The loving they'd shared, the heights they'd traveled, had been beyond her wildest imagination and she couldn't wait to make love to him again.

Eirica fell into step with the other chatting women but couldn't keep focused on their conversation. Dreams of James, of their love and the promise of a future filled with love and laughter played over and over in her mind. When she heard a horse approaching from behind, she turned, her look hopeful, but it wasn't

James, only Wolf riding his monstrous black beast. Her shoulders sagged.

Yep, it was going to be a long day.

Alison called out to the wagon master and asked if she could ride with him. He stopped and looked to Eirica for permission, which she gave. Alison was becoming as horse crazy as Kerstin, Anne's daughter.

Wolf settled Alison in front of them, then glanced down at the women. He winked at Eirica. "By the way, congratulations, Eirica. Welcome to the family."

With a look of pure devilment directed at his wife who had stopped and was looking from Wolf to Eirica, he rode away, Alison clutched firmly in front of him.

Jessie watched him ride off with a frown, then rounded on Eirica who resumed walking, trying to control her laughter at the very pregnant silence behind her. It didn't take long before Jessie, Coralie, Anne and Sofia caught up and crowded around her. Their questions came fast and furious.

"James did it, didn't he? He finally proposed?" Jessie walked backward in front of Eirica, her green eyes alight with excitement.

Deciding to play it out, Eirica said, "Actually, he stated his intentions a long time ago—right after we left Independence Rock."

"And you two didn't say anything?" This from Coralie.

"I told him no." Rounded eyes and open mouths greeted that news.

Having fun, Eirica brushed her palms down her apron. She waited a heartbeat. "Last night, I told him yes." Happy shouts mingled with congratulations and set the tone for the rest of the day.

* * *

That night, three women huddled in a small circle in Coralie's tent, sewing frantically by the light of a lard-burning lantern. Sofia, Catarina and Rook entered, with Catarina holding high another lantern to brighten the cramped area.

Rook set a small trunk down on the floor, then eased himself down, perfectly at ease among the women. Sofia opened the trunk and pulled out a pile of tiny new baby things, each made by the assembled women. Some were sewn, some knitted. The bounty included a couple of small blankets and quilts.

Coralie tied a knot and held up a small gown. "There, finished." She opened a leather pouch she'd acquired in trade with a group of Indians they'd encountered along the Platte River. From inside, she pulled out two more simple gowns, each a little bigger. "Here's three more to put in the trunk." She set them on top of the growing pile.

"What about you, Jessie?" Anne asked.

Jessie grinned broadly and placed her contribution into the middle. No one made mention of the lopsided hems or that one sleeve was obviously shorter than the other on one gown.

Anne, Catarina and Sofia each drew their contributions from their sewing baskets and added them to the growing pile.

"Oh, my," Coralie breathed, fingering the exquisite lace Anne had fashioned and stitched along the yoke of one small sacque. Sofia's and Catarina's also had lace and ribbons. "I'll never be able to do this."

Sofia laughed. "You will learn, both of you. All it takes is practice."

Both Jessie and Coralie groaned, but Coralie was determined to be able to sew such fine garments. But there was one skill she had—one her grandmother in

Boston had insisted she learn—embroidery, and she was very accomplished in her stitches.

Biting her lower lip, she glanced toward a corner where one more package lay hidden. She wanted to surprise everyone and planned to give it to Eirica when they presented the rest of the infant clothes and blankets. It never crossed her mind that Eirica's baby would be anything other than a girl.

After carefully packing the bounty back into the trunk, the women got out their quilt squares. Now there was a wedding quilt to sew, along with finishing the baby quilts each had started.

Three days later, Wolf's group reached Fort Bridger, originally built by Jim Bridger. The fort was a heavenly sight to the weary travelers. The surroundings held abundant clear sweet water and good grass for the livestock. There was also a beautiful view of the mountains to the south and the high, wide blue skies.

Two days of rest were declared. Wagons needed repair and oxen with lost or worn shoes could be taken to the blacksmith for shoeing. The beasts were unable to stand on three legs, which made shoeing them on the trail nearly impossible. Letters hastily written were mailed and those with money restocked low provisions. The two days also afforded a much-needed break from the monotony of travel.

Here, Mormon emigrants, many with handcarts instead of wagons, split off to head toward the Great Salt Lake or California. Those bound for Oregon headed northwest and rejoined those who'd taken the sublet cut-off. Talk among men concentrated on trail conditions and choices in cut-offs. Women gathered to talk, exchange trail recipes and trade excesses of one food for something of which they'd run out.

Six days after leaving the fort, the emigrants arrived at the abandoned Smith's Trading Post. The structure had originally been established by Peg Leg Smith in 1848, on the east bank of the Bear River.

The very idea of amputating one's own leg left Eirica shivering. She'd heard the tale of how the man had done just that, then dressed it and fitted a wooden leg and socket in the stirrup of his saddle so he could ride.

"How could someone do that, cut off his own leg?" Eirica handed James an armload of bedding to put into the tent.

"Survival. People do what they must." Taking the blankets and quilts from her, James ducked inside and laid them down, then came back out.

Above them, the blue of the sky faded. Eirica scanned the area. Her children sat nearby petting the pregnant Sadie, who lay on her side, panting. Eirica felt for her. The dog was huge. Lara reached out to touch the dog's side, then giggled when she felt one of the unborn pups move. The white wolf lay next to his mate, good-naturedly tolerating Eirica's children, even Ian, who tended to be a bit rough.

An odd shiver ran up her spine and her gaze shifted to her surroundings. Several times over the last few days she'd felt as though she were being watched, but had never found anyone looking her way.

Mistaking her shiver for cold, James drew her against him. "How about if I cook dinner and watch the children while you rest."

Eirica sighed with longing, tempted to take him up on his suggestion. "What about the cattle?"

"I'm off tonight." He glanced down at her, his expression filled with love and concern.

"You're worrying."

"Yeah, I don't want you to be alone in case the babe comes."

"James, look around." She indicated the people and wagons crowded on each side of them. "I'm hardly alone."

He looked at her sheepishly. "Yeah, but I won't be here."

A warm glow settled in her heart. It felt heavenly to know he cared. "I am tired." An image of him joining her made her sigh. "Too bad you can't join me."

James put his hand to his heart in mock dismay. "Woman, you'll be the death of me. Give a guy a rest."

Eirica swatted him, knowing he'd purposely restrained himself the last two nights because he was worried about sending her into labor. And in truth, she didn't have much energy. Still, it was nice to just sit or lie together. If he weren't on guard duty, he rolled his bedding beneath her wagon, giving her a sense of security in knowing she only had to call out if she needed him. And usually, he lulled her to sleep with either his mouth organ or guitar.

James led her to the tent. Before she entered, he kissed her, long, deep and slow. "Dream of me." With a wink, he returned to the fire to check on the bread baking in the Dutch oven. He faced the children so he could keep an eye on them.

Again, that feeling of being watched overcame her. She made another sweep of the area but as before, nothing struck her as worrisome. *I must be tired.* Lying down, she closed her eyes. In minutes, she was asleep.

From his vantage point between the two large wagon parties, Birk watched James cook supper, then play with his children. He ran his hand up and down the smooth barrel of the shotgun. Hatred and rage filled him, urging him to get rid of the man who dared to touch his wife. But there were just too many people around. Soon. Soon, he'd have his revenge.

His glare fell to his three brats. He hated kids: hated the mess, the noise and most of all, he resented their intrusion in his life and the fact that with them around, he wasn't the focus of his wife's attention. No, he had no use for them brats.

He absently fingered the chain around his neck and narrowed his gaze, a plan forming. Well, now, maybe he shouldn't be so hasty. He might have a use for them after all. Thinking and planning, he headed back to his camp where Zeb waited.

Chapter Fourteen

Nearly a month and four hundred miles after leaving Independence Rock, the emigrants arrived at Fort Hall. The fort, abandoned a scant year ago, stood upon the level bottomland of the Snake River with miles of good pasturage surrounding it, making it a good place to spend a night or two. Like Fort Laramie, the good-size fort was built of unburnt brick.

In the distance, snowcapped mountains were constant reminders of the need to make haste lest they find themselves still on the trail when the first snows fell. In all, the travel-weary emigrants had come twelve hundred miles in three and a half months.

They arrived at the fort in early afternoon, which allowed the animals a few extra hours of rest and plentiful grazing. Wolf chose an area several miles from the fort, downriver. Anyone who wanted to explore the fort had ample time to do so that afternoon, as

237

Wolf didn't plan to stop for long. Tomorrow they'd continue onward.

Eirica watched Sofia and her family along with Jordan, Coralie, Elliot, the Svenssons and Wolf and Jessie leave for the fort. She smiled at the sight of Elliot and Catarina walking side by side, their shoulders occasionally touching. She had a feeling there'd be another wedding when they reached Oregon.

As much as Eirica longed to see some of the trail sights, her condition left her just too exhausted at the end of the day to do anything not required of her. With an afternoon of having to do nothing but rest stretching out before her, she sighed with gratitude.

Even her children had gone to the fort. Only Rook and James remained behind with her. Rook had declared that he wanted some peace and quiet without any jabbering females driving him crazy and James, worrying over her as usual, had refused to leave her alone, even though she'd assured him she'd be fine.

Where he'd disappeared to, she didn't know, but she knew he was probably giving her a chance to rest and recoup. Today had seemed particularly rough to get through. Though they hadn't traveled nearly as many miles or as long as usual, each step had seemed harder than the last, today, each cry or whining comment from her children making her want to snap. By the time they'd stopped, all she'd wanted to do was lie down and cry. Even James and his fussing had gotten on her nerves.

Her muscles ached and she felt tired—incredibly tired, which worried her. Rubbing her lower back, she feared it wouldn't be long before the baby came. Oh, Lord, she sure wished she could put this off. Back home, she'd had her ma or a midwife to help her deliver, along with a nice soft bed with sheets; everything she needed, including privacy. But at least this time she'd have Anne and Sofia. Rounding the wagon, she saw James setting up the tent and felt some of her worry and anxiety ease. He hadn't abandoned her totally. She didn't know what she'd done to deserve him, but she thanked the good Lord for her good fortune.

Pressing her hand into her back, she continued to rub the low ache. If her babe was coming, it would be hours yet, maybe even a day, but not much more than that. With the fear of birthing foremost in her mind, she set about preparing the evening meal. There was just so much to be done yet.

James hadn't started a fire—it was hours until they'd eat—but she could fill the kettle with water and get the bread ready to bake. Fetching the cast-iron pot from the wagon, she went down to the river. As she lifted the heavy kettle out of the flowing water, a sudden and sharp pain radiated from her lower back around toward the front of her extended belly. Her womb grew hard with the contraction.

Eirica gasped and dropped the pot. It landed with a splash. She held her swollen abdomen until the searing pain passed. Biting her lip, she quickly refilled the kettle and struggled back to camp with it.

"Eirica, are you crazy? Let me have that! It's far too heavy for a woman in your condition." James took it from her.

Before she could crossly remind him that women in her condition carried water and wood and saw to their normal chores each and every day of their pregnancy, another spasm of pain struck. The intensity of it left her breathless. She stopped and hunched over, resting her hands on her knees.

James cursed a blue streak, dropping the pot of

water in his haste to reach her. "Oh, God, sweetheart, it's the baby, isn't it?"

Eirica nodded and straightened when the pain faded. She took a couple of deep, cleansing breaths. None of her other children had come this fast. "James, I need Anne or Sofia. Now."

He glanced frantically around. "Fine time for everyone to disappear on us. Let's get you back to camp and settled first." He wrapped one arm around her waist to help her return to camp.

She only managed half a dozen steps before another contraction hit. This time, she was forced to hold on to James, her fingers biting into his arms.

As soon as the contraction eased, he once again urged her forward. "Damn it, woman. Why didn't you say something earlier?"

Irritated, she glared at him. "The pains just started. They never came this fast and hard with the other three—"

She broke off abruptly and glanced down. James followed her gaze. He swore again when he saw the puddle of water between her feet. Muttering beneath his breath, he scooped her up into his arms and carried her into the tent, set her down on her feet, arranged the bedding, then stood. "Let me help you lie down."

Pacing back and forth, she shook her head. "No. Not yet."

Agitated, James surveyed the small enclosure. "Wait here. I'm going to fetch more water and get it boiling. I think Rook started his fire already. I'll be right back."

Eirica panicked and grabbed his arm. "James, what about Anne?" Her voice ended on a strangled scream. Once more she bent over. Immediately, James wrapped his arms around her, allowing her to clutch his shoulders as the contraction crested.

When the pain subsided, he tilted her chin up. "I don't think you have time, sweetheart. Looks like you're stuck with me."

Her eyes widened. "James, don't think me ungrateful, but have you ever delivered a baby?"

James grinned. "Hundreds."

At her puzzled and disbelieving look, he shrugged. "Cows and sheep, couple of horses, but what's the difference? Now, do whatever it is you women do to get ready. I've got to get some supplies and then I'll be right back." With a quick kiss to her forehead, he left the tent and ran smack into Rook.

"—Eirica's in labor."

"—Sadie's in labor."

The two men stared at each other in horror, then glanced wildly around. No one materialized to come rushing to their aid. They were alone, on their own. A muffled scream from the tent and a frantic bark from Rook's campsite spurred both men who ran in the same direction—and back into each other.

"—Out of my way."

"—Damn."

"Out of my way. I need boiling water. Eirica needs me."

Rook followed James back to his camp, cursing his broken arm. With a growl of frustration, he whipped off his sling while James set the kettle over the fire, next to one Rook already had going. James used another pan to scoop some of the boiling water out then carried it back to the tent. To add to the confusion, Wahoska paced nearby, growling low in his throat each time Sadie whimpered in the back of the wagon.

James ran back to Eirica's tent. Inside, he found a pillow and tore the case off. Feathers from the worn ticking floated in front of his face. He blew them out of his way as he tore the fabric into hand-size squares and dipped them into the water.

Kneeling beside Eirica who'd removed her dress and was on her knees, he stared down into her wide, pain-filled blue eyes. "You'll be fine, sweetheart. You'll be fine." Silently, he prayed for the truth of his words. He just couldn't lose her, not now. Not when they had a future together and so many dreams to make come true.

But deep inside, fear clawed at him. Too many things could go wrong and he knew squat about delivering babies. Why had everyone abandoned them, today of all days? He didn't have any more time to dwell on his situation. Eirica's contractions suddenly hit, one on top of another. Glancing around the tent, he found an old quilt nearly in rags and put it beneath her. Then he waited, soothing her, rubbing her back and holding her when pain wracked her body.

"Do you want to lie down, sweetheart?"

She shook her head. "No," she gasped, holding on to him as if afraid he'd leave. "Oh, God, James, I can't do this."

He smiled at the desperation in her eyes. "Sure you can. You've done it three times."

"Different," she gasped. "Not like this—"

A low guttural moan tore from her throat, a sound James had never heard before. Nor had he ever seen the intense look on another human's face as he saw on hers. Every vein stood out as if she were holding her breath and straining.

Then he realized she was. She was pushing. "Oh, God. Oh, God," he muttered over and over, torn between holding her and worrying over the babe. What was he supposed to do? Panic ran wild through him.

Suddenly, the tent flap opened and Rook burst in, dropping a length of cloth. Without any concern at the sight of her half-naked state, he grabbed Eirica's other arm. "I heard. My wife made that sound before she gave birth. I'll hold her while ya catch the babe. It won't be long now. Git that cloth. I took it from Sofia's wagon. It's clean."

James grabbed the toweling and waited, holding Eirica as she alternated between pushing and panting.

"Ah, lass, yer doing fine," Rook coaxed, urging her to rest between pushes. He grinned. "We has two pups so far. That ol' rascal wolf is prowling like any respectable man whose mate is birthin'."

Eirica smiled weakly but held on, long past the point of being embarrassed. Right now, it wouldn't have mattered if the whole damn camp crowded in to watch. Another urge to push assailed her, stronger. "James, it's coming. The babe's coming."

Her breath ended in a gasp as every ounce of effort went into pushing the babe from her womb into James's awaiting hands.

"A head. I see a head. Push, sweetheart, push. I see it."

The awe and joy in his voice gave Eirica the strength she needed for that final push. With a sound between a groan and scream, it was over. Her knees shook and her body shivered, but all she cared about was the baby.

Frantic, she glanced down, unable to see anything. Then she saw James wiping the baby roughly and using one of the wet cloths he'd dipped in the pot of warm water to wipe the tiny nose and mouth, inside and out. Holding the infant upside down, he stroked the baby's back. Then she heard it. The most beautiful sound in the whole world. Her daughter's first cry.

Eirica sagged against Rook, who hugged her. " 'ere, give the babe to me. You git yer woman settled in that bed and I'll go wash the wee lass here and bring her back." A sharp bark made him smile. "I gots ta check on Sadie, too, then I'll be right back." He wrapped the squalling infant in the towel and left, the protesting baby's wails sounding like music to Eirica's ears.

She instructed James on the rest of the birthing process. After it was over, she and James held each other. As he murmured praise and words of love, Eirica felt a stronger bond forming between her and James. He'd done every bit as good as any woman or midwife, and it didn't even bother her that Rook had come in to help. This was what family and love was about, and she reveled in it.

True to his word, Rook returned with the fussing baby, clean and wrapped in a newly laundered towel for a blanket and beneath that, one of his flannel shirts. "It's clean," he smiled, handing the baby to James. "She's a beauty, lass, jest like her ma." Then the cook left, a wide grin splitting his whiskered cheeks.

James stared down at the baby. From somewhere deep inside his soul, a strong protective urge rose as he studied this small, so incredibly tiny, human that he feared he'd crush her. He tested the weight of her in his palms; she couldn't be more than five or six pounds. Awed at the wonder of helping to bring this life into the world, he felt incapable of speech.

He pulled back the corner of the towel. A shock of golden-red hair covered the infant's head and when she opened her eyes, he was struck by their incredible blueness. He touched one soft, downy cheek. Her rosebud mouth rooted for nourishment and finding none, she screwed her face up into a look of outrage to let the world know she was displeased with her reception.

James vowed right then and there to love and protect this child. In that instant, he'd bonded with her as if she'd been his own flesh and blood. He went down on his knees next to Eirica, who lay propped against the pillows and extra bedding. She'd changed into her nightshirt while Rook had the infant. James had removed the soiled bedding and replaced it. "I think somebody wants her mama." He carefully placed the squalling infant in Eirica's outstretched arms and watched her unwrap the baby. Together, they checked toes and fingers, then James helped her lift the baby to her mother's breast.

It was just going on dusk when the happy group returned from the fort. They'd explored the area, talked to emigrants who were camped inside the abandoned buildings, and in general, they'd all had a good time.

Coralie carried Ian who'd fallen asleep. She smiled softly and glanced at Jordan. By the end of winter, she and Jordie would have their own baby, the start of their own family. The thought both excited her and made her sad. She wished her father could be there. He'd be a grandfather, and she wanted him around to spoil her children.

Behind her, Jessie, Anne, Catarina and Sofia talked while Anne's and Eirica's girls ran on ahead. The men brought up the rear, carrying on about what the fort must have been like before being deserted. They were also discussing the growing number of Indian attacks in the area. Coralie shuddered, refusing to think about it.

Susan Edwards

When they neared the camp, Jessie caught up with her. "Men." She stopped before she could continue with her disparaging comments about their morbid conversation and cocked her head to one side. "Listen, do you hear that?"

The rest of the group stopped to listen.

"Sounds like a baby," Jordan commented.

The women gasped and cried out, "Eirica!" in unison.

"Land's sake, Jessie, poor Eirica's by herself," Anne cried.

Sofia muttered something in her native tongue to her granddaughter.

Coralie gently handed Jordan the sleeping boy and together, she and the other women rushed into camp, going immediately to Eirica's wagon. They stopped when James stepped out of the tent.

Jessie ran up to her brother. "Eirica? Is she all right?" The others flanked her.

James made a shushing sound. "She's fine," he said, keeping his voice low. "Wait here."

He stepped inside, then returned with a wrapped bundle in his arms. With everyone crowding close, silent, their breaths held, he peeled away the towel to reveal one contented, sleeping baby. "Meet Summer Halley Macauley."

Ohhs and ahhs filled the air. Anne and Sofia exchanged looks. "Who delivered her?" Anne asked, peering at the sleeping babe.

James stood a bit straighter. "I did."

Jessie's jaw fell. "You? All by yourself?"

"Yep. Well, Eirica did all the work. Rook and me just helped some."

Sofia stepped forward. "James, does Eirica need help with bathing or anything else?"

246

James wore a smug, self-satisfied expression. "Nope. Everything's done." He frowned. "Course, it'd be real nice if one of you ladies volunteered to wash them sheets and stuff for me. Birthing sure makes a helluva mess."

They laughed. Sofia and her granddaughter volunteered.

"How about if Wolf and I take the children tonight so Eirica can rest?" Jessie asked.

"Great," James exclaimed. He bent down and called Eirica's children to him. "Now come meet your new sister." After a brief look, the three youngsters wandered away. "Guess it's not such a big deal to them." He turned to his sister and shrugged.

Jessie stared down at the tiny wrinkled face with awe. She glanced back at her brother who still wore a pleased grin as if he'd been responsible for the whole thing. "I still can't believe you delivered her," she said, shaking her head.

Eirica's sleepy voice came from inside the wagon. "Your brother did a fine job, Jessie."

James turned beet-red. "I told her it weren't no different than birthing calves," he muttered. More laughter followed from the gathered women.

Coralie fingered the towel and looked at James. "Could I—I mean, if Eirica wouldn't mind—"

James chuckled and put the baby in her arms.

Coralie held her breath. She'd never felt anything like the warm glow of love welling inside her as she stared down at the baby. Jordan put his arms around his wife and met her gaze with a questioning look.

"Tell them, Jordie," she urged.

A wide grin split Jordan's darkly tanned face, his mustache quivered with his suppressed excitement. Then he blurted, "I'm going to be a father."

Voices rose with excitement and the couple was

bombarded with questions. James took the baby back
into the tent, then came back out, herding everyone
away. He led the way to Rook's wagon, saying only
that he had another surprise for the group.

Jessie groaned. "I suppose this means more baby
clothes to make."

Everyone laughed then the women looked at one
another. Sofia clapped her hands. "A party. We have to
celebrate and give Eirica our gifts."

Everyone voiced their agreement. Rook met them, a
wide grin on his face, his cupped hands held close to
his shirt. "Rook, did you see the baby?" Coralie asked.

His eyes twinkled. "Sure did, lass. We has lots of
babies." He held out his arms. Cupped in his hands,
resting on his palms, lay a tiny white pup.

More excited chatter followed as everyone crowded
around the wagon where Rook had made a bed for
Sadie and her pups. Sadie received her share of praise.
She wagged her tail while six other pups, mostly black
or brown, or some combination of brown, black or
white, fought for prime nursing spigots.

Sofia put her hands on her ample hips. "I need to
plan something special for tonight." She glanced at
Wolf. "We're not leaving in the morning are we?"

Wolf shook his head. "No. We'll spend two more
days here, then see how Eirica and the babe are doing."

"Good. I'll fix Eirica a nice clear broth and some tea."

Rook set the seventh pup, the only pure white one
among the litter, and chased after Sofia. Their arguing
as to what they'd fix for Eirica's supper left everyone
in high spirits.

Wolf sat outside the tent he and Jessie had set up for
the Macauley children. He'd relieved James from duty
for a few days to allow him to remain with Eirica.

Tonight, and maybe tomorrow, Eirica's children could sleep here, to give their mom some time to rest and gather her strength. Darkness surrounded him. He hadn't bothered to start a fire as he and Jessie usually ate with the other hired hands.

Jessie came out of the tent. "Asleep and all tucked up. The girls were so excited." Jessie sat beside him, then shifted, straightening her skirts beneath her.

"You seem to be favoring your dress much more these days." His glance slid down over her curves.

Jessie grimaced. "It's more comfortable."

Wolf reared back, his brows lifted in disbelief. "Since when?"

A look of devilment, one he knew well, crept into her eyes, but she didn't say a word.

"Spill it, Jessica Naomi White. What have you been up to now?"

She giggled. "Same thing as you."

He frowned. "What is that supposed to mean?"

Jessie turned and hugged him. "Wolf, we've never talked about it, but do you want a family? Children of your own? I know running a boarding school will take our time but—"

He silenced her. "Of course I want children. We'll have our own family someday—" His voice trailed off and his gaze slid down the front of her dress to the gentle swell of her breasts. Thoughtfully, he cupped them. Demands of the trail and his responsibilities had meant little time for him and Jessie in the last couple of weeks beyond precious stolen moments to be together. Now he felt a subtle difference. His hands skimmed down to her once flat belly. There was a gentle swell there as well.

"We're having a baby?" Wolf's voice rose with disbelief.

"Yup." Jessie bit her lip, her gaze anxious.

"Are you sure?" He had to swallow several times before the words left his mouth. His gaze dipped to her breasts and her waist.

"Yup, my monthly is never late."

He closed his eyes, feeling incredibly blessed by the Great Spirit. First for giving him Jessie, then a purpose to his life, and now this.

"Are you happy?" Jessie asked.

His eyes flew open. "You've made me the happiest man to walk this land, my sweet Wild Rose." He kissed her with a need that rose inside him like an underground river rises to the earth's surface. Like the springs they'd encountered along the trail, happiness welled up inside and spilled out, encompassing his whole being. Life was good. Incredibly good. Next spring, they'd return to his people, the *Miniconjou* Sioux, in the Nebraska Territory to start a boarding school for the children of his tribe and raise their own family. His mother would also be thrilled to have more grandchildren.

Staring down into her face, Wolf lowered his head, slanting his mouth over hers. Lifting his lips when they were both breathless, he murmured, "Guess I'd best get used to seeing you in a dress."

Jessie wrapped her arms around his neck and straddled him. "Yup. I've got to admit, they are good for some things." She whispered in his ear, in great detail what she wanted.

He cleared his throat and quickly glanced around to see if anyone was in sight. Finding no one moving about and grateful for the deep shadows hiding them, Wolf loosened his breeches and pulled his wife on top of him.

Chapter Fifteen

Word spread about the birth of Eirica's baby and during the next day well-wishers dropped by to bring special treats or small gifts. The following morning, on their last day of rest, Eirica sat propped against pillows and quilts, feeling quite sinful lying abed. James refused to allow her to get up and lift a finger, no matter how many times she'd assured him she felt fine, was perfectly capable of resuming her activities.

For just a little while longer, she'd indulge in the luxury of having someone see to her needs and those of her children. Holding her infant daughter close, Eirica marveled anew at the healthy pink of her peacefully sleeping newborn. She fingered the girl's soft reddish-gold curls and ran the tip of her finger down the babe's button nose.

The baby was no longer wrapped in Rook's shirt. Before her daughter's birth, Eirica had torn an old quilt into squares to use for diapers and blankets. She'd even used one of her old dresses to make a couple of gowns. They weren't much, wouldn't last through many washings, but they'd have to do. When Summer awoke a short while later, Eirica put the baby to her breast. She loved this closeness, the bond that had already formed between her and this precious child. With Birk, she'd never been allowed the luxury of just watching her newborn child. This baby, this new life, symbolized Eirica's own new start.

When the baby fell back asleep, Eirica changed her, adding the soiled cloth to a growing mound of laundry. She wrinkled her nose. Already, a pile of dirty garments waited. Between the guilt of not starting that laundry and the growing heat in the tent, Eirica rose from her bed and made sure she was presentable. Cuddling her daughter close, she stepped outside, marveling at how well she felt. A glance down at herself made her smile. She'd soon regain her figure, and it was wonderful to be able to get up without struggling.

Warm, bright sunshine and clear blue skies greeted her. Songbirds filled the air with their sweet music, and around her, the now-familiar comforting bustle of emigrants going about their business went unnoticed. "Welcome to the world, Summer," she whispered to her sleeping daughter.

Glancing around for a safe place to lay her infant so she could start the laundry, Eirica realized she'd have to empty a box to make a temporary cradle. She spied Coralie sitting alone on a wooden crate, her back to her. Remembering the girl's worry about becoming a mother, Eirica went to her.

"Coralie, would you like to watch Summer while I start the wash? Unless you're busy," she added, noting the sewing in her lap.

A myriad of emotions crossed Coralie's features as she shoved a piece of pink material back into her sewing basket. Her gaze filled with longing as she stared at the infant stretching in its mother's arms. Delight and awe followed, quickly replaced by uncertainty and fear. "I'd love to, but I don't know what to do with her. What if she cries? What if I drop her?"

Eirica laughed and put the baby in her arms. "All you have to do is hold her. Relax and let your instincts guide you."

Coralie pouted. "I don't think I have any instincts." She cuddled the baby close to her breast. "Oh, she's so tiny, so beautiful. I hope I have a little girl."

Watching Coralie adjust her hold and sway ever so slightly in a rocking motion that came naturally to most women, Eirica knew Coralie was wrong. She had the mothering instincts, she just didn't recognize them. "I'll be by the river if you need me," Eirica said. "She just ate and I just changed her, so you get the fun part—holding her while she sleeps."

Back at her own campsite, Eirica put on a large pot of water to boil then took the dirty clothing down to the river to rinse the worst of the soil out. She had nearly finished the washing when James returned from a walk with her other three children. He strode down to the river where she was gathering the washed clothing. All that remained was to hang them to dry.

"What are you doing? You shouldn't be up yet. You should be resting."

Eirica rolled her eyes. "James, I lay abed all of yesterday and this morn. I'm fine. In fact, I've never felt so good." His concern touched her.

He stepped forward and took the wrung-out clothes from her. "I'll finish this. You go back to the tent and rest."

Susan Edwards

Her brows lowered. Well-meaning was fine and
dandy, but she wasn't an invalid. If she had to endure
any more time alone in that hot, stifling tent, she'd go
crazy. She put her hands on her hips. "James, I'm perfectly able to finish the washing. You've already done
so much."

His jaw firmed. "Not enough. You deserve to be
pampered and spoiled." As his voice softened; a hint
of pain flashed into his eyes then was gone.

Eirica knew he was remembering her past and
though his reasons were sweet, his intentions
unselfish, stubbornly she held firm. If they were to
marry, they'd have to arrive at some middle ground,
for she wouldn't allow James to treat her like an
invalid, nor would she allow him to do more than his
share of the work. Her own gaze gentled. "James, you
can't make up for the past. It's done with. Nothing can
change it."

Obstinate green eyes clashed with equally determined blues. "No, but I don't have to watch you work
hard only days after giving birth. It's bad enough that
we have to leave tomorrow, but at least you can ride."

She lifted a brow. "Or walk."

"Ride." His lips compressed.

"Are you asking or telling me?' She crossed her
arms in front of her and tapped her foot.

He threw his hands up. "Woman, what is it with
you?"

Watching him remove his hat and thread his fingers
through his thick, wavy black hair, Eirica couldn't stay
mad. She wasn't really that angry to begin with, but
she had to make her point. She stepped toward him
and held out her hand for the washed baby clothes he
held.

When he glared at her and refused to pass them

254

over, she snatched them from him with one hand and with the other, poked him in the chest with one finger. "Don't go getting bossy, Mr. Jones. I know my body, know what it can handle. If I need to rest, I'll rest. If I can't walk or get too tired tomorrow, I'll let you know. And if you're so keen on doing laundry, start with your own."

With a shove to his chest, she pushed him out of her way so she could gather the rest of the washed items.

Standing at the edge of the bank, James stumbled off balance when the soil beneath him gave way. He fell, landing with a startled yelp, on his backside. Eirica ignored his cursing as she returned to camp.

A short while later, while hanging nappies and blankets out to dry, James came up behind her. His hands slid around her from behind. "I suppose I deserved that."

She glanced over her shoulder. "Suppose?"

He had the grace to look ashamed. "All right, I deserved it. I apologize for being pushy and trying to order you around. I just worry about you."

Eirica turned in his embrace and smiled. "I know. And it's wonderful knowing someone cares. But I'm not an invalid. Nor am I a piece of fragile glass."

James ran his hands up the sides of her neck. His grin turned sheepish. "No you're not. I forget about that red hair of yours. Forgive me?"

Standing on tiptoe, Eirica kissed him on the mouth. "Forgiven." They stared at each other until a voice from behind James broke them apart.

"Ahem. If you're done with your laundry, Eirica, we have a surprise for you." When Eirica turned, she saw that Jessie stood there, watching, amusement lurking in her dark green eyes.

Eirica blushed.

James scowled. "And what if I'm not done?"

"Tough," Jessie said, laughing. "Come on, Eirica, everyone is waiting."

"Waiting? For what?" Puzzled, Eirica glanced around, just now aware of the sound of muted whispers and laughter. To her surprise, there was a large group of women gathering at Sofia's wagon.

"For the mother of that adorable little girl." Jessie grabbed her hand. "Come on. James will watch Ian."

Curious, Eirica followed Jessie, leaving James to scowl after them.

When Eirica and Jessie arrived, the group parted, revealing a makeshift table laden with food. The women quickly sat on a large quilt spread on the ground. Jessie led her to where a pile of hastily wrapped gifts awaited. Her two daughters were jumping up and down excitedly. As soon as Eirica realized all these people were there to celebrate Summer's birth, she felt tears sting the back of her eyes. Their thoughtfulness overwhelmed her.

Mixed among the women in her own wagon party, there were several others—neighbors on the trail, much as one had neighbors back home. "Oh, my. Oh, my," she whispered, unable to speak around the lump in her throat.

"Well, come on, we're all waiting," Coralie said, looking as excited as the two little girls.

Laughing, Eirica used her apron to wipe the tears from her eyes as she took up the seat of honor. For the next hour, Eirica opened gifts—some tied in paper, others hidden in scraps of material, and others unwrapped, folded in a neat square. Excited chatter followed with each revelation. Some of the gifts were new, others used, but all given in sisterly love and support.

Eirica couldn't believe the number of snowy-white

linen gowns, quilts, blankets, tiny dresses and even the knitted sacque with matching booties sitting before her. Anne had even made matching dresses for Lara and Alison and a shirt for Ian so her other children wouldn't feel left out. She'd never had so many nice things for any of her kids and the thoughtfulness overwhelmed her. Now she knew what Anne, Jessie, Coralie, Sofia and Catarina had been doing all those evenings when she'd felt so left out. They'd been sewing, planning this all along.

Touching the wonderfully soft baby garments, tears filled her eyes. "I don't know what to say. I've never—I mean—" Once again, words failed her.

Jessie leaned forward, an impish light in her eyes. "Just say thank you, Eirica. We know."

Eirica smiled through fresh tears. "Thank you. Thank you all."

"Wait, I have one more." Coralie passed Summer to Jessie who, to the amusement of all, squeaked that she didn't know how to hold a baby.

Coralie smirked at her. "Nothing to it, my dear sister-in-law." She handed Eirica a large package.

Eirica peeled back the cut-up canvas sack and gasped. With shaking hands, she lifted up a long infant dress made of pink satin with ruffles and an undergarment of matching linen. The bodice and hem of the dress bore tiny pastel flowers and there was a pink linen blanket to match, with an embroidered center and the baby's name in one corner.

Oohs and ahhs greeted the sight. Jessie stared at her sister-in-law with a dumbfounded look on her face. "You couldn't have made that?"

Coralie preened. "Every seam and stitch. I traded for a dress from a woman I met and took it apart to use it for a pattern."

"I didn't know you could embroider." Jessie said, her gaze on the items being passed around.

Coralie, pleased by reception of her gift, tipped her chin haughtily. "I may not sew or knit very well, but my grandmother in Boston insisted ladies had to be able to embroider their own lace hankies and such."

Eirica jumped in. "It's beautiful, Coralie, but where did you get such exquisite material?"

"Just something I had," Coralie muttered, looking uncomfortable.

Jessie handed Eirica back her daughter then turned to Coralie, a look of admiration and awe in her eyes. "You had one more dress saved, for a grand entrance when we reached Oregon, didn't you?"

"Oh, Coralie, you shouldn't have cut up your fine dress," Eirica said, fingering the exquisite material.

Shrugging, Coralie waved her off and glared at Jessie. "Grand entrances just don't seem to work for me anymore. Besides, where in Oregon is a farmer's wife going to wear something like that?" There was no rancor or bitterness in her voice, just pride, as she added, "I even have some left for if I have a girl."

Eirica rose and gave Coralie a hug, then Jessie. The women all stood and Eirica made sure she thanked each and every one. Then they moved to the food and pots of tea and cocoa Rook had brought over. The merrymaking went on until it was time to start supper.

Several hours later, as the sun lowered, leaving the sky above turning orange and pink, Eirica knew she couldn't be happier. With the baby sleeping, and her children giggling at something James had said while they ate, she watched. Could life be better? She had three happy children, a healthy newborn and a man who loved her.

Nope, life couldn't get any better than this.

*   *   *

Nearly three weeks later, a broken axle on Elliot's wagon forced the emigrants to stop for the night early. No one minded, though. With the first of September right around the corner, they'd been pushing themselves and the animals very hard. They'd come more than thirteen hundred miles, and had another six hundred to go before the snows arrived.

"Well, I for one am not sorry we are stopping here," Anne said, staring at the myriad falls before them.

Eirica agreed. The view was glorious. Immediately opposite, a subterranean river burst from the middle of the basalt cliffs, sending cascades of foamy white water spewing forth to spill over the rock and sage to the river below. There had to be a thousand waterfalls, some no more than thin ribbons of quicksilver water, others raging torrents.

"This couldn't be a better place," she sighed. After leaving Fort Hall, they'd followed the Snake River. Its banks were sometimes impossible to get down due to precipitous, practically vertical cliffs. The landscape had turned volcanic with groupings of black, jagged upthrusts of lava rock. Yet, as if trying to make up for the alien austerity of the valley, the Snake River boasted a marvelous beauty in waterfalls unlike any Eirica had ever seen.

Some were so loud, the emigrants could hear the roar from miles away.

Coralie held out her arms. "Can I take Summer for a little while, Eirica?"

Eirica smiled. "Sure." She transferred Summer to Coralie's waiting arms. "If you'd like, you can give her a bath." She hid her smile at the look of happiness that sparked in the girl's eyes.

"Really? Oh, I'd love to." Coralie checked Summer's nappies. "I'll even change her."

Jessie rolled her eyes when her sister-in-law rushed off. "This means she's not helping Rook and me with supper again. She's going to be impossible when her own baby is born."

Eirica chuckled. "I think she'll be a good mother."

Wrinkling her nose, Jessie muttered, "Better than a bread baker, that's for sure."

The women laughed and headed back toward their own wagons to get a start on the evening chores. Though Eirica longed for a cup of tea, she settled for a long drink of tepid water from the small water barrel on the back of her wagon. The sooner the meal was cooked and clean-up done, the sooner she and James could spend time together, unless he had first watch that night.

As she worked, she let her mind wander over her day. James had spent the day with her, alternating between helping her with the children and her wagon. Now that she wasn't with child, she insisted on doing her share and had no trouble handling the team.

True to his word, he'd started teaching her what she would need to know, including how to protect herself in case of trouble. But she wasn't very good with a knife or shooting. She hated the thought that she might someday need to use one in defense, but knew that never again, would she be a victim.

When the others learned that James was teaching Eirica to handle weapons, Rook insisted the rest of the women learn some measure of self-protection. When Coralie and Catarina both declined his suggestion, he'd sat them all down and purged from his soul the sad tale of how he'd lost his wife and daughter. For the first time ever, with Sofia sitting beside him, holding his hand, he even mentioned losing his unborn second child. After that, there were no more protests.

Eirica's days and evenings were filled with lots to do, but her favorite time came each evening, after the children were abed and it was just her and James. They'd stroll in the dark. Sometimes, they talked. Other times, they'd take advantage of a secluded place to kiss. Heat suffused her when she thought of what else they'd done in the deep shadows of the night.

James had shown her just what pleasure he could bring her with his fingers and even more amazing, had taught her to pleasure him with hers. They'd pleased each other several times since she'd given birth to Summer, but it wasn't the same as having James make love to her. Eirica yearned to experience true love-making with him and share that incredible oneness that only happened when they were joined. But knew she had to wait a bit longer for her body to fully heal from giving birth. Soon, she comforted herself. Soon she'd be able to make love with James again.

As if he knew that she was thinking of him, James walked over to her after tending the oxen and the tent and pulled her into his arms for a deep, soul-searching kiss. "I couldn't wait another minute for that."

Eirica flushed. "James, someone will see."

He grinned. "Everyone knows how I feel about you, sweetheart. I have to go check on the cattle. Can you handle things here?"

"Go. I'm fine."

"I'll try to be back in time for supper."

Eirica watched him mount and ride off. With a sigh, she checked on her children. As usual, Alison and Ian were running around together, playing chase with Hanna and Kerstin, while Lara played on her own by

261

the tent. Coralie still had Summer with her, which left Eirica free to start supper.

Around them, people came and went. Men with thick beards, hats pulled over their heads, and exhaustion written in the slump of their shoulders, pushed handcarts high-piled past where she worked. Others led mules and oxen to the water. Newcomers arrived, full-loaded wagons bumping along as families sought to find an uncrowded spot near the river. Tents went up and a multitude of sounds rode on the wind. Another ending to a day on the trail.

Eirica served three plates of beans and bacon, then called her children. Alison and Ian came running, each kneeling down around a wooden box. Ian immediately used his fingers to pick up his beans one at a time and pop them into his mouth. She poured three tin cups of milk. "Now where is your sister?" Lara sometimes had to be coaxed to eat as she hated to stop whatever she was doing. "Lara!"

Eirica strode to the far side of the tent where she'd last seen her daughter playing in the dirt with the wooden figures Rook had carved. The toys were there, scattered among mounds of dirt and rock, but where was Lara? Eirica frowned and turned in a slow circle, searching for her daughter. Bidding Alison to stay with Ian, Eirica went to the Svenssons' camp. Maybe her daughter had followed Anne's children. But Lara wasn't there either. Unease skittered up her spine. Where was she? She wouldn't wander off, not Lara.

Eirica went from camp to camp, her steps quickening as her panic grew.

James rode toward Eirica's wagon, as always, eager to see her again. Jeremy and Jordan, along with three other hired men rode toward Rook's campsite, each arguing as to who'd be first in line to see what Sofia had fixed for their supper.

Passing the meal line, James sniffed. Whatever Sofia had fixed sure smelled right tempting to a hungry man. His stomach agreed then protested when he rode past.

Before he reached Eirica's wagon, he heard her voice.

"James!"

At the sound of her high-pitched cry, James spun his horse around. He jumped down and caught her as she ran up to him. "Lara's gone. I can't find her. I've checked everywhere." Eirica's voice rose with panic.

James ran his hands up her arms. "She's here somewhere, sweetheart. Don't worry. We'll find her. Where did you last see her?"

Eirica led him to the side of the tent and the forgotten wooden animals. "She was right here. When I called her for supper, she was gone." Big blue eyes rounded with fear stared up at him. "James, Lara wouldn't wander off."

James knew Eirica spoke the truth. Unlike Ian, who habitually wandered off, Lara tended to stay close, only wandering amidst the Svenssons'. While the boy had given him and Eirica this same scare at Fort Bridger when he'd gotten lost, this seemed out of character for the older girl. His unease grew. If Lara weren't here, where was she?

He snapped his fingers. "Did you check the wagon where the pups are?"

Relief showed on Eirica's features. "No. I didn't look there. Do you think?"

"Let's go check."

Together, they ran to one of Rook's wagons. Since many of the supplies had been used up, Rook had

263

cleared a large area in one to make a nice secure shelter for Sadie and her litter. He peered in. Sadie greeted him with a soft woof. Squeals of protest followed when she stood and came to him, eager for an ear rub. Absently, he petted her, his gaze searching the interior of the wagon. No Lara.

"Go back to your babies, Mama," he told the dog then strode over to Rook. In a low voice, he asked the old cook if he'd seen Lara.

"Ain't seen the little lass since earlier, when I gave her another wooden toy."

"What's wrong?" Sofia joined them, her dark eyes going from James to Rook.

Realizing that it would be dark soon, James stuck his fingers between his lips and gave a shrill whistle, bringing silence to the hired men who were eating. He explained that Lara was missing. "Listen up. I need everyone to spread out, in pairs, and search for Lara Macauley." He dispatched one man to go fetch Wolf, while he organized the Svenssons along with Dante and Elliot. The first two had rushed over when they'd heard the commotion.

When he'd done all he could, James led Eirica back to her wagon and her waiting children. She grabbed his arm and stared up at him with stricken eyes. "Oh, James, I wasn't paying close enough attention. I lost my daughter."

"No. You can't blame yourself. As you said, Lara never wanders off."

Summer's cry interrupted him. Coralie walked up to Eirica with the fussing baby. "I'm sorry, Eirica, but I think she's hungry."

James took the infant and handed her to Eirica. Then he tipped her chin up and stared into her eyes. "I'll go look for Lara."

Eirica gently rocked the crying baby in her arms. "James, what if—"

"No. Don't say it. We'll find her."

Tears fell from Eirica's eyes. "I should go with you."

"No, you have other children who need their mama. Besides, if Lara comes back or someone finds her and brings her to the camp, you need to be here." Summer's wails grew as Eirica unfastened her blouse and shielded her nudity with the baby's blanket. The baby stopped crying as soon as Eirica gave her what she needed.

Alison ran up to them just as James turned to go. "Ma! James! I found Lara's blankie in the dirt. She must've dropped it and now it's real dirty."

Both adults glanced down at the little girl. In her hands, she held a small filthy blanket with a large footprint ground into it.

Eirica tightened her hold on her baby as she and James exchanged glances. Both knew if Lara had wandered off, she'd have taken that small security blanket with her.

"Find her, James. Find my little girl."

James reached down and kissed her, then bent to hug Alison. "I'll find her."

Moving among wagons and tents, Birk pushed a handcart, with a hastily made cover stretched across it, over the rough ground. A high-pitched whimper from inside made him stop. He peeled open the cover and glared inside at the tear-streaked face of his daughter.

"Not a sound, Lara girl, or else. Ya hear me?" He held his fist in front of her face.

The whimpering stopped. Lara sucked harder on her thumb and stared at him with wide, frightened eyes.

Satisfied that she'd do as she was told, Birk replaced the cover and continued on. What a stroke of luck. Of all his brats, she was the only one he could count on to obey him. She'd always been afraid of him.

He pushed the cart, his steps hurried. Curses followed in his wake as he shoved past anyone in his way. Finally, he reached the sheltering outcrop of rock where Zeb waited.

"Where ya been?"

Birk snickered and whipped the top off the cart, revealing his frightened child.

"Dammit man, what the hell are you doin'?"

Birk reached in, grabbed Lara and pulled her out. "This here's one of my brats, ain't ya, Lara girl?"

Lara shrank from his hold, but Birk pulled her close, kneeling down beside her. "I got a use fer her."

Zeb ran his fingers through his matted beard. "Man, they's gonna be lookin' fer her."

"Yeah, that's the plan." Using his knife, he cut several curls of her hair and a wide swath of fabric from her skirts, then took her shoes, a tiny pair of moccasins.

Beside him, Zeb paced. The two horses they'd stolen grazed nearby. "We can't take a kid with us. People will see and be suspicious."

Tucking away one of the curly tresses, the fabric and the shoes, Birk stood, handing Zeb the second lock of hair. "Oh, we ain't keepin' her." He removed a medallion from around his neck, the one his ma had given him and made him wear. The woman had been so religious, so fanatic in her beliefs, she'd made his life a living hell with her insistence that he ask forgiveness for his sins, real or imagined. He'd endured her beatings, believing he had to pay for his misdeeds. Now others would pay.

He placed the chain around Lara's neck. "Ya leaves that on, Lara girl."

He turned to Zeb. "That bitch is gonna know I's here, that I's watchin' her whorin' ways. Law says she belongs to me, and she might as well know I can come after her or them brats anytime I wants."

"I thought tha plan was ta wait till Oregon."

"Still is. But no harm in lettin' her know jest where she stands. I seen her and that bastard kissin'." Birk's hands clenched into two tight fists. "He'll die fer touchin' her."

Inside, Birk burned every time he thought of Eirica with that Jones man. What really riled him was watching that damn Jones bastard act as if he had a right to be with *his* children. Well, Birk had news for the pair of them. The bitch was still his. Them brats was his. It was time both of them knew she still belonged to him.

Putting Lara back inside the handcart, he gave Zeb instructions as to what to do with the lock of hair.

"Meet me back 'ere, then, Birk ordered. "And be ready to ride."

Chapter Sixteen

Eirica knew James was right. Someone had to stay at the campsite while others were off looking for her daughter, but she hated feeling helpless. "Oh, Lara girl, where are you?" Fear made her feet feel like lead. The sight of that dirty blanket Lara never let go of, except when Eirica insisted on washing it, deepened her apprehension. As she nursed Summer, her gaze searched the landscape, desperately seeking her daughter.

Suddenly, it was there, that odd sensation of an unseen watcher. Shivering, she turned in a slow circle, her gaze roaming over men and women taking advantage of the fading daylight. Over the last few weeks, usually in the evenings, this same feeling had come and gone at odd moments, and yet she'd never found anyone suspicious looking her way.

She shook off the eerie feeling, putting tonight's episode down to her frazzled nerves. Over and over, she prayed for Lara's safe return. When Summer finished nursing, Eirica rubbed her tiny back. After a satisfying burp, she laid Summer down in the wooden crate she'd padded, making it into a makeshift bed. Picking it up, she took the infant into the tent, out of the cooling night air. Then she cleaned up Ian who was nearly asleep and put him to bed.

Alison was still staring at her plate, her food untouched when Eirica returned. Eirica knew her eldest child was remembering her own ordeal of being kidnapped a few months ago. She bent down and pulled Alison into her arms. "We'll find Lara, sweetheart. How about helping me by picking up the toys?"

"Yes, Mama." Alison went to do her bidding, her steps slow and dragging.

Feeling a cold chill slide through her, Eirica went into the tent to fetch her shawl. Alison entered a few minutes later with her skirt bunched in her arms, the wooden toys from Rook neatly gathered there. She dumped them in one corner of the tent, then sat, her gaze wide and worried. "James will find Lara, Mama. He found me." Her voice shook and her lower lip trembled. Tears followed.

Eirica knew her daughter's words stemmed from a desperate need to believe that James would make her world right again. Wiping the silent tears from her daughter's face, she smoothed tangled strands of hair from Alison's face then gathered the child close, searching for the words to reassure her. Eirica knew she had to be strong, had to reassure her daughter, but what could she say?

Alison pulled away. "Maybe bad people got Lara like they got me and Jessie." Her blue eyes were wide, her chin trembling.

Eirica's composure nearly broke. It went against her

grain to give her daughter false hope, but hope was all that kept Eirica from becoming hysterical. "Let's not think bad things. Lara probably just wandered off and got lost like Ian did a few weeks ago. Now, let's get you into bed, sweetheart."

Alison sniffed, but let Eirica remove her dress and wipe her face and hands with the wet cloth she had brought to clean the worst of the dirt from Ian.

With Alison laying silent in her bed, Eirica fled outside, afraid she'd break down in front of the child. She didn't want to scare her eldest, yet she couldn't hold her own tears at bay any longer. Alone in the growing darkness, Eirica paced outside her tent, trying to penetrate the gloom covering the land, searching for one small little girl.

James will find her. She found herself clinging to the same hope as her daughter. Trying to keep busy, to keep her mind off the unthinkable, Eirica loaded her food back into the wagon. Bending down, she reached for a sack of beans and froze. On top of the tied-off bag lay a small lock of golden-red curls. Prickles of unease skittered up her spine and the back of her hand flew to her mouth. It looked like some of Lara's hair. She picked it up rubbed the soft strands between her fingers, then clenched the lock in her fist.

Her heart thumped hard in her chest. How did this get here? More importantly, who'd put it there? Moving away from the wagon, away from her camp, Eirica felt totally confused and frightened. What should she do? Where was James? She needed to show him her find.

Frantically, her gaze roamed the area behind her wagon, toward the river, moving outward, looking for something, anything out of kilter. But everything looked normal. There were many families she knew, many she didn't. Men and women walked back and forth from the river, some with dishes, others with pots heavy with water. She tracked one couple back to their wagon.

A short, stocky man tore around a wagon and shoved past them, knocking the woman over. The couple's angry shouts made Eirica shake her head. Some folk were so rude. Suddenly, something about the man who'd hurried by penetrated the fog of fear holding her in its grip. Scanning, she spotted him just before he disappeared between two more wagons. If she hadn't known better, she'd have thought it was Birk, but that was impossible. Not only was Birk dead, this man's figure wasn't as heavy as Birk had been.

Her gaze went from the lock of hair clutched in her hand back to where the man had disappeared. He was gone. "Now you're seeing ghosts," she chided herself, yet she couldn't shake the notion that something was terribly wrong. He'd moved like her husband, certainly. And it was just like Birk to shove his way past anyone who dared to be in his way.

Suddenly, Eirica had to know. Though she told herself she was being silly, overreacting, she flagged down Catarina and Marco and asked them to stay with her children. Holding her skirts above her ankles, Eirica ran, searching among the crowded campers for the man who brought back memories that caused her whole being to tremble with terror.

"Lara!" Over and over, James called the little girl's name. He stopped everyone he came across and described the little girl, but no one had seen her. On he went, calling her name, asking questions. As the light faded, his fear grew. Where was she? Surely she hadn't wandered this far on her own, which pointed to an even worse.

Stopping, he ran his fingers through his hair. Not too many people were moving about now. Most had retired to their tents or were sitting in front of fires. After several more fruitless minutes of searching, he replaced his hat and headed back, following the river. God, he hoped she hadn't fallen in. He shuddered at the thought.

A short ways from camp, James spotted Eirica running in the direction he'd already searched. He frowned, his gut tightening. He ran after her. "Eirica!"

When she turned and saw him, he feared the worst. Her face was devoid of color, her eyes wide and frightened. He grabbed her shoulders. "What is it? Did you find her?"

"No." Her voice came out on a long sob. "Someone took her. Someone took my baby. I think it was Birk."

James folded her into his embrace. "Honey, we don't know that for sure." The full impact of her breathless cry hit him. He held her away from him, looking closely at her. Had the strain of the last hour somehow confused her mind? Birk was dead.

"Eirica, sweetheart, Birk can never hurt you or your children again."

"What if he isn't dead? What if he didn't drown? We never found his body. She held up a lock of hair. "I found this, near the wagon. Someone came into my camp while I was in the tent with the children and left this. It's Lara's hair." Her voice broke.

"When I was looking around to see if I could see who'd put it there, I saw him. I saw a man who looked like Birk."

Stunned, James shook his head. "That's not possible. He drowned." James took the lock from her, rubbing the silky softness between his thumb and forefinger, more concerned than ever. "Did you see his face?"

Sobbing, Eirica shook her head. "No. I only saw him from the back. I ran after him but he was gone." She grabbed ahold of him. "I'm so afraid, James."

James didn't know what to think. "Eirica, are you sure this wasn't there before you noticed Lara missing? Could she or Alison or one of Anne's daughters have cut her hair?"

"No. It wasn't there. I'm positive." She hugged herself. "What am I going to do if Birk has her?" Terror laced her question.

James rubbed the back of his neck. The thought of that man getting ahold of even one of the children horrified him as well, yet he had to hold on to reason. Right now, they didn't know for sure that the man Eirica saw was actually Birk.

"Calm down, Eirica. Think. There must be hundreds of men out here who look like him from behind."

Eirica squeezed her eyes shut. "True. But not many are so rude." She explained the behavior she'd witnessed. "Besides, who else would kidnap her?"

The bleak certainty in her voice chilled him to his soul. He also had to agree the rudeness coupled with kidnapping his own child sounded exactly like something Birk would do. He thought about what Eirica had told him. Something occurred to him. "Eirica, if you saw Birk, that means he didn't have Lara. She has to be around here somewhere."

"The river," Eirica cried. "He was coming from the river."

In horror, they stared at one each other, then took off running. "God, he wouldn't hurt her. Oh, please," Eirica sobbed, stumbling.

James kept ahold of her arm as they made their way back to the river. The sound of frantic barks and howls made them break out into a run. As they drew nearer, They heard the shrill sound of a child's screams mingling with ferocious barking. Eirica gasped. His pulse quickened.

"Lara. That's Lara!"

"Don't get your hopes up, sweetheart." But James felt hope swell in his own chest. If it was Lara, she had to be alive. "It's coming from behind those rocks near the river!" Together, they rounded the boulders and stopped behind a group of men and woman gathered before the water, each drawn by the hysterical screams and the barking. Eirica and James shoved their way through. Sitting a foot deep in the water, James saw an abandoned handcart. The screams were coming from inside it.

In front, standing in the shallow water, the white wolf Wahoska stood guard, allowing no one near. His teeth were bared, his fur ruffled and his tail swishing in and out of the water. Deep growls kept the onlookers away.

James ran into the river, reassuring the wolf who stopped barking, but not growling. The two animals ran off when James reached out to tear the cover off the wooden handcart. The sight of Lara, screaming her head off, was the most beautiful sight he'd ever seen. He spoke softly, his voice hoarse with relief. Gently, he lifted the crying child out. Turning, he handed her to Eirica who waited with arms outstretched. Cheers went up around them, but he barely heard them over the child's hysteria.

"Lara. My sweet little girl, it's all right. Everything is all right." Over and over Eirica murmured her daughter's name.

Beyond calming, Lara clutched at her mother, her voice growing hoarse from screaming. James put his arm around Eirica and led her back through the crowd. "Come on, Eirica, let's get her back to camp."

By the time they reached Eirica's wagon, Lara's screams had subsided to choking gasps. James stoked the fire and brought over Eirica's lard-burning lantern, then he stepped into the tent to grab a quilt. He took a few minutes to reassure Alison that her sister was safe. Then he wrapped the quilt around mother and child and held them both.

Eirica stroked her daughter's head, examining the girl as best as she could in the firelight. Threading her fingers through Lara's hair, she felt the blunt ends where Lara's hair had been sheared short. "Why," she whispered, holding the strands up. James ran his fingers along hers. "Why did someone cut her hair?"

Unspoken between them lay the fear that somehow Birk had survived and was behind this. "I don't know, Eirica. I don't know." None of it made sense to him.

Finally, the little girl fell into an exhausted sleep. With James assisting, they uncovered her to check for injuries. She seemed unhurt, with no marks or bruises. Eirica frowned. "Her dress has been cut, James. The whole bottom hem is missing and her shoes are gone, the ones that Wolf's mother and sisters made." She glanced at him, questions he couldn't answer lurking in her gaze.

James had never felt so helpless. And he'd often felt that feeling raising his siblings, especially Jessie. He reached around Eirica to finger a gleaming chain peeping through the skewed neckline of Lara's dress. "What's *this*?"

"I don't know." Soft whimpers from inside the tent warned that Summer was waking.

Susan Edwards

James carefully lifted the chain from around Lara's neck and held it up to the lantern. It glittered in the lamplight. He looked to Eirica.

She stared at the round medallion dangling from his fingertips. Eirica's face lost color, her lips were pinched and she covered her mouth to muffle her startled cry. "Oh, my God," the words broke off, full of horror. "That looks like—it's Birk's—"

"It could be anyone's, Eirica. Maybe Lara found it." Even as he said the words, James knew he was wrong. Someone had deliberately put it there.

Her hands shook when she reached for it. Before she touched the chain, she jerked her fingers back as if afraid it would burn her. "No. No. It's his. The back. Turn it over."

The front showed the virgin mother Mary with baby Jesus, not something James could imagine Birk wearing, though now that he thought of it, he recalled having seen a gold chain around the man's neck on several occasions. He just hadn't paid it much mind. He turned over the gold piece and held it close to the lantern. "Looks like it says Proverbs 13:24."

" 'He that spareth his rod hateth his son; but he that loveth him chasteneth him betimes.' " Eirica recited the verse. She doubled over, nearly crushing Lara in her arms. "God, how many times have I heard him recite that damn verse. Before he beat us—if he wasn't in an uncontrollable rage—he used to make me, or the children, kiss his belt or the wooden cane, or whatever he'd chosen to use against us. Said his mother had taught him the value of penitence with that verse, that it was his duty to see we paid for our sins." Her voice broke off on a moan. "No. Oh no, it can't be him!" She gasped, fighting fear and horror.

James didn't want to believe it but he held the evidence in his hand. How could Birk be alive? No one could have survived falling into the snow-fed, swollen Platte River where they'd crossed. Disbelief gave way to fury when he thought of what the man had done to his own child and now to Eirica. He shoved aside his own fears, his own pain and worry. First he had to see to Eirica, to Lara, to this family he loved more than life.

Fearing she'd wake Lara with her soft sobs, James took the spent girl from her mother and put her to bed in the tent. It took a few minutes of his softly rubbing Lara's back for the child to fall back into a restless slumber. Alison crawled over to sit by her sister, her big blue eyes filled with silent worry. He ran his fingers through the five-year-old's curls. "It'll be all right, Ali. I'm going to stay here tonight. Watch over Lara while I tend to your ma."

Back at the fire, James picked up the quilt and wrapped it back around Eirica, then drew her against him. She pressed nearer. Her anguished sobs broke his heart. Every protective instinct within him rose. He'd be damned if the man would ever again get within a stone's throw of the woman he loved and her children. "Shh, sweetheart. I'm here. I'm not going to let him near you."

Eirica couldn't speak, couldn't voice her worst nightmare. Her eyes were swollen; her jaw hurt from clenching it so she wouldn't scream and cry out at the unfairness of it, but the worst of her pain came from her heart. Her heart lay in torn ruins, hope bleeding from her.

Birk was alive. The disbelief and horror left her numb. She lifted her head to stare at James. She'd been so close to finding happiness and it had been ripped from her. "He's alive, James. Birk was here. He took Lara from where she was playing." The mere thought of him being that close made her stomach roil.

"He left that lock of hair here, left her where she'd be found, knowing that when I saw that medallion, I'd know it was him. He's warning me that he'll take the children from me. Next time, he might actually kill one of them to punish me."

"Eirica, there won't be a next time. Birk will never get near any of you again." The anguish in James's voice mirrored her own.

Shivering, Eirica recalled those moments when she'd felt watched and realized that he'd been following, watching. Anger coursed through her. She clenched the piece of jewelry in her fist, then tore free from James and ran down to the river where she tossed it as far from her as she could.

How dare he play with her in this manner? How dare he frighten her child? She cursed Birk. She blamed herself for being that innocent young girl who'd fallen for every one of his lies. Anger, fear and guilt washed over her in waves. She hurt, so much. How could she survive this? Just knowing Birk was out there, watching, waiting for his chance to reclaim her, left her numb with fear.

Then the full realization hit her. She wasn't a widow. She was still a married woman. She hadn't thought she could hurt more than she already did, but she was wrong. Piece by piece, she was slowly dying.

James had followed. He pulled her into his arms. "I won't let him hurt you or those children ever again," he repeated. "He won't get near any of you. I'll die before I let that bastard touch any of you again."

His words, harsh and full of deadly promise, hung over their heads. Suddenly, it wasn't just her and her children in danger. James was in danger as well. Her fury drained. She turned in his arms and gripped his shoulders, frantic to make him understand. "No. No, you can't. You can't stay here. He'll kill you the first chance he gets."

"I'm not leaving."

"Yes, you have to—"

James took her mouth with his in a desperate kiss, which she returned. He pulled back, his voice harsh. "He can't have you. We belong together, you and I. Damn it, we belong."

Shaking her head, unable to fight with him, Eirica ran sobbing for her tent.

James watched her go, his heart frozen, his soul shattered. How could this happen? He paced, needing to rid himself of some of the fury roaring beneath the surface.

As the night deepened, he vowed that Birk would not destroy their love or their chance at happiness. Once they reached Oregon, he'd look into divorce laws. If it took all his share of the money he had stashed for a new start, he'd find a way to free Eirica of her mean and sick-minded husband.

Late into the night, brooding before the fire, James heard Lara crying, followed by the baby. He didn't hesitate to remove his boots and slip into the tent. Eirica started, a strangled scream in her throat.

"Shh, it's just me. Give me the baby."

He changed Summer while Eirica calmed Lara. Then he handed the infant to Eirica to nurse and gathered Lara in his arms, rocking her. Alison crawled over to him and he held her beside him. When both girls were back asleep, he covered them, then lay down behind Eirica, his arm draped around her waist. Summer lay in front of her, content until her next feeding.

Eirica leaned into him, her voice desperate in the dark. "What am I going to do, James?"

His lips moved across the back of her neck. "We'll take it one day at a time, sweetheart, one day at a time. It's all we can do."

Laying there, his face buried in her hair, surrounded by her scent, he held the woman who'd become infinitely precious to him. Around them, the children made noise. Ian slept soundly as normal while Alison and Lara moved restlessly, moaning occasionally in their sleep.

Though at least two hours had passed, he knew from her breathing that Eirica was still awake. He doubted either of them would sleep. He took comfort in the cocoon of warmth even though it couldn't dispel the chill in the recess of his heart. Everything had changed and he worried what the new day would bring.

James closed his eyes, desperately afraid he'd lose this woman. Though they were snuggled, a wide chasm separated them. His hold tightened and she pressed back into him. He felt the tremors run through her as she fought her own demons and vowed to do whatever it took to keep her and her children safe.

The next morning, Eirica rose, feeling stiff, sore and exhausted. She felt drained and wondered how'd she'd make it through the day. She'd spent the night fighting nightmares of the past and fears for the future. Even though James had held her throughout the long night, she hadn't been able to sleep. Her world had been turned upside down and she wasn't sure it would ever be right again. But she'd made one decision during the long night: She would not allow James to put himself at risk on her behalf. How could she live with herself if anything happened to him? Birk was out there, mean as ever. Any man who'd kidnap his own flesh and blood, his own daughter, and put her through this hell wouldn't hesitate to kill a man he saw as a threat.

Long into the night, Eirica had lain awake, thinking and planning. When she arose, she knew what she had to do. She had to distance herself from the man she loved. But she knew James well enough to know she'd never be able to convince him of the danger to himself. He wouldn't care.

He'd already started coffee brewing and when she joined him, he handed her a cup. "You okay?"

Eirica shook her head, feeling like she'd never be okay again. "James, you can't be here, not anymore."

As if he'd expected this from her, he stood abruptly, hot liquid sloshing over the edge of his cup to drip on his boots. "I'm not leaving you alone to face him. Don't try to tell me it's for my own good."

He knew her well, Eirica thought. She went to her second plan. "You have no choice. I'm still a married woman."

"So? You can divorce him. We'll find a way, but we're not going to let him drive us apart. I won't leave you."

This was the one time Eirica longed to lean on him, to allow him to shield her, protect her, but she couldn't. He didn't know Birk, didn't know what he was capable of. This time, she had to be strong. *She* had to protect James.

"You said you'd listen to me, consider my wishes. Were you lying? I'm asking you to do this my way."

James tossed his coffee to the ground. "That's unfair. It's one thing for me to ask if you need help with washing or if you want to take a walk, it's another to ask me to walk out of your life and leave you vulnerable to that bastard." He shoved both hands over his head. "I'm not leaving. I won't let him waltz in and resume where he left off."

Eirica straightened her shoulders. "Your being here isn't what's stopping him, James. It's Wolf, your brothers, Lars. It's everyone. He's too much of a coward to face them all. He proved that last night when he took Lara. He could've kept her, or—or harmed her— but he didn't, because his intent was simply to remind me that I'm still a married woman—his woman."

"You're not his woman."

Eirica smiled sadly. "You're right. I'm not. I won't live like that ever again, but if he's alive, then you and I can't be together."

James stalked around the fire, his heels churning up the dirt. "Hell, Eirica, there's no one around who would even dare think badly of you, especially since everyone thought you were a widow."

Standing up to James, fighting for his safety, was the hardest thing Eirica had ever done. She knew Birk would continue to watch her. If James wasn't around her, it was less likely that her cowardly husband would go into a rage and possible hurt or kill him. As much anguish as it caused her to hurt James in this manner, she had to stick to her resolve.

"What everyone thought no longer matters. I'm not a widow, was *never* a widow. Has it occurred to you that *I* might care what others think? If you love me, James, you'll do as I ask. You'll stay away."

"Are you asking me to forget that I love you, that you love me?" His voice rose with disbelief.

"No. I'm asking you to prove your love by doing as I ask." Eirica prayed he'd leave, and fast, so that she wouldn't break down in front of him. She wanted to shout, to scream at Birk, wherever he was, for what he was doing to her, to James to her babies. She wanted to tell him she'd found happiness that not even he could destroy—but he could. If he killed James, she'd be devastated, and that was exactly the type of punishment Birk would deem fitting: Kill the one person who meant the world to her.

James jammed his hat on his head and glared at her. "If that's what you want, fine. But we're not finished, Eirica, not by any means." He stalked away, mounted his horse and tore through the camp.

She watched until he faded from sight. "No," she said softly, "this isn't what I want. I don't want you to forget me or our love. I do love you, even if I'm not free to do so. But at least, you'll be safe. Please, Lord, keep him safe."

With tears running down her cheeks, she started her tasks, relying on routine to guide her as she couldn't think, couldn't feel. Her movements were jerky, clumsy. Visions of her grand future withered and died, but nestled deep in the core of her soul, safe from harm, hid one small gem, her love for James, more precious than any gemstone and rarer than the finest metal. She'd do whatever she had to do to protect him.

When she saw Jessie coming toward her, concerned and with the same stubborn look on her face as her brother, Eirica knew the others had heard her and James arguing. Eirica shook her head and walked into her tent. No one, not even Jessie, could make her change her mind.

Travel resumed as usual. Jessie and Coralie each took up positions on either side of Eirica. Her wagon had been placed between Rook's supply wagons. And if this morning, Rook had his rifle slung over his shoulder, no one made mention of it. Nor of the rifle Jessie carried. And those who'd heard Eirica's exchange with James that morning pretended not to have heard.

Eirica wasn't willing to risk the lives of the others either, but she knew from the determination on their faces, they weren't going to abandon her. Even Sofia and her family had taken positions around her. No words were spoken, but she understood and accepted their support for her children's sake. She'd learned her lesson well the day she'd nearly lost Ian when he'd fallen from the wagon. She'd never risk them.

The day passed without incident, as did the following day and the next after that. The emigrants crossed Three Island Crossing without any problems. But the atmosphere around the wagon train was dampened by what had happened to Lara, and to Eirica and James as a result.

Everyone, including Eirica, knew James spent his nights guarding Eirica's tent, arriving after she was in bed, gone before she rose. Eirica refused to talk about it to anyone. She'd closed herself off. Even Rook and Sofia's daily arguing had stopped. It was as if everyone was walking around on tiptoes for fear of not knowing what to say or how to act.

Everyone worried over Eirica. Gone was the pretty and blossoming woman who'd emerged after Birk's supposed drowning. Her easy smile and laughter had vanished along with the sparkle in her eyes. She kept to herself and with each passing day, her face thinned, and her eyes grew more haunted.

But it was little Lara who worried them most. She refused to let go of her mother except when Eirica had to feed the baby, then she'd let only Jessie or Rook take her. But she refused to talk, and she hadn't said a word since James and Eirica had found her. She refused most of the food she was served.

Even Kerstin and her brothers failed to draw her out of the silent world she'd retreated to. She sat, sucking her thumb, regarding anyone who came near with wide-eyed terror. Even Rook and his offering of another toy carving, this time of a bird, couldn't garner reaction from her.

Nearly two weeks later, Sofia joined Eirica, bringing her a pot of tempting stew. "Let me take the *bambino* for a bit while you eat."

"I'm not hungry, Sofia, but thank you." Eirica sat on the ground beside a blanket where the baby lay kicking her tiny feet and waving her arms.

"Nonsense. Enough moping." Sofia planted her hands on her ample hips. "What good are you to your children if you get sick? You're not eating, and you're not sleeping. You look like you're going to collapse and out here, that's the first step to dying."

Eirica lifted red-rimmed eyes to her. Dark shadows marred the delicate skin beneath her eyes. "I can't eat. I just feel so sick. Look at her." Eirica dropped her voice, her gaze filled with tears as she glanced down at the sleeping child who lay across her lap.

Sofia cleared the emotion from her throat. Eirica didn't need her sympathy. "Right now, it's Lara's mother I'm concerned with. If you don't eat and snap out of it, neither will she. And the child has lost more weight than she can afford, as have you. You need to stay strong, for them, for your man James." Sofia's heart went out to the young woman. She reached down and took the baby, who was awake and trying to play. Sofia cooed and got a gurgling smile in response.

"You have much to fight for, Eirica. You have your life and the life of your children, and your futures. And there is also a certain young man who's hurting every bit as much as you are. True love stands the test of many hard trials. You are denying both of yourselves this chance to work and solve your problems together."

"Having my husband alive is more than just a trial. I can't let James risk his life. And he would, Sofia." Her voice begged the woman to understand.

Sofia hardened her own heart. "Seems to me it's a question of faith and trust. Why would our God give James to you then return you to that man who doesn't deserve his family? And what about trust? By sending that young man of yours away, you're telling him that you don't trust him to make his own decisions. Weren't you the one all fired up when he tried to tell you what to do? Think about it. Think about James and think about your children, especially Alison. That little girl doesn't understand why her mama sent him away. The children need him as much as he needs all of you."

With that, Sofia walked off.

Sitting quietly, Eirica thought about Sofia's words. She pulled the rock James had given her from her pocket and rubbed her fingers over the smooth surface.

Trust yourself.

She closed her eyes, tried to gather the scattered pieces of her heart together. She had to be strong. She had to fight for what she wanted. Did she want James, happiness, love and laughter, enough to fight for it— with her life if need be?

She sat a bit straighter. "Yes, I do. I do," she whispered. For the first time since discovering Birk was alive, she glanced at her children who sat silent and watchful, their eyes full of fear—fear she was conveying to them.

Sofia was right. It was time she proved to herself that she was strong, that for them, she'd fight for what was right. And James was right for them. They needed him. *She* needed him. They'd take it one day at a time—as he'd suggested—if it weren't too late.

Standing, she served up bowlfuls of Sofia's aromatic stew and drew Alison out of the tent. She even managed to coax some of the broth into Lara's mouth. And all the while, she talked, trying to build back her family. She wouldn't shut them out. They needed to learn by her example how to be strong and fight for what was right. When Alison's features firmed, sharing her mother's determination, Eirica felt like maybe everything would be all right.

Sofia returned to Rook who waited behind one of his wagons. She spoke softly to him. He grinned and nodded, then fetched a small pan of food, mounted his old nag and rode out to the cattle. When he found James, he called him over and dished him up a bowl filled with chunks of meat, noodles and spices, most of which he still had no idea what they were.

James shook his head. "I'll eat later."

Rook drew his bushy brows together. "The hell ya will. You's starving yerself like the lass. What good will ya be ta her if ya falls sick?"

James turned away. "It's over. Eirica doesn't want me. She won't even speak to me."

Rook's bushy brows rose. "And why do ya suppose that is?'

Scowling, James adjusted his hat. " 'Cause she's married!"

"And ta protect ya."

James made a rude noise. "She's the one who needs protecting."

"Then why are ya way out here and not watching o'er that sweet woman and her children?"

James heaved a huge sigh. "I promised to listen to her, to do it her way."

"Women, they's funny creatures. If I'd listened to my Annabelle each time she spoke, we's never would have had a life together. Most of the time, if I did as she said, I wound up in deeper trouble. Sometimes, ya has to ask yerself if that's what they really wants. Or if that's what they really need. Sometimes, a man has to do what's right, no matter what his woman says."

Mulling over Rook's words, James took a bowl of chow without even being aware of it. "Still don't help me none if she don't want me around." James frowned into the bowl, the spoon halfway to his mouth. He dropped it once again unable to eat.

"Do ya love the lass?" Rook knew the answer would be yes. When James nodded, he stated, "And she still loves you. Seems a mighty funny way ta show it to the other, with ya here and her there."

Noticing that James was suddenly not only eating but in deep thought, Rook rode away, pleased. He and Sofia sure made a good team these days.

By the time James finished the meal, he felt warmed, inside and out. Hope welled inside him. By golly, Eirica needed him, now more than ever and he was a fool to have given in to her request. He hadn't wanted to run roughshod over her, to force her into accepting his help, so he'd given in, trying to prove his love.

But she was wrong. The way to prove his love to her was to return to her side and stand by her through thick and thin. He had to convince her that they had to lay the foundation for their future by working together, starting now.

Tonight, he'd take up his usual watch. Tomorrow morning, they'd talk.

Chapter Seventeen

The next morning, James waited outside Eirica's tent for her to emerge. He paced, firming in his mind his arguments and reasons why they had to stay together. Long into the night, he'd thought about Eirica and the situation. If anything happened to her because he'd stayed away, he'd live with the guilt forever. Rook was right. His place was here, and if his insistence on remaining angered her, then so be it. His mind was made up. Birk would have to go through him to get to Eirica.

James still had a hard time accepting that the man had survived. It was incredible. Normally James wasn't vindictive and would never wish death on anyone, but not so with Birk. Any man who'd terrorize a sweet little child like Lara deserved to be strung up by his toes as his sister used to say of Coralie after their many altercations. Hell, the bastard deserved much worse. Eirica and her children had suffered more than enough at his hands. Keeping himself busy, he put on a pot of water to boil. By the time Eirica stepped out of her tent, he had two cups of cocoa waiting.

"Eirica," he greeted, taking in her ragged appearance. She looked as worn around the edges as he felt.

"James." Her voice trembled slightly and she stood there, staring at him as if uncertain of her reception.

He tossed his hat into the back of the wagon and held out his arms, eager to hold her close, yet afraid she'd refuse to talk to him. To his relief, she cried out and flew into his arms. James held her tightly, afraid to let her go. The children still slept, so it was just the two of them. Somehow, in the short amount of time he had before they woke, he had to convince her that together, they could stand up to Birk and win.

"God, I've missed you, sweetheart. Don't send me away. Not ever again." His heart sang. They could work this out. Somehow, their love would make it all right. "Let me stay and help you. Together we'll take care of each other, and the children. Together, we'll fight for *our* future, yours and mine and theirs."

Eirica shook her head against him. "I won't. Not ever again. I love you so much it hurts."

"You have no idea how much I needed to hear you say that," he groaned. He pulled back and tipped her chin. "I love you, Eirica. You are my life. Without you, there is no sun. No warmth, no beauty, just a frozen, bleak world. Your love is the light that gives my heart and soul life."

Eirica trailed the back of her fingers across the stubble staining his jaw. "God help me but how can I send away a man who speaks like a poet and sings like an angel? Yet how can I ask you to stay and risk your life?"

James wiped the tears streaming down her face.

"Nothing will happen to me. We'll be safe, at least until we reach Oregon City."

"And then?"

"Then we have to make new plans. But for now, we'll just take it one day at a time. You have to trust me, sweetheart."

For the first time in days, Eirica smiled. She drew out his rock. "Wrong, Mr. Jones. We have to trust each other." She placed the rock in his palm and covered it with her own palm.

Together they sat, clasping the stone between them until James couldn't wait any longer to kiss her, his soul starved for her touch. He dropped the rock back into her pocket and drew her close.

Eirica responded, her arms tight around his neck, her fingers buried in his hair. Their lips met for a long, searing kiss. Frantic need to believe him consumed her. Somehow, she had to believe he and Sofia were right. Somehow, everything would work out. Surely God wouldn't be so cruel as to show her what true love was, then deny it to her? Her hands slid around to his back; his encircled her. Neither paid attention to the lightening sky or the movement of others around them.

"I love you, Eirica. I'll love you no matter what."

Eirica pulled back, reluctantly ending the kiss. She felt torn between their love, her need to touch him and have him touch her, and by what was right for both of them. "I'm married," she reminded him. "What if I can't get a divorce from Birk? What if I'm never free of him?"

James took several deep breaths. "No matter what, Eirica, I'll be there for you. We'll win, sweetheart." He kissed her again, slowly, tenderly.

Summer's hungry wail ended their kiss and their time alone. "I know you're married and I respect that. We won't make love until you're free but don't ask me not to touch you or kiss you."

"But you need children of your own." Eirica couldn't stand the thought of never making love to this man again.

He smiled at her, so sure, so strong. "I have four children whom I love. And one of them needs her ma right now. Wait here. I'll bring her out."

A few minutes later, James returned with Summer cradled in his arms. Eirica loved the sight of this big man holding her infant daughter. He held the baby out in front of him, her body supported by his palms as he smiled and cooed at her, trying to stop her hungry wails. He was so gentle, so loving, a natural father. She couldn't remember her pa or Birk ever holding any of their children.

Using the blanket Anne had knitted to shield herself from the others, she allowed James to put the baby to her breast. He sat next to her. She blushed as he watched Summer latch on to the engorged nipple. Part of her rejoiced at his pleasure in something so natural, so elemental. She turned her head to look at him. His hand slid up her throat and drew her lips to his in a tender kiss.

"I'll start cooking. I stole some of Sofia's pancake batter. We'll surprise the children." He stood and went to the back of the wagon.

Eirica knew, and so did he, that it would take much more than sweetened pancakes to make her children feel secure again. But at least they could see that she and James, together, were there to love and protect them. When she finished nursing, she joined James, working alongside him as if they'd done it for years rather than weeks.

When the whistle sounded to head out, they were ready. Jessie came over and took charge of the oxen to free James to help Eirica. James picked up Lara. Alison and Ian walked in front of them, while Eirica carried Summer. James put his free arm around Eirica's shoulder.

At his touch, the warm strength holding her securely against him, Eirica stiffened, fighting a moment's panic as she glanced around. Then his scent, warm and savory surrounded her, soothing her raw nerves. But she couldn't help watching, wondering when Birk would show himself.

"Relax. It's all right. He's not going to jump out at us. He's hiding."

Eirica knew James was right. Birk would wait until night, spying on them, hidden by the crowds and the cover of darkness. Still, she couldn't help but stare around her. It took a few minutes, but Eirica became aware of a difference in the formation of the wagon trail. Rook rode next to Jessie who kept the oxen moving by cracking her whip over their backs when they hesitated.

Turning her head, Eirica noted that Jordan was with Coralie behind them. She frowned. Jordan never stayed with the wagons during the day. Even Wolf was still with them, riding in the lead instead of returning to the cattle as was his habit if there were no problems with any of the wagons or the trail.

Sofia and her family along with Lars and his flanked them on the other side.

"Where's Elliot?"

James snickered. "Riding drag."

She lifted her brow. "He's helping with the cattle?"

"Yep." Though the words were light, Eirica realized that everyone had rallied to form a protective circle around her and James. Birk wouldn't be able to get to either one of them during the day.

"Did you arrange this?" She waved her hand at the placement of people they knew so well.

James smiled. "No. But that's what family is for, Eirica. We protect our own and stand together."

Eirica marveled at the thought that these people would give so much, and without thought. Looking at each and every person, she realized that she'd do the same. There wasn't a single person she wouldn't defend or help as they were protecting her. Again she was struck by the true meaning of family. James was right when he'd told her that her own relatives had failed her.

Eirica glanced at her children, then at James, and she felt a warm glow settle in her heart. The six of them looked like a family. A happy one. She took a deep breath. Somehow, they'd make it and starting right now, they'd stick together as a family should.

Hidden deep in a gully near Farewell Bend, Birk finished off his meal of hard biscuits and dried salmon that he and Zeb had gotten from a squaw near Salmon Falls. Smacking his lips, he uncapped his flask of rotgut and drank deeply, then stretched his arms over his head.

After another long drink, he set the flask down and crawled on his belly to the edge of the gully to look down onto the trail following the Snake River. He scanned the long line of wagons that moved past and frowned. Glancing up at the sky, he studied the position of the sun.

"No sign of 'em yet," he muttered to himself. "They should've got here by now."

Letting out a belch, Birk scrubbed his lips with the back of his hand. After taking Lara to warn his wife he was there, he and Zeb had ridden hard to get ahead and find a safe place to hide and wait for them. This secluded nook between hills overlooking the trail was the perfect spot. But after spending the last three days watching and waiting, he was beginning to fear they'd somehow missed them. Taking one last look up and down the trail, he yawned and slid back down. Pulling his stolen hat down over his eyes, he fell asleep.

By late afternoon, a layer of dark clouds swept across the sky and a splattering of raindrops fell.

Zeb's return woke him. "They's a-comin'."

Both men moved back to the top of the hill. After awhile, Birk spotted the large herd of cattle in the distance and scanned the wagons approaching. It was hard to make out individuals, so he moved down the hillside, staying low and in the narrow gullies. Finally, he saw her and his brats, but what made him tighten his hold on a nice, shiny new rifle he'd stolen three nights ago was the sight of his wife walking next to that woman-stealing Jones bastard. His lips twisted and in his fury, he forgot to breathe. His face reddened, his chest hurt and red swam before his eyes.

As if flaunting their disregard of his warning, James put an arm around Eirica's shoulder and shifted the infant to his other side. Birk nearly stood and shouted at them, so great was his fury. She was his; she knew that and was deliberately defying him. He stroked his weapon, lifted it and took aim at James. All he had to do was pull the trigger. Then, bang, the bastard would be gone. He'd teach that bitch to look at another man.

Unlike his shotgun, this one could bring down prey at a distance.

Maybe he should just kill *her*. All this was her fault. He moved the barrel and sighted her. Nah, if he killed her, he'd do it slowly so that he could watch her suffer. Smirking, he trained the rifle on each of his children.

Damn brats. His heart raced and he returned the sight to James. It struck him how happy the damn lot of them looked. He narrowed his eyes. Not for long. They'd suffer, all of them.

It wasn't fair. Fury over his lot in life washed over him, making him forget his surroundings. In his mind's eye, he saw his ma, heard the contempt in her voice as she demanded he sit in a corner, on his knees, for hours and pray for her sins.

And he had. He'd prayed when his ma demanded it, he'd obeyed her, submitted to her beatings and carried out her beliefs but what had it gotten him? A runaway, two-timing wife and a bunch of whining brats. Where was his reward? He was due. By God, he was due. Taking sight, he moved his finger to the trigger. And what better reward than watching them die one at a time?

A sudden growl off to the side penetrated the foggy haze of his need for revenge. Startled, he scooted around and saw a large white wolf standing on the small rise just below him. The beast eyed him with fangs bared. The animal stood between him and his target. Then it was too late. His wife and her lover were out of range. Below him, Wolf's men were now passing with the cattle. Damn. He didn't dare do anything now, including killing that damn wolf. They'd be up on him as soon as they heard the shot. "Just you wait, wife-of-mine," he whispered.

Escaping the wolf who seemed content to stay where it had been, Birk scurried back to where Zeb was helping himself to the flask of whiskey. He'd bide his time, wait as originally planned for them to reach Oregon. Then he'd get his revenge on them all. He had time. Lots of time. "Let's move out. They's gone."

They walked over to the pack mules grazing nearby along with the horses. When Zeb mounted, Birk asked, "Did ya do as I said with that last lock of hair?"

Zeb nodded. "Yeah, that wife of yers won't be able to help noticing our little present." He snickered, then belched.

Birk gathered his belongings and tied them behind his saddle. But before he could mount, he saw a flash of white coming straight for him. Yelling for Zeb to get his shotgun, Birk leaped into the saddle, but not before he felt the stab of fangs sinking into his buttocks. He kicked his booted foot at the wolf and heard the tear of cloth. Glancing down, he spotted Jessie's dog beside the wagon master's wolf, both barking and growling.

"Shoot them," Birk yelled to Zeb. He himself was barely able to control his mount, let alone handle his shotgun. But Zeb was having the same trouble. Together, the two managed to wheel their screaming horses around, grab the reins of their frightened pack mules and take off, galloping deeper into the hills.

Finally, having escaped their canine pursuers, they turned westward, staying ahead of the travelers.

Jessie and Lara sat in the wagon with Sadie and her puppies. Jessie hoped the puppies would draw a smile or some reaction from the little girl but they'd done nothing so far. Suddenly, Sadie growled, the sound a low rumble in her throat. The dog jumped from the moving wagon, her growls turning into warning barks as she ran for the hills. Jessie started to follow, but Lara's cry stopped her.

Knowing she couldn't leave the little girl, Jessie yelled, "Sadie, come!"

The dog ignored her, stopping at the top of a hill. Jessie could just make out a flash of white ahead of Sadie. She frowned. Something had riled both animals. What was it? Birk? She pulled her Sharps rifle nearer without letting Lara see, then she watched, all the while talking softly to Lara and the pups.

When Sadie and the wolf returned, Jessie noted their ruffled fur. Wahoska had something in his mouth and the white fur beneath his chin was stained pink. She reached down and pulled a bit of cloth from his fangs. Conscious of the child behind her, Jessie patted both animals on the head. "Good job," she whispered. "I'll have Rook give you both a nice big bone." Both wagged their tails. Muffled squeals and sharp barks came from behind Jessie and she moved aside.

"Now get back in here with your babies." Jessie's husband had removed one plank from the tailgate so the dog and wolf could hop in and out easier, though now that the pups were four weeks old Wolf would soon have to put it back to keep them in. Sadie leaped up. Immediately, her pups converged upon her, fighting one another to reach a free nipple. A soft giggle came from Lara. One of the pups, not interested in food, was giving the girl a hearty face-washing.

Jessie noted the markings. "I'll bet you and your sisters and brother would like a puppy of your own, right, Lara?"

The little girl nodded shyly, then went back to sucking her thumb, her blanket clutched tightly in her fist.

Jessie already knew James wanted at least one of Sadie's litter. He'd always loved her dog and Jessie and Wolf would take the dog and wolf back with them when they returned from Oregon. Jessie reached out to stroke Sadie's fat, furry body. Lara squeaked. When the puppy had realized he was losing out on his meal, he'd returned to fight among his litter mates for a teat of his own.

Though Lara wasn't yet speaking, Jessie felt pleased that she'd gotten a happy reaction from her. James and Eirica would be thrilled with that news. However, that bit of joy would fade when she showed them and Wolf what Wahoska had brought back with him. The watching and waiting was telling on all of them. Birk was out there, trailing them. Of that, there was no doubt. Wahoska would not attack someone indiscriminately.

"I sure wish Ma and Pa would let me have one of your puppies, Jessie."

Jessie turned to see Rickard—the Svensson boy— looking in over the back of the wagon. Behind him, the team of oxen in his charge plodded along slowly. He laughed when Sadie licked each pup, eliciting squeals of protest from them and stirring the furry pile into happy playing. The jostling of the wagon made the pups tip over and roll on the padded wagon bottom.

Seeing Rickard's wistful expression, Jessie grabbed a small female with a white face. Jessie knew it was Rickard's favorite. She'd already planned on giving it to him—with his parents' permission. But she'd wanted it to be a surprise, so she hadn't told him. Instead, she handed the pup to him. "Would you like to take her for a while?"

Susan Edwards

Rickard's gaze widened. "You don't think Sadie will mind, do you?"

Jessie glanced at her dog, but Sadie seemed to prefer napping while the other little dogs climbed over her body in their puppyish antics. "She trusts you."

"Gee thanks, Jess. Well, I gotta get back to work." With that, the boy tucked the yawning pup inside his shirt and resumed his place beside the oxen.

Jessie hopped out of the wagon, then lifted Lara down, too. Thinking of the wolf's find, she stood a moment, indecisive as to what to do. With her hands on hips, she scanned the area, looking for the animal, but saw no sign of him. He'd run off. Oh well, Wahoska could take care of himself. She hurried up to fall into step beside Eirica some ways ahead. Lara walked between them, tightly holding on to her mother's hand.

Jessie offered to carry Summer for a bit. Coralie wasn't the only one who needed to practice and learn what to do with a baby, though she and Wolf hadn't told anyone yet. Still, both knew it wouldn't be long before the others guessed for themselves. Though not as far along as her sister-in-law, she already had to leave her pants unbuttoned and use a length of rope to hold them up. Good thing she had some loose flannel shirts. The one dress she owned was already too tight. She sighed with a mixture of disgust and dismay. Guess she was going to have to ask Anne to help her sew some new dresses.

Chapter Eighteen

"We have to go over those?" Coralie squeaked, her eyes round with disbelief.

"I'm afraid so," Eirica replied, torn between relief at having made it this far and fear of the last leg of the journey. From where the now close-knit group of women stood, the mountain range on the other side of the valley loomed large and imposing.

She glanced down. The descent into the valley below was so steep, it required the use of several switchbacks to zigzag their way to the bottom. She stared at the wagons already heading down. The noses of one team of oxen nearly touched the back wheels of the wagon in front of it.

Eirica glanced sideways at Jessie who for once wasn't eagerly anticipating a new "adventure." In fact, the woman looked quite pale, sick even. "Are you all right?"

Coralie took her sister-in-law by the arm. "Come

on, Jessica, buck up and let's get this over with. The sickness will pass before you know it. If it gets too bad, ask Rook to fix you his special tea."

"What sickness? I'm just tired." Jessie resisted and tried to put some spirit behind her denial but failed. None of them were fooled.

Coralie rolled her eyes and clucked her tongue, shaking her head, her blond curls swaying across her shoulders. "Do you honestly think you can hide your delicate condition from us? We all know. Even Jordan knows."

Jessie straightened with a jerk. "What! My brother? How can *he* know? Wolf promised he wouldn't say anything."

Coralie pulled her onward. "Boy, is your mind muddled. How can you possibly think you could hide the fact that you've suddenly developed a figure? I'd like to see you try to bind your breasts now. That wouldn't work." She laughed. "Sadly, Jessie, your days of passing yourself off as a boy are over." Coralie frowned for a moment, staring at Jessie's middle. "And those shirts don't hide the swelling, though how you can already be showing when I'm just barely showing is beyond me."

In front of Jessie and Coralie, Anne and Eirica turned their heads. Pleased smiles confirmed that Coralie was right. They knew. "All right, I didn't want anyone to worry," Jessie grumbled, rubbing her stomach. "Wolf is bad enough." She wrinkled her nose then sighed. "Well, since you're so smug about it, you're helping Rook tonight. I'm so tired, all I want to do is sleep."

Laughing, Coralie nodded, her blue eyes sparkling with happiness. "Guess what? I think I felt my baby move yesterday. It was just a strange little flutter, but

Anne and Eirica said that's what it feels like at first."
Coralie looked pleased, one hand pressing against her
abdomen.

Eirica and Anne joined in for a lively discussion and
soon all of them were chattering excitedly, their trepidation about the descent forgotten as the woman
exchanged knowledge and discussed possible baby
names. By the time they finished the climb down,
Eirica and Anne had promised to help Jessie make
some more dresses.

Coralie nudged Jessie. "I'm going to make your
baby a frilly pink dress."

Everyone laughed. Eirica couldn't imagine Jessie
dressing any daughter of hers in frills and lace.

"I have so much, you and Coralie could share,"
Eirica offered, thinking of all the wonderful gifts
she'd received. She appreciated the work that had
gone into her own baby gifts and was eager to join in
on the new sewing marathon to come. Coralie had
already given her some material to make Jessie a
wrapper dress. And Eirica knew Sofia and Anne were
also busy with their sewing projects. But she had so
much, she felt guilty.

"Nope," Jessie said with a laugh. "I have a feeling
my brother will want more children. You'll need
them."

Eirica blushed. "I'd like to have James's baby," she
said softly, staring down into her daughters wide, blue
eyes. "Maybe a boy next time—with his daddy's black
hair and green eyes."

Everyone sighed happily. "I can't believe how
much has happened in the last five months. We've had
a wedding, a birth and now the two of you are with
child."

"And soon to be another wedding." Jessie smiled.

Eirica felt her eyes tear up. "I hope so." She kept to herself her fears of the future.

"You don't know my brother. Stubborness and determination are the traits of us Joneses."

Coralie looked smug for a moment, then whispered, "If you want my opinion, we're going to have *three* more weddings." She glanced at Sofia and Catarina.

Talk turned to Catarina and Elliot's courtship, then to the blossoming romance between Sofia and Rook. Lost in her own dreams of her own future, one Eirica clung to, she and the others began the walk across the Grande Ronde Valley.

A few days later, the emigrants ascended into the densely wooded Blue Mountains. Towering pine spruce and balsom all but blocked the narrow trail through the thickly forested mountain. Beside the trail, tall grass and weeds were a welcome sight after the choking dust of the arid desert, and the bracing air and deep shade were a relief after the parching heat.

The sound of birds singing overhead completed the pastoral scene and made Eirica feel as though they'd stepped into another world. Echoing throughout the woods, voices of fellow travelers were heard, though the emigrants could only see those who were directly in front of them on the winding road through the forest. Even the sky above was nearly blotted out by the gigantic trees. Though the sounds gave a sense of unity in their one common goal, the thickness of the forest retained a feeling of privacy.

Periodically, gunfire sounded. Game was once again in abundance for those who sought it, as were berries and other edible plants. And for the first time in months, firewood was plentiful.

They were into the fourth week of September, so

fear of snow kept them moving, pushing themselves and their animals ever forward. The going was slow and rough, but the mood was lighter, filled with hope. They were nearly to their destinations.

During what would probably be one of their last days of rest, Eirica and James sat in front of the Macauley tent with a fire burning brightly. The flames took the edge off the chill in the air, though James also had made it bigger than normal to set the mood. He cradled Eirica between his thighs, her head resting in the crook of his neck and shoulder. In silence, they sat in the warm glow with a canopy of stars, bright as sparkling jewels peeping through the treetops overhead.

James sat lost in thought. He didn't see the golden-orange and red flames as they licked at the generous pile of logs and twigs. Nor did he hear the occasional sparks as they popped and floated toward the starry heavens only to cool and fall back to the earth.

Fear of losing Eirica once they reached Oregon ate at him. A restless panic was beginning to assail him and it grew steadily worse with each mile covered. He tried to hide it from Eirica, but he knew she, too, feared what awaited them. Birk had made sure they knew he was in front of them.

They'd found Lara's mocassin hanging from the limb of a tree just that morning, not far from where they'd camped for the night. And they'd found another lock of Lara's hair stuck in the bleached-white broken skull of an oxen shortly at Farewell Bend. Only the cut hem of her dress hadn't been found. Either Birk was saving it or they'd missed it.

Though Lara had finally begun talking again, she still wouldn't go off without either James, Eirica, Rook or Jessie. James knew it'd take a long time for her to again feel safe. And her frightening ordeal had affected Alison as well. It'd taken James a lot of work to bring back the eager, adventurous child who dogged his steps whenever she could.

What would happen to them when Birk came after them? And he would. Sooner or later, that bastard would show up and undo all the work he and Eirica had accomplished with the two girls. He sighed, wishing he knew what to do.

The mere thought of losing Eirica filled him with such despair, he couldn't bear to think of it. Somehow they had to find a way for Eirica to divorce Birk. Then came the harder task of safeguarding her and the children once Eirica was free. But how? He couldn't be around them every minute of the day. His own sense of helplessness nearly drove him crazy. He hated this. He hated the wondering and waiting and worrying.

Eirica glanced up at him then lifted one hand to his taut jaw. "There's not much we can do now, James. As you said, one day at a time."

James leaned into her hand. "The fear of failing you hurts. What if I can't keep you safe in Oregon?"

Eirica turned in his arms, sitting sideways across his lap. "You've told me more times than I can count to be strong. Now I'm telling you the same thing. We have to be strong, and we can only do our best." She closed her eyes for a moment. "I'm afraid, too, James. But we've taken precautions, the rest is a waiting game and my husb—Birk knows it. We can't allow fear to rule us, or come between us. If we do, he wins. We have to stay calm and alert. That is how we will win against him. Once Birk gets angry, he loses all control. But we'll have plans. We'll outsmart him."

James stroked her hair. "He could be out there, watching us even as we speak. Maybe this fire isn't a good idea." James peered into the surrounding darkness, hating the idea of Birk watching them, and wondering what might push the man over the edge.

"This fire is heavenly. Sitting with you in front of it makes me want to do this for the rest of my life. I'm determined we will spend our evenings together in front of a beautiful fire like this one. If Birk is out there, there's nothing much we can do now but ignore it."

Eirica took his hand in hers and brought it to her face. Where once she'd been afraid of his hands, now she loved the feel of his rough, calloused palm against her face. She leaned into his hand, seeking the words to comfort him as he'd always done for her.

"With Sadie and Wahoska prowling the area, Birk won't be anywhere near us." Unspoken was the knowledge that the wolf had attacked Birk. Jessie had told them of the cloth she'd found. Several times lately, both animals had started barking for no apparent reason. James felt some measure of comfort in her words. She was right. Neither animal would let Birk too close.

Eirica watched James, willing him to put his worries aside. She, too, feared what the future held in store for them, and worried about Birk. But that only made her more determined to take advantage of each and every minute with James. If their time together was short, she refused to allow Birk to taint it. She'd done what she could to protect her family. Without James's knowledge, she'd made arrangements with Jessie to take care of her children if something happened to her and James. Birk would not get his hands on them. Jessie and Wolf had promised to do whatever it took to protect them and raise them. Her friends would hide them, then take them back to the Nebraska Territory when they went.

She waited for James to say something, hating to

see the worry clouding his gaze. Like her daughter Lara, James was a worrier, and tended to stew, regardless if there was much he could do about the situation. Rising onto her knees, she pressed her lips to his in a quick kiss, then she sat back on her heels.

"James Noah Jones, you will stop this instant! I won't have our time together ruined by the man I had the unfortunate error as a young, naive girl to marry. I have to believe that the Lord, who has shown me what love is, will protect us and allow us to marry and live without fear." She wrapped her arms around his neck and stretched her fingers into the hair at the nape of his neck. "Now kiss me. No sense letting this beautiful fire and wonderful night go to waste."

She sighed when he finally gathered her close.

"Anyone ever tell you that you're getting mighty bossy?" he whispered in her ear, his breath warm.

Eirica playfully bit his earlobe. "You, every night for the last week." She pulled back so she could look at him. "But tonight, I'm serious. We're a team, remember? We'll work it out together."

She pulled out the stone and dropped it in his palm. "Trust me."

James clenched the rock and smiled at her, his eyes full of love and tenderness. "With all my heart." Then he lowered his head.

If there was a hint of desperation in their embrace, in the frantic need each conveyed to the other as their mouths met for a long kiss, it left them both breathless and aching for more.

Eirica fought her desire for James. Though they'd not made love since discovering Birk was still alive, she couldn't cut off all contact with James. Sitting together in the evenings, stealing a kiss here and there, had to suffice. And if they couldn't marry, well, she'd decide then what to do with the urges and needs welling inside her. But the one thing she didn't want to risk was becoming with child. As much as she wanted James's baby, she wanted that baby born with *his* name—a legal part of her family, not bastard-born.

Eirica sighed when James lifted his head to stare at her, his eyes unreadable.

"I love you, James," she whispered.

"Not as much as I love you." He angled his mouth back over hers.

By the time they broke apart and turned to the fire, cuddled together, there was no struggle as to who loved whom more. It was a tie, and their love continued to build—which made their vows to fight for the future even stronger.

A week later, the emigrants stood teary-eyed at a point before the Dalles. The Svenssons had decided to leave Wolf's party and take the river route the rest of the way into Oregon. They planned on ferrying down the Columbia River to Fort Vancouver, then navigate up the Willamette River to claim their new land. With the herd of cattle and the horses, Wolf had decided to take the overland route through the Barlow Road.

Jessie, Coralie, Eirica, Sofia, Catarina, and Anne stood hugging and crying, their handkerchiefs sodden with their farewell tears. "I'm going to miss you, Anne," Eirica cried, hugging the woman. She'd become a good friend and role model. One day, she, too, would have a marriage as wonderful as Anne and Lars, did. She stepped back to allow Jessie her turn to hug the woman. Jessie wore the new calico dress Anne had made with fabric Coralie had given to her. Eirica smiled. It was odd to see Jessie in a dress, a beautiful woman instead of the tomboy they'd met at the beginning of the expedition.

Anne sniffed. "We'll see you in Oregon City. I'll leave word where we go. We'll find each other again, I promise you all." Anne then turned to the others. "Who knows, we might be neighbors," she offered in an effort to make the parting less painful.

Wolf, Jordan, James, Rook and Elliot stepped forward to each claim his woman. "Dry your tears, woman," Lars ordered his wife gruffly. "It's time to go."

Lars led Anne away. She turned and waved. Eirica picked up Lara and together, they waved to Hanna and Kerstin. How she'd miss them. Behind her, Jessie's frantic voice drew her attention.

"Wolf, where's Rickard? I haven't said my good-byes. They can't leave until I see him."

"Jessica, you'll see them soon."

Jessie turned away and ran to her wagon, tears streaming down her cheeks. She hadn't realized how much she'd miss Anne's youngest boy. He'd become the younger brother she didn't have: someone who looked up to her, wanted to be like her. She'd spent the last five months teaching him everything she knew. She smiled through her tears, recalling his difficulty in handling the oxen on the day they'd left Westport. She'd resented him, hated the idea that he was to be in charge of her team. That was back when Wolf hadn't trusted her. But Rickard's own lack of experience had triggered something in her; she'd been the one who taught *him* to snap a whip and handle the oxen.

And when he'd shot himself in the foot trying, along with the rest of the emigrants, to keep the stampeding herd of cattle from their wagons, she'd taught him how to handle his weapon. Pride filled her. While he still was not as good a shot as she was, he was improving. And with the whip, he'd excelled. When he cracked it now, it sounded like lightning.

"Jessie?"

She turned at the sound of his voice. Letting out a cry of relieved joy, she ran to him. They held each other tight. "I'll miss you, Rickard."

"I'll miss you, too, Jessie. I ain't never had an older sister till I met you."

Jessie sniffed. "You take care. Don't shoot yourself or fall in the water or do anything else stupid. If you do, you'll answer to me."

Rickard grinned. "I won't." His gaze slid toward the wagon where the pups were yapping, protesting at having to be confined to the wagon.

Lars shouted for Rickard. The boy shifted from one foot to the other. "I guess I gotta go."

Jessie grinned with anticipation. "Wait. I have something for you."

She reached inside the wagon and pulled out the pup with the white face, his pup, complete with a collar around its neck and a length of rope attached. A pink bow attached to the collar was Coralie's insistent contribution. "She's yours. You'd better take care of her, you hear?"

Rickard's face split into a wide grin. "Oh, wow! Gee, thanks, Jess!" He hugged the pup close and giggled when the furry animal twisted around to lick his face. After a final hug, he ran back to his parents with his precious bundle stuffed down his shirt.

All too soon, Wolf indicated that it was time for the rest of them to move out as well.

For the two men hidden along the trail, revenge was nearly within their grasp. Birk and Zeb lay on their

Susan Edwards

bellies, concealed beneath some bushes high on the
hillside. Birk had been relieved that the group had
split, there were now fewer of them to deal with in
Oregon.

Right now, Wolf and the Joneses posed his biggest
problem in getting to Eirica, them and those damn animals. Anytime he got too close, he'd stumble across
the dog or wolf prowling around the perimeter of the
camp. And whenever Eirica left the camp, it was
always with them damn Joneses. They never let her or
his brats out of their sight. He fingered his shotgun.

Before this was over, James Jones would be a dead
man.

Somehow, he'd get Eirica back. Maybe he'd just grab
her, the hell with his children. They were too much trouble. He frowned, knowing it'd take him a while to get his
wife back to being submissive again. He didn't like the
changes he'd seen in her when spying on her. She'd gotten too independent. Perhaps he'd have to take at least
one of his brats with him. Maybe Lara, the quiet one. He
could keep her, at least until he had Eirica away from the
others. He planned on heading down to California, taking her as far from those friends of hers as he could.

While Zeb scouted ahead, checking on Wolf's
wagon train—they'd decided to fall behind and tail the
group so there was no chance of losing them—Birk
helped himself to the whiskey flask. It was nearly
empty. They'd have to find more, maybe tonight. He
lay there, in the thick pile of leaves and compost on the
forest floor, and let his mind wander to the enjoyment
of reclaiming Eirica.

Imagining her fear, her cowering before him made
him squirm with excitement. Damn, his need was
growing. He needed release. Though he'd eased his
stiffness many times on his own, his body wouldn't be

312

satisfied until he was able to lie between her legs, see her fear and hear her cries as he forced her to submit to his dominance of her body.

He groaned, emptied the bottle and tossed it away. Suddenly, Zeb returned from his scouting. "Now's our chance. Them women is up ahead, alone. One of the wagons broke an axle and the menfolk are dealing with it. It'll be a while afore they get it goin'. I say we get 'em now."

Zeb fingered the deep scar that ran the length of one cheek. He took his knife from his sheath and ran his finger down the long blade. "I gots me a score to settle with that bitch with tha whip."

Birk ignored Zeb's ravings as he tried to clear his drink-muddled mind and think. Could they nab the Jones woman and his wife and get away? Would that half-breed track them down? He grinned. Maybe they could get far enough to have some fun with the Jones woman then get rid of her. He slid a glance at Zeb. As soon as he killed his wife-lusting, drinking buddy, it'd just be him and Eirica. Without any of them brats they'd be able to go faster, and if she gave him any trouble, maybe he'd just take care of her, too.

Maybe it would just be easier to get himself a new bride, one he could train new to please him. The more he thought of it, thought of the trouble Eirica had caused him and the very idea that another man might have had her, the less he wanted her back. Yet he had a strong, powerful need to vent himself on her. Deciding to think about it some more later, he stood. "Show me where they are and we'll see. When I take my woman back, I don't want no one interfering again!"

Zeb rubbed his hands together. "It'll be perfect. Them women are all alone. We jest take them all into

these woods a ways and have some fun. And with that
blond beauty with them other two, there's more 'n
enough to go 'round. All we's got ta do is gag them
and nobody will know." Zeb's voice was a hoarse
whisper.

They stopped where they'd hidden their bulging
packs. They'd traded their pack mules and horses for
more food and drink once they'd entered the mountains. It was too hard to conceal their presence with
the four animals. Birk grabbed the hem of his daughter's dress in case they needed it to use as a gag and
shoved it in his pocket, then he hefted his pack onto
his back. Both men grabbed ropes and their shotguns.
Birk carried his Sharps rifle. The sound of wagons
creaking along the trail and raised voices concealed
their presence.

They passed where the women walked and Zeb led
Birk to where the trail ended at a steep hill. "They's
gonna have to stop here at Laurel Hill ta wait fer the
others. They still don't know they are way ahead of
them others in their party. And with the broken wagon
blocking the trail, all we has ta do is wait for the wagons ahead of them ta get down—then we's takes what
we wants. Nobody around ta stop us. Man, I can't wait
ta taste heaven with that angel," Zeb said, his voice
rough with lust.

Birk felt his face redden and his pulse pumped with
renewed fury. Whether he kept Eirica around or not,
no one else was touching her, especially not Zeb.
"Eirica's mine. The bitch will pay for what she done."
He pulled at the front of his trousers in an attempt to
ease his painful erection.

Zeb narrowed his beady eyes. "Wadaya mean,
yours? Ya promised to share her. What with all that
red hair, yer wife should be real spirited and spunky."

Flipping the rifle at his side, Birk pointed the weapon right at Zeb's middle. "Yeah, well, I've changed my mind. You'll have to settle for that Jones bitch, and maybe that spoilt woman who married into that there Jones family. Eirica's mine. Ain't nobody touchin' her but me. Understand?"

"Yeah, I understand all right," Zeb growled, backing away.

Birk lowered the gun but kept an eye on the man. When the trail cleared, they both hunkered down to wait for the women to arrive. He heard their voices in the distance.

Chapter Ninteen

Following the south shoulder of majestic Mount Hood, Wolf's party continued their slow and arduous trek along the Barlow Road. Each day, the weary emigrants came closer to their goal: Williamette Valley, now less than a week away.

Eirica, Jessie and Coralie walked together, ahead of the wagons, which were following single file behind them. Alison and Ian walked ahead of them. Lara had stayed behind with James. Running around the children's feet, the pups pounced and barked at anything that moved. Sadie plodded along following them.

Holding Summer, Eirica enjoyed the quiet walk. It was so peaceful, a perfect day. The bite of winter was in the air, but when they hit patches of sunny trail, the temperature warmed, enough to dispel the chill. Above her head, squirrels went about their business of preparing for winter and birds glided through the branches. Each was content to just savor the day.

Soon, their days would be filled once again with the hard work of setting up new households.

After a while, another noise intruded, ruining the perfect harmony of the setting. Loud shouts, the same combination of panic and excitement that hit men at difficult spots in the trail as they battled against the roadblocks nature put before them, warned Eirica they were coming upon what most considered the worst obstacle of the overland trip—Laurel Hill.

When they reached it, she made the children step back as all three women gasped with horror. "Land's sake, this is much worse than Windlass Hill," Eirica whispered, staring down at the scree-covered chute. It was so narrow, she couldn't imagine there was enough room to walk alongside the cattle. And the trail itself looked dangerous. The soil had been worn down five to seven feet in some places, leaving steep banks on both sides.

But what left the three women breathless with fear was the two-hundred-and-forty-foot vertical drop-off. Eirica and Coralie shook their heads in denial. Impossible, Eirica thought, her gaze wide. And to top it off, she knew from James that this was only one of two such chutes. Beyond the sharp right angle at the bottom of this chute waited another sixty-foot drop.

"It's worse than *anything* we've seen." Coralie glanced back at the way they'd come. "Maybe we took a wrong turn somewhere," she offered hopefully.

Jessie shook her head, her hand pressed to her stomach. She sat on the stump of a tree near the edge of the trail. "No, we didn't take a wrong turn. But I'm not going down this until the others catch up." They all glanced behind them but there was no sign yet of the wagons.

Eirica joined Jessie, eager for the rest, cradling

Summer in her arms. She frowned when she felt the wetness seeping through the baby's blanket. "Drat, she's wet again." Sadie also plopped down in the shade, keeping an eye on her rambunctious pups.

Coralie held her hands out. "Here, let me take her. I'll go change her and let the others know what awaits them. I just cannot see how they are going to get the wagons down this without them ending up splintered at the bottom."

Eirica handed the baby over. She and Jessie smiled as Coralie retreated, the two bored children following. "She's going to make a wonderful mother," Eirica said.

"Yeah. She will." Jessie sounded tired.

"So will you, and you'll get past this part soon."

"Yeah right. I'll believe it when it happens." Jessie leaned back, basking in the filtered sun.

With no children to keep an eye on, Eirica removed her bonnet to let the breeze slide across her neck and relaxed, content to gather her strength for the ordeal to come.

James and Wolf stared at one of the wagons. Another broken axle—and they had no spares and no time to make one. They'd already discussed trying to repair it, but Wolf knew it wouldn't make it down Laurel Hill. Now, as they mulled over what to do, each was conscious that they were holding up the line of wagons behind them.

"Why don't we just unload it, put the stuff in the other ones and dump it," James decided. He hated to lose the wagon but he could always make another. Right now, it was more important to get to Oregon City. He glanced at Coralie when she came up to him with Summer in her arms, Alison and Ian at her side. Looking around, he asked, "Where's Eirica?"

Coralie made a face. "She and Jessie are waiting for everyone up at Laurel Hill. I came back to change this sweet little thing. What happened?"

James ignored her. He met Wolf's gaze, both men frowning. "Are they alone?"

"Well, Sadie and the pups are there. They aren't going to go on ahead. Trust me, that hill is going to be a nightmare."

James put his hands on his hips. "I didn't realize they'd gone ahead. Wolf, I don't like them up there by themselves. I think I'll go up and get them."

Wolf frowned, his hands on his hips. "I'll go with you. Coralie, get your husband to come take care of this. Elliot, too."

Coralie stopped them, her eyes wide. "You don't think they are in danger, do you? I thought you said Birk would be waiting in Oregon."

"Just in case," James said, reaching into the wagon for his Sharps.

Wolf grabbed his and together, they took off on foot, leaving Jordan and the others to deal with unloading the wagon and getting things moving. They hadn't gone far when the sharp report of a gunshot echoed through the forest. Both men broke into a run.

Eirica was startled from her thoughts when Sadie growled, then let out a string of furious warning barks. Twisting on the boulder, she saw the dog hunch her shoulders and lower her head, her lips pulled back, revealing sharp fangs. Immediately, her pups scampered around, confused as to where the danger lie.

"What's wrong, Sadie?" Jessie asked, jumping up to survey the wooded area on either side of them.

Two men emerged from behind the concealing trees, guns pointed at them. Eirica felt her heart freeze.

"Birk!" Her mouth went dry and a chill ran through her as she stared at her husband.

Birk narrowed his eyes, pointing the rifle in his hands at Sadie. "Call off the dog, missy, or I'll shoot it," he warned Jessie, his voice low and threatening.

Jessie grabbed Sadie by the scruff of her neck and backed away, moving onto the trail in the direction they'd just come.

Eirica followed on shaking legs. She glanced down the trail. Where was everyone? They should have caught up to them a long time ago.

"That's far enough," the second man said, eyeing both women with a gleam in his eyes. "I gots a score ta settle with you," he addressed Jessie, tracing his scar. But his gaze drifted back to Eirica.

Eirica swallowed. She recognized him. He was the one who'd tried to rape her long before, that night by the river. And he would have if it hadn't been for Jessie. Her gaze shifted from him back to Birk. Her husband stood staring at her, hatred in his eyes.

Beside her, Jessie spoke, her voice loud. "The others are right behind us. If you value your lives, you'll leave."

Birk grinned, then spat on the ground as he advanced on Eirica. "Nice try, missy, but I know they's back a ways, dealin' with a broken wagon. By the time they git here, we'll be gone and they'll think you went on." He leered at Eirica. "When they git down that hill and find you're not there, it'll be too late. Now, move up the hill behind you. We's gonna take a nice walk through them trees." Zeb moved over to Jessie, his shotgun trained on her and the dog that Jessie struggled to control.

Eirica and Jessie exchanged worried glances. If they left the trail, they stood a chance of never being rescued. Somehow, they had to stall the two men. When Coralie returned without her and Jessie, maybe James or Wolf would come to let them know about the delay. It was their only chance.

"How did you survive, Birk? We thought you'd drowned."

Birk narrowed his eyes. "Did ya mourn me, wife? Did ya miss me?"

Eirica noted the clenching of the one hand steadying the butt of the gun. She braced herself before answering honestly. "No. You're a mean, sick man, Birk Macauley."

Birk reached out and grabbed Eirica, pulling her against him, his arm tight around her neck. "We's gonna go have us a nice long talk, wife," he sneered. "You've sinned. You need punishing."

Eirica struggled against his hold. "My only sin was in marrying you, and believe me, I've paid dearly for it."

"Why, you smart-assed bitch!" He threw Eirica to the ground, laughing at her involuntary cry of pain as she crashed to the rocky ground.

Eirica fought for breath. Her thigh throbbed where he'd kicked her and her hip ached from hitting a stone in the trail. When he came at her, she braced herself for the kick she knew was coming. She turned slightly, catching the heel of his boot in her thigh instead of her ribs or stomach, where he usually aimed. This time, she swallowed her cry of pain, refusing to give him the satisfaction. Nor would she cower. She glared at him.

Furious when she didn't react as he expected, he grabbed a fistful of her hair and yanked her onto her knees. "Yep, we's got lots to catch up on."

Though scared, Eirica kept telling herself that the longer she was able to goad Birk, the better chance she and Jessie would have to survive. Taking a deep breath, knowing he couldn't possibly hurt her more than he had in the past when he'd battered her body or the pain he'd put her through by taking Lara, she twisted around to face her husband.

Hatred for everything he'd put her and the children through filled her and gave her courage. "What's the matter, Birk, haven't had any helpless women or children to kick around? Is that the only way you can prove you're a man?"

Seeing the look of utter rage come over him, she tilted her chin. "You don't know the meaning of being a man. You're a coward. A big, bullying coward!" With her fisted hand, she drew back and struck him as hard as she could between the legs. James had taught her that was the best place to aim to bring down a man.

Birk jerked and yowled in pain, dropping his weapon. He clutched his injured part through his pants, but her punch hadn't carried enough force to double him over. It had just made him furious and more dangerous than ever.

When his fist connected with her face, she flew back, landing perilously near the brink of Laurel Hill. Pain radiated from her jaw and stars floated in front of her eyes. Still, she got to her knees. *I have to stall him. I have to save us.*

She had no idea where Jessie or Sadie were but through the buzzing in her ears, she heard the dog's growls and knew her friend was still there, watching. This time, though, Jessie couldn't save her.

Wild with an insane fury, Birk grabbed her arm, twisting it as he dragged her over to where his rifle had fallen. "You'll die for that, you bitch. You're gonna die!"

She lay on her back. He stared down at her, the gun in his hands. When she saw his foot lift, she tried to scramble away, but Birk used his foot to stop her by stepping on the side of her face. He applied just enough pressure to grind her cheek into the dirt. From far away, she heard Jessie shout at him, but she couldn't make out the words.

When Birk shoved the hard, cold steel of his shotgun into her throat, Eirica knew her time had run out. She squeezed her eyes shut and held her breath. Tears trickled down the corners of her eyes, falling onto the leaves blanketing the ground.

Please, God, take care of my babies. Keep James safe.

Chapter Twenty

Jessie feared to look away from where Eirica's husband held a shotgun to the woman's throat. She had to do something to help Eirica. She'd never seen a man so enraged. She looked at the ground, pushing herself to her feet, but a sudden blast made her cover. "No," she cried out, her heart thudding, her eyes welling.

"No," she sobbed again, lifting her head. But to her shock, Birk toppled back, a hole in his gut. Shock widened his eyes, then he fell, teetering on the edge of the narrow chute before falling backward, out of sight.

Her gaze sought Eirica's and to her immense relief, her friend was alive, unhurt by the blast. Help had arrived, she thought, then she saw Zeb point his double-barrel shotgun at Eirica. He'd been the one to shoot Birk!

"Git up and don't give me no trouble. Don't want ta haf ta hurt ya afore we finish our business." He speared a look at Jessie. "An' this time, yer young friend here won't be able ta help ya."

He bent down and picked up Birk's weapon, keeping the shotgun trained on Eirica as he addressed Jessie. "Tie and muzzle that dog. I'll take care of her when we git's away from here. He tossed Jessie a length of rope and the torn hem from Lara's dress.

Jessie caught it, the sound of Zeb's laughter sending a chill up her spine. "You know you'll die if you don't let us go. My husband—"

"I know all about yer breed-husband. But his family ain't here ta help him this time. And by the time he gets here, we'll be gone." He licked his lips.

Jessie pretended to be having trouble subduing her dog. "They'll hear the gunshots."

"Yeah? Jest hunters is all they'll think. Now hurry it up. I rather fancy samplin' each of you while the other watches." His eyes turned ugly as he stared at Jessie who looped the rope around the dog's collar. "Yep, should be lots of fun to pay you back for what ya did ta me." He moved closer to the edge and peered down, then he laughed. "Maybe you'll think of a real nice way to thank me fer killin' that worthless husband of yers, Angel-face."

Jessie bit her lip, her heart thudding painfully. Around them, the puppies were running frantically, whining and crying. Zeb kicked one away when it got too close to him. The pup's frightened squeal made Sadie's growls grow wild.

Taking advantage of the distraction, Jessie slid her hand down to her boot where she'd hidden a knife but she couldn't draw it out and throw it as Wolf had taught her. Eirica stood between her and Zeb.

Jessie sent a silent plea for her husband to hurry.

Susan Edwards

Surely as soon as Coralie returned alone, both Wolf and James would come. She knew both her husband and her brother well. Jessie looked at Eirica, trying to signal her to move. She had to disarm Zeb. Desperation filled Jessie. With Birk dead, Eirica was now free to marry James, but if they couldn't get free of Zeb, neither would enjoy their newfound happiness.

"Fergit the dog. It's easier ta jest shoot it." Zeb sent nervous glances behind them and motioned for Eirica to move closer to Jessie. Only a few feet separated them now.

Jessie dug her fingers into Sadie's coat, a silent signal to attack when she released the dog. Time was running out. Using Sadie to draw the gun from Eirica was their only hope. Again, she tried to use her eyes to signal Eirica to be ready to move.

Suddenly, she heard another low warning growl coming from somewhere in the forest behind her. It was followed by the sound of furious running through the underbrush.

She released Sadie and threw herself at Eirica, knocking them both to the ground just as a streak of white fur went sailing overhead.

Wahoska landed with all four paws square on Zeb's chest, his fangs sunk in the man's throat. Another shot rang out. Eirica, beneath Jessie, cried out.

Jessie lifted her head just in time to hear Zeb's bone-chilling garbled scream. The force of the Wolf's attack knocked him off balance and he staggered back. Before Jessie could scream, both man and wolf fell down Laurel Hill.

"Oh, God," she cried. Both women jumped up and ran with Sadie to the edge of the chute where Zeb and the wolf were tumbling down over the rocky ground. Then they were gone.

With tears in her eyes, Jessie started to follow but Eirica grabbed her. "Jessie, no. It's too late. No one could have survived that. Think of your baby. If you fall, you'll lose it." Eirica sobbed, drawing Jessie into her arms.

Around their feet, six pups sat on the edge, looking lost and puzzled. Sadie lifted her nose to the wind and sniffed. After a few minutes, she sat on her haunches and lifted her muzzle to the sky. Her howl of agony echoed throughout the forest.

That night, camped a short distance from Laurel Hill, James and Eirica walked, arms around each other's waist, uncaring of who might see them. "That was too damn close," James whispered hoarsely, knowing he'd never forget those heart-stopping minutes after he'd heard gunfire. It had seemed like forever before he and Wolf had arrived on the scene. Relief had followed quickly when he found Eirica and his sister safe. But those moments would haunt him for a long time to come.

"It's over, now. It's truly over, right James?" Eirica still sounded shocked.

He drew her into his arms and held her tight, feeling his eyes grow moist as he buried his face in her hair. "Yes, sweetheart, it is. It's over. He'll never harm you or your children, again." James knew it'd take a long time for Eirica to heal. The bruises and cuts on her face and thigh would fade quickly enough, but those wounds in her heart and soul would take longer.

"I stood up to him. I actually stood up to him." Her voice sounded faint, as if afraid to confess what she'd done.

Another shudder tore through him. If she hadn't stalled Birk by enraging him, both her and Jessie would have been killed. "I know. Jess told me." He looked down at her, a beam of moonlight illuminating her features. "I'm proud of you."

She bit her lip. "Really? I was afraid you'd be upset."

He was. Or rather, he was horrified, but he'd never let her know that. She'd done what she had to do; that earned her his respect. But he didn't know what he'd have done if Zeb hadn't killed Birk.

"I'm so proud of you. Together, we are gonna make one hell of a team."

Eirica wrapped her arms around his waist. "How about if we start now?"

James tipped his head to the side. "Start what now."

"Teamwork. Being partners. Being close partners." She pressed her breasts against him. "*Really* close."

"Let's go somewhere where no one will come upon us."

Eirica glanced around. "There's no one here. I need you, James. Now."

She reached between them and tore at the buttons on his shirt, tracing the dark curls down into the waistband of his denim pants. "I love you, James Jones."

"God, Eirica, slow down." He moaned when she made quick work of the fastening of his denim trousers. His breathing turned to short gasps when she reached inside and stroked him. He was so ready for her, he felt as though he'd burst.

He reached for her, needing to feel her skin against his fingers, her mouth against his, but she ducked out of his embrace and slid his pants down. Cool air raced across his buttocks. Her hand wrapped fully around his shaft and she stroked it, bringing him to a fevered pitch.

Knowing he'd end this quickly if he didn't stop her,

he dropped down onto his knees in front of her, pulling her into his arms and fell to the carpet of dried leaves beneath them, shielding her. Then he rolled over on top of her. "I love you, Eirica."

His need to touch her matched hers. He shoved her dress up, his hands sliding up the inside of her thighs. When he found her moist center, he slid a finger inside, her moan threatening the thin thread of his control.

Arching nearer to him, Eirica gasped. A second finger joined the first and his thrusts grew faster and deeper. "No, not yet," she moaned.

"What do you want?" James asked, his voice hoarse.

"Inside," she gasped, on fire for him. "Inside. Take me to that special place. Now." She pulled his hand away, begging him to come to her. Her body craved the release only he could give her. She moved her hips, begging for him to work his magic.

"I want to kiss you, taste you."

"Kissing isn't enough," she panted. While she loved kissing him, tonight she wanted more. She wanted it all. No barriers. No fears. No more teasing and no more unfulfilled desires. And she didn't want it slow.

James lifted her skirts and urged her feet further apart. "I think you'll like this kissing."

The minute his mouth touched where his fingers had been, she felt flames of desire heat her body. How she kept from screaming and alerting everyone within a mile radius she didn't know. She bit the soft fleshy part of her hand to keep from crying out. The intensity of need pulsing through her made her hips buck against him as his mouth and tongue touched all the intimate places crying out for his loving.

Then it began, the urge to let go and fly. Eirica dug

her fingers into his hair as it built, holding him to her as she flew apart, gasping her cry of pleasure into her clutched fist.

"Beautiful," James whispered when her body calmed. He rose over her. "Again, Eirica. Again."

"Yes. Oh yes, James. Yes." She wrapped her legs around his waist and sighed when he slid into her. "We're one. Finally."

"Forever, sweetheart, forever." He lowered his lips to hers and stroked them both to a feverish pitch until they reached fulfillment as one, each a part of the other as they soared through a night of shimmering stars and white heat.

Five days later, one hundred seventy days after leaving Westport, the emigrants were just one day from their goal: Oregon City. Milling to one side of them, the cattle grazed contentedly. By mutual consent, Wolf's party stopped to let their weary gazes feast on the fertile soil and the wide open space. The sky above was a deep blue and the air was clean and bracing. They drew in deep breaths.

Eirica leaned against James, surrounded by her three older children. Summer lay sleeping, secure in the cradle of James's arm. Eirica glanced down at her sleeping infant. This child, and all the ones to follow, would know only love, security and happiness. Laughter would be as much a part of their lives as eating and breathing.

"We made it, Eirica," Coralie said. She and Jordan stood on one side of her with Jessie flanking James. No one knew where Wolf had gone, but the lingering sadness in Jessie's gaze told them he was still coming to terms with losing Wahoska.

Eirica hugged Coralie. Soon they'd be sisters. She, Coralie and Jessie were bound together by the hardships and miracles of traveling so far together, as well as marriage. She leaned across James and laid her hand on Jessie's arm. "I'm so sorry, Jessie." She couldn't help but feel guilty over the wolf's death. If not for her, for Birk and his attempt to kidnap her, the wolf would still be alive.

A voice from behind them advised, "Don't be."

All turned to find Wolf standing there, Sadie and her pups at his feet. Jessie went to him and, unmindful of her audience, kissed him tenderly on the lips. Hugging her to his side, Wolf absently reached out to smooth her growing abdomen.

"I knew when that wolf followed me West there was a reason, a purpose. I found him injured as a youngster on my way back to my people. It was right after I decided I'd had enough of the white man's schooling. Wahoska stayed by my side, even going to town with me, but he'd never accompanied me overland before, always turning back to await my return to my people." Wolf leaned down to rub Sadie behind her ears. For a long moment, the two stared at one another, as if sharing a secret.

Finally Wolf met Eirica's teary gaze, then he glanced down at his wife. "He lived a long and full life and, in the end, he chose to give his life to save yours and Eirica's. And for that I will forever be grateful to the spirits for sending him to me."

A sharp, high-pitched bark drew everyone's attention. A single white pup, the only entirely white pup in the litter, sat on his haunches, its paws lifted. Everyone chuckled when Wolf bent down to pick him up. A wet tongue-licking followed.

Eirica and James exchanged smiles. The pup had obviously chosen Wolf for his new master. Though Wahoska had been left behind, his legacy would not be forgotten.

James smiled down into Eirica's eyes. "Have I told you today how much I love you, Eirica?"

Eirica grinned and lifted her lips to his. "No, and for that, you must tell me every day for the rest of our lives." James handed the baby over to Coralie and drew his love close, kissing her fully.

Suddenly, a gruff voice broke apart their kiss. "What's the hold-up? Everyone's going smarmy on me, again!" Rook's gruff voice drew shouts of laughter from the small close-knit group. At his side, Sofia jabbed him in the ribs.

"Hush, you old fool. This is beautiful, touching." She glared at him. "And romantic." They went on, their bickering fading.

Wolf lifted a brow and eyed his wife's family. "Shall we go?" Jessie took his hand and allowed him to lead the way.

"You bet," Jordan answered, handing Summer back to James. He and Coralie followed, arguing as to whether they would share a home with the rest of the family during the winter or rent a room where they could be alone.

James glanced down at Eirica, then at the three children watching him. They were his children now. In his arms, Summer reached up to put her hands in his mouth and Ian lifted his arms. "Up. Ride."

Eirica took the baby who protested with a howl. James settled Ian on his shoulders. Happy and content, she held on to Lara's hand while Alison took hold of James's hand and stood between them.

James looked at her. "Ready?"

Eirica stared at her family. So many new beginnings lay before them: a new home; a new husband as soon as they found someone to marry them; new additions to their family to plan; and so many new dreams to dream. But her dream of love and laughter had already come true.

"Ready?" she echoed. She smiled at James. "For anything."

Epilogue

April 1857

"Mama! Mama! They're here. They're here," Alison shrieked, running through the simple log cabin. She skidded to a stop in the room Eirica and James slept in. "Pa says to hurry."

"I'm coming," she called out. It still thrilled her to hear her children call James Pa. They were his and no one loved them more fiercely than he. "Now hold still, Summer Jones, and let Ma finish dressing you." Her daughter, now eight months old, squirmed and fought, but finally, she was dressed and her hair was combed.

"Need help?" James asked from the doorway.

Hearing her father's voice, Summer squealed. Her hands opened and closed rapidly, her quiet demand for her father to pick her up. "Come on, sweetpea. Your aunt, Jessie, is here." He held out his hand for Eirica.

Eirica took his hand, thankful to have such a loving, wonderful man. True to his word, he'd made sure she knew how to take care of herself and her children here. They were a team and had worked together to build their house and clear their land. Soon, they'd plant some fruit trees and purchase more cattle to add to the small herd Wolf had given them as a wedding present.

But the gift James had presented to her on their wedding day was what really made him dear to her heart. He'd given her the deed to the land. So much had changed during the last year and there were more changes to come. Thinking about them brought tears to her eyes.

"Oh, James, I can't believe Jessie and Wolf are leaving in the morning, or that Rook and Sofia are going with them." Tears fell from her eyes. Her husband handed her a clean handkerchief. "I'll miss them so much."

"I know." His own eyes darkened with sadness. Not only was he losing his sister, but Jeremy had surprised them all that morning by announcing his intention to go with Wolf and Jessie.

For a moment, they held each other, much to Summer's displeasure.

His voice broke. "Come on. Everyone else has arrived."

From the main room of the three-room cabin, Eirica heard raised voices, then she heard a rough voice demand, "What's keepin' them two? They's best not be gettin' all smarmy again."

Rook poked his head into the room. "Git out here, you two." He stepped in. "There's my li'l lass." Summer reached for him, arms outstretched, a huge toothy grin covering her face. She squealed and clapped excitedly when he took her from her father.

Susan Edwards

James shook his head and grinned ruefully. "She's fickle-hearted already."

Eirica laughed, feeling lighter of heart. She straightened her apron, a clean, crisp new one to go with her new green calico dress. Together she and her husband joined bedlam, there was no other way to described the absolute chaos that greeted them.

Coralie and Jordan had arrived, bringing their two nearly grown puppies, reuniting them with the two pups she and James had kept. Alison, Lara and Ian dashed after the animals, creating a racket of excited shouts and barking dogs.

Eirica sighed. James left her side to corral the dogs and chase them outside. Eirica greeted Coralie who held her newborn son. The two women hugged, then Eirica pulled the blanket Coralie had knitted off the baby's face. Jordan, Jr., slept peacefully. No one would ever guess that Coralie had once doubted her ability to be a mother. She and Jordan doted on their son.

"He's so precious." Eirica smiled to herself as she ran a finger over the baby's soft mat of curly black hair. She hadn't told anyone, not even James, but she suspected that she herself was pregnant again. Maybe she'd have a son, a miniature of his father.

Sofia and Rook joined them. More hugs followed, then Eirica burst into tears. "I can't believe you and Rook are leaving as well." How could she bear to lose these two wonderful people who'd stepped in and filled a void in her life? They were returning with Wolf to help with his and Jessie's boarding school.

Rook bounced Summer in his arms. The little girl was dressed in the pink dress Coralie had made her, and to see this big, barrel-chested old man holding a dainty little thing like her daughter made Eirica want to laugh and cry at the same time. He drew her into a bear hug. "You'll do jest fine, lass."

After a few minutes of talk and tears, Sofia slid her husband a knowing look. "Time to get the meal started." She headed for the stove. Rook, still carrying Summer, followed fast on her heels, arguing over who'd do what.

"Well, some things haven't changed," Coralie giggled. Then she glanced around. "Where is Jessica?"

"Right here, Cory," a breathless voice said.

Jessie joined them. In her arms, she held her daughter, Sarah, named after Wolf's mother. Eirica reached out to take the pink bundle. Peeling away the blanket, she revealed a tiny matching pink dress lovingly adorned with embroidered stitches.

Coralie nodded approvingly at Jessie's choice of garment for her daughter. "There's hope for you yet, Jessica."

Jessie wrinkled her nose, an impish gleam in her eyes. "Don't count on it, Cory. She's only wearing a dress today cause you made it and we're leaving. I figured if you went to the trouble to make it, the least I could do was let Sarah wear it one time."

Jessie and Coralie continued their good-natured bickering. James rejoined them and Eirica grinned at her husband. "Some things haven't changed," she mouthed.

Glancing around, Eirica frowned. "Where is Samuel?"

Jessie motioned to Wolf who was talking to Jordan. Wolf came over, looking every bit the proud papa, carrying a tiny blue bundle.

Coralie stepped back to widen the circle. Soft sighs filled the immediate area. Twins. Jessie had shocked them all by giving birth to a son and daughter, both with curly black hair.

Susan Edwards

After several more minutes of talk, everyone spread out. Eirica handed the baby back to Jessie and smiled. She'd gotten her wish. Love and laughter filled her house.

James caressed her shoulders from behind. "Happy, sweetheart?"

She tipped her head back, leaning against him. "Oh yes." A sudden crash and a yowl of protest broke them apart. On the other side of the room, Ian had knocked over a chair in his attempt to get to the food on the table. His uncle Jeremy rescued their feast and was carrying the half-screaming, half-laughing boy away holding him high overhead.

"Welcome to the family, sweetheart." James murmured into her ear.

Eirica laughed softly. Rook and Sofia continued to argue over the wood stove, with Summer adding her opinion in her high voice. Elliot had his arms around a very pregnant Catarina. There had been so much hardship on the trail, but so much joy at its end.

Joy and happiness filled her heart as she watched these people she held dear to her.

What a family they were.

Lair of the Wolf

Chapter Five

Martha Hix

Lair of the Wolf also appears in these *Leisure* books:

COMPULSION by Elaine Fox
includes Chapter One by Constance O'Banyon

CINNAMON AND ROSES by Heidi Betts
includes Chapter Two by Bobbi Smith

SWEET REVENGE by Lynsay Sands
includes Chapter Three by Evelyn Rogers

TELL ME LIES by Claudia Dain
includes Chapter Four by Emily Carmichael

On January 1, 1997, *Romance Communications,* the Romance Magazine for the 21st century made its Internet debut. One year later, it was named a Lycos Top 5% site on the Web in terms of both content and graphics!

One of *Romance Communications'* most popular features is The Romantic Relay, an original romance novel divided into twelve monthly installments, with each chapter written by a different author. Our first offering was *Lair of the Wolf,* a tale of medieval Wales, created by, in alphabetical order, celebrated authors Emily Carmichael, Debra Dier, Madeline George, Martha Hix, Deana James, Elizabeth Mayne, Constance O'Banyon, Evelyn Rogers, Sharon Schulze, June Lund Shiplett, and Bobbi Smith.

We put no restrictions on the authors, letting each pick up the tale where the previous author had left off and going forward as she wished. The authors tell us they had a lot of fun, each trying to write her successor into a corner!

Now, preserving the fun and suspense of our month-by-month installments, Leisure Books presents, in print, one chapter a month of *Lair of the Wolf.* In addition to the entire online story the authors have added some brand-new material to their existing chapters. So if you think you've read *Lair of the Wolf* already, you may find a few surprises. Please enjoy this unique offering, watch for each new monthly installment in the back of your Leisure Books, and make sure you visit our Web site, where another romantic relay is already in progress.

Romance Communications

http://www.romcom.com

Pamela Monck, Editor-in-Chief

Mary D. Pinto, Senior Editor

S. Lee Meyer, Web Mistress

Chapter Five
by Martha Hix

"You would answer me, Lady Meredyth." A northern tongue of spring wind lapped the yard, causing Sir Garon's chain mail to rattle. "What will you yield to spare the lives of your rebellious Welsh fools?"

"I am considering your question, Sir Garon."

Meredyth willed her tears not to fall. Tears would show weakness to the Wolf. To win against his superior strength, she must never again allow the cur an advantage. Wits were what she needed, especially now, while his men at-arms herded her loyal people to the dungeon, Owain, the smith, being prodded forward by the tip of a broadsword.

Sir Olyver, also girded in chain mail, strolled up to stand behind his liege lord, viewing the devastation from the riot encircling them. Meredyth's eyes pleaded with the older man to intervene, to help her.

He seemed merely to smirk behind his beard. Her last hope fled.

What should she do? How could she defend the people of Glendire? What were her choices?

"If you think to flout me by saying nothing, Lady Meredyth, you should think again." Sir Garon glared down at her, a gloved finger tapping her nose. "I would have your answer before the blackbirds roost and our vows are exchanged."

How she would love to spit in his English face! "You are the conqueror, my lord. You must name my punishment."

"Nay. Speak, Lady Meredyth."

"Wales forever!" was what she allowed.

"Glendire is English now. You would do well to remember that. And to act accordingly."

"I act according to my conscience," she retorted.

"You wear my patience thin."

"I'm sure I do. About as thin as the food stores of Glendire." Catching sight of Bertha, the alewife, as the poor, demented woman tried to scavenge the black pot she'd used in the attack, Lady Meredyth took a deep breath. " 'Twas folly, ordering so much food prepared for the wedding feast. My people are hungry. We must use sparingly from the larder."

"Bear this in mind. The welfare of *my* people depends upon the peace between the lord and his lady. There is enough strife in the land without our adding to it."

Unfortunately, she had begun to realize the truth of his statement. To openly agree with him, however, would go against her convictions, the very essence of her will. If only she could rid herself of him . . .

"I would hear your answer now, my lady. What will you yield to me?" When she said naught, Sir Garon gestured toward the entrance to the dungeon.

"Shall I call a guard and have him retrieve one of the prisoners? A pikestaff with a Welsh head upon it would add decoration to the gatehouse."

Stiffening her spine, Lady Meredyth said, "You would not dare. I would cut your pumping heart from your chest and feed it to the hounds."

Gauntlets going to his lean waist, the castle cur threw back his shaggy head and laughed. Then his hands made fists, and he shoved his face into hers.

"Name your punishment, green-eyed shrew. Name it now, or I will call for a prisoner."

The Wolf didn't make veiled threats, of this she felt certain. She glowered at the knight who matched her in stubbornness. One of them would win, one would lose. Yet, as her mother, the Lady Gwyneth, used to say, wars be not lost with the sacrifice of a single battle. Somehow Glendire must survive. Thrive. Prosper. The fighting among victors and vanquished must cease, at least until the Celtic lords of Wales could rally. The replanting of the barley fields must begin.

The marriage couldn't be stopped. Meredyth need wed Sir Garon. And she must yield to her punishment.

She didn't have to be pleased about her fate. Longshanks might have stolen her property and given it to an ambitious knight, but she'd be no lamb sacrificed to Longshanks' Wolf.

A plan came to her, one that refreshed her spirit. Why should she not play on Sir Garon's meager decency? After all, he hadn't allowed his knaves to rape the women or pillage the halls. He had even shown signs of gentleness this morn, in chamber.

And he'd charged to Meredyth's defense during the fracas between the soldier and Alyce.

Meredyth took a chance. " 'Twould be fitting if you lashed me, for all to witness."

He blinked. The fists at his sides opened, flexed, then closed again. His face paled a shade. "Go to your chambers. I will think on your offer."

Lash the Lady Meredyth?

Never!

"No woman has ever known the sting of my hand," Garon said to his liege man, and he paced the chamber he'd demanded, where the Lady Meredyth would spread her comely legs for him.

Would that her knees opened willingly, he mused. Favors taken under duress had never appealed to him. "I will not lash her."

Olyver Martain gave over the last of his chin chain mail to a squire, who took it away. "You will show weakness to the Welsh dogs if you do not. She has challenged you, Wolf."

"No one heard her offer. None but you."

Would that Sir Olyver had not overheard. Never had Garon truly enjoyed the knight's company, even though the older man showed him every courtesy, in public displaying almost the same sycophantic respect as did the others of the garrison. In private, though, Garon sensed that this knight knew well where to strike a blow and how to turn the dagger.

Bonhomie betwixt the two knights being naught, Garon had been annoyed to learn the bearded noble would accompany him to Wales, at King Edward's behest. Despite his fair-minded reputation, the king sometimes possessed a streak of fiendishness.

Sir Olyver, smirking, drew his trimmed beard between a thumb and forefinger, stroking his chin. "You remember your youth, when your father flogged your mother until it brought you to cravenly tears. You have carried this weakness all your twenty-five years, Wolf. You are but a pup, yelping in the litter, if you do not show your might."

Garon glared at the look of smug superiority in Sir Olyver's creased face. Pouring a flagon of tested mead, he tipped the contents down his throat. The fermented honey coated his voice but could not coat his anger. "You should take care with gossip. It becomes none but old women."

"Longshanks himself told me about your kin, sire. Surely you don't criticize your king, accusing him of rumor-mongering?"

"Do not put words into my mouth. I am the king's man, as well you know."

Garon walked to the lancet window and looked out, yet he paid little heed to the yeomen who lit torches and cleared the yard below. He thought of his family in Devon.

The Saunders household of that land of slate and limestone was no more, of course. The soil had gone fallow under Garon's father, who'd never made much of himself, too deeply had Sir Cedric Saunders been in the wineskin. Often had he vented spleen on his wife and sons over his own incompetence. The beatings had shortened Lady Ebalinn's life, taking her to her grave before Garon, her youngest son, saw his tenth year.

Soldiering had been a welcome relief to Garon, a way to leave his father and his sad memories of Devon behind him.

Last year, before taking that arrow meant for his king, he'd learned that Sir Cedric had died after drinking tainted wine. Garon had found nothing to mourn.

All he had now was the future. Even though he hadn't wanted the gift of Glendire and its defiant chate-

Martha Hix

laine, Garon had had to accept the prize his king had offered. And he would do all in his power to honor it.

Sir Olyver picked at a thumbnail. "If her ladyship were mine, I'd take the lash to her."

"Then we can all be thankful she's not yours," Garon said, vowing that someday he would grind Olyver Martain's nose into the floor. "You can shame me not with my low birth. I have risen above it." Garon set the cup down. "Nor am I ashamed to honor damsels. Even defiant ones. Think you on this, Sir Olyver. Lady Meredyth would not be worthy as lady of Glendire were she amiss in her loyalty her people. 'Tis my duty to bend her to my will—and Longshanks'—not to break her."

The moment the older knight's mouth opened to reply, a page burst into the chamber.

The skinny lad much resembled a twig and had a twitchy air to him. He said to Garon, " 'Tis time for the exchange of vows, sire. The chaplain asks after you. The candles are burning low. The Lady Meredyth is in the narthex, waiting."

Garon pictured the lady in his mind, and wondered if it had taken ropes and pulleys to keep her "waiting" in the chapel. Ah, the Lady Meredyth. The young maiden who, out of loyalty to her land, had behaved as a lad. Who, out of loyalty to her people had defied the wolf to lash her. A knight could gain much from an alliance with such as Lady Meredyth, little of that gain having to do with her castle or its riches. Garon knew he wanted much more than her hand in a convenient marriage. He yearned for her body and spirit to be his alone.

He brushed at his sleeves and tugged at the hem of his wedding jerkin. "Let us not keep my bride waiting."

Sir Olyver caught his arm. "You would marry the Welsh woman without first settling her debt?"

"Her debts will be settled. When and where are not for you to decide. Take your hand from my arm, Sir Olyver."

The older knight released his grip and bowed in too-obvious concession. "As you wish, my lord."

Garon, breathing deeply through his nostrils, hurried down the staircase to the chapel. The day of setting down Sir Olyver couldn't come too soon for Garon.

But for this day—and this night!—he must deal with the defiant Lady Meredyth.

And defiant she was as she met him at the altar. Instead of bowing her head reverently, as she should, she tipped up her chin at him, vowing, "You shall never be the husband of my heart."

"Beware, lady bride," he whispered. "Eaten words have not the savor of sweetmeats or blackbird pasties."

She chose that moment to grind her heel into his little toe.

Forsooth, though she should be trembling in fear of her forfeit, she continued to try to nettle Garon. Too long did she tarry before reciting her vows. She even chuckled at his and the chaplain's discomfiture. She paused to pluck a stray thread from her garments.

Yet Garon would not be shaken, though the breathtaking sight of her almost unnerved him where her acts of rebellion did not. How lovely she looked in her wedding attire, with her cropped hair hidden by an embroidered mantle.

At the moment they should have sealed their vows, she muttered, "I would sooner kiss a pig than touch my lips to yours."

Someone behind Garon sniggered—Olyver Martain, no doubt.

"Since you think me swine, lady wife, I shall take your remark as consent."

With that, his lips claimed hers. Her mouth did not open for him. He lifted his head, vowing silently to gain her passion, to make her ache for his kisses. What would it take to win her love?

A gentle hand?

Force?

Garon pondered his dilemma while taking his wife's arm to escort her from the chapel. Of one answer he was certain. It would take patience to win the heart of the fair Lady Meredyth . . . and he had little patience.

The bridal couple retired to the chamber that had belonged to Meredyth's parents. Thankfully, Longshanks' Wolf didn't lunge like his namesake upon his bride. He sipped ale; with his long legs stretched toward the fire, he slumped in the hide chair. 'Twas the same seat her father had used to doze in at even-tide, when troubadours would sing, the chaplain would speak of God, or Bertha, the alewife, had entertained the lady and her court with farfetched premonitions.

Skelly-eyed Bertha believed her second sight much clearer than her first, but both were bad. The very idea of torches that burned without pitch, or a big box hovering in the heavens to snap graven images of the stars, or strange, single-eyed machines that put distant people in communication with one another so that scantily clad ladies might drool over a galaxy of sinewed men with long hair and exposed knees—it was all pure nonsense.

Truly, how could Meredyth even be thinking of Bertha the alewife at a moment such as this?

She did not settle into the chair where Lady Gwyneth had worked needle and loom with her talented fingers. Now that Dame Allison had finished assisting her into a nightgown, Meredyth nervously paced the rushes. Stalling for time before Sir Garon would claim his husbandly rights, or her punishment, or both, she studied the chamber.

Nothing was the same as it had been.

The Wolf had already made this his lair. His chain mail sat atop the carved wooden chest where Lady Gwyneth's threads had been stored. Battered armor stood in one corner. A hairbrush and comb, both of masculine design, were scattered where the departed lady's casket of jewels had rested. On a table betwixt the two chairs was a plate of foodstuff—cheese and apples, with hunks of dark bread.

"My mother never allowed food in the sleeping chamber," Meredyth said. "It attracts rats."

Sir Garon tore his dark gaze from the licking flames and settled it on her. His eyelids were heavy, his expression bland. "Never fear. Beelzebub is captain of rat control."

Meredyth eyed the big black tomcat curled atop the fur throw that covered the bed. She stuck her tongue out at the creature, though she secretly gave thanks that it, and not she, was currently, occupying her parents bed. Although she imagined her mother had gone to it without the fear, hesitation, and disquiet that beset the daughter.

"I don't like cats," she stated.

Sir Garon chuckled and popped a piece of cheese into his aggravating mouth.

"Beelzebub may care not for you, either, lady-bride. You will both adjust."

Meredyth kicked up rushes as she huffed to the lancet window nearest the staircase, then plopped down in the embrasure to stare at the keep below. During times of peace, she'd sat here to gaze upon the barbican, to dream of Welsh knights in shining armor passing through the drawbridge.

Mayhap this English knight would find a reason to take his cat and retreat through the drawbridge. She coerced a smile. "What are your plans for the future, my lord? Will honor guide you? Or will religious beliefs?" If he had either, he'd yet to show them, she believed. "If you are religious, as am I—"

He interrupted her thought with a guffaw. "You? Religious? Do not make me split my sides, lady-bride. You worked sacrilege at your own wedding."

She winced but continued, pursuing the slimmest of hopes for her and Glendire's salvation. "But do you not plan to join a Crusade?"

"I plan to rear sons and daughters."

"Would it not be exciting if your progeny were able to tell their children of their grandfather's bringing the land of Christ into the English fold?" she persisted.

"No Crusades."

"Would not a knight of rank be dissatisfied to spend his fighting years nodding before a fire, when his peers are off to Crusade?"

"No Crusades," this knight repeated.

"Should not a knight of your esteem be in the north lands with his king, then, bringing the Highlands to its knees?" she attempted.

"No Scotland."

"Are not the French causing trouble for your king? Or mayhap Longshanks gave you Glendire to retire you. Mayhap you aren't up to knightly deeds. Are you in disfavor, my lord?"

Sir Garon's gaze now smoldered, and burned into her eyes. "There will be plenty of tales for our children to hear. Many lessons to be learned from both knightly honor and knightly villainy. But the latter tales will not be about their father." He looked away. "They will be about their grandfather. My father. An ignoble knight. My progeny will learn always to take the proper path, and their mother and father will set such an example."

For the first time, Meredyth felt a certain sympathy for her new husband. Always she had known her father's strength of character. Dafydd Llewellyn had lived valorously and died a hero. How awful it must be, feeling shame over a parent.

Quickly she warned herself to be unmoved; sympathy to a foe could become an opening to defeat. As well, a cry from the vicinity of the dungeon reminded her of matters left unsettled between her and her enemy. "You have not answered me about my punishment," she said.

"You will not be lashed, lady bride," Sir Garon said quietly.

She hid a smile. He had played into her hands. Yet to think she'd tamed the Wolf would be a foolish notion. She trusted him no more than she did the alewife's premonitions.

"I am eager to know my people freed." The stone embrasure cold and hard against her spine, she tucked her knees beneath her chin and hugged her legs. "What will my punishment be?"

"Like you, I must take my time to consider. I am thinking on it."

"You surprise me, Lord Wolf. I should think you'd have—"

"Garon. My name is Garon. Call me thusly."

"I call no one by a familiarity when I am not friendly to him."

"Before this night is over, we shall be familiar," he assured her.

Meredyth shivered. That. While undressing, she'd spoken more with Dame Allison about the event to come. And despite her trepidations, she found herself curious on one matter. "Sir Garon, will you not have witnesses to our marriage bed?"

He tilted his head toward her. "I do not need witnesses."

"How, then, will you be able to prove to your minions that I am virtuous? Perchance I am not."

Sipping from the chalice, he raised his eyebrows. "Then, like a wolf on the prowl, he rose from the chair and crossed the room to her. "When you gorged on the drugged mead you would have had me drink, I did not find your responses to be those of a lady of experience."

Meredyth froze. "You didn't touch me. I felt no pain."

"You were drugged. How could you recall the pain?" He fingered the strings of her nightgown, untying the neck. "Not all women experience pain. For instance, have you ever ridden a palfrey?"

"Of course I have."

"Riding many times can tear the maidenhead. If it was gone to begin with, then you'd have had no pain."

"For shame," she said and shook her head. "Honorably, you refuse to mark my flesh with your whip, yet dishonorably you would touch me without marking my memory. I should think most knights would wish to arouse a lady, even a drugged lady, to memory."

He laughed. "You think too freely, my lady. But not, mayhap, wisely."

She sprang up from the window seat. "What, pray tell, did you do to me?" she demanded.

He laughed again and, catching her by one arm, led her to the hide chair and tugged her onto his lap.

She shoved at his chest, which seemed as hard as the castle walls. "Sire!"

"Garon. My name is Garon." His breath fanned the opening of her nightgown. "Call me by my name, lady-bride."

"I will not."

His arm supporting her back, his fingers splayed against her midriff. "You will."

"No."

She tried to pry his fingers off, but her squirming accomplished nothing—except to excite a part of him that nudged at her derrière.

"Oh!" she gasped, surprised at the feel of it.

"The Dark Warrior surprises you, Merrie? Did you not think you would awaken him?"

She gasped again. "You make crude references. Yet, since you are a cur, why should I expect anything but crudity?"

"I would say that makes you a cur's wife, then. Indeed, I could say the cur's bitch, but I would not so dishonor my bride." He ran a hand down her leg to inch up the hem of her nightdress and grasp her knee. He rotated his hips, nudging upward. "I seek, rather, to honor you, with my mighty warhorse, the Dark Warrior."

If she had good sense, Meredyth knew she should acquiesce, should give in, should give up. Surrender. Be done with it. And her traitorous flesh suddenly ached for such capitulation. But, rebellious to the core, she would not so shame her purple blood.

"Have I not already been dishonored with a visit from your destrier, sire?" she taunted. "I have no use for lusty beasts in my bedchamber."

357

"Have you not, Merrie?" A finger traced her chin as he slipped her earlobe betwixt his teeth and nipped gently.

Warmth settled into places within her Meredyth had never known existed.

"Merrie, bride, when you were drugged on your dastardly mead I did no more than kiss your sweet, rounded Welsh forehead and your charming, uptilted Welsh nose. Dark Warrior yearned to charge at your gate, yet a knight such as I would allow him no quarter. I did not seek to dishonor my highborn bride-to-be. 'Tis no lie, I've known the charms of many women. But for my lady-wife, I have high esteem. And even a cur can at times be noble."

"You speak the truth?"

His thumbnail grazed her nipple, causing the warmth in her private parts to whip into storm clouds of desire. Then his lips replaced his nail. She gasped. She moaned. And she murmured his hated name.

"Ah, my sweet. That is better." Tenderly, he enveloped her in his arms. "Yes, I speak the truth. Be it known, Lady Meredyth, I will never lie to you."

He would not lash her. He would not dishonor her. He would not lie to her. These were fine qualities in a husband, were he Welsh. Yea, but he was English, uninvited and unproven. And, alas, here to stay.

"Let me carry you to our bed, comely Merrie. 'Tis I, Garon, who will breech your gate, not the mindless warhorse of lust. Allow me to make love to you. Give me all of yourself. I seek your mind as well as your passion."

Such mead-rich words, tendered with lips that grazed her throat, fingers that caressed her with boldness yet a certain gentleness. They coaxed her even further into the tempest of fleshly awareness.

Into her ear he whispered, "Let us become lord and lady, united in body and soul, as I guide my people to riches and prosperity."

"My people," she rallied to protest.

"No. The Lord Garon's people. They will serve me, I will see to their welfare, and you will serve by my side."

She seethed. At moments such as this, she wished to have been her father's son. Daughters got hideously short shrift in this world—wifely servitude and the begetting of cur progeny.

"Unlock the dungeon, sire, and I am yours." In body. Never in soul.

"No. Not until you are my wife indeed."

She leapt to her feet, marched to the bed, jostled Beelzebub to the floor, and yanked the fur throw into her arms. She stomped to the fire, tossing the bedcover before the hearth. Nose in the air, she settled into fur. "I will not take to the marriage bed until the dungeon is emptied."

He loomed above her. All she dared study were his feet.

"I have decided on your punishment."

"What?" Meredyth jerked her gaze upward.

He was yanking off his jerkin, exposing his bare chest. It was ribboned with scars, the most prominent being close to his heart. That silvered mark most surely had come from an arrow. Again she felt a pang of sympathy. And again she quickly squelched it, thinking darkly that mayhap someday her dagger would make the pierce of an arrow seem paltry in comparison.

"How shall I pay?" she asked, being careful not to whine.

Sir Garon bent at the knees to hunker down on his

haunches. "On the morrow, at first light, you will present yourself in the yard. You will demand fealty to Sir Garon Saunders from the people of Glendire. And you will proclaim your own. Then you will declare your undying affection for me."

She cursed him silently. "What about this night?"

He stood and took a step backward. "That is up to you, Lady Meredyth. The question is, will you, the daughter of kings, lie to the people of Glendire? Or will you give your husband the chance to rouse your affection and devotion before dawn's light?"

Watch for Chapter Six, by Deana James, of Lair of the Wolf, *appearing in May 2000 in* In Trouble's Arms *by Ronda Thompson.*

AUTHOR'S NOTE

Dear Readers,

I hope you enjoyed Eirica and James' story and the completion of the Oregon Trail. As Jessie and Wolf travel back to the Nebraska territory (to get Jeremy there in time for book six), Star Dreamer (Wolf's sister), has decided to leave the tribe. Can she find peace away from her land and people? Join her and Grady O'Brien as these lost souls find a new chance at love and happiness in *White Dreams*, book five in my *White* series. Check out my website for excerpts and reviews at: <u>http://members.aol.com/susanedw2u</u> or write to me at:

> Susan Edwards
> P.O. Box 766
> Los Altos, CA 94023-0766
>
> **(SASE greatly appreciated)**

WHITE WOLF

SUSAN EDWARDS

Jessica Jones knows that the trip to Oregon will be hard, but she will not let her brothers leave her behind. Dressed as a boy to carry on a ruse that fools no one, Jessie cannot disguise her attraction to the handsome half-breed wagon master. For when she looks into Wolf's eyes and entwines her fingers in his hair, Jessie glimpses the very depths of passion.

___4471-4 $5.50 US/$6.50 CAN

MADELINE BAKER

The West—it has been Loralee's dream for as long as she could remember, and Indians are the most fascinating part of the wildly beautiful frontier she imagines. But when Loralee arrives at Fort Apache as the new schoolmarm, she has some hard realities to learn...and a harsh taskmaster to teach her. Shad Zuniga is fiercely proud, aloof, a renegade Apache who wants no part of the white man's world, not even its women. Yet Loralee is driven to seek him out, compelled to join him in a forbidden union, forced to become an outcast for one slim chance at love forevermore.

____4267-3 $5.99 US/$6.99 CAN

Dorchester Publishing Co., Inc.
P.O. Box 6640
Wayne, PA 19087-8640

Please add $1.75 for shipping and handling for the first book and $.50 for each book thereafter. NY, NYC, and PA residents, please add appropriate sales tax. No cash, stamps, or C.O.D.s. All orders shipped within 6 weeks via postal service book rate. Canadian orders require $2.00 extra postage and must be paid in U.S. dollars through a U.S. banking facility.

Name_____

Address_____

City_____ State_____ Zip_____

I have enclosed $_____ in payment for the checked book(s).

Payment must accompany all orders. ☐ Please send a free catalog.

Spirit's Song

MADELINE BAKER

She is a runaway wife, with a hefty reward posted for her return. And he is the best darn tracker in the territory. For the half-breed bounty hunter, it is an easy choice. His was a hard life, with little to show for it except his horse, his Colt, and his scars. The pampered, brown-eyed beauty will go back to her rich husband in San Francisco, and he will be ten thousand dollars richer. But somewhere along the trail out of the Black Hills everything changes. Now, he will give his life to protect her, to hold her forever in his embrace. Now the moonlight poetry of their loving reflects the fiery vision of the Sun Dance: She must be his spirit's song.

___4476-5 $5.99 US/$6.99 CAN

Dorchester Publishing Co., Inc.
P.O. Box 6640
Wayne, PA 19087-8640

Please add $1.75 for shipping and handling for the first book and $.50 for each book thereafter. NY, NYC, and PA residents, please add appropriate sales tax. No cash, stamps, or C.O.D.s. All orders shipped within 6 weeks via postal service book rate. Canadian orders require $2.00 extra postage and must be paid in U.S. dollars through a U.S. banking facility.

Name_____
Address_____
City_____ State_____ Zip_____
I have enclosed $_____ in payment for the checked book(s).
Payment <u>must</u> accompany all orders. ☐ Please send a free catalog.
       CHECK OUT OUR WEBSITE! www.dorchesterpub.com